Praise for

holly hepburn

'The Star and Sixpence sparkles with fun, romance, mystery
and a hunky blacksmith. It's a real delight'
JULIE COHEN

'Warm, witty and laced with intriguing secrets! I want
to pull up a bar stool, order a large G&T and soak
up all the gossip at the Star and Sixpence'
CATHY BRAMLEY

'You'll fall in love with this fantastic new series
from a new star of women's fiction. Filled to the brim
with captivating characters and fantastic storylines in
a gorgeous setting . . . I want to hear more!'
MIRANDA DICKINSON

'A fresh new voice, brings wit and warmth to
this charming tale of two sisters'
ROWAN COLEMAN

'Like the dream pub landlady who always knows exactly
what you want, Holly Hepburn has created the most
delightful welcome to what promises to be a brilliant series'
KATE HARRISON

'Warm, witty and utterly charming . . . It left me
with the most wonderful happy glow'
CALLY TAYLOR

'A super sparkling star of a story'
ALEXANDRA BROWN

Holly Hepburn is the much-loved author of commercial women's fiction. She lives near London with her grey tabby cat, Portia. They both have an unhealthy obsession with Marmite. Follow Holly on Twitter @HollyH_Author.

Also by Holly Hepburn

A Year at the Star and Sixpence
The Picture House by the Sea
A Year at Castle Court

Last Orders at the Star and Sixpence

holly hepburn

**SIMON &
SCHUSTER**

London · New York · Sydney · Toronto · New Delhi

A CBS COMPANY

First published individually as ebooks, titled *New Beginnings at the Star and Sixpence*,
Christmas Kisses at the Star and Sixpence, *Cosy Nights at the Star and Sixpence*
and *Last Words at the Star and Sixpence* in Great Britain by
Simon & Schuster UK Ltd, 2018, 2019
A CBS COMPANY

This paperback edition published 2019

1 3 5 7 9 10 8 6 4 2

Simon & Schuster UK Ltd
1st Floor
222 Gray's Inn Road
London WC1X 8HB

Simon & Schuster Australia, Sydney
Simon & Schuster India, New Delhi

www.simonandschuster.co.uk
www.simonandschuster.com.au
www.simonandschuster.co.in

A CIP catalogue record for this book
is available from the British Library

Paperback ISBN: 978-1-4711-7031-7
eBook ISBN 978-1-4711-7032-4

Typeset in the UK by M Rules
Printed and bound by CPI Group (UK) Ltd, Croydon, CR0 4YY

MIX
Paper from
responsible sources
FSC® C020471

To Emma Capron.
I miss your comments in the margins.

PART ONE

New Beginnings
at the Star and Sixpence

Chapter One

A Taste of Autumn

at the
Star and Sixpence

The leaves are turning gold and there's a chill in the air,
so why not join our new chef, Gabe Santiago,

for an evening of smoky flavours and zinging cocktails
as he introduces his new brand-new menu.

Booking essential.

Thursday 25th October

It was a crisp mid-September morning, the kind that began with dewy grass but promised warmth as the sun rose higher in the sky. Nessie Chapman leaned back against the wrought-iron bench in the garden of Snowdrop Cottage and let her eyes drift shut. Soon, she'd have to walk over to the neighbouring Star and Sixpence and help her sister, Sam, welcome their new chef on his first day. But not right this second. She could steal a moment or two to appreciate the chirp of birdsong and gentle buzz of a nearby bee; Sam wouldn't begrudge her that. In fact, knowing Sam, she might even prefer to be alone to greet the undeniably gorgeous Gabriel Santiago, although she'd insisted after they'd agreed he was the right person for the job that she was only interested in his prowess in the kitchen.

The truth was, Sam didn't begrudge Nessie much. She'd cheered to the rafters when Nessie had finally got together with Owen Rhys, the blacksmith who lived next door to the Star and Sixpence, and she'd continued to cheer even when her own love affair with cellarman Joss ended in another tumultuous break-up. And she hadn't objected a few months later when Nessie tentatively mentioned that Owen had asked her to move in with him, even though it meant Sam would be living in the pub on her own. She'd simply beamed in delight and declared that she couldn't wait to have the place to herself.

There was a faint creak behind Nessie, alerting her that the back door of the cottage had opened.

'A penny for your thoughts,' a deep, Welsh-accented voice said.

Nessie smiled and opened her eyes. 'If I had a penny for every time you've said that ...'

Owen smiled back, his dark eyes crinkling beneath his coal-black brows and unruly curls. 'You'd have around twenty pence, I expect. I should up my rates.'

He dipped his head to brush her lips with his and she felt the same familiar rush of delight mixed with incredulity that she still got every time Owen kissed her. Would it ever get old? she wondered, gazing up at him. It was hard to imagine at the moment, when every kiss still felt like their first.

'So,' he said, raising an eyebrow. 'Do I have to guess what you were daydreaming about?'

Nessie laughed. 'You won't be surprised to hear I was thinking about the pub. Sam wants to make sure everything is gleaming for the new chef's arrival.'

'Ah, yes,' Owen said wryly. 'The much-anticipated Señor Santiago. I popped into the bakery yesterday and Martha was like a cat on hot bricks. I hope he's ready to become Little Monkham's new heart-throb.'

Nessie pictured the brooding Spanish chef and pulled a wry face. 'Something tells me he's already used to that kind of attention.'

'I can imagine,' Owen replied. 'How does Sam feel about him?'

The question was innocent enough, but Nessie felt herself bristle slightly at the implication behind the words; Sam had been at the centre of village gossip on more than one occasion in the past. Or at least her love life had. Then Nessie reminded herself that this was Owen, who didn't have a gossipy bone in his body, and she forced herself to relax. 'She's looking forward to it, I think,' she said cautiously. 'We both are. He'll be a breath of fresh air.'

Owen smiled. 'He'll certainly cause a lot of sighing, if his photo is anything to go by. Luke is hoping you'll be able to sneak some puddings home.'

An image of Owen's nine-year-old son popped into Nessie's head; blond-haired and blue-eyed, he was the opposite of Owen's dark Welsh looks, but they shared the same appetite. In fact, Luke didn't so much eat food as inhale it and Nessie could just imagine him licking his lips at the thought of the kind of desserts that might be going begging at the end of the night in the Star and Sixpence kitchen. 'I'll see what I can do,' she promised.

'And now I suppose we'd both better get to work,' Owen said, casting a rueful glance towards the pub. 'You know where I am if your wonder chef decides to whip up an impossibly fancy lunch, although a decent steak sandwich would be just as welcome.'

Nessie laughed. 'We'll let him unpack before we start demanding meals, shall we?'

Owen accepted the teasing rebuke with a cheerful nod. 'I suppose you've got a point. See you later, then.'

Dropping another kiss onto her forehead, he crossed the yard and disappeared into the forge.

Nessie sat for a moment longer, then roused herself with an

inward sigh; Owen was right, she'd better get moving. Sam might not begrudge her sister's happiness, but she definitely wouldn't appreciate cleaning the pub on her own.

Nessie wasn't sure she'd ever seen Sam as anxious as she was right before Gabriel Santiago was due to arrive. She paced the floor in front of the gleaming bar, casting fretful glances back towards the door that led to the newly fitted kitchens.

'You did steam-clean the floor, didn't you?' she asked Nessie, running a hand through her usually sleek blonde bob. 'After you'd done the oven and swept up the dust?'

Nessie summoned up her most soothing voice. 'You were there when I did it, Sam. And I've double-checked the spare room, before you ask – everything is ready. All we need is the man himself.'

Sam checked the time. 'He said he'd get here around ten o'clock, depending on traffic.' She took a deep breath and glanced towards the spotlit bottles that lined the back of the bar. 'God, this is stressful. Is it too early for gin?'

'Relax, Sam,' Nessie said, frowning a little. 'Would it help to think of him as just another new employee?'

Now it was Sam's turn to frown. 'An employee who just happens to be an internationally respected Michelin-starred chef – one we've been boasting about for weeks. There's a lot riding on making sure he settles in fast and sticks around.'

'He's also a professional,' Nessie reminded her. 'And he's

already inspected the kitchen, before he agreed to work with us. A speck or two of dust won't scare him off.'

For a moment, Nessie thought her sister would argue, but then she sighed. 'You're right. I don't know why I'm so worried.'

Nessie thought she knew: Sam had been different since her relationship with Joss had fallen apart. It had been a difficult break-up – neither had wanted to accept that the bad times had begun to far outweigh the good – and Nessie suspected her sister had been considerably more hurt than she'd ever admit when Joss had made the decision to leave Little Monkham 'for both their sakes'. He'd been Sam's first serious love affair and the ensuing fallout had dampened her usual optimism, making her more wary of everything. Including, it seemed, their new business venture.

'I thought I was supposed to be the worrier,' Nessie said, her tone gently teasing. 'Connor and Tilly will be here soon – they'll get everything ready for opening. Why don't we go upstairs and grab a cuppa?'

Connor was the burly ex-fireman who looked after the pub's cellars, and Tilly was their nineteen-year-old barmaid; both were stalwart members of the Star and Sixpence team. And Nessie wouldn't be surprised if Tilly's mother, Martha, abandoned the village bakery to catch an early glimpse of the pub's new chef – he'd been all she had talked about for weeks.

Sam puffed out a long breath. 'Okay, deal.'

The first-floor rooms were a far cry from the gloom and woodchip wallpaper that had dominated when Nessie and Sam had first moved into the Star and Sixpence. The bedrooms hadn't needed much; a lick of paint on the wood-beamed ceilings and plush new carpets to take some of the chill out of the early winter mornings. The kitchen had been another story – Sam hadn't wasted any time in stripping out the boxy wall units and replacing them with something sleek and tasteful. The outdated appliances had gone too, including a fridge that was so vintage it had almost come back into style. In the living room, there were now two matching teal sofas that went beautifully with the oak coffee table and bookshelf, plus a flat-screen TV that Sam and Nessie had rarely found the time to watch. The rooms were still recognisably part of an old building but updated and modernised, in the same way that the pub downstairs was a fresher, more inviting version of the sixteenth-century inn it had been.

'It'll be weird having a flatmate again,' Sam said, as they sat around the small table in the kitchen, sipping tea. 'And even weirder that it won't be you.'

'I'm sure it will just be a temporary arrangement,' Nessie said. 'I imagine Gabe will want his own space too, once he's settled in a bit.'

Sam gazed at her over the top of her mug, her expression pensive. 'We are doing the right thing, aren't we, Ness? Expanding the business, I mean.'

Once again, Nessie was struck by the reversal in their roles. Sam had always been impetuous and confident, while Nessie was more thoughtful and reticent. But those differences had grown less marked over the last year and not all of it was due to Sam's broken heart; Nessie felt more settled in her role as the official landlady of the pub, in her place among the Little Monkham community too. Being with Owen had helped – his placid strength gave her something to lean on and the future no longer looked dark and unknowable. She could see the years stretching ahead, comfortable and safe, and the thought gave her more peace than she'd ever known.

'Of course we are,' she told Sam, with a smile of encouragement. 'We need to keep growing if we're going to bring home that National Pub of the Year award.'

Sam nodded slowly. 'I know. But are we being too ambitious? We could have gone for a lower-profile chef.'

'We could,' Nessie agreed. 'But when have we ever taken the easy path? More importantly, when have you?'

Sam said nothing.

'We chose Gabe because he's a rising star – fresh and exciting and not afraid to take a few risks,' Nessie went on. 'Anyone can do good pub grub. We want more than that.'

'Go hard or go home,' Sam said, a wry smile tugging at her mouth. 'Okay, you've convinced me all over again.'

The thud of feet on the stairs made them both glance towards the kitchen door. 'Good,' Nessie said. 'Because it sounds like he might be here.'

Tilly appeared in the doorway, her cheeks unusually pink. 'There's a man at the door asking for you,' she said, sounding flustered. 'It's ... He's ...'

Nessie took pity on her. 'Gabe Santiago, I presume?'

The barmaid nodded.

'Thanks, Tilly, we'll be right down,' Nessie said. She glanced at Sam. 'Ready?'

Her sister lowered her cup and squared her shoulders. 'As ready as I'll ever be.'

Chapter Two

Sam let Nessie lead the way, thankful her sister hadn't worked out the real reason she was second-guessing their decision to appoint Gabe. Deep down, Sam knew they'd absolutely made the right choice in striking a deal with an up-and-coming, talented chef; as Nessie had rightly pointed out, they wanted to innovate, not follow. In fact, the problem wasn't so much with Gabe Santiago as Sam herself; she'd felt a treacherous burst of attraction from the very first moment they'd met, and the appeal hadn't lessened with successive meetings, no matter how hard Sam had tried to crush it. And now they'd be practically living in each other's pockets, seeing each other every day . . . Sam had no idea whether the attraction was mutual, or even whether Gabe was single, but she'd made the mistake of mixing business with pleasure once before and she was determined not to do it again. No matter how gorgeous their new employee was.

All her good intentions evaporated when she saw Gabe standing beside the bar, however. She'd forgotten how tall he was – well over six feet – and his dark hair was tousled, as though he'd just rolled out of bed. A layer of stubble covered his jaw; along with the messy hair, it should have made him look unkempt, but somehow he pulled it off. His forehead was furrowed as he studied the cocktail menu, like he was mentally pairing each drink up with one of his recipes. He had no right to look that good after a four-hour drive, Sam thought irritably as she stepped out from behind the bar. Especially not when she absolutely shouldn't be noticing.

'Sam, Nessie,' he said, an easy smile lighting up his tanned face. 'It's good to see you again.'

Nessie beamed in return. 'Welcome back, Gabe. I hope you had a good journey?'

'Very smooth,' he replied. 'Hardly any traffic at all.'

His accent was every bit as sexy as Sam remembered, something else that irked her. Squashing the irrational annoyance as much as she could, she summoned up a clipped tone. 'Hi.'

His intense, dark-eyed gaze became cool as he tipped his head at her, every bit as professional as she had been. 'Hi.'

'Let me introduce you to Connor, our cellarman, and Tilly, who works the bar,' Nessie said.

Gabe turned his attention to the rest of the Star and Sixpence team and the breath Sam hadn't even realised she'd been holding escaped in a barely concealed sigh. Luckily, no one was paying her the least bit of attention; Connor was busy shaking Gabe's hand and Tilly had blushed a deep rosy red before smiling shyly. 'Nice to meet you.'

Once the introductions were done, Nessie cleared her throat. 'You've already had the grand tour, Gabe, but we'd be delighted to show you round again once you've settled in. Wouldn't we, Sam?'

If only you knew, Sam thought grimly, wishing she'd had the presence of mind to arrange an unavoidable appointment that would allow her to flee. 'Of course. I've got some urgent paperwork to do, but I'm sure you can do the honours, Nessie.'

Her sister opened and closed her mouth. 'I think the paperwork can wait until this afternoon,' she said, firing a half-frown Sam's way. 'There are bound to be questions I can't answer. But, before that, you must be tired after your long journey, Gabe – what can we get you to drink?'

He held up his hands. 'Don't let me get in your way. Point me towards the kettle and I'll make my own drink.'

Sam's unfounded irritation grew; once again, she hid behind professionalism. 'Whatever you'd prefer. Connor, would you be able to help Gabe get his things upstairs?' She glanced at the chef. 'As I'm sure you'll remember, there's a kitchen on the first floor, just along from your room. There's tea, Nespresso and milk – help yourself.'

Was it Sam's imagination or did Gabe raise an eyebrow before he and Connor headed towards the pub entrance.

The moment their backs were turned, Nessie grabbed Sam's arm. 'What the hell was that about? You were almost rude.'

Sam met her gaze. 'I'm starting as I mean to go on. And I wasn't rude – just businesslike.'

Understanding dawned in Nessie's eyes. She lowered her voice. 'Lightning doesn't strike twice.'

'It does,' Sam said with a grim shake of her head. 'But it's not going to strike between Gabe and me. You can count on that.'

The pub was busy for a Wednesday evening. Business had been brisk all day, with a greater number of villagers than usual popping in, either for a lingering coffee or with a tenuous excuse to chat to one of the bar staff. At first, Sam had been amused at the way their gazes travelled around the room, clearly hoping for a glimpse of the newest member of staff, but by the early evening the sensation of only having half of anyone's attention was wearing thin.

'I hope this level of interest isn't going to be permanent,' she grumbled, leaning against the glass-fronted fridges as Martha let out a loudly self-conscious laugh from her seat at the bar. 'The air of anticipation in here is getting on my nerves.'

Nessie threw her an amused look and continued to stack the cups beside the coffee machine. 'You can hardly blame them,' she said mildly. 'Gabe's reputation has definitely preceded him and you know how much they love a celebrity. Remember how they were when Nick came to visit?'

Nick Borrowdale was the star of Sunday night's flagship TV show, *Smuggler's Inn*, and one of Sam's best friends. He'd been a regular at the pub the year before, happy to lend his support to Sam and Nessie's efforts to restore the Star and Sixpence to glory. He had fought Sam's corner when she'd been hounded by the press over a one-night stand with a high-profile government advisor and had been steadfast in his loyalty. It was no surprise to anyone when he and Sam eventually got together, and Sam sometimes caught herself wondering what might have happened if she'd chosen Nick instead of Joss – would she still be single now? There was no way of knowing; Nick was currently in the US, filming a new thriller, and his career was going stratospheric. Besides, it had felt like the right thing to do at the time . . . she cared deeply for Nick but she'd loved Joss. And then he'd broken her heart.

'You can't compare Nick with Gabe,' she said to Nessie with an impatient shake of her head.

'Why not?' Nessie replied, staring at her. 'Let's face it, they're both pretty easy to look at – is it any wonder the village ladies are keen?'

And Sam couldn't argue with that either. In fact, she'd banked on the star quality of both when she'd sought out their involvement at the pub. What she hadn't banked on was joining the ranks of Gabe's admirers herself. But she wasn't about to admit that to her sister. 'Nick is an A-list celebrity,' she said haughtily. 'And Gabe – well, I'm sure he'd prefer to be judged on the food he creates rather than his looks.'

A momentary hush fell over the bar, followed by the buzz of many hurriedly resumed conversations. Sam didn't need to look at Nessie's wide frantic eyes to know Gabe was standing behind her. Had he overheard her scornful pronouncement? She had no idea.

Taking a deep breath, she turned. 'Gabe. I hope you're all settled in?'

'I am, thank you,' he replied. 'I tend to travel light, apart from the tools of my trade.'

His eyes sparked with some secret entertainment that Sam suspected was at her expense. 'Good,' she said stiffly.

He glanced past her to smile at Nessie. 'Your tour was very thorough – I feel as though I know Little Monkham and her villagers already.'

Another peal of laughter rang out from Martha, causing Sam to grit her teeth.

Nessie cleared her throat. 'Speaking of the villagers, it would be great to do some introductions, if you're feeling up to it?'

Gabe inclined his head graciously. 'Of course.'

Nessie's gaze flickered towards Sam. 'Do you want to—'

'No,' Sam said, lightning fast. 'You can have that privilege. I'll help out behind the bar.'

She busied herself checking the stock levels in the fridges, even though Connor had topped them all up before his shift had finished. By the time she'd worked her way along the bar, Nessie and Gabe were on the far side of the pub, chatting to Father Goodluck from the parish church. Sam straightened the last row of Pinot Grigio and frowned. Now what else could she find to do that would keep her out of Gabe's way? Could she justify a trip down to the cellar?

'If you straighten those bottles any more, you'll wear the labels off,' an amused voice drawled.

Sam looked up to see Ruby Cabernet staring down at her, one perfect eyebrow arched in curiosity. 'Just checking we've got everything we might need,' she said.

'I think twelve bottles of Pinot is enough for a Wednesday evening in Little Monkham, don't you?' Ruby's gaze was shrewd. 'If I didn't know better, I'd say you were hiding.'

'Hiding?' Sam got to her feet and forced a carefree smile. 'What on earth would I be hiding from?'

The older woman winked. 'Not what, darling. *Who*. As in that delicious new chef you've treated us all to.'

'Gabe?' Sam said, wondering whether her actions were so transparently obvious to everyone. 'Why would I be hiding from him?'

'That is the sixty-four-thousand-dollar question,' Ruby replied solemnly. She glanced across to where Gabe stood chatting to white-haired Henry Fitzsimmons and lowered her voice so that only Sam could hear. 'I'd quite like to eat him for breakfast and perhaps again for lunch, so why wouldn't you? Or is that the problem?'

Sam sighed. Ruby's relationship with Sam and Nessie's late father meant she took a particular interest in their lives. And before her retirement to Little Monkham, she'd spent years working as a stage actress – not much got past her, especially now she'd stopped drinking.

'He'll be great for the pub,' Sam said, reaffirming the mantra she'd repeated to herself all afternoon.

Ruby tilted her head. 'But less so for you. Is the attraction mutual?'

Sam's cheeks burned as she glanced around to make sure no one was listening. 'No! And it's hardly an attraction – more an inconvenient crush.' She folded her arms. 'It'll pass and then everything will be fine.'

Ruby patted her red hair, which was tucked into an elegant chignon, and smiled. 'Of course, he might prefer a more mature lady. I'd be happy to keep him busy.'

Sam smiled. Ruby had been a great beauty in her youth and although that beauty had dimmed a little with age, she was still an eye-catching woman. 'And what would Micky think about that?' she teased, referring to the will-they-won't-they dalliance Ruby had been conducting with silver-fox rock star Micky Holiday.

'I doubt he'd bat an eyelid,' Ruby said, with a delicate snort. 'I've known Micky for a long time and he's never been one for monogamy.'

Sam knew Micky too; she'd seen him turn on the charm with women half his age and get away with at least their phone numbers. But she'd also noticed the way he acted around Ruby during his increasingly frequent visits to Little Monkham; the soft admiration in his eyes when he knew she wasn't watching him, his refusal to drink a drop of alcohol even though he was a famous party animal. He was still as roguish and rude as ever, but Sam thought he scaled things back around Ruby.

'He might surprise you,' she said.

Ruby shook her head wryly. 'Micky stopped surprising me a long time ago. Now, it looks very much as though your sister and Gabriel are moving this way. Why don't I head them off so you can make your getaway?'

'Thanks, Ruby,' Sam said, warm with gratitude.

But the other woman was already moving away. 'Not at all,' she murmured, her tone distracted. 'It will be my pleasure to help.'

Just as Sam was about to bolt for the cellar, she saw the pub door open and Franny Forster, the chair of the Little Monkham Preservation Society, walked in. Sam almost groaned aloud. If Franny spotted her there would be no chance of escaping to the cellar or anywhere else; as the widely acknowledged ruler of the village, she would demand that both sisters were there as she cast her eye over their latest employee.

'Sorry, Ness,' Sam mumbled, making hurriedly for the door that led downstairs. 'You're on your own this time.'

And she fled into cool darkness with a heartfelt sigh of relief.

Chapter Three

Thursday was Nessie's day off.

She awoke just after seven o'clock, unsurprised to see Owen's side of the bed was already empty; he was an early riser, born of many years of getting up to look after Luke. Normally, Nessie got up to help make breakfast, but after a busy evening in the pub, she was under strict instructions to stay in bed. She propped herself up against the pillows, listening to the thud of Luke's feet as he tore around the cottage, gathering up everything he would need for the day. Occasionally, she heard the rumble of Owen's voice and that made her smile. She loved the way the lilt of his accent made everything sound like poetry. And then the rumble became a roar and Nessie winced; there was nothing poetic about bellowing at Luke to move his dirty trainers.

Minutes later, Owen poked his head around the door, a cup of tea in one hand. 'I thought we might have woken you,' he said, his expression sheepish. 'Sorry.'

'Don't worry. I was already awake,' Nessie replied, smiling.

He placed the cup of tea on the bedside table and sat on the edge of the bed. 'What are your plans today?'

Nessie stretched as she gave the question some thought. 'I don't know,' she said eventually. 'I thought maybe we could take a walk by the river later, if you're not too busy? There were some blackberry bushes there that had a few unripened berries last week – I thought Gabe might be able to use them in the kitchen.'

Owen shook his head. 'I'll be slaving over a hot fire all day, I'm afraid. I've got an order for some bespoke ironwork that needs to be delivered tomorrow.'

Nessie hid a smile; she'd half expected as much. Owen took his craft very seriously and it showed in the work he produced, so much so that his reputation was growing. He was working harder than ever and often kept the forge fires blazing until late in the evening. It was one of the things his sister, Kathryn, had warned Nessie about when she'd first agreed to move in to Snowdrop Cottage. 'Lay down the law,' Kathryn had said, with a knowing look. 'No working past seven-thirty in the evening. He won't work on a Sunday, but make sure you insist Saturdays are family days too, or you'll end up a blacksmith's widow.'

Nessie had been far too shy to take her advice, but there were times she wished she had. 'That's a shame,' she said to Owen now. 'But maybe we could go at the weekend – we could take Luke.'

'You're on,' Owen said. 'We'll pack a picnic, make an afternoon of it.' He stood up and moved to the door. 'You could join me for a sandwich at lunchtime, if you're around?'

It was better than nothing, Nessie supposed. 'Sure. Around one o'clock?'

Owen smiled. 'Perfect.' He cocked his head and listened. 'It's awfully quiet down there. I'd better go and see if Luke's gone through with his threat to run away from home.'

In the end, Nessie spent her morning catching up with things she hadn't had time to tackle earlier in the week. Running a pub wasn't a nine-to-five job; there was always something to keep her busy, even though she and Sam now had a reliable team to help. Nessie tried hard to keep away from the Star and Sixpence business on her day off, but it wasn't always possible. And Sam's reluctance to have much to do with Gabe was already causing problems; Nessie had spent the best part of an hour with him that morning, working through a list of preliminary supplies for his recipe testing. Then she'd headed home to place an advert for a sous-chef to help in the kitchens once they opened – the Star and Sixpence would only be offering food three days a week to start with, but both Sam and Nessie suspected demand would be high enough to merit additional days in time. They might as well get a strong team together now and start as they meant to go on.

Her stomach began rumbling around midday, and she half considered popping over to the pub to see whether Gabe had whipped up anything tasty. But it made more sense to keep out of the way, at least for today; Nessie understood Sam's reason for wanting to keep her distance from Gabe, but he was going to be impossible to avoid – there would be a lot of occasions when it was just the two of them. The sooner Sam got over her current awkwardness, the better.

Instead, Nessie walked down to the bakery to pick up a fresh loaf. The sun continued to shine, bathing the still-parched village green in golden warmth and causing Nessie to smile. It wouldn't be long before the grass was emerald green and tinged with silvery frost, she thought. And then Christmas would be just around the corner. The thought made her excited and anxious at the same time: it would be her first Christmas with Owen and Luke – the first in Snowdrop Cottage – but it was also one of the busiest times at the pub. She was going to have more than ever to juggle ...

The smell of freshly baked bread helped to soothe some of her anxiety away. Martha wasn't behind the counter; instead, Nessie was greeted with a cheerful smile by her apprentice, Isabelle, and she couldn't help feeling grateful for having avoided Martha's inevitable cross-examination about Gabe. They chatted politely for a few moments, then Nessie made her excuses and left. By the time she'd called into the butcher's for some ham and discussed Gabe's request for some top-quality sirloin steak, it was twelve-thirty.

She tapped on the door of the forge just before one o'clock. A few seconds ticked by before Owen's voice rang out, letting her know it was safe to enter. Pushing back the door, Nessie braced herself for the wave of heat that she knew would envelop her the moment she entered the forge. She often wondered how Owen bore it, especially during the long blistering summer they'd just had, but he told her he was used to it. He'd dampened the gas level so that the coke embers would cool down while he wasn't using the fire, but, even so, Nessie wasn't surprised to see sweat beaded on his forehead as she approached him; smithing was hard work even when the temperature outside was autumnal.

'You cooked,' he said, nodding at the laden tray in her hands.

'Hardly,' she replied, smiling. 'But I did go and grab some fresh bread and ham. Where shall I put the tray?'

Owen reached for the towel that lay on a workbench and wiped his face. 'It's too hot in here. Shall we go into the office?'

He meant the small room off to one side, which had windows that opened wide onto the yard outside the cottage. It was cluttered and cosy, but Nessie knew it would be much cooler than the forge itself. 'Okay. I brought some iced water too – I thought you might be in need of a drink.'

Owen grinned. 'I half hoped you might have brought me a pint of Thirsty Bishop, but I suppose water will do.'

'It most certainly will,' Nessie said, with mock-severity. 'The last thing we need is for you to be drunk in charge of an anvil.'

'You're as wise as ever,' Owen agreed. 'Come on, then. Let's eat.'

Nessie filled him in on her morning as they ate, taking care not to mention Sam's aversion to Gabe. Owen grumbled about the intricacies of the ironwork he'd been working on.

'I like the challenge of the fancy stuff,' he said, pushing his empty plate away, 'but you know how it is. You only have so much time to get the metal into the right shape before the temperature drops and then it needs to be heated again.'

Nessie smiled. 'Strike while the iron's hot.'

'Exactly,' Owen said. 'Except that it's all so fiddly. I'll be glad when it's done and I can get back to the simpler stuff.'

'Anything I can do to help?'

His eyebrows rose. 'In the forge?'

She'd often seen him work before, but it had only ever been in passing, fleeting glimpses of sparks and deep concentration. And, suddenly, she was curious about the way he spent his days. 'Why not?' she said. 'At the very least I could keep you supplied with tea. Unless I'd be in the way?'

He thought for a moment. 'No, you wouldn't be in the way. But I'm sure you have better things to do than listen to me swear at a lump of iron.'

Nessie laughed; she wasn't sure she'd ever heard him swear. 'Probably, but I'd like to see what you do.'

'I can't promise it'll be exciting,' he warned. 'But I'd never say no to your company.'

They walked back through and Owen found her a worn leather apron like the one he wore. He pointed to a stool tucked underneath the high bench along the wall furthest away from the silver-hooded fire. 'You'll be safe enough over there, although you will have to wear plastic goggles, I'm afraid. Forge policy.'

Once she was settled, he turned up the gas to bring the fire up to temperature.

'That'll take a few minutes,' he said. 'I can show you the section I made this morning, if you like? To give you an idea what I'm aiming for.'

Nessie could see immediately why it was painstaking work. The client had requested two wrought-iron gates with swirling loops covered in delicate leaves that wove around the frame like Sleeping Beauty's thorn forest. Each leaf had to be hammered thin and shaped before being embossed with a pattern. Once they were all complete, Owen needed to attach them to the frame of the gate and twist tendrils of iron around them like vines. It was going to look magical when it was finished.

'Wow,' Nessie breathed, reaching out a finger to trace the lines on one perfect oak leaf. 'It's amazing. Really beautiful. You're so clever.'

A ruddy tinge crept into Owen's cheeks, but Nessie thought he looked pleased. 'It's easy when you know how.'

'I bet it's not,' Nessie said firmly. 'You're an artist, Owen. This is a work of art.'

He shook his head stubbornly. 'Blacksmiths aren't artists. It's mostly brute strength and understanding how metal and heat work together. You could do it if you wanted to.'

She stared at him in disbelief. 'I could not.'

'You could. Look, I'll show you.'

He handed her a pair of thick leather gloves. 'Put these on.'

Nessie gazed at the gloves; they looked as though they would come up to her armpits. Doubtfully, she pulled them on and flexed the fingers. 'They're so stiff. How do you work with them?'

27

'You get used to them,' he said, shrugging easily. 'And they've saved me from a nasty burn on more than one occasion. Now, here's your hammer. It has to be heavy, I'm afraid, or it won't do the job.'

She hefted the hammer in one hand. No wonder Owen's muscles were so well-developed; her arm hurt just holding it. She placed it on the anvil as Owen held up a thin iron rod.

'You're going to turn this into a leaf.'

'Impossible.'

'Totally possible,' he said, smiling. 'The first thing you need to do is heat the iron.'

He led her over to the fire and showed her how to grip the rod with a pair of tongs and bury it in the hottest part of the glowing embers. She watched in fascination as the black metal changed colour; red, orange, yellow and then almost white.

'Carefully draw it out and carry it over to the anvil,' Owen said, just behind her shoulder. 'Don't rush, take your time.'

Concentrating, Nessie did as he instructed. Her hands shook as she squeezed hard on the tongs, determined not to drop the hot iron. 'What now?' she asked, as she rested the rod on the cool anvil.

'Now we need to flatten it out,' Owen said, holding out the hammer. 'Take this in your strongest hand and use the other to grip the tongs. Then, when you're ready, hit the tip of the iron as hard as you can.'

She focused on the metal and brought the hammer down hard. A shower of sparks flew up and a round dent appeared in the rod.

'Good,' Owen said, steadying the arm that held the tongs. 'Do that again.'

Nessie did and was gratified to see the metal flattening out with each strike. When the iron lost its bright glow, Owen helped her to reheat it and then continue to hammer. Once she'd flattened the rod end, he showed her where to strike so that the shape of a leaf began to appear. Nessie wiped the sweat from her forehead and studied the iron through critical eyes. It didn't look anything like Owen's delicate handiwork, but it was recognisably leaf-shaped. With a bit more work, it might even look half-decent.

'You're a natural,' Owen said, taking the tongs from her and plunging the iron into a a nearby bucket of water. Steam hissed and rose in a cloud.

Nessie lowered the hammer and flexed her arm, wincing at the ache in her muscles. She removed her goggles. 'I don't know about that. I think I just had a very good teacher.'

Owen dampened the fire and stripped off his leather gloves. He crossed the floor to pull her into a hug with a smile. 'We make a good team.'

He smelled of smoke and cinders, Nessie thought, the way he always did when he'd been working. She inhaled deeply; beneath the smokiness there was an unmistakable Owen scent, something that was always there, even when he'd just stepped out of the shower. It often caused Nessie's insides to contract – a sudden stab of wanting that still caught her by surprise. She sighed, wondering whether he felt the same when he held her; probably not right at that moment, when she was hot and tired from her unexpected brush with smithing. In fact, he was more likely to be regretting the decision to let her to stay – hadn't she promised not to get in the way?

Nessie was about to apologise when he spoke. 'Your hair smells like the forge.'

'Sorry,' she said, blushing. 'I'll get a shower.'

'I like it,' he said quietly and Nessie felt his fingers gently caress the small of her back, through her T-shirt. She glanced up, uncertain whether she'd imagined it, but his expression was intent. Before she could reply, he bent down and kissed her.

The urgency surprised her; his lips were firm and insistent, as though he'd been waiting for an opportunity to kiss her. The wanting she'd felt earlier caught light, filling her with a warmth that had nothing to do with the heat of the forge. One of his hands slid underneath her T-shirt to caress her skin. She shivered and returned the kiss with matching urgency. And then she tried to bury her fingers in his black curls and remembered she was still wearing the stupid gloves.

Owen realised a heartbeat after her. Breaking the kiss, he took her hands and carefully tugged at the leather, freeing first one hand, then the other.

'Better?' he murmured.

'Much better,' she replied, reaching up to push a curl from his face. 'But you've got work to do – I should go.'

He pulled a wry face. 'Work is the last thing on my mind right now.'

She cleared her throat, almost embarrassed to ask the

question that was on her lips. 'Do you want to go over to the cottage?'

He studied her for a moment, his dark eyes hesitant. 'Actually, I thought we might stay here. I – I could lock the door, so we won't be disturbed.'

The thought made Nessie burn with embarrassment and temptation. She'd never admit it to anyone, but she'd had several fantasies about what she'd like to do with Owen in the forge, lit up by the glow of the fire. Never in her wildest moments had she dreamed he might have had similar fantasies. And now he seemed to be suggesting that they might . . . that they should . . .

'Nessie?' he said, brushing her lips tentatively with his own. 'It was just an idea. We don't have to.'

She stared up at him, feeling the heat swirl inside her again, and took a deep breath. 'You'd better lock the door.'

He did.

A moment later, he was standing in front of her again. He pulled at the string of her apron and lifted it gently over her head, then bent to kiss her with the same insistence as before. Nessie let herself melt into him, resting against the anvil for support as she sank her fingers into his hair. His hands slid under her T-shirt once more and stroked her skin, causing her to break the kiss with a soft moan. She fumbled with his apron; he took over and dropped it to the floor. And then it was her turn to slip her hands beneath his shirt, to caress his skin and slide them over the muscles of his broad chest, down towards his waist.

'Nessie,' he murmured, raining feathery kisses on her face. 'Don't stop.'

Emboldened, she undid his jeans. In return, he drew her T-shirt over her head and dropped a line of kisses along her collarbone. She pulled him close, savouring the feel of his hot skin against hers, and let her hands drift downwards. Now it was his turn to moan and whisper her name again.

Afterwards, she worried that the sound of their mingled cries must have been loud enough to carry on the afternoon air. The thought made her blush as she and Owen dressed, but the fierce kiss he gave her on the doorstep of Snowdrop Cottage chased her embarrassment away.

'That was amazing,' he said, shaking his head in wonderment. 'Although how I'm supposed to concentrate at work now is anyone's guess. My head will be filled with thoughts of you and what we did.'

She couldn't help smiling. 'Sorry. Although I'm not really.'

'Me neither,' he said, planting another kiss. 'Have I told you how much I love you, Nessie Chapman?'

Nessie felt her smile grow even wider. 'Not for at least ten minutes. I love you too, Owen.'

His eyes shone as he gazed at her. 'And that makes me the happiest man alive.'

Chapter Four

Without ever discussing it, Sam and Gabe developed an instinctively choreographed routine over the weeks that followed. It helped that he was a night owl and she'd become a lark over the last year; she was always up first, preparing breakfast for the guests staying in the luxurious rooms on the top floor of the Star and Sixpence, and he was often out in the afternoons, sourcing produce and checking out the local competition. If Sam timed it right, she could sometimes avoid seeing him for the whole day – although she told herself she wasn't actually avoiding him. She was pleasant and polite when they did run into each other, and she was happy to discuss business issues, but he clearly picked up on her coolness and saved most of his questions for Nessie. And that professional distance was no bad thing, Sam reminded herself. He might consider her aloof, perhaps even unfriendly, but she'd rather that than repeat the mistakes of the past.

The arrangement worked well until Gabe invited Sam and Nessie to a sample menu tasting.

'Can't you do it on your own?' Sam asked her sister, when she passed on the invitation. 'Or take Owen – he likes to eat.'

Nessie stared at her. 'No, Sam. He invited you. It would be rude to send someone else.'

'But—'

'No buts,' Nessie said firmly. 'He already knows something is off and skipping this won't help.'

Sam's heart sank. Nessie was right; it would be churlish and petty to send Owen in her place. But the thought of spending an hour or more with Gabe, tasting the amazing dishes he'd created from scratch, filled her with quiet panic.

Nessie's voice softened. 'I don't often tell you what to do, Sam, but I'm your big sister and sometimes I have to. You need to get over this problem with Gabe – have you considered getting to know him a bit better?'

Sam summoned up a mental image of Gabe charming his way around the Star and Sixpence when he'd first arrived. 'I don't think that's going to help.'

'You never know,' Nessie said. 'Maybe he picks his nose or bites his toenails or has really rampant ear hair.'

Sam shuddered. 'That's gross, Ness. And at least two of the three are entirely undesirable in a chef.'

Her sister gave her a triumphant look. 'But they are all major turn-offs. Do they make him any less fanciable?'

Once again, Sam pictured the chef, with his brooding

dark eyes and stubble-edged jaw. The trouble was that she couldn't imagine him doing any of the disgusting things Nessie had suggested; her imagination automatically leapt to much more desirable thoughts. But Nessie had been right about one thing; Sam needed to get over her crush on him. It was eating away at her professional pride and that was something she couldn't bear. 'Okay, I'll come. Maybe I'll even talk to him.'

'Good girl,' Nessie said, smiling in relief. 'And I hesitate to say this, knowing it's the last thing you want to hear, but . . . you're both adults. There are some people who say the best way to get over someone is to get *under* them.'

Sam felt her jaw drop as she stared at her sister's bright pink, embarrassed expression. It was the most un-Nessie-like thing she had ever heard her say and she was uncomfortably aware of a matching tide of mortification creeping up her own cheeks. 'I – well, I don't think that's the way to go, but thanks anyway.'

Nessie nodded, still blushing but apparently determined. 'So I'll tell him you'll be at the menu tasting, right?'

'Uh – yes,' Sam said faintly. 'Yes, I'll be there.'

'Good,' Nessie said, and turned away. 'You've got to start somewhere.'

She wasn't wrong, Sam thought, gazing at her sister's back in stunned silence. But she was pretty sure a fling wasn't the best way to get over her attraction to Gabe Santiago. In fact, she could only imagine it making things worse.

*

Sam had to admit, every single dish Gabe had created was a little taste of heaven.

'And this is a goats' cheese ravioli in a black truffle cream sauce,' he said, pointing to a bowl filled with soft yellow pasta that Sam had no doubt was freshly made. 'Beside it you'll see a garlic flatbread and slow-roasted tomato chutney.'

She took a forkful of the melt-in-the-mouth ravioli and savoured the sharp tang of the cheese as it mingled with the creamy sauce. The flavour was equal to anything she'd eaten in the best London restaurants, although she didn't know why she was surprised; of course Gabe's food was incredible. That specific talent was the reason they'd hired him.

Nessie groaned with delight and dug her fork into the sauce for a second parcel of pasta. 'This is amazing, Gabe. You should definitely put it on the menu for the Taste of Autumn evening.'

Sam tore off a strip of flatbread and dipped it into the chutney. An explosion of tart rich crimson lit up her taste buds. She waited for the flavour to fade before shaking her head in admiration. 'Wow.'

'Wow, as in good?' Gabe asked, studying her expression. 'Or wow as in, "I can't believe we've let this guy loose in our kitchens"?'

A wave of discomfort washed over Sam at the hint of apprehension behind his words and she gave herself a brisk inner shake. Nessie was right; he knew something was off. She met his gaze with the most reassuring smile she could manage. 'Wow as in great. What else have you got for us to try?'

'Just one or two things,' he replied.

It was the understatement of the year, Sam thought, as he unveiled dish after dish. Some were based on familiar pub meals – steak and chips or sausages and mash – but each one had a twist that elevated it into something better. And, of course, the ingredients were all locally sourced and fresh. The desserts were Sam's favourites, though; the passion fruit crème brûlée was the most mouth-watering food she'd ever tasted. Nessie evidently agreed because she let out an unembarrassed sigh of pure satisfaction as she put the empty ramekin down on the kitchen worktop. 'I think I am going to have to join a gym, or I'm going to be the size of the pub by Christmas.'

'Me too,' Sam said, inwardly acknowledging another Gabe-related temptation she was going to have to negotiate. 'Thanks for all your hard work.'

He shook his head. 'Now the hard work really begins – narrowing down the choices to decide what to serve at the taster evening. Did you have any favourites?'

It really was a shame they couldn't serve them all, Sam thought, listening to Nessie and Gabe debate the dishes. As they talked, her eyes kept straying back to Gabe; his face was alive with enthusiasm for his recipes. That passion was one of the things that had made him such an obvious choice for the Star and Sixpence. The problem was that it wasn't doing anything to dampen the fires of Sam's crush.

'What do you think, Sam?' Gabe said, turning to her. 'The tiramisu or the coconut and pineapple upside-down cake?'

Sam hesitated for a moment, her gaze fixed on the kitchen work surface. 'Both,' she decided, looking up at him. 'Who says you can't have your cake and eat it?'

He smiled, his eyes fixed on hers. 'That's exactly how I feel.'

And Sam had to remind herself that they were only talking about food.

It was a quiet Friday afternoon. Nessie was covering Connor's break, keeping one eye on the scattered regulars who were reading the paper or chatting among themselves. The weather had taken a turn for the worse and the pub windows were covered in a light film of drizzle. They might even need to light the fire for the evening, Nessie thought, casting a glance at the enormous chimney breast that dominated the bar. And then autumn would really have arrived.

The stranger came in just before three o'clock. At first, she assumed he was looking for the toilets; he stood in the middle of the pub, gazing around him as though taking everything in.

'The loos are just through there, on the left,' she called cheerfully, smiling in welcome. 'Help yourself.'

The man didn't return her smile. 'I'm looking for Vanessa and Samantha Chapman,' he said, walking to the bar.

Nessie frowned. Now that he was nearer, she could see that he was in his mid-twenties. He was good-looking, in spite of his unfriendly air, with a strong jaw and decent cheekbones. In fact, there was almost something familiar about him. They couldn't have met before – not if he didn't know who Nessie was – but there was definitely something about him she couldn't quite put her finger on. Someone from the Health and Safety Inspectorate, maybe? Except they usually had their identification clearly displayed and this man was altogether too casually dressed.

'I'm Vanessa Chapman,' she said. 'How can I help?'

He blinked, his green eyes reflective. 'I should have known – you look like him.'

Nessie's frown deepened. 'Pardon?'

The man ran an agitated hand through his short blond hair. 'Is Samantha here? What I have to say concerns both of you.'

'She's not, I'm afraid,' Nessie said and her feeling of disquiet grew. Who was this man?

'When will she be here?' he asked, glancing around almost as though he thought Sam might be hiding behind the bar.

'Later,' Nessie said tersely. 'Can I ask what this is about?'

He shook his head. 'It's better if I come back.'

Nessie had had enough. 'Who are you? What do you want with Sam and me?'

'I'm Laurie Chapman,' he said, and hesitated, throwing her an uncertain look. 'The brother you never knew you had.'

'What?'

Sam leaned back against the sofa, stunned, as Nessie let out a long sigh. 'That's exactly what I said. But he refused to go into more detail, just left a mobile number and suggested we call when it's convenient to talk.'

'But how ...' Sam began, then trailed off. 'I mean, obviously, I understand how we might have a brother, or a half-brother, more likely. But I don't get how we didn't know about it – surely Ruby would have told us?'

Nessie shrugged. 'Maybe she didn't know, either. It's not impossible that Dad didn't know, in which case he couldn't have told Ruby.'

Sam rubbed her face, her expression still bemused. 'Wow.'

'Yeah,' Nessie agreed. 'Wow.'

'I suppose there's a chance he could be lying,' Sam said, after a few seconds had passed.

Nessie remembered Laurie's green eyes and blond hair, so like the memories she had of their father. She shook her head. 'Maybe. I don't know. He looked a bit like Dad.'

Sam puffed out a breath and managed a shaky laugh. 'Then we'd better learn how to play Happy Families,' she said, reaching for her phone.

The White Hart pub wasn't as pretty as the Star and Sixpence, Nessie thought as she and Sam pulled up outside on Saturday morning, but it would do very nicely as neutral ground to meet Laurie.

'Is that him?' Sam asked, nodding at the back of a blond-haired man disappearing through the door of the pub.

'I think so,' Nessie said, squinting after him. 'Hard to tell from one meeting.'

Sam pulled on the handbrake and switched off the engine. 'Let's go and find out.'

Nessie knew as soon as they walked into the White Hart that it had been Laurie; he'd taken a seat facing the door and rose the moment she and Sam came into view.

'It's him,' she murmured to Sam.

'So I see,' Sam whispered back. 'He's the only other person in here, apart from the barman.'

Nessie did her best to smile as they approached the table he'd chosen. 'Hi, Laurie.'

He nodded at her, then turned his green-eyed gaze towards Sam and held out a hand. 'You must be Samantha. Nice to meet you.'

Nessie watched Sam's guarded expression as she shook Laurie's hand and wondered if her own face was similarly wary. There was no doubting Laurie's confidence in who he was; he believed he was their brother. The question was, what did he want?

He cleared his throat. 'I was about to get a drink – can I get you something?'

Nessie felt her tension lessen; he sounded nervous. Then again, meeting two half-sisters for the first time probably was a little nerve-racking. 'A latte, please,' she said, trying to soften her voice and sound friendly.

'An espresso for me,' Sam said, her tone clipped.

Laurie nodded and headed towards the bar.

Sam leaned towards Nessie. 'I see what you mean, he does look a bit like Dad, only twenty years younger.' She paused and frowned across the room. 'Before the drink got to him, obviously.'

'I know. Who do you suppose his mother is?'

Sam spread her hands. 'Who knows? Presumably some-one Dad met after he left us, but before he arrived in Little Monkham. I'm sure Franny would have said if he'd sown any wild oats under her jurisdiction.'

Nessie swallowed an urge to laugh at the idea of Franny keeping a list of all the illicit relationships that had undoubt-edly been part of village life over the years. Then her smile faded away as she realised it was probably nearer to the truth than anyone wanted to admit. 'Franny would definitely have known,' she said, glancing at Sam. 'She probably writes it all in a special notebook and locks it in the Post Office safe.'

Moments later, Laurie was back bearing a tray of steaming coffee. He handed a small espresso cup to Sam and placed a frothy latte in front of Nessie.

'So,' he said, once he'd taken a seat with his own flat white. 'I suppose you're wondering why I've suddenly appeared out of the blue.'

'Got it in one,' Sam agreed. 'You've got to admit, it's a bit like the start of those TV shows where a mysterious rela-tive turns up out of the blue and starts to terrorise the main characters.'

Laurie attempted a wolfish grin that didn't quite work. 'Yes, I've come to cheat you out of the Star and Sixpence,' he said. Then his smile faded. 'Or perhaps it's just that I decided it was time to find the sisters I've always known I had. You decide.'

The second explanation sounded plausible enough, Nessie

thought. But could it be true? Had Andrew Chapman fathered a son?

'Okay,' Sam said. 'I'm going to ask the obvious question. What makes you so sure we're related?'

He raised his eyebrows. 'Apart from the fact that we look alike, you mean?'

Sam glanced at Nessie. 'There are a lot of blonde-haired, green-eyed people in the world. Hardly any of them claim to be our long-lost brother.'

Laurie spread his hands. 'Dad told me about you. He used to talk about you a lot; although my mum hated it, so it was always our little secret. "They're lovely girls, Laurie," he used to say, "a proper pair of crackers. When you're old enough, you need to find them. They'd love to know they've got a little brother."'

'He never mentioned you,' Sam said flatly. 'Not once.'

'That doesn't surprise me,' Laurie replied, taking a sip of coffee. 'He also told me he hadn't seen you for years and wasn't sure he'd ever see you again. Something about your mother, I think.'

Nessie felt Sam bristle and hastily stepped in. 'Speaking of mothers, what about yours? Does she know you're meeting us?'

Laurie glanced away. 'Mum died a few months ago.'

'Oh,' Nessie said, a hot rush of guilt storming through her. 'I'm sorry to hear that.'

'It's taken me a while to get her affairs in order,' he went on. 'I looked for you as soon as I could.'

Sam's expression was closed. 'I'm sure we're both very sorry for your loss. But I still don't understand how you and your mother fit into what we know about Dad's life. How old are you, for a start?'

'Twenty-six,' Laurie answered, without hesitation.

Nessie did the maths in her head. She was thirty-seven, which meant an eleven-year age difference between her and Laurie. Andrew had abandoned them when she was ten, so Laurie had been born within a year or so of him leaving. It was tight but perfectly possible, she thought. 'And he lived with you?' she asked, giving Sam a troubled look.

'For a while,' Laurie said. 'Mum said he turned up in the local pub one night, saying he had nowhere to go. She took a shine to him, invited him to spend the night on her sofa and he didn't leave the next morning. A year later, I was born. He finally went when I was six.'

He looked away then, but not before Nessie saw the hurt in his eyes. It was a pain she knew well; the ache of abandonment, of wondering what exactly you'd done wrong to make your daddy go away. She warmed to him a little more, in spite of her misgivings.

'And you can prove all of this,' Sam said. 'I mean, you've got a birth certificate that names Andrew Chapman as your father?'

Laurie reached into the bag that lay at his feet and pulled out a large brown envelope. 'I thought you'd probably ask that. Here.'

He pushed the envelope towards them. Nessie lifted the

flap and slid the paperwork out. They sat for a moment, staring at the words and names that confirmed Laurence John Chapman had been born to Helena Marsh and Andrew Chapman twenty-six years ago, in Peterborough Hospital.

Nessie studied the birth certificate until the writing blurred before her eyes. She exchanged an uncertain glance with Sam. 'It looks like we have a little brother,' she said finally.

'It does,' Sam said, and let out an incredulous huff of laughter. 'Even now, Dad is messing with our heads.'

Laurie looked back and forth between them. 'I'm sorry to spring it on you like this. I didn't know how else to do it – a letter seemed too formal and email didn't seem like the way forward either. So I went for face to face.' He gave a self-conscious laugh. 'Surprise!'

For a moment, neither Sam or Nessie spoke. Then Nessie got to her feet and spread out her arms. 'Welcome to the family, Laurie. It's good to meet you.'

Chapter Five

It was gone closing time on Saturday evening. The last merry stragglers had been safely herded out into the night and the bar was clean and set for the next day. Nessie waved Connor off and shot the bolts across the thick wooden door, before sinking into an armchair in front of the glowing fire.

She glanced across at Sam, who was swirling the remains of a gin and tonic around her glass. 'How are you feeling?'

Her sister sighed. 'Tired. Confused. Frazzled. Like I've been hit in the chest with an emotional cannonball.' She managed a wry smile. 'The usual, basically.'

'Except that this isn't usual,' Nessie observed, reaching for her own drink. 'I mean, it's not every day that you discover you have a brother you never knew existed.'

'No, I can definitely say it's a first,' Sam said. 'How are you feeling about it?'

It was a good question, and one Nessie wasn't sure she

could answer right at that moment. Like Sam, she felt a little unsettled, as though the world was a snow globe that had somehow been shaken up. There'd been a lot she'd wanted to ask Laurie but had held back, deciding there would be plenty of time to unravel the whole story as they got to know him better. And the idea that she and Sam had a brother, that they were now three when it had always been just the two of them, was taking some getting used to.

'It's still sinking in,' she said eventually. 'I suppose we'll have to give it time.'

Sam nodded. 'I can't decide if it's a good thing that he's moved to Purdon, though. What if we don't get along?'

Purdon was a small village not unlike Little Monkham, around ten miles away, and Laurie had announced he'd rented a cottage there. 'It's not like I have anything to keep me in Peterborough now,' he'd said, with a sad smile.

'I think it's a good thing,' Nessie said slowly. 'We can't get to know each other if we never see him.'

'True,' Sam said. 'Although he'll have to weather the storm of village gossip first. Franny will probably want to recruit him as a spy for Little Monkham's intelligence agency when she finds out – you know how competitive she is.'

That was true; there was already a fierce rivalry in the pub quiz stakes, with Franny's Inquizitors fighting off the Purdon Warriors on a regular basis to keep the much-coveted trophy, and the Best Kept Village prize was just as hotly contended.

Nessie smiled. 'Poor Laurie. I hope he's got a talent for espionage.'

'Maybe we should offer him a job here,' Sam joked. 'For his own protection.'

Nessie sipped her drink thoughtfully. 'That's not a bad idea, actually.'

'I wasn't being serious,' Sam said, staring at her as though she'd lost the plot.

'No, but think about it,' Nessie said, leaning forwards. 'It's the perfect way to introduce him to the village, and for us to get to know him better too.'

Her sister looked far from convinced. 'We don't need any new staff.'

'We will, once Gabe starts pulling in the customers,' Nessie said reasonably. She softened her voice. 'And ... reading between the lines, it doesn't sound like Dad got any better at fatherhood after he left us. Maybe the Star and Sixpence owes Laurie something too.'

'I don't know—'

'We don't have to decide now,' Nessie said. 'But one of the reasons Dad gave us this place was to make up for all the things he knew he'd got wrong. Maybe he'd want us to extend that to include Laurie.'

Sam raised her chin. 'If that's true, why didn't he include Laurie in his will?'

It was something Nessie had wondered herself. 'I don't know. Maybe they'd lost touch, or maybe Dad was trying to keep things simple.'

'Or maybe he knew something we don't,' Sam said pointedly. 'It's just too early to offer Laurie a job – he's virtually a stranger.'

'So is Gabe,' Nessie countered. 'Connor was too, before we got to know him.'

'The difference is that they both had professional reputations to fall back on,' Sam replied. 'We took up references too – I can't imagine doing the same with Laurie.'

Nessie drew in a deep calming breath. 'I'm sure he'd give us the name of his previous employer, if we asked.'

'But that's just it,' Sam said. 'We can't ask. If you're going to work for family, you expect them to trust you as standard, not demand to see proof that you're a competent human being.'

Arguing with Sam was like trying to grip smoke, Nessie decided. 'It's just an idea – a less contrived way for us all to get to know each other.'

Sam's mulish expression softened. 'I know. And it's typically you – kind and warm-spirited. But let's take things one step at a time, eh?'

'Okay,' Nessie said, giving up. 'Just don't blame me if Franny sends him undercover first.'

'Then you can definitely say I told you so,' Sam replied with a half-smile. She glanced at the clock and stretched. 'I'd better get to bed. I've got a long lie-in planned for the morning.'

'I know, it's my turn to do the breakfasts.' Nessie yawned. 'It's been a bit of a day, hasn't it? I feel wrung out.'

Sam grimaced. 'Tell me about it. Let's hope tomorrow is less eventful.'

On Sunday morning, Sam awoke to the soft rattle of rain against her bedroom window. She pulled the duvet up around her ears and lay still in the gloomy half-light, listening to the steady patter that was only broken when a gust of wind snatched up the raindrops and threw them against the glass. A quick look at her phone told her it was eight-thirty; Nessie would have delivered breakfast to the guest rooms by now and be tucked away in the office downstairs, printing off invoices for check-out. There was no sound beyond the rain.

Sam relaxed and stretched her toes to the end of the bed, wriggling them blissfully against the cool cotton sheet. There was no need to fret about peering out at the landing before she padded to the bathroom today; Gabe was spending a few days in London and she could dance naked around the first floor if she chose. Although it wasn't unheard of for Connor or Tilly to pop upstairs from time to time, so maybe she'd make sure she was fully dressed before she fired up Spotify.

Just after ten o'clock, Sam made her way along Sixpence Street to Weir Cottage, where Ruby had promised her eggs Florentine for breakfast. It was a once-a-month, Sunday-morning ritual they had; there was something indescribably soothing about sipping a Virgin Mary and tucking into a delicious brunch while listening to Ruby's endless supply of scandalous stories from her acting days.

As always, Ruby looked as though she'd just finished a

screen test when she opened the door that morning. Her lustrous red hair was twisted into a low bun that sat at the nape of her neck, and her make-up was so flawless that Sam was half-tempted to ask for a tutorial. She was dressed in slim capri pants and a black polo neck jumper that only enhanced her high cheekbones and contrasted with her red lips. Her feet were encased by fluffy kitten-heeled mules that Sam would never dare to wear and there was a tantalising hint of Chanel in the air. Ruby was every inch a star and, as always, Sam had a moment of disconnect as she followed her along the hallway to the sunlit kitchen at the back of the house. She'd never known Ruby anywhere other than Little Monkham and couldn't think of a place better suited to her, yet there was always a subconscious sense that she didn't quite belong in that world – like a rare orchid kept alongside tomato plants.

Weir Cottage itself was as cool and elegant as its owner. There were no photos from Ruby's glory days as a darling of London's theatre scene on display; Sam knew she kept them all tucked away out of sight in the spare room – there when she wanted to step back in time but hidden from her everyday life. In fact, the only photos for public viewing were the ones Ruby claimed made her the proudest; pictures of her son, Cal, and his wife, with their arms around Ruby's adored granddaughter. Ruby hadn't been part of her son's life as he grew up – her drinking had caused a rift she'd never dreamed would mend – but Sam and Nessie had made it their business to bring the family back together.

'I've just been Skyping with Cal,' Ruby said, waving at the laptop on the kitchen worktop. 'Little Ruby has started drama classes – she's auditioning for the lead role in the school play.'

Sam smiled. 'Good for her.'

'And Cal is already talking about Christmas.' Ruby stopped talking and gazed down at the stick of celery in her hand. 'Would you and Nessie mind terribly if I didn't spend the day with you?'

'Of course not,' Sam said, with an amused shake of her head. 'Nothing would make us happier than for you to be with your family at Christmas.'

Ruby puffed out a long breath. 'Well, you girls are my family too. I'll miss you both.'

'And we'll miss you,' Sam said. 'But we get to see you every other day of the year, it's only right that they get to spend Christmas with you.'

Ruby twisted the pepper grinder over the drinks and gave each celery stick a final flourish. 'Here's to families and happy ever afters.'

Sam chinked her glass against Ruby's and took a sip – it was as delicious as ever – then she cleared her throat. 'Speaking of families, something unexpected happened yesterday.'

Ruby listened as she cooked, the frown lines in her forehead deepening as Sam described the meeting with Laurie.

'So, I suppose what I wondered – what Nessie and I both wondered – was whether you knew?' Sam said, as Ruby placed a steaming plate of spinach and eggs on the table in front of her. 'About Laurie, I mean.'

Ruby didn't answer immediately. She manoeuvred into her seat, wincing a tiny bit as she sat; Sam knew she still sometimes suffered stiffness after a nasty fall the year before that had ended in a hip operation. But Ruby's troubled expression didn't clear once she was seated. 'No,' she said in a quiet voice. 'I didn't know Andrew had another child. He never mentioned it.'

'It would have been long before you knew each other,' Sam said. 'Before he came to Little Monkham, actually, so perhaps it isn't such a surprise that he didn't tell you. I'm not sure whether he would even have remembered, the amount he drank.'

Ruby stopped pushing the food around her plate and raised her chin. 'He would have remembered. Alcohol made him forget a lot of things, Sam, but not how many children he had.'

The reproach in her voice made Sam want to shrink into her seat. 'No, you're right. I'm sorry. What I mean is, maybe he preferred not to remember.'

'That's more likely,' Ruby conceded. 'Although he never held back from talking about you and Nessie. Something awful must have happened between him and Laurie's mother for him to bury it so deep he couldn't tell me he had a son.'

The news had hurt Ruby; Sam could see it in her eyes, although she was far too good an actress to let it show anywhere else. 'I'm sure he had his reasons,' she said softly. 'I don't suppose we'll ever know what they were, but please don't let it upset you.'

Ruby looked up, a determined smile on her face. 'No, I shan't. And I'm being horribly selfish, anyway – this isn't about me. How are you and Nessie taking the news?'

'Cautiously,' Sam replied. 'Or at least, I am. Nessie is more open to the whole idea, but we both know she's a sucker for a sob story.'

'Is there a sob story then?' Ruby's eyes were suddenly sharp.

Sam hesitated, turning Laurie's tale over in her mind. He didn't seem to want anything, other than to make contact and perhaps get to know his half-sisters, which wasn't an unreasonable expectation. It had been Nessie's idea to offer him some work, not his. And everything he had told them sounded pretty likely; Andrew had very real form for loving and leaving his children, no matter how good his intentions. So there was no reason for Sam to feel anything other than astonishment and curiosity at Laurie's arrival in their lives. And yet, she was still wary.

'No,' she told Ruby. 'But he'd recently lost his mother and I did pick up an air of vulnerability about him. I think it appealed to Nessie's maternal instincts.'

'Yes, I can see how that might happen,' Ruby said. Her mouth twisted into a rueful smile. 'Not something that really troubles you, however.'

Sam laughed. 'No. I'm the least maternal person in the world. Ness wants to give him a job – I think she'd probably invite him to stay in the spare room if it wasn't for Gabe.'

The irony of being suddenly grateful for Gabe's presence was not lost on Sam.

'You know, I think I'd like to meet Laurie,' Ruby said, sinking her knife into the golden yolk on her plate. 'I want to hear his story for myself. Is that something you can arrange?'

'I'm sure it is,' Sam said, pleased to have an ally. 'And if Nessie gets her way, I might not have to arrange it at all – you'll find him behind the bar of the Star and Sixpence.'

'It might not be a bad thing if she does,' Ruby said thoughtfully. 'Keep your friends close but your enemies closer.'

Sam smiled; had Ruby ever missed an opportunity to be overdramatic? 'I wouldn't go so far as to call Laurie an enemy.'

Ruby's eyes narrowed. 'Maybe not, but if there's one thing I know about Little Monkham, it's that secrets don't stay secret for long. If he's got anything to hide, we'll soon winkle it out of him.'

'Poor Laurie,' Sam said, suddenly feeling sorry for him. 'He's got no idea what he's let himself in for . . .'

Chapter Six

Sam hated the involuntary lurch her stomach gave when Gabe walked into the Star and Sixpence on Tuesday afternoon. She dropped her gaze, glowering instead at the pint of Thirsty Bishop she was pulling for Henry Fitzsimmons.

'Steady on, Sam,' Henry said, his short white moustache quivering in alarm as creamy foam slopped over the side of the glass. 'It'll be all hops and no head if you keep on like that.'

'Sorry,' Sam mumbled, taking more care with her next pull of the pump.

When she looked up again, there was no sign of Gabe. She presumed he'd strolled right past, without bothering to say hello, and that caused another unreasonable flash of irritation. It was fine for her to pretend he didn't exist but entirely not fine for him to ignore *her*.

She took the money Henry was offering her and slammed it into the till drawer. 'Your change,' she said, placing the coins into his outstretched hand. 'Thanks, Henry.'

He cleared his throat. 'I get the feeling all is not well, Samantha. Has your new chef gone off the boil already?'

Sam summoned up a brisk smile; she wasn't about to tell Henry anything, not when he would report straight back to Franny. 'Not at all. I can assure you Gabe is still sizzling hot.'

Henry grunted. 'So I keep hearing. Martha told me today that she's thinking of learning Spanish, and Franny has ordered his recipe book. You and Nessie seem to be the only women in the village immune to his charms.'

'I'm sure that's not true,' Sam said, hoping the truth wasn't written all over her face. 'Now, I hope we can count on your support at the karaoke evening next week? I'm looking forward to hearing your Elvis again.'

His faded blue eyes narrowed slightly and she knew he was torn between wanting to boast and maintaining his dignity. 'Of course I will be there,' he said stiffly. 'You know how Franny and I like to support your endeavours. But I doubt I'll be taking a turn with the microphone. Not after last time.'

Sam kept her face perfectly straight. The look on Franny's face when he'd begun to thrust his pelvis in time to 'Jailhouse Rock' had been priceless, so Sam wasn't entirely surprised he'd been rapped over the knuckles. Even so, she was quietly confident that, when the time came, he wouldn't be able to resist the siren call of performing again.

'That's a shame,' she said. 'I know a lot of women find a man who can sing quite sexy – myself included. But perhaps tone down those moves of yours – we don't want Franny getting jealous of all those fluttering hearts, do we?'

Henry turned so red that she half worried his own heart was doing more than fluttering. But he shook his head and some of his embarrassment receded. 'I'll certainly consider it,' he said, just as Gabe appeared at Sam's elbow. 'Someone's got to give these young whippersnappers a run for their money, what?'

Sam turned, wondering how much of the conversation Gabe had heard and decided it was most of it, judging from the amused expression he wore. 'It would be a very cold day before you'd catch me singing Elvis Presley,' he told Henry solemnly. 'Your crown, and your lovely wife, are both safe from my clutches.'

Henry huffed into his pint. 'She's not my wife, actually. We're just stepping out together, that's all. Early days and all that.'

Sam stared at him. 'Hardly that, Henry. It's been more than a year since you and Franny got together.'

His bushy eyebrows shot up. 'Has it? Good lord, I think you're right.'

'It was Valentine's Day last year,' Sam reminded him. 'Surely you can't have forgotten?'

He gave her a guilty look. 'The months tend to blur as you get older. I took her out for dinner, though. On Valentine's Day. And I bought her some flowers.'

Sam smiled. 'I'm sure you did enough, Henry. Franny isn't one to hide her displeasure, is she?'

'No, she's not,' he replied, with a shudder of obvious recollection. 'Well, well. Almost eighteen months. How time flies.'

'I'll remind you next February,' Sam said in sympathy. 'So you can make more of a fuss.'

Henry looked grateful. 'Thank you. Appreciate that.'

Almost reluctantly, Sam turned her attention to Gabe. There was a heavier than normal layer of stubble covering the lower half of his face; it suited him. Determined not to get distracted, she summoned a purposeful smile. 'Welcome back. Is there something I can do for you?'

Gabe nodded. 'As a matter of fact, there is. As you know, I'm trying to use local fresh produce in the kitchens here and autumn is the perfect time of year to go foraging. In particular, I'd like to find some wild mushrooms and I wondered whether you might know if there are any grow-ing nearby.'

Sam blinked, moderately insulted. Really, did she look like the kind of woman who went digging about in the dirt for mushrooms? 'I don't think I do.'

'Archer's Wood,' Henry chipped in briskly. 'Take the bridge over the river and follow the path until it forks. You'll find plenty of fungi growing there – tasty with a good fry-up.'

'There you go,' Sam said. 'Mushroom city.'

'That is good news,' Gabe said thoughtfully. 'Although I am not much of a woodsman and I don't know the area at all. Perhaps you could come too, Sam?'

She wanted to laugh. Seriously, hadn't he even noticed her carefully maintained highlights and perfect manicure? But from the corner of one eye, she could see Henry watching with interest, and his observation about trouble with Gabe floated back into her mind.

'Of course,' she said easily, hoping neither of them noticed her crossed fingers. 'I'd be more than happy to help. Maybe at the weekend?'

'Perfect,' Gabe said, smiling.

'Perfect,' Henry echoed, looking back and forth between them.

'Perfect,' Sam muttered under her breath, picturing a soggy stomp through the dripping trees that surrounded Little Monkham. 'Just bloody marvellous.'

'And finally, this one leads to the cellar.' Nessie pointed to the thick wooden door at the top of the cellar stairs. 'That's Connor's kingdom, although he occasionally lets one of us mere mortals venture down there, if we promise not to touch his beer barrels.'

Laurie nodded. 'The cellar is out of bounds. Got it.'

Nessie smiled. 'So that's the guided tour over and done with. Any questions?'

'I don't think so,' Laurie said, glancing around the bar. 'Or maybe just one. Who is that woman with the red hair? She hasn't taken her eyes off me from the moment we came in here.'

Nessie followed his line of sight, although she knew exactly who he meant. 'That's Ruby. She was Dad's girl-friend after ... after your mum, I suppose.' She sighed and squared her shoulders. 'Come on, I'll introduce you.'

Ruby's welcoming smile didn't reveal any of the reservations Nessie knew she had about Laurie.

'How wonderful to meet you,' she said, taking his outstretched hand. 'Nessie and Sam have told me so much about you.'

Laurie managed an awkward smile. 'Nice to meet you too.'

A busy silence stretched, during which Nessie could see Ruby sizing Laurie up. Was she searching for evidence of Andrew amongst his features and mannerisms? Of course she was. And Laurie must know that too.

'We'd better get back to work,' Nessie said, with an apologetic glance at Ruby.

'Goodness, don't let me keep you,' Ruby said, raising her eyebrows. 'From the sounds of things, there'll be plenty of time for Laurie and I to get to know each other.'

Laurie waited until they were safely behind the bar to lean towards Nessie. 'Was she really Dad's girlfriend?'

'I know. You'd never put them together, would you?'

'No,' he said, firing a swift glance in Ruby's direction. 'No, I wouldn't.'

Nessie gave him a sympathetic look. 'She means well. And she was devoted to Dad, so I suppose it's only natural that she's curious about you.'

'I suppose so,' Laurie conceded, although he looked far from convinced.

'Now,' Nessie said, 'let's see if you can put those pint-pulling lessons to good use. Father Goodluck is in need of another pint over there.'

Laurie wasn't what Nessie would call a natural barman. He frothed up Father Goodluck's pint to such an extent that it had to be abandoned. He gave three customers the wrong change, making Nessie relieved that most of their payments came via cards – the last thing they needed was for the till to be down at the end of the night. And he accidentally insulted Franny by serving another customer before her; the glower she fired across the bar could have outburned the sun.

Once or twice, Nessie sent him out to collect glasses and run the gauntlet of the curious villagers, although she hadn't revealed his relationship to her and Sam. Ruby seemed especially keen to talk, but Laurie was careful to avoid her. Eventually, as closing time drew near, she gave up all pretence of nursing her tonic water and watched his every move. She showed no sign of leaving and Nessie couldn't say she was surprised; when Ruby wanted something she usually got it. And in this case, she wanted answers from Laurie.

'How was your first evening?' she asked, once the pub was empty of customers. 'Do you foresee a new career as a barman?'

Laurie gave another awkward smile as he leaned against the bar. 'I can't say it was top of my childhood list.' He looked around, as though taking everything in. 'But this place has a nice vibe. I can see myself getting used to being here.'

Ruby returned the smile, but Nessie could see it didn't quite reach her eyes. 'I'm sure your father would be glad. He loved the Star and Sixpence.'

He grinned. 'I bet. What's not to love about living in a pub?'

'It has its ups and downs,' Nessie said, thinking of all the times she'd longed for a nine-to-five job instead of the long days it took to make the Star and Sixpence run as though it were no effort at all.

'I can imagine,' Laurie said. 'You and Sam are doing fantastically. Much better than I expect Dad did.'

The temperature dropped several degrees. Nessie could have groaned out loud.

'What do you mean?' Ruby's voice was perfectly even and measured.

Laurie shrugged. 'It's no secret the old man liked a drink – Mum told me he could barely stand up most nights. I can't imagine he was good at handling the business – he probably drank the profits.'

Ruby's expression might be frozen but her eyes were blazing. She opened her mouth to speak, but Nessie got there first.

'It's been a long day,' she said hurriedly, hoping to defuse things before Laurie could do any more damage. 'And you've got that drive back to Purdon.'

'Yeah, you're right,' Laurie replied, with a shrug. 'I suppose I'd better be on my way.'

But Ruby was not to be deterred. 'I can assure you, your father was more than capable of managing the Star and Sixpence,' she said, her tone tight. 'Yes, he had a drinking problem, and yes, he lost his battle with it more often than he won, but he still fought every day.'

Laurie sighed. 'I'm sorry, Ruby, but spare me the lecture about his *struggles*. You should have been there when my mum fought to put food on the table because he didn't pay her enough money to feed me properly. He wasn't exactly father of the fucking year.'

Ruby sucked in a breath, as though he'd wounded her. 'I understand you had a fraught relationship, Laurie, but that doesn't entitle you to be disrespectful.'

'It does, though,' Laurie fired back, his own eyes suddenly alight with fury. 'I've got every right to disrespect him if I want to, because he never showed any respect for me or my mum.'

'Laurie,' Nessie said unhappily. 'I don't think this is the time or—'

He pushed away from the bar, a violent movement that set alarm bells jangling in Nessie's head. But he sucked in a deep breath and made a visible effort to control himself. 'No, you're right. I'm sorry. I just don't like being told what to think about a man who didn't think about me at all.' He walked towards the door. 'Night, Nessie. See you tomorrow.'

The silence he left behind was punctuated only by Ruby's fast breathing.

'It isn't true,' she said, gripping Nessie's wrist urgently. 'I know Andrew sent money – sometimes, I even helped him out – although I didn't know what it was for until just now.'

Nessie stared at her. 'You helped? What do you mean?'

The older woman shook her head. 'I mean that sometimes the books simply wouldn't balance and I had to subsidise them. It was never very much, but it did mean I saw the money coming in and out.' She fixed Nessie with a frank look. 'And there was a regular payment going to a woman I didn't know right up until Andrew died. I think you'll find that was Laurie's mother.'

'Oh, Ruby,' Nessie said, seeing the shimmer of tears behind her eyes. 'Why didn't you tell us you'd helped out financially? Sam and I would have paid you back, with interest.'

'It's not about that,' Ruby said stubbornly. 'I don't want money, which is why I've never mentioned it. I just hate to think of you believing everything Laurie says, that's all.'

Nessie thought back over Laurie's comments and sighed. The trouble was that both she and Sam had first-hand experience of their father's haphazard approach to money. And Laurie's accusations had a familiar ring of truth about them; Andrew Chapman had never been the most reliable of people, as their own mother had discovered after he vanished. But hadn't she also told her daughters that he had never written to them? That had turned out to be a lie ... Maybe there were other things their mother had lied about, Nessie thought. And maybe Laurie's mum hadn't been entirely truthful with her son, either.

'Your father wasn't a bad man, Nessie,' Ruby went on, her tone quiet and even. 'He had his demons, but he tried his best to do what was right by you and Sam. I refuse to believe he didn't extend the same courtesy to Laurie, no matter how much the boy bad-mouths him.'

And that was part of the issue, Nessie thought an hour later, as she lay in bed beside Owen, unable to sleep. Because Andrew Chapman clearly *hadn't* treated Laurie the same way he'd treated his daughters; he hadn't named him in his will. Had he done it out of vindictiveness? Or forgetfulness? Or had he been trying to pretend he didn't have a son at all?

Whatever the reason, Nessie felt honour-bound to try to make up for it with Laurie. All she had to do now was convince Sam to take the same view. And persuade Ruby that Laurie wasn't the disrespectful son she'd cast him as. That was probably going to be the hardest challenge of all.

Chapter Seven

Sam was tempted to ignore the knock on her bedroom door at seven o'clock on Saturday morning. What she really wanted to do was pull the duvet over her head and pretend she'd never agreed to go mushroom picking in the woods with Gabe. But it was far too late to back out now.

'Be there in a minute,' she called, trying to mask her reluctance. 'I'll have a coffee if you're making one.'

Hauling herself out of bed, she crossed to the shutters that covered the latticework leaded windows. She expected to see grey skies and persistent drizzle, but the weather surprised her with a peaches and cream sunrise and the hint of blue skies behind the wispy gold-tinted clouds. Immediately, her mood lifted. It would be damp and muddy in the woods, but at least the sun was doing what it could.

Gabe was waiting in the kitchen, sipping a steaming mug of coffee. His dark hair was even more untidy than normal and one cheek was sleep-creased and yet he still caused a treacherous stir inside Sam, which resulted in a grumpy frown. He had no right to look so good when he'd clearly just got up, she thought, raising a self-conscious hand to her own frizzy blonde bob. It wasn't fair.

'No need to ask how you feel about the prospect of an early morning mushroom hunt,' Gabe observed, eyebrows raised.

Sam thought about denying it and then allowed herself a sheepish groan. 'Is it that obvious?'

'No more than usual,' he replied. 'I don't know how you like your coffee so couldn't make you one.'

There was no reproach in his voice – if anything, Sam thought she detected resigned amusement. 'Dark, strong and not too bitter,' she said, reaching for her favourite coffee pod.

'Noted,' Gabe said, watching as black liquid poured into the espresso cup. 'Do you want to eat before we go? I could make you an omelette when we get back, if we find enough treasure.'

The thought of golden eggs wrapped around hot, buttery mushrooms made Sam's mouth water, but it would undoubtedly mean spending more time with Gabe. 'You could,' she said, cautiously.

Gabe's mouth quirked at her obvious reluctance. 'It's an offer to cook breakfast, Sam. Not a proposition.'

'I didn't think it was!' Sam exclaimed, heat racing across her cheeks.

'We can include Nessie if it will make you more comfortable,' Gabe went on, flashing her a wide-eyed look.

He was teasing her, Sam realised with a further rush of

mortification. And then she felt a cold plunge of certainty; he knew exactly why she was acting the way she was. He *knew*.

'Let's just get going,' she said, forcing herself to sound as though she had no idea what he was getting at. 'You can't make a mushroom omelette without any mushrooms.'

'That is true,' Gabe said solemnly. 'But I'm sure we'd manage to cook something up between us.'

Sam downed her coffee in one mouthful, wincing as the scalding liquid hit her throat. The kitchen felt small, too full of Gabe, and she was suddenly keen to get out to the space of the woods. 'Let's go. Before I get hangry.'

'We wouldn't want that,' Gabe agreed, finishing his own drink. 'Lead on, Sam.'

Dew glistened on Sam's sturdy walking boots as they cut across the village green. Gabe had looked surprised when he'd seen her feet, as though he didn't believe she owned such practical footwear, and Sam didn't feel the need to explain that she'd borrowed them from Nessie. Maybe the best way to handle Gabe Santiago was to convince herself that she didn't care what he thought of her. If she could manage to do that, everything would get a lot easier.

The air was earthy and moist as they crossed the bridge that spanned the river and entered Archer's Wood. There was no early morning village buzz here; the only sound was the delicate chirping of the birds. The trees were well into their autumn glory; the leaves were a riot of amber, gold and russet and Sam found herself breathing deeply as she and Gabe passed beneath the patchy network of branches.

'Do you walk here often?' Gabe asked.

'Not as often as I probably should,' Sam said, taking another lungful of fresh air. 'Nessie and Owen come here a lot, especially when they want Luke to run off some energy.'

Gabe nodded. 'I can imagine Little Monkham is a good place to raise children. I grew up in the Seville heat and would have loved to escape somewhere like this. It's the opposite of home – almost like Narnia.'

The reference made Sam smile; Narnia had been one of her and Nessie's favourite escapes when they'd been younger, but she hadn't thought of it for years. She could easily imagine how the cool, damp woods might have a magical feel to someone who'd grown up on the sun-scorched streets of southern Spain. 'There's no White Witch in these parts, although Franny sometimes acts like she rules us all.'

He laughed. 'I don't know what you mean – she's been lovely to me so far.'

'That's because you haven't crossed her,' Sam said darkly, but her shudder was half-hearted. Franny might have been her nemesis when she and Nessie had first arrived in the village, but she'd proved a kind and fiercely supportive friend many times since then. Although it had to be said that both sisters had taken great care to stay on the right side of the postmistress since those early days at the Star and Sixpence; neither of them wanted to risk her wrath again.

'She reminds me of my grandmother,' Gabe said. 'She is always telling me how done she is with everyone's shit.'

Now it was Sam's turn to laugh. 'Your grandmother sounds like a character.'

He tipped his head. 'She is. Both she and my grandfather helped to raise me after my father left my mother. We're still very close.'

Sam was silent for a moment, processing the new information. 'I didn't know about your father. I'm sorry – that must have been hard.'

Gabe sighed. 'In some ways, yes. But he wasn't an especially good man and so life was easier after he left. My mother began to smile again.'

Sam's eyes prickled with unexpected tears. 'So did mine. Although my father wasn't a bad man. He drank and that made everything more difficult.'

'I understand,' Gabe said, flashing her a sympathetic look. He paused, as though trying to find the right words. 'Meeting Laurie will have opened some old wounds, I think.'

His perceptiveness caught her off guard; she took a moment to reply, concentrating on putting one foot in front of the other on the compacted muddy path. 'It has. But nothing that won't heal again.'

'Good,' he said. 'It's healthy to revisit those feelings sometimes. Especially as time gives you a better perspective. The older I get, the more forgiving I become.'

She looked up then and found his gaze resting thoughtfully on her. 'You're right, it is healthy. As long as you don't get too tangled up in things you can't change.'

'True,' he acknowledged. 'I think that is a lesson Laurie has not yet learned.'

Once again, Sam was surprised by Gabe's insight. 'I'm not sure I had at twenty-six.'

Gabe shook his head. 'Nor had I. But I was never as angry as Laurie seems to be. He tries to hide behind derision, but you can almost feel his rage.'

She had to concede he was right; Laurie definitely had some unresolved anger towards the father he felt had abandoned him. 'Being at the Star and Sixpence will help,' she said slowly. 'I know it's only a building, but there's such a soothing quality about it – almost as though it radiates contentment.' She gave a self-conscious laugh. 'You probably think I'm mad.'

'Not at all,' he said, shaking his head again. 'My mother's house in Spain is exactly the same – I find a curious sense of peace when I am there. Everything makes sense.'

Sam smiled. 'Then you know just what I mean. Maybe the Star and Sixpence will work her magic on Laurie too.'

'Maybe,' he said, matching her smile.

A companionable silence grew, during which Sam turned the conversation over and over in her mind. No matter how much he infuriated her, she'd never disliked Gabe, although she mistrusted his charm and good looks. But now she'd caught a glimpse of who he was beneath that charm and discovered she approved of what she saw; he was smart and perceptive, and emotionally intelligent too. She'd had no idea he was observing Laurie's arrival with such interest, either, or her and Nessie's reaction to it. Why should he, when it was no concern of his? And yet his observations made sense. There was no doubt about it, she decided, giving him a curious sideways glance; Gabe Santiago ran deeper than she'd imagined. Her heart sank a little as she realised what that meant: inevitably, it only made him more attractive.

'And there's no one special back home?' she blurted out, almost without meaning to. 'A woman, I mean. In Spain.'

His gaze was level as he glanced at her. 'No. Nobody special anywhere.'

'Oh,' she croaked in reply. 'I'm – uh – sorry to hear that.'

Sam spent the next few minutes berating herself for being so crass. But Gabe seemed to sense her discomfort and started to talk about the river that flowed through the heart of Seville and the building he missed the most. By the time he stopped and gestured off the path to the base of a tall beech tree, Sam had almost forgotten her stupidity.

'Look,' he said, pointing to a cluster of creamy yellow buttons. 'They look like chanterelle mushrooms to me. Shall we go and take a closer look?'

'That is why we're here,' she said, managing a small smile. 'You can't make a mushroom omelette without mushrooms, remember?'

'I remember,' he said. 'And I have a good feeling about these ones. I think they're going to blow your mind.'

Sam laughed. 'I hope they're not those kind of mushrooms. I'm not sure Little Monkham is ready for hallucinogens.'

Gabe knelt beside the tree and peered at its base. 'They're

not. But in the right hands, the taste of these will be almost as good.'

He drew out a knife and began to slice the stems, gathering the mushrooms into brown paper bags. As Sam watched his careful, deft movements, she couldn't help wondering what else those hands were good at. Maybe Nessie was right, she thought, watching his long fingers work, maybe it was time to find out what other talents Gabe had.

The sound of a key in the lock made Nessie, Owen and Luke all look up as they ate their evening meal.

Owen frowned. 'It can't be . . .'

Luke leapt up, his face aglow, and hurried to the hall. 'It is! It's Kathryn!'

A moment later, Owen's sister appeared in the doorway, with Luke's arms locked around her waist and a huge smile on her face. 'Surprise!'

'Kathryn!' Nessie exclaimed, her heart filled with astonished delight. 'I know I've lost my diary but hopefully not my marbles – please tell me we weren't expecting you.'

'You weren't,' the dark-haired woman said, her Welsh lilt teasing. 'That's why I said surprise.'

Owen got to his feet and wrapped her in a hug. 'It's good to see you. To what do we owe the pleasure?'

'Our drummer has broken his arm. So we're taking an enforced break from touring while he recovers.'

Luke beamed. 'Does that mean you're home for good?'

Kathryn ruffled his hair. 'Not good, no. But for a month

or so, at least.' She paused and sent a swift look Nessie's way. 'If that's okay, obviously.'

'Of course it is,' Nessie said, joining in the group hug. 'I can't think of anything I'd like more.'

'Good,' Kathryn replied. 'Now, if you'd all like to let go, I'll take my coat off.'

Nessie insisted on finding something for Kathryn to eat, so she could join them at the dining table. It had been just less than ten months since Kathryn had left Little Monkham to tour with her band, Sonic Folk, and she had plenty to tell them about life on the road, although Nessie was sure some of her stories were being hastily edited for Luke's benefit. It was good to have her back, she decided with a rush of warmth.

'And how are things between you two lovebirds?' Kathryn asked, once she'd run out of tour tales. 'No need to ask if you're enjoying sharing a nest – you're both glowing with contentment.'

Nessie glanced shyly at Owen, who smiled. 'We're very happy,' he said. 'Life couldn't be better, in fact.'

Kathryn widened her eyes. 'Oh?' she said innocently. 'Not even with the pitter-patter of tiny feet?'

Nessie drew in a sharp breath of embarrassment; having more children wasn't a subject she and Owen had discussed. It wasn't that either of them had avoided the topic, more that they were still getting used to living together. The thought of adding a baby seemed a step too far at the moment, but it was something Nessie hoped might happen in the future.

'No chance of that,' Owen said, with a rumble of amusement. 'Between the forge and the pub, we're far too busy for babies. Right, Nessie?'

'Right,' Nessie echoed, wondering why his pronouncement made her feel so flat inside.

'Awww,' Luke said, frowning. 'I wouldn't mind being a big brother.'

Owen fired a sideways glance at Kathryn. 'Believe me, Luke, it's overrated. Stick with being an only child.'

'You loved it when I arrived, Owen,' Kathryn said, grinning unrepentantly. 'Admit it.'

He smiled with genuine affection. 'I think I can honestly say it was the worst day of my life. You've been driving me nuts ever since.'

The conversation descended into good-natured squabbling, with Luke chipping in with cheerful insults where he could. Nessie did her best to join in but eventually let her gaze drop to her empty plate. At least now she knew how Owen saw their future without having to ask – he didn't want any more children. And that was fine, really it was; Luke was a wonderful stepson and she loved him more than she would have thought possible. But there had been a tiny part of Nessie that had assumed she and Owen might one day have a baby of their own together. And the knowledge that she'd so clearly been mistaken was going to take some getting used to.

'Nessie?' Kathryn's voice broke into her thoughts. 'Everything okay?'

She forced herself to smile. 'Of course. Now, why don't I fill you in on what's been happening in Little Monkham? You won't believe who Mr Bickerstaff eloped with . . .'

There was no doubt about it: Martha's Beyoncé left a lot to be desired. Nessie glanced across at Laurie, who was watching the performance on the karaoke stage with an expression that was somewhere between horrified fascination and grudging admiration.

'You get used to it after a while,' Nessie murmured as she eased past him behind the bar.

'Really?' he whispered back sceptically.

Nessie thought hard and sighed. 'No. But you do learn to tune it out, which is a very useful skill on karaoke night.'

Laurie grunted. 'I can imagine.' He glanced across at the whiteboard that held the list of upcoming performers. 'I dread to think what the vicar is going to sing. "Amazing Grace" or some other banger, I suppose.'

His withering tone caused Nessie to frown; she hoped none of their customers had heard it. But she could see where Laurie was coming from – Martha's performance didn't inspire confidence in the other Little Monkham residents' vocal talents.

She waited until she'd finished serving her customer before responding. 'Father Goodluck does a nice "Sweet Caroline", actually,' she said, her own voice upbeat. 'And Henry loves a bit of old-school Elvis, so I imagine he'll be singing something along those lines. They both might surprise you.'

Laurie looked unconvinced. 'We'll see.'

But it was Kathryn up next and even Laurie couldn't pull a face at her smoky rendition of 'Son of a Preacher Man'. In fact, Nessie caught him watching her with undisguised admiration more than once. And he wasn't the only man admiring Kathryn; Gabe looked impressed as he leaned against the bar. Nessie didn't dare ask Sam whether she'd noticed; there'd been a definite thaw in her sister's behaviour towards the chef, but Nessie didn't know whether that was because she'd got over her crush or decided to go with it. Best not to stir the pot, Nessie decided, as Kathryn finished the song and enthusiastic applause rang out around the bar.

George, the DJ, took the microphone and raised it to his mouth. 'Now, I know how much you enjoy fresh meat – I mean, fresh *talent* – here at the Star and Sixpence, so I'm delighted to welcome a debut performer to the stage. Let's hear it for Gabe Santiago, singing "Hero".'

A loud 'ooooh' of female appreciation swept across the bar. Nessie's head whipped around to find Sam, who was staring open-mouthed at Gabe as he wove through the crowd to take his place.

'He's either incredibly brave or unbelievably stupid,' Laurie said, shaking his head. 'If he's good, they'll never let him out of here fully clothed. And if he's bad . . .'

Ruby smiled. 'I have a feeling they'll forgive him.'

It became obvious the moment Gabe started to sing that no forgiveness would be needed. His voice was warmer than spiced honey, with the faintest raspy edge, but that wasn't what sent shivers down Nessie's spine; it was the fact that he was entirely ignoring the lyrics on the screen and singing the song in Spanish. And judging from the spellbound silence that had fallen over the audience, others felt exactly the same way.

More than once, Nessie's gaze strayed to her sister, who was somehow managing to look as though she'd heard Gabe sing a thousand times before. But Nessie wasn't fooled; there was a telltale flush along Sam's cheekbones that suggested she was far from immune to the effect of his voice. Interesting, Nessie thought, with a secret smile.

The applause was rapturous when Gabe stopped singing.

Martha leaned against the bar and fanned herself with a beer mat. 'Is it me or is it suddenly a bit warm?'

Ruby took a sip of her elderflower spritzer. 'It's not you – it's hotter than Burt Reynolds' chest hair in here.' She gave Nessie an arch look. 'I hope you're got plenty of ice back there.'

'Good point.' Nessie caught her brother's eye. 'Could you bring some more ice through when you've got a minute, please?'

Laurie nodded and disappeared through the door that led to the kitchen.

Ruby sniffed. 'I'm glad to see you're putting him to work. You might make a barman out of him yet.'

'I know you're not convinced by him,' Nessie said, lowering her voice so that only Ruby could hear, 'but give him another chance. At the end of the day, he is Dad's son.'

The older woman was silent for a moment, her eyes fixed on the swirling ice cubes in her glass. Then she looked up, a faintly reminiscent look in her eyes. 'You're right, as always, Nessie. Everyone deserves a second chance.'

Nessie opened her mouth to reply, but Kathryn chose that exact moment to materialise at Ruby's side. 'I need a long drink of something very cold and I need it right now.'

Wordlessly, Nessie poured her a pint of ice-cold lager and set it on the bar.

Kathryn took a long draught, then wiped the foam from her lips and fixed Nessie with a determined look. 'And now you're going to introduce me to your hot new chef.'

'You might want to wait,' Ruby said, nodding towards the stage. 'It looks like Henry is about to perform and you won't want to miss it.' She winked at Kathryn, who looked back and forth between her and Nessie.

'I've heard Henry sing before. What am I not going to want to miss?'

'His moves, darling,' Ruby said, eyes twinkling. 'He's added a few flourishes to his performance and it's like Elvis himself has come back to delight us all.'

Understanding dawned on Kathryn's face. 'All the more reason to find something else to do. Where did Gabe go, anyway?'

'He's being mobbed by Martha and her friends,' Nessie observed. 'Come on, he probably needs rescuing.'

But they hadn't got more than halfway across the pub floor when the opening bars of Henry's chosen song started to play. Both of them stopped: it definitely wasn't an Elvis song.

'Is that—' Nessie began.

Kathryn nodded. 'Bruno Mars. Well, well, it seems Henry has updated his repertoire.'

The lyrics began to roll across the screen. Henry started to sing. The tune was pitched a fraction too high, Nessie realised with a sinking feeling, but he pushed on, his gaze fixed on Franny the whole time. And as he took a breath, Kathryn let out a gasp of astonished recognition.

'Oh my god. It's *Marry You*. You don't think—'

'He's proposing to Franny,' Nessie breathed, taking in Henry's earnest expression and the shaking microphone in his hand. 'Yes, I think he might be!'

Franny's disapproving frown was slowly melting away as she understood what was happening. Her eyes widened and her mouth became a circle of astonishment. All around her, grins of delight materialised.

'Go on, Henry!' Martha's husband, Rob, shouted amid other calls of encouragement.

Nessie couldn't help grinning as she spotted Owen's amazed face on the far side of the pub. Had anyone, apart from DJ George, known what Henry was planning? She didn't think so. And yet why shouldn't he propose to Franny? It was true that most men would quake with terror at the idea, but Nessie had seen the fierce village postmistress soften since she and Henry had got together. And right now, her cheeks were flushed a girlish pink that told Nessie she was thrilled at the unexpected gesture of love.

As the last ding-dong of musical notes faded away, Henry

stepped briskly from the stage and fumbled in his jacket pocket. His white moustache bristled as he sank on one knee in front of Franny and cleared his throat. 'My dearest Frances,' he began gruffly, only the tiniest bit out of breath. 'Will you do me the very great honour of becoming my wife?'

He opened up the ring box to reveal a sparkling diamond on navy blue velvet. It felt to Nessie as if the entire population of Little Monkham held its breath, almost as though the Star and Sixpence herself was waiting. But Franny's pink cheeks deepened into a scarlet glow that lit up her face with a pure, unaccustomed joy.

'Yes, Henry,' she said, in a thick voice that sounded very much as though she was fighting back tears. 'Yes, I will marry you.'

The room erupted into cheers; whoops and applause rang out as Henry slid the diamond ring onto the third finger of Franny's left hand and planted a chaste kiss on her cheek. And then people were clapping him on the back, taking Franny's hand to admire the new ring and Nessie saw nothing but wall-to-wall smiles all across the pub.

Sam appeared at her side, looking amused. 'I can't decide whether Henry has taken leave of his senses permanently or just temporarily, but I think he's made Franny the happiest woman in the world.'

'Me too,' Nessie said. 'Look at her smile. If there's any tricky Preservation Society business we need her on side for, now's the time to ask.'

Sam nodded. 'And Henry definitely wins most original

marriage proposal. I had no idea he even knew who Bruno Mars is.'

'He's a dark horse,' Nessie replied, laughing.

Sam glanced over one shoulder. 'I'll tell you who else is a dark horse. Gabe. Did you have any idea he could sing like that?'

Nessie blinked. Henry had stolen the show so completely that she'd almost forgotten Gabe's performance. 'Of course I didn't. Did you?'

'Nope,' Sam said, then lowered her voice. 'But it didn't help me to see him as just our chef.'

'The good news is that you're not the only woman who feels that way,' Nessie said wryly, her gaze travelling across the bar to where Kathryn was introducing herself to Gabe. 'But if you're really interested, I think you might have some competition. Kathryn was very keen to meet him.'

Sam's expression grew suddenly neutral. 'Oh. I see.'

'Does he have any idea you feel like this?' Nessie asked.

'No,' Sam replied instantly, then gnawed on her lip. 'I can't see how he would. I've been careful.'

She glanced over at Gabe, who was smiling at Kathryn, and Nessie caught a flash of the attraction Sam was trying so hard to fight. 'Why don't you tell him?' she said kindly. 'How many times did you tell me to do the same with Owen? And how long did it take us to actually get together?'

'Too long,' Sam said, with a sigh. 'But you and Owen didn't work together. What if Gabe doesn't see me that way?'

'Then you patch up your wounded pride and move on,

with your head held high,' Nessie replied. 'But if you don't tell him, you run the risk of someone else getting in there first. And I think you need to ask yourself how that would make you feel.'

Nessie was pleased to see that her words seemed to galvanise Sam into action, who straightened her shoulders. 'Okay, I'll pick my moment.'

'Good,' Nessie said, with a nod of satisfaction. 'Now, we should probably go and say congratulations to the happy couple.'

Sam dragged her gaze away from Gabe and Kathryn. 'Of course. Shall we gift them a bottle of champagne too? I think they'd like that.'

'Great idea,' Nessie said. 'We've got a couple in the cellar – I'll go and get one.'

'Let me,' Sam replied. She gave Nessie a lopsided smile. 'I could do with a minute to myself, actually.'

Nessie smiled. 'Don't take too long or I might have to send Gabe down to look for you.'

Sam managed a weak grin. 'You know, that's not the worst idea you've ever had.'

'Just go,' Nessie said, laughing. 'And don't forget to bring the champagne.'

Chapter Eight

As the Autumn Taster Evening approached, life at the Star and Sixpence whipped into a whirlwind. The bar was buzzing most evenings, with more customers than usual even on the quieter nights, which Sam suspected was due at least in part to the feel-good factor that followed Henry and Franny's engagement. Sam had also been kept busy sourcing the wines Gabe had specified to go with his menu, something Nessie had uncharacteristically forgotten to do; her lost diary still hadn't materialised and seemed to be impacting on them in all kinds of unexpected ways. It was more than just the stress of a missing diary, though; Sam thought her sister seemed subdued in other ways too. She'd asked Laurie to fill in for three of her evening shifts over the last week, claiming Owen had a big project underway and needed her help to look after Luke.

'Can't Kathryn step in?' Sam had asked, but Nessie had shaken her head.

'I think she has other plans,' she'd answered cryptically.

It didn't take one of the Bletchley Circle to work out what she meant, Sam realised; Kathryn was spending most evenings in the Star and Sixpence, hoping for a glimpse of Gabe. Sam could hardly blame her; that was probably another reason the pub felt busier – half the village ladies were there most nights to sigh and swoon over him, and Sam herself was one of them. She might spend a large part of each day with Gabe, but she was fairly sure he saw her exactly the way she'd intended him to see her – as a colleague and fellow professional and nothing more. To make matters worse, since the karaoke evening, she'd found it almost impossible to flirt with him; it was as though she'd forgotten how to talk to him. Thank goodness Nessie wasn't at the top of her game, Sam thought with bewildered gratitude after another excruciating encounter; an inability to flirt was so remarkable that her sister would probably try to take her temperature.

Things hit crisis point on the morning of the Taste of Autumn event itself. Nessie was running late – some complication with getting Luke ready for school meant Sam had to see to the departing guests in the rooms upstairs at the same time as checking through the order for the kitchen.

'Why don't you leave the kitchen delivery with me?' Gabe said, leaning against the living-room door frame as Sam raced up the stairs for the fourth time in as many minutes. 'At least I'll have the benefit of remembering what I ordered.'

Out of the corner of one eye, Sam could see an expanse of tanned chest and she knew – just *knew* – it would be stippled with fine dark hair. She kept her gaze firmly averted as she reached the landing. 'I can manage.'

'I have no doubt you can,' Gabe said, his tone dry. 'But I'll be checking the delivery for myself the moment you finish. And it looks like you have enough to deal with right now – why don't you let me help?'

He sounded so reasonable that Sam forgot she shouldn't look at him. The sight of him lounging half-dressed in the doorway set her already racing heart thumping even more. 'The delivery note is in the kitchen downstairs,' she said tightly. 'Thank you.'

Gabe tipped his head. 'No problem. And I know you and Nessie usually share the job of preparing breakfast for the guest rooms, but if you ever want some help, I'm happy to chip in sometimes.'

The offer was so generous that Sam managed to smile in spite of her stress. 'That's not your job.'

'No,' he said, shrugging in a way that made his golden skin shimmer. 'But we're a team here. I'd be a pretty poor teammate if I didn't help out, not to mention a bad chef.'

His voice echoed in Sam's head long after he'd gone to find a shirt and she'd busied herself with ensuring the bed and breakfast guests were looked after. A team, she thought dreamily and then gave herself a mental shake. It was probably a good thing he had no idea what kind of team she'd like them to be.

Nessie appeared not long after nine-thirty. Sam took one look at her pale, clammy face and sat her down in the empty bar with a glass of water.

'What is it?' she asked in concern, as her sister pressed the glass to her cheek. 'Is it a cold, or the flu? Franny says we should get the jab – she said pubs are full of germs at the best of times, but winter is the worst.'

Nessie managed a weak smile. 'It's nothing. Probably just a touch of food poisoning.'

'What? Has anyone else got it?' Sam asked, frowning. 'Owen or Luke?'

'No,' Nessie replied. 'But I was the only one who had the prawns in the takeaway we shared last night. Obviously, they weren't quite as fresh as they should have been.'

Sam eyed her sister with concern: she looked as though she might blow over in a stiff breeze. And if it was food poisoning . . .

'Go home,' she said as kindly as she could. 'Apart from anything else, you look terrible and you're probably breaking a hundred health and safety rules just by being here.'

Nessie shook her head. 'I can manage some admin. The order for next month's barrels needs to go to the brewery and—' She stopped and put a hand over her mouth.

Sam stood up. 'You know I say this with love and sympathy, Ness, but please don't throw up on the carpet. We'll never shift the smell before tonight.'

With a stricken look, Nessie got to her feet and hurried for the toilets. When she returned a few minutes later, she wore an expression of resignation. 'I'm sorry to let you down like this.'

Sam let out a huff of exasperation. 'You're not letting anyone down. Now go and get better. Tell Owen to stop banging away in the forge and make him look after you – lots of rest and fluids and mopping your fevered brow.'

'He's out doing deliveries today,' Nessie replied. 'I'll just go to bed and wait for it to pass, I think. Sorry again.'

'Stop apologising,' Sam said loudly, then softened her tone. 'Try to sleep if you can and let me know if you need anything – I'll come and check on you later.'

'There's really no n—'

'There's every need,' Sam said, holding up a firm hand to forestall the inevitable argument. 'Now come on – I'll walk you back to the cottage.'

Once Nessie was safely tucked up in bed, with a jug of water and a bucket beside her, Sam made her way back to the Star and Sixpence and checked the staff rota. The plan had been for Nessie to help Gabe in the kitchen while Sam managed the front of house, but that was out of the question now. Her fingers hovered over the list of names; Connor and Laurie were manning the bar, with a team of Tilly and a pair of temporary waitresses called Charlotte and Sarah handling the food orders. But she still needed an extra pair of hands either to help in the kitchen or to greet the diners as they came in and seat them according to the table plan Nessie had drawn up. And the difficulty was that anyone Sam might normally call on was booked in to dine. In fact, the only person who hadn't booked was Kathryn.

Sam reached for her mobile and waited while it rang. Nessie had said she was the only one who'd eaten the dodgy prawns, hadn't she? Fingers crossed that Kathryn wasn't ill too . . .

'Hello you,' Kathryn said, her voice warm in Sam's ear. 'What's up?'

Taking a deep breath, Sam explained.

'And I'm really hoping it hasn't got you too,' she finished.

'No, I'm perfectly fine,' Kathryn reassured her. 'Poor Nessie – I had no idea she wasn't well. What can I do to help?'

'I know you're not coming along for the taster, but I'm really hoping you're in Little Monkham this evening,' Sam said. 'I could do with another pair of hands if you are.'

'As long as it's not waitressing,' Kathryn said. 'People are more likely to end up wearing the food instead of eating it if you make me do that.'

Sam laughed. 'No, we're sorted for waitresses. What I need from you is . . .' She glanced down at the paper in front of her and hesitated. What did she want Kathryn to do – front of house or help Gabe in the kitchen? The choice ought to be straightforward; Kathryn had spent years helping Owen to look after Luke, she knew one end of a saucepan from another. Whereas Sam was great at dealing with people but much preferred to leave the cooking to others – the thought of spending an evening in a steam-filled kitchen didn't fill her with enthusiasm. Except that Gabe would be there. And who knew what might happen if Kathryn was there too? Despising herself just the tiniest bit, Sam closed her eyes. 'If you could take over the front of house, that would be amazing. You'll know almost everyone who comes in – all you'll need to do is sit them down in the right places.'

'No problem,' Kathryn said cheerfully. 'I might even dig out an LBD for the occasion. Do you think Gabe might appreciate a nice fitted dress?'

'Definitely,' Sam said, pushing down a wave of guilt. 'Can you be here for six o'clock?'

If Gabe had any doubts about Sam's ability to assist him in the kitchen, he kept them to himself as she outlined the revised plan.

'I hope Nessie feels better soon,' he said sympathetically. 'Prawns get a bad press, but there's no doubt they need careful handling.'

Sam kept her eyes on her sheet of paper; Gabe was leaning against the stainless-steel counter, dressed in his crisp chef whites, and each time he moved Sam caught a hint of a citrus and musk scent that caused a flurry of butterflies inside her.

She cleared her throat. 'So you're okay with having me for a sous-chef?'

'Sure,' he said, spreading his hands and fixing her with a direct look. 'As long as you do everything I tell you to do, at the precise moment I tell you to do it, things will work out fine.'

Sam swallowed and glanced away, unable to resist a tiny

shiver of apprehension. Gabe might only be talking about cooking, but food certainly wouldn't be the only thing on Sam's mind that evening.

By seven-thirty, Sam had lost any expectations she'd had that working with Gabe might be sexy. There was her outfit, for a start; he'd taken one look at her fitted jeans and white T-shirt and insisted she wear an apron that almost drowned her. Her freshly straightened hair was scraped back into a severe bun and tucked into a net that reminded Sam strongly of stodgy school dinners. And her manicured fingers were encased in unattractive latex gloves that made handling everything more difficult. But she found the work itself surprisingly absorbing; Gabe had been scrupulous in his preparation. The fixed nature of the taster menu meant that there were no surprises and a lot of the hard work had already been done. But each plate still needed to be put together; Gabe's instructions were precise and authoritative, but he never raised his voice and Sam soon found herself anticipating his directives.

It wasn't quite how she'd pictured things, and she couldn't exactly call it fun, but there was a certain satisfaction to be taken from presenting a perfectly dressed plate for Gabe to work his magic over, and sensing his silent approval. Between the two of them, they were creating something that would give a moment of delight to the person who ate it. And that was a thought that made Sam smile, in spite of her intense concentration.

At ten o'clock, the last wave of desserts went out and Sam allowed herself a sigh of relief. They'd done it; nothing had been broken, no mistakes had been made and Gabe hadn't bellowed in the style of Gordon Ramsay once. And judging from the stream of compliments being relayed by Tilly and the other waitresses as they returned the empty plates, the taster menu had been a resounding success.

'Well done,' Sam told Gabe, as yet another glowing comment came in. 'I mean, I'm not in any way surprised that everyone loved the menu, given how amazingly talented you are.'

Gabe shrugged. 'It's me who should be thanking you, Sam. I know it can't have been easy to step in for Nessie, especially when you've never done anything like this before, but you did a great job.' He smiled. 'You can be my sous-chef again, if you like.'

The way he looked at her sent a sharp burst of heat through Sam's abdomen. She opened her mouth to reply, but the kitchen door opened and Kathryn came in. She beamed at both of them in obvious delight. 'That was what I reckon you PR types would call an absolute triumph. Franny practically fell off her chair when she tasted that roast beef and she's already talking about Gabe stealing Nigella's crown.'

Sam laughed and glanced at Gabe. 'Let's get the restaurant up and running first, shall we? Then we can discuss world domination.'

Kathryn grinned. 'Good idea. I was going to ask if the two

of you wanted to come out and meet your adoring public, but I'm guessing you might want to freshen up a bit first.'

Sam raised a suddenly self-conscious hand to her steam-frizzed hair; she was willing to bet that all her carefully applied make-up had melted away in the heat, leaving her face shiny and naked. Gabe, on the other hand, looked the same as he always did: good enough to eat. It really wasn't fair. 'No, I'll stay here and get on with the cleaning up.'

Gabe frowned. 'We're a team, Sam. You should come and take your share of the praise.'

She managed a rueful smile. 'It's not me they came for, Gabe. And a good PR always knows when to stand back and let the talent shine.'

For a moment, she thought he would argue; his gaze was brooding as he studied her. But after a few seconds, he tipped his head and followed Kathryn out to the bar. Sam heard the start of enthusiastic applause before the kitchen door swung closed, leaving her alone. She stood still, letting the adrenaline drain away and feeling bone-weary exhaustion take its place. And then she pulled open the dishwasher and began to load the plates.

She was elbow-deep in washing-up suds, rinsing the last saucepan, when Gabe reappeared some thirty minutes later, bearing two flutes of what looked a lot like champagne.

'Please tell me that is what I think it is,' she said, her mouth watering in anticipation.

'It is,' Gabe answered, placing the flutes on the work surface and gently lifting her hands from the water. 'There was just enough left over from the bottles we bought and I decided we deserved them more than Laurie.'

The breath caught in Sam's throat as he reached for a towel and dried her hands. It was a curiously intimate thing for him to do and yet somehow it felt like the most natural action. She ought to say something, Sam thought distractedly, but, as often seemed to be the case around Gabe these days, no words presented themselves. Instead, she took the glass he offered her and gazed up at him as he chinked it delicately against his own.

'To teamwork,' he said.

'To teamwork,' she repeated, cursing her lack of original-ity. But the way Gabe was looking at her made it difficult to think about anything other than how dark and deep his brown eyes were.

The champagne was blissfully cool. Crisp bubbles burst on Sam's tongue, sending waves of buttery deliciousness across her taste buds. She closed her eyes for a moment, savouring the sharpness, and opened them to find Gabe was still watching her.

'I'm glad you've decided to let us be friends,' he said, a faint smile pulling at one corner of his mouth.

The polite thing would be to deny it, Sam thought in a panic-fuelled fluster. But then she saw the gentle amusement in his eyes and her panic lessened. She took another sip of champagne. 'Me too. Although it wasn't ever a reflection on your professional abilities.'

He raised an eyebrow. 'I am glad to hear it.'

Sam glanced at the door, weighing up the odds of someone

walking in at the exact moment she admitted the real reason she'd been so frosty; it was definitely a risk. But she'd also seen the way Kathryn had turned to Gabe as they'd left the kitchen, a flirtatious smile at the ready. If she didn't seize the moment now, Sam wasn't at all sure she'd get another chance. She gripped the stem of her champagne flute and tried to summon up some of her old PR charm.

'In fact, it wasn't a reflection on you at all,' she said, forcing herself to sound light. 'It was me, trying to pretend I wasn't attracted to you.' She glanced upwards, half-expecting to see him looking surprised but he simply nodded.

'I know.'

'You *know*?'

Gabe sighed. 'I didn't know immediately. At first, I was confused – you'd been so warm when we met in London, so full of enthusiasm for how we might work together. And then I arrived here and you were like a different person.'

Sam resisted the urge to fold her arms. 'So you naturally assumed I must fancy you, is that it?'

His gaze held hers. 'No. It took a little while, but I gradually came to recognise that you felt the same thing I did when I was with you.' His mouth curved into a soft smile as he took a step nearer to her. 'But I didn't know for sure until that day in the woods, when you asked whether there was anyone special back home in Spain.'

Her head was spinning. Had he really just said he felt the same way as her? 'I thought I'd better check,' she murmured. 'Just in case you had a wife and six beautiful babies.'

'No wife,' he replied, closing the distance between them to a few centimetres. 'No babies. I'm as single as you are, Sam.'

Before she could stop herself, Sam reached up to brush her fingers along the shadow that lined his jaw. 'Good,' she said. 'Because I think I'm going to kiss you.'

She stood on tiptoe to press her lips against his. The moment her mouth touched his, she felt the shiver of a million goosebumps break out across her skin as every hair stood on end.

Gabe leaned into her with gentle insistence, parting her lips. Sam's eyes drifted shut as her fingers burrowed into his hair, pulling him nearer. Kissing him was everything she'd hoped it would be: soft, yearning and satisfying all at the same time. He placed one hand on the small of her back, pressing his body against hers, and Sam gave herself up to the kiss.

When they finally parted, Sam found she needed to hold onto Gabe to stop herself from shaking. The passion in his eyes faded as he studied her in concern. 'As much as I'd like to think that was me, I don't think I can take all the credit. What's wrong?'

Sam frowned. 'I'm not sure ...' And then the answer presented itself: she'd skipped dinner. 'Oh – I think I might be hungry!'

Gabe smiled. 'Well, luckily we can do something about that. When it comes to late-night snacks, I'm definitely your man.'

Leaning her against the work surface, he crossed to

the fridge. Sam watched him go, hugging the warmth of his embrace to herself. If that kiss was anything to go by, Gabe was going to be every bit as wonderful as she'd anticipated. But there was no rush, she decided as he pulled containers from the fridge shelves and reached for a saucepan. She'd learned her lesson from charging into a relationship with Joss: this time, she was definitely going to take things slowly.

Chapter Nine

Sam found it hard to look Kathryn in the eye the following morning.

'I thought we should finalise plans for Franny's hen do,' the dark-haired woman said across the bar. She held up a square box emblazoned with the logo from Martha's bakery. 'I brought freshly baked macarons.'

Guilt sent spidery tendrils crawling over Sam; she did her best to scorch them. She hadn't done anything wrong – not really. And Gabe had been equally involved, although Sam couldn't see that he had anything to feel guilty for; Kathryn wasn't his friend. That was the problem – Sam had betrayed an unwritten rule of womanhood; she'd known her friend fancied Gabe and she'd still gone ahead and kissed him. It didn't matter that they hadn't gone any further than kissing. The treachery was still there.

She summoned up a smile, hoping it didn't look as false

and worthless as it felt. 'I'm always up for Martha's macarons. Why don't you come upstairs?'

They settled in the kitchen.

Sam set a pot of tea on the table and tried to ignore the subtly inquisitive glances Kathryn sent along the landing towards Gabe's room. 'I haven't heard from Nessie – how is she? Any better?'

Kathryn pulled a face. 'Not much. She looked quite poorly this morning – Owen was trying to persuade her to go to the doctor, but she said she'd rather get some rest.'

Unease blossomed in the pit of Sam's stomach. It was very unlike Nessie to take time off from work and even less like her to take to her bed. 'Has she eaten much?'

'Owen made her some toast this morning,' Kathryn replied. 'But I don't know how much of it she managed.'

'I'll pop over and see her later,' Sam said, frowning. 'Maybe I can persuade her to go to see Dr Armstrong.'

'I'm sure she'd love to see you,' Kathryn said as she poured the tea. 'And I imagine she'll want your take on last night. I gave her the edited highlights, of course, but she might want to hear how Gabe performed up close.'

More guilt flooded Sam's cheeks, despite knowing that Kathryn had no idea just how close she and Gabe had become. She took a sip of too-hot tea to cover her embarrassment. 'I'm not sure there's much to tell her. We were run off our feet for most of the evening.'

Kathryn sighed. 'I wouldn't mind being run off my feet by Gabe.'

And now Sam was certain her face must be flaming red. She busied herself by opening the cake box. 'Oh, you brought a couple of the pistachio ones. They're my favourites – thank you.'

Kathryn reached for a bright pink raspberry cake. 'You're welcome. Martha said she's happy to provide the cakes for the hen do, by the way. All we really need to decide is how we're going to get Franny to the venue without raising her suspicions.'

Sam laughed. 'I'm not sure that's going to be possible. I bet her spies have already revealed all our plans.'

The Welsh woman winked. 'They can't know about the game of pin the willy on the groom I've got planned.'

'You haven't!' Sam gasped.

'I have. I'm hoping Henry will let me draw his outline, but Owen can step in if not.'

She looked so pleased with herself that Sam couldn't help grinning. 'Can you imagine Franny's reaction?'

Kathryn smirked. 'I bet she'll love it. She's not as prudish as she makes out, you know.'

'I hope you're right,' Sam said, with a slight shudder as she imagined an incensed Franny when confronted by the task. 'For all our sakes. Now, how are we going to get her over to Purdon next Saturday?'

It was early evening. Sam gazed around the café she'd hired for Franny's hen do and allowed herself to bask a little in the glow of a job well done. All the village women were there, wearing various hot-pink hen party accessories: Ruby and Nessie were debating the perfect Virgin Mary recipe, Martha was putting the finishing touches to the *Magic Mike* gingerbread men they'd baked and Tilly was giggling with Kathryn over some photos of Franny as a baby. It had all gone much better than Sam had dared to hope, although there'd been a split second at the start when they'd removed Franny's blindfold and presented her with her undeniably tacky Bride-To-Be throne that she'd worried she and Kathryn had got things horribly wrong. But the smile that had split Franny's face a moment later laid all Sam's fears to rest. And now, several cocktail pitchers for the better, the party was in full swing. Kathryn hadn't yet found the courage to bring out her pièce de résistance, but Sam was as certain as it was possible to be that Franny would enter into the spirit of things.

She watched now as Franny got to her feet, bridal-white deely boppers waggling, and made her way unsteadily towards her.

'This is lovely,' she said, only slurring her words a little. 'Really lovely. Jus' what I wanted.'

Sam hid a smile; she wasn't sure she'd ever seen Little Monkham's most formidable resident drunk before. 'I'm pleased to hear that. How's Henry's stag do going?'

Franny peered owlishly at her phone. 'Very well. He says he won the beer pong, whatever that is.'

Sam pictured the scene at the Star and Sixpence and grinned. 'Good. And are you feeling happy about the wedding itself? It's only a few weeks away now.'

'It's all under control,' Franny said, tapping her nose in a conspiratorial way. 'Henry has been sensible enough to real-ise I know best – we haven't had a single argument.'

Once again, Sam wanted to smile. Henry might come across as curmudgeonly with everyone else, but he was obviously head-over-heels in love with Franny and it was hard to imagine him disagreeing with her over anything to do with their wedding day. 'He's a good man,' she said warmly.

'He is,' Franny replied, then fixed Sam with a solemn stare. 'But what about you, Samantha? I worry about you being all alone now that Vanessa has Owen. We need to find a good man for you.'

'Don't worry about that,' Sam said, touched by her con-cern. 'I'm not in any hurry.'

Franny swallowed a hiccup and raised a finger of warning. 'That's what I used to say. And then forty years went by.'

'But then you found Henry,' Sam pointed out. 'And he's the perfect match for you.'

'We need to find you a Henry,' Franny said. Her gaze sharpened. 'Not my Henry. Another one. A younger one.'

'Ideally,' Sam said, her mouth twisting in amusement.

A shadow fell across them and Sam looked up to see Ruby standing there, glamorous as ever in the hot-pink sash all the guests wore. 'Sorry, Sam, I'm under instruc-tions from Kathryn to retrieve Franny for important hen duties,' she said.

Sam glanced over at Kathryn, who was holding a

suspiciously bulky armful of paper. 'Far be it from me to monopolise the bride-to-be,' she said. 'Off you go, Franny.'

Ruby slipped a hand under Franny's elbow and guided her over to her throne.

Nessie took advantage of the empty seat and slid in beside Sam with a smile. 'How's our hen?'

'Bearing up,' Sam said. 'More importantly, how are you doing?'

Nessie gave her a weary smile. 'Not bad. A little tired of being tired, but I'm sure that will pass soon enough. It has to, it's been a week! Who knew prawns could be so much trouble?'

Sam gave her sister a sideways look. 'You're sure that's what it is, then?'

A frown creased Nessie's forehead. 'What else could it be?'

'Let's see . . . what else might cause a woman to throw up every day for over a week?'

'Oh, that,' Nessie replied, her confused expression clearing. 'There's no way I could be pregnant. We're far too careful.'

Sam studied her; there was no doubt that Nessie was certain. And surely she would know. 'You're not late or anything like that?'

Nessie shook her head. 'It's all clearly marked in my diary – I'd know.'

Sam paused. 'The diary you lost?'

And now it was Nessie's turn to hesitate. 'Yes, that diary. But I'm sure, Sam. I can't be pregnant.'

'Okay,' Sam said, reassured. 'Because it's been bad enough not having you around for this last week. I'm not sure I could cope with you abandoning me for maternity leave.'

Nessie raised her eyebrows. 'Have things been that tricky? You and Gabe seem to be getting along like a house on fire now.'

Sam couldn't help it; she blushed. And it wasn't lost on Nessie.

'Sam?' she said incredulously. 'Is there something you want to tell me?'

There wasn't, Sam thought desperately. Nothing at all. But at the same time, she knew it was too late; Nessie wasn't going to let go. 'We might have kissed,' she admitted in a low voice. 'After the Taste of Autumn evening.'

Nessie's face lit up. 'But that's good news. Why didn't you tell me?'

Sam cast an unhappy look in Kathryn's direction. 'Because there's a complication. And until I've spoken to her, I don't know whether Gabe and I can move forward.'

Understanding dawned on Nessie. 'Oh, I see. She'll understand, though. And besides, she'll be off touring again in a few months.'

'I know,' Sam sighed. 'Maybe I'm just being a coward.'

Her sister smiled. 'Sam Chapman, you are the least cowardly person I know. Terrified of getting your heart broken again, maybe. But never a coward.'

The warmth in her voice lifted Sam's spirits. 'So you think I should talk to Kathryn?'

'I think you should stop creating complications,' Nessie said firmly. 'You like Gabe, he clearly likes you. I can't believe I'm having to tell you this, but why don't you both have some fun?'

It made sense, Sam thought; was she putting barriers in the way where none really existed? It certainly wouldn't be the first time.

'Be honest with Kathryn,' Nessie said, as Sam cleared her throat. 'She'll cope. And, more importantly, be honest with yourself.'

'Okay, I will,' Sam promised.

At that moment, Kathryn held up a hand for silence. 'And now for something that will stand Franny in good stead on her wedding night.' She held up a packet of drawing pins and flashed a wicked grin. 'It's time to find out which of us can tell Henry's arse from his elbow!'

Chapter Ten

Nessie slept late on Sunday morning.

Snowdrop Cottage was uncharacteristically silent when she woke up; Owen and Luke were out at football, and Kathryn was snoozing off the effects of the seemingly endless cocktail pitchers that had kept appearing at their table the night before. Nessie was relieved she'd chosen to drive; she didn't envy Kathryn the hangover she'd undoubtedly have when she woke up. She felt awful enough as it was; her stomach was rolling unpleasantly in a way she'd become all too familiar with over the last week.

She lay in bed for a moment and watched the sunlight play across the ceiling, then glanced at the tuft of paper poking out of her handbag and sighed. She'd made an excuse to duck out during yesterday's celebrations, her illness providing the perfect excuse to pop to the pharmacy. Though it was purely a formality; something to set her mind at rest after her sister's interrogation at the hen party. But if she was going to do it, she ought to do it now, before Owen came home and got entirely the wrong idea.

She read the instructions twice, then took a deep breath and followed them to the letter. It was strangely unsettling to sit staring at the smooth white stick as the long seconds ticked by, waiting for it to confirm what she already knew. But at least this way she could confidently tell Sam that she was wrong and concentrate on getting better.

Her phone beeped, alerting her that the three minutes were up. Impatiently, Nessie stared at the test, waiting for the words *Not Pregnant* to appear. When only half the message materialised, she waited for the word 'Not' to emerge. It didn't.

A cold feeling of panic squeezed at her heart as she gazed downwards. *Pregnant* loomed back at her, undeniable and certain.

She sat back on the edge of the bath. It couldn't be. *She* couldn't be ... *Oh my god,* she thought, clenching her eyes shut. *How am I going to tell Owen?*

She was still perched on the edge of the bath when he and Luke arrived home ten minutes later.

'Ness?' he called from the other side of the bathroom door. 'Are you in there? Luke needs a shower – he's got mud in places you wouldn't believe.'

Nessie looked down at the pregnancy test again, hoping the message might have miraculously changed. It hadn't.

With a leaden sensation dragging at her stomach, she stood and opened the door.

'What?' Owen said, the moment he saw her expression. 'Are you ill again?'

She drew in a shaky breath and held up the test. 'Not exactly.'

His eyebrows beetled together furiously, then shot up towards his hairline as his lips worked wordlessly for a few seconds. 'But how?' he finally managed. 'When?'

'The forge, I suppose,' she said, studying him with anxious eyes to gauge his reaction. 'It's the only time we didn't take precautions.'

His gaze dropped to the test once more, and then slid back to her face. 'And how do you feel about it?'

It was a good question, Nessie thought. 'Stunned, mostly. I was so sure it was the takeaway that was making me feel so awful that I never stopped to consider anything else.' She gnawed at her lip. 'How do you feel?'

He didn't answer. Nessie felt tears prick the back of her eyes; surely he wasn't going to remind her he didn't want any more children? She blinked hard, determined not to cry. And then his hand moved to curve protectively around her belly and he gave her a smile so wide she thought her heart would crack. 'How could I be anything other than over the moon, Nessie? We're – we're going to have a baby!'

She burst into tears. Owen pulled her into his arms, raining kisses onto the top of her head as she sobbed into his chest. Moments later, Luke and Kathryn appeared in the doorway, their startled faces pale.

'What's going on?' Kathryn demanded. 'What's wrong?'

Owen turned to beam at her. 'Nothing's wrong.' He took a deep breath and gave Luke an encouraging nod. 'Do you remember what you said about being a big brother?'

Luke's face lit up. 'Seriously? SERIOUSLY?'

'Seriously,' Owen laughed and looked at Kathryn. 'And I'm afraid that means you're going to be an auntie again.'

'I knew it!' Kathryn crowed, her expression shining with happiness. 'Bloody hell, I can't think of anything I'd like more.'

It was all too much for Nessie, who broke into a fresh peal of sobbing that only subsided when Owen tilted her face upwards and gently wiped her tears away. 'I can't think of anything else I'd like more, either,' he said, planting a soft kiss on her lips. 'You're going to be a wonderful mother, Nessie. Everything is going to be fine.'

He wrapped his arms around her and held her tight. And her feeling of panic vanished, to be replaced by a lightness she hadn't felt for weeks. She touched her stomach wonderingly and allowed herself the smallest of smiles. 'I'm not sure I believe it yet,' she whispered back. 'But everything *is* going to be fine.'

PART TWO

Christmas Kisses
at the Star and Sixpence

Chapter Eleven

CALLING ALL GINTHUSIASTS!

**Sam, Nessie and Laurie Chapman
are proud to invite you to a
FESTIVAL of GIN**

at the Star and Sixpence.

Sample gins from award-winning boutique distilleries
and tickle your taste buds with our bespoke cocktails.

Don't miss the chance to meet our Author in Residence,
the *Sunday Times* Bestseller, Lola Swann.

Thursday 6th – Sunday 9th December

St Mary's Church was packed. Nessie didn't think she'd ever seen more people crammed into the dark wooden pews, not even for the Christmas Eve carol service and that tended to be a full house. Today, every seat was taken and there were more people standing shoulder to shoulder at the back, pink-cheeked in spite of the late-November chill outside. They had run out of hymn sheets and the order of service cards, but nobody seemed to mind; in fact, they seemed happy to share. But there was a very good reason for the full church, Nessie reflected as she gazed at Father Goodluck in his white and gold robes: it wasn't every day that Franny Forster, the for-midable Chairwoman of the Little Monkham Preservation Society, got married. In fact, Nessie very much doubted that anyone had had the guts to turn down the bride's command to attend.

Beside her, Sam fidgeted. 'If I'd known these seats were so uncomfortable, I'd have brought a cushion,' she muttered in Nessie's ear.

Nessie hid a smile. Her sister was an infamously reluctant churchgoer and seized on any excuse to avoid the regu-lar occasions throughout the year when the rest of Little Monkham's residents gathered en masse under St Mary's vaulted roof. But, like everyone else, she wouldn't have missed witnessing Franny and Henry tie the knot.

'I'm not sure I'll believe it until I see it happen,' Sam had told Nessie as they'd left the Star and Sixpence that morning to walk the short distance to the church. 'I still can't get my head around the idea of Franny as a married woman.'

Nessie knew exactly what she meant; Franny had seemed perfectly content to conform to the stereotypical 'Spinster of this Parish' role life had dealt her. But she also suspected that much of Franny's spiky exterior was merely armour against the disappointments of the past. It had taken Henry some time to negotiate his way past the barriers and into her heart but, now that he was there, Nessie suspected he'd made Franny the happiest woman alive. And one look at her glowing face as she spoke her vows confirmed it.

A short sigh issued from Nessie's other side. She glanced across to see that her half-brother, Laurie, wasn't even trying to conceal his expression of boredom.

'What?' he whispered when he saw her watching him. 'I hate weddings.'

She shook her head and wished, not for the first time, that it was Owen beside her instead. She imagined entwining her fingers with his as the romance of the wedding swept her away, exchanging a tender look and feeling the warmth of his love flow along her arm and into her belly, where their baby might somehow feel it too. But Owen was at the front of the church, along with his nine-year-old son, Luke, fulfilling the responsibilities as part of the church choir. Nessie had to content herself with the occasional mutual glance and the admitted pleasure of hearing his delicious baritone rolling across the congregation during the hymns.

'Not long now,' she murmured to Laurie, as Henry's best man stepped forward with the rings.

Laurie threw her a grumpy look. 'There's ages left. I wish I'd stayed at the pub.'

Nessie straightened and watched Franny slide the ring onto Henry's finger, determined not to let either of her siblings spoil the moment for her. Sam had sworn off marriage years ago, describing it as a total waste of money and paper, although Nessie knew she had no problem going to the parties that followed. And Nessie had yet to uncover Laurie's views on matrimony, but his grumbling now suggested he wasn't a fan. She thought once again of the baby inside her. What if the next wedding Sam and Laurie attended was Nessie's own; surely they'd be more gracious then? Although she had no idea yet whether Owen wanted to get married. He'd been unexpectedly thrilled at the news she was pregnant, but she knew he was entirely oblivious to her longing to do everything 'properly'; to Nessie, getting married was the next step, both romantically and logically. And if Owen did agree with her, then the next wedding Sam and Laurie attended probably would be their sister's. She'd have to give them both important jobs to do, to keep them busy . . .

An expectant hush fell over the congregation as Ruby Cabernet made her way to the pulpit, exquisitely dressed in a figure-hugging emerald-green dress, her vibrant red hair gleaming under the soft lights. Pausing to offer a smile that was both practised and warm, she began to read.

'Set me as a seal upon your heart, as a seal upon your arm,' she said, causing a rush of goosebumps to race across Nessie's skin as she recognised the Song of Solomon. 'For love is as strong as death, passion fierce as the grave.'

Ruby went on, her voice sizzling with all the emotion her many years of acting could muster, and Nessie felt her gaze drawn to Owen once more. She expected to find him watching Ruby, but his eyes were fixed on hers, dark and intense. Nessie felt a shiver dance down her spine as something unspoken passed between them.

'Many waters cannot quench love, neither can floods drown it.' Ruby soared to a rich crescendo. 'If one offered for love all the wealth of one's house, it would be utterly scorned.'

The reading had been so expertly delivered that a smattering of applause broke out. Nessie barely noticed; she was too mesmerised by the expression on Owen's face.

'You two are going to get thrown out if you're not careful,' Sam whispered in her ear, sounding amused. 'I'm not sure the Church of England holds with such unbridled yearnings.'

Heat flooded Nessie's cheeks and she broke eye contact to throw a sheepish look at her sister. 'Sorry.'

'Don't be,' Sam replied, grinning. 'That reading is scorching hot. It's the one Harry and Meghan had at their wedding, right?'

Nessie nodded. 'Yes, that's it.' She glanced at Franny and Henry, who only had eyes for each other. 'Not quite what I expected, to be honest.'

'Me neither. I think Franny has hidden depths.' Sam's grin became a smirk. 'Poor Henry.'

Father Goodluck replaced Ruby at the pulpit and spread

his arms wide. 'Marriage is what brings us together today . . .'

His cheery sermon on the redeeming quality of love gave Nessie the opportunity to calm her racing pulse and discreetly fan her too-warm face with the order of service. The number of people packed into the pews wasn't helping her cool down, although the memory of the way Owen had gazed at her was having its own effect on her body. She forced herself to focus on Father Goodluck and tried not to join her siblings in wishing the service was over.

The shuffling that had broken out during the vicar's sermon ceased the moment nineteen-year-old Tilly began to sing, as Franny and Henry vanished to sign the register. Her pure soprano voice sounded achingly flawless as she climbed through the high notes of 'Ave Maria'. Nessie exchanged a look of pride with Sam at their talented barmaid and, in the pew ahead, Martha was clutching her husband's arm and failing to hold back tears at her daughter's perfect performance.

And then Father Goodluck led the bride and groom back to the altar for the final blessings. With a triumphant burst of chords, the organist played 'The Wedding March' and a radiant Franny walked down the aisle on Henry's arm, beaming at anyone who caught her eye. Applause filled the church, along with whoops and cheers that sounded both right and wrong to Nessie, and she couldn't hide a broad smile of her own as she joined in. Even Laurie was clapping, despite his boredom earlier in the ceremony. Sam was grinning from ear to ear too as she watched the happy couple pass by. And then she turned to Nessie and Laurie, her grin becoming considerably more businesslike.

'Father Goodluck said we can sneak out through the vestry. We need to get back to the pub before this lot, otherwise Gabe's going to be crushed in the stampede at the bar.'

'Excellent plan,' Nessie said, pulling on her coat. 'Let's get going.'

Owen reached out a hand to clasp hers as she passed him in the aisle, but there wasn't time to do more than squeeze his fingers.

'See you later,' she mouthed before he was swept along towards the rear of the church.

She cast one final look towards him as Sam ducked through the smaller door into the vestry and saw a face that made her heart plummet. Standing among the assembled guests, staring as the sisters hurried away, was Joss Felstead. The man who'd broken Sam's heart.

The Star and Sixpence filled up fast. Sam busied herself behind the bar, forcing Nessie's whispered warning to the back of her mind. The news that Joss was at the wedding had caused an unpleasant lurch in Sam's gut that had unsettled her more than she'd ever admit. It shouldn't be a problem, she'd told herself fiercely as they'd hurried across the green towards the pub. He had just as much right to be at the wedding as she had; maybe more, since he'd been a Little Monkham resident for a lot longer than her before his sudden move to Chester. And relationships failed all the time – surely enough time had passed for them to be civil, if not quite friends . . .

All the same, Sam wasn't ready to look into his familiar, summer-blue eyes when he appeared at the bar. A moment of panic clutched at her heart and she considered backing away, leaving him to Laurie. But then the corner of Joss's mouth twitched beneath his beard, as though he knew what she was thinking, and she straightened her shoulders.

'What can I get you, Joss?'

'A pint of Thirsty Bishop and a glass of Prosecco, please,' he replied, his expression as polite as hers.

Sam resisted the temptation to gaze over his shoulder for a plus-one; Nessie hadn't been able to work out whether he'd been alone in the church, but the Prosecco suggested he hadn't. It wasn't any of her business who he'd brought, Sam reminded herself as she tucked a glass under the beer pump and heaved the handle slightly harder than was necessary,

'Steady, Sam,' Joss said, his sandy eyebrows raised as the beer sputtered and foamed. 'Don't tell me you've forgotten everything I taught you.'

She fought the rising tide of crimson creeping up her neck and eased her grip on the pump, pouring all her concentration into pulling the perfect pint. *Don't tip it over his head*, she told herself sternly as she summoned up her coolest smile and placed the glass on the bar in front of him.

'No need to pay,' she said, waving away his money once the Prosecco was beside the beer. 'It's a free bar.'

'Oh. Thanks,' Joss said. His eyes lingered on her and, for

a moment, he looked as though there was something more he wanted to say. But, instead, he simply nodded and picked up the drinks.

Sam turned away, hoping she didn't look as flustered as she felt, and realised Laurie was watching her with undisguised curiosity. She allowed herself a small inward groan; round one to Joss. Her gaze flickered to the door that led to the kitchens, where Gabe and his little team were working hard on canapés and the buffet for the guests – at least he hadn't witnessed her less-than-dignified first encounter with her ex. Then again, perhaps he wouldn't care; there'd been precious few kisses since the one they'd stolen during the Taste of Autumn evening the previous month. Nessie's morning sickness meant Sam's workload had doubled and, together with the pressure on Gabe to get the restaurant menu up and running, they had both been too stressed and exhausted to manage much more than some half-hearted flirting whenever they met on the landing of the accommodation they shared above the pub. And now that the restaurant was running four nights a week, things were even more hectic; neither had time for a personal life – not with anyone. At least, that's what Sam told herself. In her darker moments, she wondered whether Gabe had lost interest in her entirely.

Giving herself a brisk shake, Sam smiled at the next customer, who happened to be Owen. 'Let me guess,' she said, before the dark-haired Welshman could speak. 'A pint of the Bishop, right?'

He flashed her a good-natured grin. 'Am I that predictable?'

'You are,' Sam said, feeling some of her tension ease as she returned his smile. 'It's very soothing, knowing that some things never change.'

'Happy to be of service,' Owen said sombrely. 'Kathryn would like a Silver Sixpence cocktail and Luke has asked for a Coke, but he'll be getting an orange juice.'

As Sam busied herself with his order, she noticed him watching Nessie with a look of tender concern. And, for the first time, she felt a stab of envy at the way things had worked out for her older sister. Nessie had everything: a gorgeous home, a partner who adored her and a ready-made family that she was sealing with the new baby. And while the thought of motherhood filled Sam with horror, she had to admit she was quietly jealous of Nessie's contentment. She didn't begrudge her a moment of happiness, of course, but she couldn't help wishing for a slice of that happiness for herself. Or at least a sliver of stability.

God, Sam thought, swirling the silver-coloured cocktail around the glass with a stirrer, *I must be getting old.*

She was grateful when the bar grew so busy that she barely had a moment to think. By the time Franny and Henry arrived, rosy-cheeked from posing for the wedding photographer in the chilly November air, the drinks were flowing freely and the waitresses were weaving their way through the crowd with trays of Gabe's mouth-watering canapés. As Franny and Henry made their way around the guests, accepting congratulations, Sam made her way over to Nessie, who was collecting empty glasses.

'Time for you to take a break,' she said firmly. 'Owen and Luke are over there – why don't you go and sit with them, take the weight off your feet?'

Nessie looked as though she wanted to argue, then her hand curved around the small bump that had already started to show. 'Okay, if you're sure you can manage?'

Sam nodded. 'I've got Connor and Laurie. We can spare you for a while.'

Her sister gave her a grateful smile. 'In that case, I'll do as I'm told.'

It wasn't until Sam was behind the bar once more that she noticed Laurie was nowhere to be seen. There wasn't time to track him down, however; several people were waving empty glasses at her. Gritting her teeth into something resembling a smile, Sam hoped Laurie had just nipped to the loo. This was no time to take an unscheduled break.

Laurie still hadn't reappeared when the guests began to trickle out of the heated marquee on the village green. As the crowd thinned, Sam scanned the pub for her brother. She caught sight of him vanishing into the kitchen and was about to follow when she was accosted by Henry's best man, demanding drinks to take into the meal. By the time she'd furnished him with several pints, the bar was empty enough for her to see Joss laughing with Tilly. He glanced over, catching her staring, and she couldn't help muttering a not-quite-inaudible curse.

'Back in a second,' she told Connor, who nodded and continued to serve the remaining customers.

If Sam had expected the kitchen to be an oasis of calm after the bustle of the bar, she was in for a disappointment. Steam clouded the air, and Gabe's staff had their heads down, concentrating on their work. The atmosphere was thick with tension and Sam instantly understood why; there seemed to be some kind of argument going on between Gabe and Laurie.

'We ordered what you asked for,' Laurie said, his tone adamant. 'Beef and prawns for the canapés. Salmon for the starters.'

Gabe's lip curled in disgust. 'I needed topside of beef, not the cheapest cut you could find,' he said, his Spanish accent growing thicker in his fury. 'And these prawns barely deserve to be called that – look how small they are. As for the salmon . . . it tastes as though it was smoked in a tobacco factory.'

'Have you seen the price for topside?' Laurie countered. 'We're running a business here, Gabe. And in case you hadn't noticed, we don't have a Michelin star. No one expects that kind of quality, and they're certainly not paying those sorts of prices.'

Sam stepped in between the two men, a hot rush of embarrassment sweeping over her. Laurie's chin was raised high in challenge and Gabe's fists were clenched, as though he might punch the younger man at any moment. 'That's enough,' she said sharply. 'What's going on here?'

Gabe gestured to a silver tray, half-full of canapés, a furious glint in his eye. 'Look at those. I have never known these to go uneaten before. Never.'

Sam frowned. She'd tasted plenty of Gabe's test recipes and they'd been melt-in-the-mouth delicious. It was surprising that the hungry wedding guests hadn't snapped them up.

'Try one,' Gabe went on, thrusting the tray under her nose. 'You'll soon understand.'

Suddenly reluctant, Sam did as she was told. The problem was immediately clear: instead of crumbling in her mouth, the beef was tough and chewy. She worked her jaw hard, struggling to break up the meat enough to swallow. Wordlessly, Gabe handed her a napkin and she took it with a grateful nod.

'I ordered exactly what you told me to,' she said, once her mouth was clear of the stringy meat.

'And Laurie decided he knew better,' Gabe replied, glaring sideways. 'So instead of my fresh, high-quality ingredients, I have been forced to put up with substandard produce. And this is the result.'

A rush of incredulity washed over Sam as she turned to Laurie. 'Is this true? You changed the order after I'd placed it?'

Laurie's face became mulish. 'I was trying to save money. You and Gabe seem to think it grows on trees.'

'But—' Sam felt her jaw gape a little. 'That wasn't really your decision to make. And this is Franny's wedding – the woman who wields more power than the Queen around here. If there's one day we need to pull out all the stops and bring our A game, it's today.'

Once again, Laurie glowered with self-righteous certainty.

'They're all drunk – no one is going to care whether the beef is topside or skirt.'

'I care!' Gabe roared, slamming his hand onto the stainless-steel work surface. 'It is my professional reputation that's at stake here – a chef is only ever as good as his last meal. And this –' he pointed at the silver tray with open disgust, 'this is unacceptable.'

Sam took a deep breath and replayed the conversation slowly in her head, wondering how to rescue the situation. What else had Gabe been complaining about? The prawns and the salmon?

'Right. Tell me what else is wrong,' she said, her voice determined.

Laurie tried to interject, but Sam waved him away. She listened to Gabe's impassioned complaints, to his conviction that the food was going to be well below the standard that he was used to serving, and privately agreed with every word he said. But she was well aware that Laurie was throwing her mutinous looks, as though she'd crossed to the enemy by even allowing Gabe to complain; as much as she agreed with Gabe's objections, she didn't want to undermine her brother completely by telling him their chef was absolutely within his rights to demand the best ingredients – it was part of their contract, after all.

'What can we do to fix it?' she asked, once Gabe had finished his tirade.

He scowled. 'Nothing. There is no time to do anything. If this was a normal restaurant sitting, I would close the kitchens and refuse to send out any food at all.' His scowl softened a little. 'But I will not ruin a wedding by doing that.'

Laurie let out a bark of disbelieving laughter. 'You should hear yourself. I've got news for you, Gabriel. You're not in charge here. We are.'

Sam's cheeks burned with mortification as the rest of the kitchen staff stared with avid interest. Did Laurie have any idea how well-regarded Gabe was in the culinary world? He'd hosted his own television show, for heaven's sake; he was a superstar. And they were lucky to have him.

'And I have news for you, you little *gilipollas*,' Gabe snapped. 'You're not in charge of anything.'

The word wasn't familiar to Sam, but the meaning was; whatever Gabe had called Laurie, it was deeply insulting.

'Are you going to let him talk to me like that?' Laurie demanded, rounding on Sam.

She puffed out her cheeks. 'I'm not sure I understand what it—'

'It means "stupid dick",' Gabe said, suddenly calm. 'And I stand by it.'

Laurie's outrage was almost palpable. 'That's it,' he said, clenching his fists. 'You and me, outside.'

Sam was suddenly overcome with weariness. 'Oh, stop it,' she told Laurie. 'There's no need for that.'

He squared his chin. 'There's every need. He called me a stupid dick.'

He sounded so petulant that Sam had to suppress a wild giggle. She bit her cheek until the urge subsided and shook

127

her head. 'That isn't how we do things, Laurie. Get back to the bar and help Connor. And, Gabe, do the best you can with what you have.'

Both glowered at her and she thought for a heartbeat that they might refuse. But then Laurie swore under his breath and wheeled about. A second later, he was gone, leaving Sam to face Gabe's wrath. Except that he didn't seem angry with her; he looked disappointed. And that was somehow worse.

'This cannot happen again,' he said. 'If it does, you will be in breach of contract and I will walk out.'

Sam tried not to wince at the coldness in his voice. 'It won't. I promise.'

Gabe turned away. 'Good. Now get out of my kitchen. We have a disaster to avert.'

The dismissal was so breathtakingly rude that it rooted Sam to the spot. She was hyper-aware that six sets of curious eyes were watching her, waiting for her next move. And so she damped down her own furious response and pressed her lips together. With a single tight nod, she spun on her heel and made for the door. It was only once she was safely on the other side that she allowed herself to gasp and press the heel of her hands against her eyes. How had Gabe dared to speak to her that way? And what the hell had Laurie been thinking?

'Sam? Is everything okay?'

And now Sam had to swallow another despairing groan, because Joss was the last person she wanted to see. But she forced herself to open her eyes. 'Of course. Perfectly fine.'

He looked at her askance. 'You don't seem fine. You seem a bit . . . frazzled.'

Sam let out a sigh and glanced around the bar, which was mercifully empty of both customers and staff. She didn't know where Laurie had gone and, right at that moment, she didn't actually care, as long as he steered clear of the kitchens. And she supposed everyone else must be in the marquee, getting ready to hear the speeches.

She passed a shaky hand across her face. 'I need a bloody drink.'

Joss studied her in silence for a moment, then gave her a lopsided smile. 'Luckily, that's one of my superpowers. What do you fancy?'

Once upon a time it would have been a loaded question, but Sam saw nothing but concern in his eyes. She let out a long puff of air. 'I don't care. Just make it a double, please. And make it fast.'

Chapter Twelve

When Sam woke up the next morning, it was to the faint buzz of a drill. She lay still, trying to work out where it might be coming from, but it was hard to establish anything over the pounding in her head. Opening her eyes a fraction, she tried not to wince at the stab of pain caused by the murky morning light filtering through the shutters. Her mouth felt dry and her stomach queasy; exactly how much had she drunk last night?

She groped on the bedside table for a bottle of water and pressed it to her lips, frowning when she realised they were tender, maybe even bruised. It was almost as though she'd spent the whole night—

A sudden icy suspicion drenched her like a tidal wave. She fired a sharp glance at the other side of her bed and let out a silent groan at the sight of the misshapen duvet. It wasn't a drill she could hear buzzing, it was snoring. And there was only one man she knew who snored like that.

Taking a deep breath, Sam lifted the duvet a touch and peered underneath. She dropped it again, lightning fast, and clapped one hand over her eyes as the room lurched. There beneath the covers, every bit as naked as Sam, was Joss. And suddenly she remembered everything.

'Shit,' she whispered in horrified dismay. 'Shit, shit, *shit*.'

She hadn't meant it to happen. In fact, she'd actively kept her distance throughout the evening, despite catching him watching her several times. The run-in with Gabe hadn't helped; he hadn't spoken to her once and his expression had been thunderous each time she'd seen him. So when Joss had grabbed her hand to pull her onto the dance floor, she hadn't wanted to resist, not when his laughter had been so infectious. And then there'd been more drinks, which had blurred her boundaries even more; drinking always brought out the flirt in her and flirting with Joss had been like coming home after a long trip away – comforting and easy and right. The sex had been like that too, with the hint of unfamiliarity that came with six months apart. There was no denying that it had felt good at the time.

She lay back against the cool cotton pillow and closed her eyes, sifting through the jumble of emotions. It wasn't the first time she'd woken up feeling like this; back in London, shame and regret had often gone hand in hand the morning after a night out, although she'd told herself she was empowered and free to sleep with anyone she fancied, providing they were single. But this wasn't some random man she'd picked up in a bar at closing time; this was Joss, with whom she had a long and complicated history. And that made everything trickier. Being in her own home meant Sam couldn't dress in the half–light and slip away before he woke up. She'd have to face the consequences of her behaviour this time, no matter what they might be.

Joss let out a loud snort and shifted under the covers. Sam bit her lip; how was he going to react? Had he planned for this to happen or had it been a spur of the moment thing, brought on by being back in Little Monkham? She hoped it was the latter; as good as the sex had been, that was all it had been. Part of her would always love Joss, but she knew beyond any doubt that she wasn't *in* love with him any more.

A quick glance at her phone told her it was just after eight o'clock. It made sense not to be in bed when Joss did surface, Sam decided, and slid her feet to the floor. He didn't stir as she pulled on her dressing gown and eased open the bedroom door. Breathing a thankful sigh of relief, Sam headed for the kitchen; she was going to need coffee before facing the music.

She hadn't expected to find Gabe there. He sat very still at the kitchen table, wearing a stony expression that suggested he knew exactly what had happened. Mortified and ashamed, Sam almost turned tail and ran. But her craving for coffee, and maybe some ibuprofen, was stronger than her shame.

Straightening her shoulders, she walked in and fired a careful smile in Gabe's direction. Part of her hoped he was so incensed that he'd ignore her entirely, but it was a thought that vanished the moment she stepped into the room and dredged up a good morning; his muteness felt accusatory, she decided, and pretty much anything else would have been preferable. Swallowing hard, Sam slipped a pod into the coffee machine and set about warming some milk.

'I should probably warn you that Joss is here,' she said, after a few moments of heavy silence. 'We – erm – well, he stayed over last night. In my room.'

She half-expected him to pretend he hadn't heard, but instead he merely nodded. 'I know.'

The confirmation of her suspicion made Sam's cheeks flame. 'It's not what you think.'

His gaze was level. 'It sounded as though you were doing exactly what I think.'

'Oh.' Sam cringed at the thought of what he might have overheard. 'Sorry. But it wasn't something I planned – we'd both had a few drinks and I suppose we got a bit – uh – carried away.'

'There is no law against that.'

'No,' she said, a little stung by the fairness of his words. 'But I can understand why you're not happy—'

Gabe stood up, pushing his chair back with a screech. 'On the contrary, I am glad it happened. You and Joss make a good couple.'

'It isn't like that. Joss lives in Chester and I live here. We're not getting back together.'

'It's not really any of my business,' Gabe said, and there was an edge to his voice. 'You and I might have kissed a few times, but it's hardly a lifelong commitment. You're free to sleep with whomever you choose, Sam.'

She battled to keep her expression from flinching. 'Of course.'

'And so am I,' he added, heading towards the door.

Sam concentrated on making her coffee, trying to ignore the panicky, sick feeling that was threatening to overwhelm her. Did his parting comment mean he had his eye on someone else? Could that someone be Owen's sister Kathryn? Although judging from his tone, Gabe didn't consider it to be any of Sam's business, either.

What a mess, she thought despondently as she slumped into the seat he'd just vacated and cast a guilty look along the landing towards her bedroom door, where Joss awaited her. Things were about to get a whole lot messier.

She sipped her coffee, putting off the moment for as long as she could, but eventually acknowledged it was time to face the inevitable shame. She carried a mug of strong, sweet tea along the landing, pausing outside her bedroom just long enough to take a deep breath, and opened the door.

Joss was fully dressed, sitting on the edge of the bed and lacing up his boots. He glanced up as she entered the room and the look of mingled sheepishness and embarrassment in his eyes almost made Sam drop his tea. Was it possible he was just as mortified as she was? Or was it trepidation that was making him look five years younger?

'Hi,' he said and cleared his throat. 'So this isn't at all awkward, is it?'

She held out the mug, her mouth twisting into a wry smile. 'On a scale of one to ten, I'd say it's an eleven.'

'At least,' he said as he took the tea. 'Look, I know you probably won't believe me, but I didn't plan for this to happen.'

Sam waited while he took a drink, clearly thinking something through. *Please don't say you still love me*, she thought as needles of apprehension stung her nerves.

'I was supposed to stay at a mate's place last night,' Joss continued. He ran a hand through his hair and sighed. 'Obviously, I knew I'd be seeing you at the wedding, but I thought it would be okay. I thought I was over you.'

'Joss—' Sam began.

'No, you've got to hear me out,' he said, shaking his head vigorously. 'I thought I was over you – that I'd be able to see you and not feel anything. I even thought we might be friends, maybe have a laugh together. But I was wrong.'

She felt a dull ache begin in her chest. 'Joss—'

'I should have known we wouldn't be able to keep our hands off each other. But, in my defence, you did look amazing last night.' He met her gaze with a wistfully appreciative smile. 'You still do, in fact.'

The compliment gave Sam a tingle of pleasure, despite the awkwardness of the situation. 'So do you,' she said gently. 'But it doesn't change the fact that we shouldn't have done what we did. It was a lot of fun, but we still should have known better.'

She held her breath as he stared into his cup of tea. Each second felt like a minute. But finally he grinned. 'Yeah. Still, there are worse mistakes to make, right?'

Sam recalled the hardness in Gabe's voice when he'd told her it was none of his business who she slept with. 'Yeah,' she echoed, doing her best to sound carefree. 'There are worse mistakes.'

'Friends?' he said, getting to his feet and opening his arms.

'Friends,' she said as she accepted the hug. 'But definitely not with benefits, okay?'

His snort of laughter ruffled her hair. 'Agreed.' He released her and stepped back. 'Want to go and wave Franny and Henry off on honeymoon together? Or shall I sneak out the back way so we can pretend this never happened?'

Sam frowned as she tried to remember who'd been there at the end of the night, when she and Joss had stumbled upstairs. Nessie and Owen had been long gone by then, as had Tilly and Connor; not that any of them would say anything. But Sam had been aware of Ruby's gaze throughout the evening, sharp-eyed and appraising, and she knew the older woman would have a pretty clear idea of where Joss had stayed.

'It'll be fine,' she said eventually. 'And Franny is away for two weeks – everyone will have forgotten by the time she and Henry get back.'

Joss lifted one eyebrow in surprise. 'I wouldn't be too sure about that. It's easy for me – I'm going back to Chester this afternoon – but you have to live here.'

'Sod it,' Sam said, folding her arms. 'People are going to gossip anyway, we might as well give them something to gossip about.'

His self-assured smirk reminded Sam of everything that

had drawn her to him in the first place, all those months ago. 'I've never been too worried about the wrath of Franny. Her bark is worse than her bite.'

'Liar,' she replied fondly. 'Now go and wait in the living room while I get a shower. And no, I don't need any help.'

There were some bleary-eyed Little Monkham residents among the crowd assembled on the village green at ten o'clock. Martha was wearing sunglasses, in spite of the overcast skies, and looked as though she'd rather be asleep. Nessie was pale, Sam saw with a frown and she made a mental note to look at the pub's schedule to see whether there was an extra day off her sister might take. Ruby, on the other hand, was as fresh-faced and glamorous as ever; she picked her way across the emerald grass in a pair of short, sky-blue Hunter wellies that gave Sam instant boot-envy.

'Prepare for the inquisition,' Joss murmured.

'Good morning,' Ruby said, as soon as she was within earshot. 'How are those heads today?'

'Fine,' Sam said with a smile. 'How are you feeling? I saw you dancing the night away with Father Goodluck.'

'He's got surprisingly decent hip action for a man of the cloth,' Ruby replied. She fired a sideways glance at Joss. 'And speaking of smooth ...'

He took the unspoken enquiry in his stride. 'I've got a smooth hip action too, Ruby.'

Sam hid a smile, which wasn't lost on Ruby. 'I'm sure it wasn't only your hips that got some action last night,' the actress observed, arching one eyebrow. 'Are you officially back together or is it – what do you young people call it now – a booty-call situation?'

Joss spluttered into his coffee and Sam felt her mouth drop open.

'Neither,' she managed, after a few seconds had elapsed. She glanced around to make sure no one was listening and lowered her voice. 'We've decided to chalk it down to a drunken mistake.'

'Something I know all about,' Ruby said, with a knowing wink. 'Still, at least you had some fun. The only hot stuff I went to bed with was a mug of Horlicks.'

Once again, Joss dissolved into coughing.

'Anyway,' Sam said, throwing him a pointed look. 'Obviously we don't want everyone to know, so if you could keep it to yourself, we'd be grateful.'

'Oh, of course, darling. You can count on me.' Ruby's eyes danced in amusement. 'But I feel I should quote a little Oscar Wilde here. There is only one thing in the world worse than being talked about, and that is not being talked about.'

'Not in this case,' Sam said firmly, as a cheer rang out around them. 'This time, I'd rather not be talked about at all.'

Ruby tapped her nose in a conspiratorial fashion. 'Say no more, darling.'

Franny and Henry had emerged from the Post Office, suit-cases in hand. Franny gave the crowd a regal wave, beaming from ear to ear.

'She hasn't changed,' Joss said, amused.

Sam laughed. 'Did you expect her to?'

And now Franny was holding up a hand, appealing for quiet. Obediently, the well-wishers on the green fell silent.

'Henry and I wanted to thank you for joining us, both yesterday and today,' she called. 'It seems strange to be abandoning you, and I almost wish we didn't have to go, but tradition is tradition. I'm leaving the Post Office in the hands of Kathryn Rhys, who I'm sure will do her best to fill in for me. Thank you again, and see you all in two weeks!'

Spontaneous applause broke out. Sam glanced across at Kathryn, who was whispering in Nessie's ear and no doubt giggling about the back-handed compliment Franny had just paid her. And then there was a toot of a car horn and a taxi pulled up alongside the bride and groom. Moments later, it was driving away, whisking them to Italy and leaving the villagers to watch it disappear from view.

'Well, that's that,' Joss said, yawning. 'I suppose I'd better get back to Chester. Unless—'

Sam was relieved to notice that she felt absolutely no pangs at the thought of his absence. 'Absolutely no chance,' she said, smiling at the unspoken suggestion. 'Safe journey.'

'Yeah.' He paused to give her one final look, then returned her smile. 'Take care of yourself, Sam.'

'You too,' she said, as he turned to walk away. 'See you around.'

He waved an arm but didn't look back.

'It's all for the best,' Ruby said, her voice quietly sympathetic. 'Now you can focus on the delicious Gabriel, hmmm?'

'I don't think so,' Sam said, her amusement melting away. 'He wasn't very impressed with me this morning. In fact, he basically told me he was interested in someone else.'

'Nonsense,' Ruby replied briskly. 'If that's true, why can't he take his eyes off you?'

Sam felt a jolt of surprise and instinctively sought out Gabe, on the other side of the green. Sure enough, his gaze was fixed on her, although he looked away fast when their eyes met.

'See?' Ruby said in satisfaction. 'I've had more than my fair share of smitten suitors over the years, and let me tell you, I know when a man is captivated. Mark my words, Sam – Gabe Santiago is into you.'

Could it be true? Sam wondered. She might have believed it before her night with Joss but now? She let out a shaky laugh. 'Thanks, Ruby, but I think I'm swearing off men for a while.'

'Of course you are,' the older woman said, with a look that told Sam she saw right through the lie. 'Playing a little hard to get has never failed me yet.'

Sam opened her mouth to argue, then closed it again. It was easier to let Ruby think whatever she wanted to think. But the truth was, Sam had no intention of playing games with Gabe, or anyone else. She'd said it before, but this time she meant it; it was strictly business at the Star and Sixpence from now on.

Chapter Thirteen

December arrived in a flurry of cold, starry nights that gave way to silver-frosted mornings and helped to fill Nessie with an irrepressible sense of anticipation. She loved to see the seasons change around Little Monkham; autumn had been particularly spectacular, with the woods blanketed in amber and russet leaves, but Nessie recalled the winter before, when the village had been covered in thick snow and looked like a painting. Then again, spring and summer had their own charms, Nessie considered as she leaned against the ancient wood timber of the pub door and watched her neighbours go about their day. She was lucky to have made her home here, she thought with a warm swell of contentment. It had given her more than she'd ever dreamed possible.

'Shouldn't you be sitting down?'

The matronly edge in Sam's voice made Nessie smile. Her sister had become increasingly bossy with her in the weeks since Franny and Henry's wedding; Nessie had often found herself the subject of concerned scrutiny and grown used to being told in no uncertain terms to rest more. It didn't matter that her morning sickness had eased off considerably, or that her energy levels had improved – Sam seemed determined to wrap her in cotton wool and had recruited almost everyone around them to the cause, including Owen, Laurie and Gabe. All of which meant Nessie frequently found herself watching everyone else work, with strict instructions not to help – something she found endearing and frustrating in equal measure. She hoped the well-meaning interference would settle down now that she'd reached the all-important twelfth week; she and Owen were due at the hospital for their scan in a few days and constantly being told to rest wasn't really practical when there was a gin festival to organise and a famous author to accommodate.

'I've been sitting down all morning,' Nessie told Sam mildly. 'And the final delivery from Silent Pool is due any minute, so I thought I'd keep an eye out.'

Sam had worked her PR socks off for the festival, contacting a number of small but well-regarded gin distilleries to invite them to showcase their products. She'd placed large orders and suggested they send representatives, with promises of great media coverage and an enthusiastic welcome. It helped that the travel editor for the *Observer* had grown up in Little Monkham and had been only too pleased to not only feature the festival in the paper, but to pull some strings with her journalist friends to ensure it was widely covered. Sam had managed to place it in several of the glossiest women's magazines too. And now it was the eve of the festival and all they could do was hope people came. If they didn't, it wouldn't be through lack of effort on Sam's part, Nessie thought with a familiar stab of guilt that she hadn't done more to help.

'Do I have to remind you that you are making a whole new person in there?' Sam asked, with a pointed look at Nessie's slightly rounded belly. 'I know you want to help, but you need to look after yourself too.'

'I am,' Nessie protested. 'I'm pregnant, Sam. Not an invalid.'

Sam gave her a hard stare, then sighed. 'I suppose you do look a bit less pale than normal,' she allowed in a grudging tone. 'Not what I'd call blooming, but better.'

'Thanks,' Nessie said with dry amusement. 'That's the nicest thing anyone's said to me all morning.'

'You know what I mean,' Sam said, with a half-smile. 'The morning sickness has been rough on you.'

Nessie couldn't argue; it had been so bad at first that she'd assumed she had food poisoning. 'Some women don't have any sickness at all,' she said. 'Lucky things.'

'And some throw up for the whole pregnancy,' Sam replied, with a delicate shudder. 'Just ask the Duchess of Cambridge.'

Nessie was about to reply when a large lorry swung into view at the bottom of the village green. 'This looks like it might be for us,' she said. 'Where's Connor – in the cellar?'

'You wait here – I'll get him,' Sam said before Nessie could move. 'You know how steep the cellar steps are.'

Swallowing a sigh, Nessie watched her sister hurry away. The sooner everyone stopped treating her like she might break, the better.

By midday on Thursday, the inside of the Star and Sixpence had been divided up into six decadent gin parlours, each boasting a bar that catered for the different distilleries and a cocktail list that made Nessie want to try them all. She normally didn't mind being teetotal, but the low-lit parlours and their divine-sounding menus looked so inviting. Which, she supposed, was the whole point; customers could order a gin and tonic any day of the week, but it might not be infused with pink peppercorns and served in a bone-china teapot, and they might not perch on a velvet chaise longue to drink it.

'Here,' Sam said, holding out a tall glass of something that looked a lot like a cocktail. 'This is from SJ over at the House of Virtue parlour. Don't worry, it's non-alcoholic.'

Nessie frowned at the drink as she took it. 'Are those . . . peas floating underneath the cucumber?'

Her sister nodded. 'Yep. Try it. I promise you won't be disappointed.'

Unsure what to expect, Nessie took a sip and was pleasantly surprised by the delicate flavours of elderflower and cucumber mingled with the quinine from the tonic. She let the drink flow across her taste buds and swallowed. 'You're right,' she said, smiling. 'I'm not disappointed.'

Sam took another mouthful of her own drink. 'Good, isn't it? Although the real test will come later, once Ruby gets here.'

'She said she'd stop by just before we open,' Nessie said, sipping again. 'Apparently, our guest of honour is an old friend of hers.'

'Is there anyone famous that Ruby doesn't know?' Sam asked wryly.

Nessie grinned. Ruby might be long retired, but her career as one of the leading lights of British theatre meant that her address book was starrier than most and her celebrity anecdotes were legendary. Of course she would be friends with the gin-loving Lola Swann.

'No,' Nessie replied. 'If they're worth knowing, Ruby knows them.'

'I bet they've put the world to rights over a bottle of Bombay Sapphire or two, over the years,' Sam said. 'Although obviously times have changed since then.'

Nessie tipped her head in acknowledgement; Ruby had fought hard against her addiction to alcohol and freely admitted she'd often been tempted to have a drink. But she was coming up to her one-year anniversary and seemed more determined than ever not to give up her hard-won sobriety. Nessie was sure she'd be able to reminisce with Lola Swann without taking the trip down memory lane too far.

'True. At least there are plenty of mocktails to choose from.' Nessie glanced towards the closed kitchen door, behind which Gabe was working on canapés to accompany the drinks. 'And lots of delicious distractions.'

The faintest hint of pink crept across Sam's cheeks. 'He's definitely distracting.'

'I meant the snacks,' Nessie said, half-laughing. 'But since you've raised the subject . . . how are things between you?'

'Not great,' Sam admitted, with a barely disguised sigh. 'I mean, workwise, we're fine – we discuss the orders, plan menus, talk about wines. But that's the best I can say – he's polite and professional.' She paused and threw Nessie an anguished look. 'And I try my hardest not to care, but it's driving me insane.'

Nessie could understand her sister's frustration; having decided she wanted Gabe, Sam now found she couldn't have him. And the reason she couldn't have him was entirely down to her own impulsiveness. It was like that Christmas years ago where Sam had eaten all her own Advent calendar chocolate on the first day of December and then demanded that Nessie share hers for the rest of the month. Except this time, Sam couldn't lie down on the floor and scream until she got her own way.

'Give it some time,' Nessie advised, not unsympathetically. 'Gabe's ego is bruised and you know how delicate those can be.'

Sam groaned. 'I can't believe I was so stupid. It didn't even mean anything.'

'I know,' Nessie soothed. 'We've all done it.'

There was a faintly accusatory look in Sam's eyes. 'You haven't.'

'Not this exact thing, no. But I have done plenty of things

I've regretted the next day.' Nessie gave a rueful shake of her head and ploughed on, 'And while spending the night with Joss wasn't the most sensible thing you could have done, it's not a life-changing mistake.'

'It feels like one,' Sam said morosely.

She looked so downcast that Nessie wanted to give her a hug. 'It's not as though you weren't single at the time. If Gabe really likes you, he'll get over it.'

Sam was silent for a moment, then sighed again. 'And if he doesn't? Like me, I mean.'

Nessie thought of the way Gabe's gaze followed Sam when he knew she couldn't see him, and of the kind-but-firm way he'd responded to any other woman who tried to flirt with him, including Kathryn; it was obvious to anyone with half a brain that he only had eyes for Sam. But Nessie knew her sister well – she valued something more when she'd had to work for it. And although there was no doubt Gabe had been disappointed and hurt when Sam had slept with Joss, Nessie couldn't help wondering whether the Spanish chef had also worked out what made her sister tick. Maybe he'd taken a leaf out of Ruby's book.

'Time will tell,' Nessie advised. 'Give him some space and see what happens.'

'I'll try,' Sam said, managing a wavering smile. 'Thanks, Ness.'

She gave Sam's arm a swift squeeze. 'No problem. That's what sisters are for.'

*

There was an expectant crowd for the opening of the festival. Any doubts Sam had harboured about Lola Swann's ability to hold the attention of her audience had vanished the moment she'd entered the Star and Sixpence that afternoon; the elegant, blonde-haired author had swept in, paused dramatically in front of the roaring fire and gazed around in obvious approval.

'Ruby was absolutely right – this is my kind of place,' she'd announced, beaming at Sam and Nessie. 'And there's no need to introduce yourselves – I know exactly who you are.'

She'd hurried forwards to clasp their hands, resplendent in a lilac floral dress and matching silk scarf, and Sam instantly felt as though she'd known her for years.

'I'm so thrilled you invited me to stay,' Lola went on, once Sam and Nessie had greeted her. 'I've been hankering to write about Little Monkham for years and being your writer in residence means I can.'

Nessie's welcoming expression slipped a little, as though she was alarmed at the prospect of the village being immortalised. 'What do you think you'll write about?'

Lola smiled. 'This place, of course. I can't imagine a better place to set a story than a village pub. I'm sure you girls have some stories to tell.'

She fixed them both with an inquisitive gaze, but Sam shook her head. 'Being a licensee is a sacred trust, I'm afraid. What happens at the Star and Sixpence stays at the Star and Sixpence.'

'How wonderful!' Lola exclaimed, her eyes gleaming. 'Do you mind if I write that down?'

She'd been delighted with her guest room, tucked away in the eaves of the pub, and had questioned Sam about the ghost of Elijah Blackheart, whose spirit was said to haunt the building. There was nothing that didn't interest her; she'd charmed Connor by asking him to show her the cellar and engaged Gabe in a detailed conversation about his home town, Seville, which she'd visited as book research.

'We'll have to watch what we say around her,' Nessie murmured, as Lola laughed at something Gabe had said. 'If we're not careful, we'll end up in her book.'

The thought made Sam grin. 'I don't mind – just think of the PR possibilities!'

And now Lola was holding court in front of the bar, a rounded Copa glass brimming with peppery pink gin and tonic at her elbow. 'Dickens would have us believe that gin was how the poor escaped their miserable lives,' she said, her voice bubbling with mirth, 'but I prefer to think they were just early adopters. And thank goodness they were, because if it hadn't been for the gin shops they used to visit, we might never have had the wonderful variety you see here today.' She paused to raise her glass in salute. 'To Dickens, gin and the wretched poor. I now proclaim this festival open!'

Next to Sam and Nessie, Ruby lifted her mocktail and then smiled at Sam. 'Isn't she wonderful?'

'She is,' Sam replied, watching the audience make a determined beeline for the gin parlours. 'And the perfect patron for the festival.'

'Absolutely,' Ruby agreed. 'She drinks like a fish, but that's authors for you. I've hardly met one who didn't.'

Sam laughed. 'How long have you known each other?'

'More years than I care to remember,' Ruby said. 'We met at a party – I forget whose now – and hit it off straight away. That was before she topped the bestseller lists, of course, but we've been friends ever since.'

'I can see why,' Sam said. 'You're actually quite similar.'

A wicked twinkle appeared in Ruby's eyes. 'That's what Peter O'Toole used to say. "Ruby, darling, I honestly can't tell if it was you or Lola that I woke up next to this morning."'

Sam felt her eyes widen. Ruby's tales of her acting past were often studded with mentions of famous names, but she'd never been quite this scandalous. 'And?' she demanded, her gaze travelling to the blonde author and back again. 'Which of you was it?'

Ruby smiled and lowered her voice to a throaty whisper. 'Would you be terribly shocked if I said it was both of us?'

'Ruby!' Sam exclaimed, with a burst of astonished laughter. 'You didn't!'

'It was a very long time ago,' Ruby said, with a complacent shrug. 'And he was a very attractive man – he played Professor Higgins to my Eliza Doolittle in *Pygmalion* at the Shaftesbury. Lola and I both fancied him like mad and there was a party where one thing led to another . . . Happy times.'

The revelation only made Sam even more determined to keep her own personal life away from the curious eyes of their resident writer. 'I'm glad you've stayed friends,' she said, as Lola made her way towards them. 'In spite of having the same taste in men.'

'We always will be,' Ruby said. 'But it's no coincidence that I never introduced her to your father.'

'Ruby!' Lola said, wrapping her arms around the actress in a hug that exuded warmth and affection. 'How glorious to see you.'

'And you,' Ruby replied. 'I see you've changed your hair.'

The author patted her ash-blonde curls. 'I couldn't bear the grey. Made me feel ancient.'

Ruby smiled. 'So what's the gossip? Any news from London?'

The question sounded innocent enough, but Sam thought she detected an undercurrent of disquiet behind Ruby's words, an unspoken question that clearly wasn't lost on Lola.

She frowned. 'I do have some news, but I'm not sure this is the time. Shall we talk about it later?'

Ruby shook her head stoutly. 'Anything you have to say can be said in front of Sam, here. She and Nessie are like the daughters I never had.'

Lola's hazel eyes darkened. 'Well, it's about Micky Holiday, of course. I don't think he's been entirely honest with you, Ruby. In fact, I'm certain he's lying to you. But—'

A woman bustled up, a star-struck expression on her face. 'Lola, I'm a huge fan. Would you mind signing this?'

She thrust a paperback and a biro towards Lola, who took it with a practised smile. 'Of course. Who shall I sign it to?'

Sam took the opportunity to fire a sideways glance at

Ruby. Unsurprisingly, she looked tense and unhappy. What on earth could Micky be lying about? Sam knew Ruby had doubts about his ability to stay faithful to one woman; she'd often referred to his womanising behaviour in the past, before they'd begun what might loosely be called dating, and Sam was aware he had more than his fair share of rock and roll groupies vying for his attention. Was that what was running through Ruby's mind now? Had Micky slipped back into his old ways?

Beside them, Lola continued to be perfectly charming, showing no signs of impatience with her chatty admirer even though Sam was sure she must be keen to get back to the conversation she'd just abandoned partway through.

Sam leaned closer to Ruby, lowering her voice to a whisper only she could hear. 'Are you sure you want to hear what Lola has to say now?'

The actress nodded. 'Better now, among people, than later when I might be tempted to turn to the bottle for solace.'

It was an important consideration, Sam thought. She reached out and squeezed Ruby's hand. 'Okay. I'll distract the fan.'

To Sam's surprise, Ruby's fingers tightened on hers. 'Can you stay? I need you here.'

'Of course,' Sam said, just as Lola wrapped up her conversation with the woman. 'I'll stay as long as you need me to.'

'Sorry about that,' Lola said, pulling a long-suffering face and grabbing her drink. 'Perhaps we ought to get out of here. Please tell me you've got a snug or something, Sam.'

Ignoring the murmurs of disappointment from Lola's devoted fans, Sam led the two older women out of the bar and up the stairs to the first floor. 'There we are,' she said, pushing open the door of the living room she shared with Gabe. 'You can talk properly in here.'

Lola flopped onto the sofa with an audible sigh and kicked off her high heels. 'So, where was I?' She cast a glance at Ruby's face and sighed. 'Ah yes. Micky H.'

'It's another woman, isn't it?' Ruby said, with stony resignation. 'Be honest. I can take it.'

'I don't know how much to say,' Lola replied, her tone fretful. 'It really should be Micky who tells you. I know he wants to.'

Ruby sighed. 'Thirty years ago, I'd have wondered whether it was you.'

Lola had the grace to look shame-faced. 'Not this time. I'd tell you if that's all it was.'

'So it is another woman?' Sam blurted out, before she could stop herself.

Lola ignored the intrusion. Her eyes were still fixed on Ruby. 'Ask him,' she said, as the seconds ticked by. 'It's the only way.'

For a moment, Sam thought Ruby would argue. Then she let out a long, slow breath, as though she'd been holding it for some time, and tipped her head once in acquiescence. 'Okay, I will.'

Lola visibly relaxed, as though she had been carrying a heavy weight that was now lifted. 'Soon, though. Don't wait.'

Sam felt her forehead crinkle into a frown. She wasn't sure what Lola was trying to say; Ruby might be convinced Micky had met someone new, but there was something else bubbling under the author's words. Whatever it was, it didn't sound good, Sam decided with a worried sideways glance at Ruby. It didn't sound good at all.

Chapter Fourteen

By Saturday evening, the festival was in full swing. Sam observed the crowd and the growing number of posts appearing on social media with immense satisfaction: pictures of the extremely photogenic cocktails offered by each gin parlour, excited tweets about some of the tiny little boutique distilleries whose products were waiting to be discovered. Connor and Tilly were kept busy behind the bar, selling the tokens to be exchanged for drinks in the parlours and looking after the non-gin drinkers, leaving Sam to circulate among the throng. Gabe's canapés were going down well too, although she caught several of the village women casting wistful glances at the kitchen door, as though they could summon the man himself by the power of thought. Sam pictured him in his pristine chef whites, chopping and seasoning over the shimmering gas hob, his face flushed and his forehead creased in concentration. And then she hurriedly banished the image, because that kind of distraction was the last thing she needed.

'This is amazing,' Martha said, when Sam stopped to ask how her spiced sloe gin cocktail was. 'And I love the tunes too.'

Sam cocked her head to listen. It hadn't been easy deciding on the right music for the festival, but it seemed that her Roaring Twenties playlist was hitting the right notes. 'We've got a live band tomorrow night – flapper dresses optional.'

Martha patted her ample stomach comfortably. 'I'm not sure I'm built to be a flapper. But I'll definitely be back for more tomorrow. You've worked miracles, Sam. As usual.'

'Team effort,' Sam said, as a plate of canapés sailed by. 'Have you tried these pork crackling blinis? They're pretty moreish.'

'Tell me about it,' Martha said. 'I've already had more than I should. But they all taste like heaven. Make sure you hang on to Gabe – he's a wizard in the kitchen.' She paused and let out a lusty sigh. 'Probably good at a lot of other things too.'

Sam gave her a practised PR smile and tried not to think about what else Gabe might be good at. 'We'll do our best.'

Everything was running so smoothly that it took Sam a while to realise she hadn't seen Nessie for some time. Odd, she thought, frowning slightly; it wasn't like her sister to take a break without mentioning it. But a quick glance round upstairs revealed no sign of her. Back downstairs, Sam scanned the crowd once more then girded her loins and popped her head around the door that led to the kitchen.

'I'm looking for Nessie,' she called, grateful for the clouds of steam that meant Gabe wasn't much more than a hazy outline. 'Anyone know where she is?'

Most of the staff shook their heads.

'I think I saw her heading over to the cottage earlier,' Gabe said, nodding to the condensation-covered window. 'I don't know if that helps.'

'Thanks,' Sam called and retreated into the bar to pull out her phone.

Where are you? Are you okay? x

She waited, staring at the two ticks that remained stubbornly grey. Over a minute passed before they turned blue and the words *Nessie typing . . .* appeared at the top of the message panel.

Yes! I'm at home – Luke is a bit poorly. Back soon x

Sam was about to tap in a reply when the door behind her opened. She turned around to see Gabe standing there, a concerned look on his face.

'Is everything okay?' he asked.

'Fine,' she said. 'Luke isn't well, Nessie says, but it sounds like she's got everything under control.'

'Good,' Gabe said, nodding. 'Nessie strikes me as always having everything under control.'

Unlike you. He didn't say the words, but Sam heard them all the same.

She gave him a tight smile. 'Yes, she's brilliant. I don't know how we'll manage without her when the baby comes.'

His brown-eyed gaze regarded her thoughtfully. 'She

won't be far away. And you've got a good team here. We'll pull together, keep things going until she returns.'

Ouch, Sam thought, trying not to wince. She knew Gabe didn't think much of her personally – he'd made that clear after the indiscretion with Joss – but she'd always felt he respected her professionally.

They stood in silence, Sam staring at the floor as her eyes swam, and for one wild moment she was filled with a sudden compulsion to spill out everything she'd told Nessie earlier that day: that she bitterly regretted spending the night with Joss, that the thought of never kissing Gabe again made her heart ache, that she wished with all her might that she could travel back in time and change what had happened. It was the polar opposite of what Nessie had suggested and yet an impassioned declaration was much more Gabe's style, Sam thought as her heart started to race. She looked into his eyes and came to an abrupt conclusion.

'Listen, Gabe, I think there's something you need—'

'It's the man himself!' Martha's gin-fuelled screech cut across the pub. 'Gabe! Cooee!'

Several heads turned in amusement. Sam cursed Martha's timing and shook her head with a huff of resignation. 'You'd better run. If she catches you, there'll be no escape.'

Gabe studied her, his expression brooding. 'What were you going to say?'

'Nothing,' Sam lied, willing her jangling nerves to settle down. 'Nothing important, at least.'

He considered her response, and Sam half-wondered

if he would call her out on the lie, but he simply nodded and disappeared through the kitchen door. A few seconds later, Martha arrived, with the remains of what smelled like a hot gin and ginger cocktail sloshing in her loosely gripped glass.

'Sorry, Martha, the kitchen is off limits, I'm afraid,' Sam said, as lightly as she could. 'You'll have to wait until later to see Gabe.'

The baker's face crumpled with disappointment. 'Oh,' she said, staring over Sam's shoulder with a slightly unfocused gaze. 'Oh, that's a shame. I fancied getting my hands on some more of his pork scratchings.'

Sam couldn't help smiling at the hint of innuendo. 'Never mind. Now, why don't we go and find Rob together?' she said, referring to Martha's good-natured husband. 'I'm sure he's wondering where you are.'

'I'm sure he's not,' the other woman grumbled, but she let herself be led back into the hubbub. 'The only time Rob wonders where I am is when his dinner's not on the table.'

'Look, your glass is empty,' Sam said, plucking the almost-finished cocktail from Martha's unresisting fingers. 'Why don't we get you some water? Or, better still, one of the amazing non-alcoholic cocktails they're selling?'

Martha let out an uninterested snort. 'No thanks. It's not every day a gin festival hits Little Monkham. I want the good stuff, not the mocktails.'

'Maybe later,' Sam said in a firm tone as she steered the baker towards an empty chair in front of the fire. 'Ruby here has been drinking them all evening, I'm sure she can recommend something.'

A flicker of understanding passed over Ruby's face as she glanced from Sam to Martha. 'Of course I can. We don't want you peaking too early, do we, Martha?'

'I wouldn't mind peeking at Gabe,' Martha mumbled, sinking in the chair with an exaggerated wink. 'The earlier the better, if you know what I mean.'

'Wouldn't we all, darling?' Ruby replied. 'Now what are you going to have to drink?'

'Thank you,' Sam murmured in Ruby's ear, when Martha took the mocktail list and peered blearily down at it. 'I owe you.'

'Nonsense,' Ruby replied in an undertone. 'Although I wouldn't say no to a hot mulled apple juice if you're going outside?'

The hot cocktails were being served from a fairy-lit grotto on the village green just outside the Star and Sixpence. 'Coming right up,' Sam promised, heading for the door.

It was blissfully cool outside, and much quieter. A small crowd clustered around the grotto, with a few drinkers sitting at the nearby tables and chairs, chatting and laughing. Sam took a deep breath of the chilly night air and tilted her face back to gaze up at the stars twinkling down from the December sky. Her eyes came to rest on Sirius, the brightest star, and she found herself making a wish almost before the idea had fully appeared in her head: *I wish Gabe would forgive me.*

'You look lost in thought.' Nessie's voice cut across Sam's yearning. 'I bet I can guess what you're wishing for.'

'Probably,' Sam admitted, turning with a smile. 'How's Luke?'

'Better now he's stopped throwing up,' Nessie said, pulling a face. 'He's sleeping.'

Sam couldn't quite suppress a shudder. 'Urgh. This is why I'd make a terrible mother – no stomach for bodily fluids.'

Nessie grinned and patted her tummy. 'But you're going to be this little one's favourite auntie. Nappy changing and burping after feeds are part of the job description.'

'Not a chance,' Sam replied. 'I'm going to be the kind of cool auntie who sweeps in with half of Hamley's and then vanishes when it's time for anything unpleasant.'

'You are not,' Nessie said, laughing. 'I think you're going to be a very hands-on aunt.'

Sam thought back to Gabe's unspoken suggestion that Nessie was the dependable sister and straightened her shoulders. 'Maybe. In fact, I might just surprise everyone,' she said. 'Including myself. I've got plenty of time to get used to the idea after all.'

'True,' Nessie said. 'If you want to get some practice in, then I'm sure Kathryn wouldn't mind giving up her place as Luke's nurse for the evening.'

'No thanks,' Sam said, lightning-quick. 'Do you fancy a mulled apple juice? I'm getting one for Ruby.'

'Sounds great,' Nessie replied. 'And you can fill me in on what I missed while I was mopping up puke.'

'Ness, please,' Sam said in a pained tone. 'And you didn't miss a thing, actually. I had everything under control.'

Nessie linked her arm through Sam's. 'Of course you did. I knew you would.'

'We'd better keep an eye on Martha, though,' Sam went on, as they headed for the grotto. 'If she keeps knocking back the cocktails, Luke won't be the only one we have to look after tonight.'

'I'm sure you've got that under control too,' Nessie said.

'I do,' Sam said, basking in the warmth of her sister's approval. 'See? I can cope without you. For twenty minutes or so, at least.'

Nessie sat back in her seat on Tuesday morning, staring at the spreadsheet on her laptop. 'Wow,' she said, not quite able to believe what the figures were telling her. 'We should throw a gin festival every weekend.'

Owen glanced across the kitchen table. 'Good news?'

'Better than good,' Nessie said, turning the screen around so he could see it. 'Our takings are six times better than the same weekend last year. In fact, I think it might be our most successful weekend ever.'

'It's like Dickens said,' Owen stated solemnly. 'People love gin.'

Nessie checked the numbers again and let out a shaky laugh. 'Apparently they do. I can't wait to tell Sam – she worked so hard to make the festival a success. She's going to be thrilled.'

Owen glanced at the clock. 'I'm sure she will. But don't

you think we ought to get going soon? We're due at the hospital at eleven and parking can be tricky sometimes.'

It was later than she'd realised, Nessie thought as she checked the time for herself. They didn't want to be late, not for something as momentous as seeing their baby for the first time. 'Okay, I'll tell her later. And I can show her the scan photo too – goodness knows she needs something to cheer her up.'

No matter how much her sister tried to put a brave face on things, Nessie knew she was still miserable over the situation with Gabe. And it couldn't be easy for her, seeing him every day. Maybe Christmas would help, Nessie thought as she pulled on her coat; there was something irresistibly romantic about it after all. It had certainly made all the difference to her and Owen at the beginning of their relationship.

The roads were wet on the way to the hospital. Nessie was glad they had plenty of time; Owen was an excellent driver and knew the country lanes well, but she much preferred not having to hurry. They found a parking spot without too much trouble, too; a heavily pregnant young woman offered them her ticket with a smile as they pulled into the space just outside the antenatal department. 'There's still an hour or so left,' she said. 'With a bit of luck, they'll still be running to time in there and you won't need to top up.'

'Half an hour early,' Owen observed as they made their way inside. 'Fancy a coffee?'

'Make it a herbal tea and you've got yourself a date,' Nessie replied coyly.

They checked in with the receptionist just before eleven

o'clock and took a seat among the other expectant mothers in varying stages of pregnancy. Some were with their partners, one or two were alone.

Owen looked around with interest. 'You know, I don't think this has changed a bit in the last ten years.'

Nessie smiled. 'It must have done.'

Owen pointed at a table stacked with dog-eared magazines. 'No, I'm pretty sure those are the same ones. I read an article that said Louboutins were the new Jimmy Choos. I've never forgotten it.'

He looked so serious that Nessie was almost convinced. Then his mouth twitched, just the tiniest bit, and she burst out laughing so loudly that the other patients turned to stare at them.

'Vanessa Chapman?' a voice called, cutting across Nessie's laughter.

She turned to see a middle-aged woman in a white coat holding a folder. 'That was quick,' she said to Owen. 'Come on.'

'My name is Elspeth and I'm going to be doing your scan today,' the woman said, as she ushered them into a dimly lit room that held a bed and a large, unwieldy computer screen. She checked her notes. 'This is your first baby, isn't it?'

'Yes,' Nessie said.

'No,' Owen said at exactly the same time, then laughed. 'Nessie's first but my second.'

Elspeth smiled. 'I understand. Well, Nessie, if you'd like to pop onto the bed, we'll get started.'

Nessie lay back, pulling up her top and unbuttoning her jeans as Elspeth instructed.

'The gel is a bit cold, I'm afraid,' the sonographer said, squeezing a snail trail of clear jelly across Nessie's stomach. 'But it's necessary.'

An explosion of butterflies fluttered inside Nessie and she knew the anticipation she felt must be showing on her face because Owen squeezed her hand.

'Here we go,' Elspeth said, smoothing the gel with the probe. 'Just a small amount of pressure, to make sure I see everything I need to.'

The screen was angled away, hiding it from Nessie's view. She resisted the temptation to crane her neck and catch a first glimpse of the baby.

'It's easier if you relax,' Elspeth said, moving the probe around and pressing into Nessie's skin.

Seconds became minutes. The sonographer slid the probe across the gel, down towards the white tissue that protected the waistband of Nessie's jeans and pushed into her groin. She took a different angle, clicking on the mouse with her other hand, and Nessie imagined each click as a snapshot, selecting the best poses. After a few more movements, she lifted the probe up and placed it on the tray at her elbow.

Nessie smiled. 'All done?'

Elspeth hesitated a fraction of a second. 'Not quite. I'm going to ask a colleague to check a few things.'

The words jangled like a discordant wind chime in Nessie's ears. 'What? Why?'

'The measurements I've taken suggest the baby is smaller than we'd expect for this stage of pregnancy,' Elspeth said, her tone giving nothing away. She got to her feet and locked the computer screen. 'I won't be a moment. Please wait here.'

The door closed with a click, leaving Nessie staring at Owen with rapidly rising panic. She sat up. 'The baby is small? Does that mean there's something wrong?'

Owen was very still, his face ashen. 'I think . . .'

'What?' Nessie said again, his pallor causing her pulse to spike even more.

He ran an unsteady hand over his face. 'I think she couldn't find a heartbeat.'

A loud roaring started in Nessie's ears and tiny dots of light danced in front of her eyes. 'No,' she whispered, the word catching in her throat. 'No, no, no.'

She lay back on the bed, fighting the blackness that came to claim her. Elspeth hadn't said anything about the baby's heartbeat – hadn't even mentioned it. Owen must be wrong.

'It's just small,' she said, barely aware she was speaking out loud. 'She said so. That doesn't mean there's a problem, does it? I mean, babies can be small, can't they?'

Owen didn't reply. When Nessie turned her head to look at him, she saw his gaze was fixed on the locked screen, as though he could see past it to the image that lay hidden behind it. A tear bloomed in the corner of her eye and slipped down her cheek, followed by another. She squeezed her eyes shut, forcing the hot ache to subside. There was nothing to cry about. Everything was going to be fine.

When the door opened again, Elspeth had been joined by another white-coated woman. 'Hello, my name is Jenna,' she said. 'I'm just going to double-check the measurements Elspeth has taken.'

'More gel, I'm afraid,' Elspeth told Nessie, her voice gentle.

No one spoke as Jenna repeated the same actions that Elspeth had made ten minutes earlier. The only sound was the clicking of the mouse. Nessie watched the faces of the two women, lit by the glow of the computer screen. Once or twice, Elspeth pointed to something and Jenna moved the probe and pressed it into Nessie's belly. Finally, Jenna wiped the device and laid it on the tray.

'I'm sorry to have to tell you that we've been unable to find a heartbeat,' she said, her voice quietly sympathetic. 'The measurements of the foetus suggest growth stopped several weeks ago – you wouldn't have been aware that anything had happened. Unfortunately, this is quite common – it's called a missed miscarriage. I really am very sorry.'

Nessie couldn't help it; she sobbed. It came from deep inside and felt as though it tore a piece of her heart away as it exploded from her mouth. Tears spilled from her eyes, hot and fast, and the pain was like nothing she'd ever experienced before. Owen sat as still as marble, his expression immovable. He didn't speak, didn't make a single sound, as he stared at the computer.

'Are – are you sure?' Nessie managed, in between sobs. 'M-maybe you just missed the heartbeat, if the baby is s-s-small.'

Elspeth reached across and took her hand. 'I'm afraid there's no doubt, Vanessa. I am so sorry.'

Nessie turned her face away and shut her eyes as a fresh wave of misery swept over her. One hand pressed her belly, the way it had so many times since she'd first seen the word *Pregnant* materialise on the white test wand. More tears forced their way through her burning eyelids and cascaded down her cheeks. Her baby. *Her baby.*

'We'll need to talk about what happens next,' Elspeth said. 'But there's no immediate rush. We'll give you some time alone now.'

Nessie didn't open her eyes. It was only when the door clicked again that she knew the two women had gone. 'O-Owen?'

For a moment, she thought he might have gone too. Then there was a faint rustle of movement and a barely audible sigh that threatened to send another flood of tears coursing across Nessie's face. 'I'm here.'

She turned her head, forcing her hot throbbing eyes to open so she could see him. 'I'm sorry, Owen.'

Her words seemed to rouse him. He blinked. 'What have you got to be sorry for? You heard them say – it happens all the time. It's nobody's fault – just one of those things.'

'But I should have known,' she mumbled. 'Should have sensed it somehow. Instead of—' She broke off to take a deep breath against the hurt that threatened to send her spiralling into uncontrollable sobbing again. 'All those weeks of singing stupid songs and talking to our baby when he or she had slipped away without me even knowing.'

'Don't,' he said quietly, taking her hand. 'Don't do this to yourself, Nessie. You couldn't have known.'

She tried to take comfort in his touch, but it felt like the hand of a stranger; there was none of his usual strength. He must blame her, no matter what he said; who else could be responsible? He was trying to be kind, that was all. Trying to make her feel better when all she wanted to do was curl into a ball and sob.

A cool breeze caused goosebumps to flower across Nessie's stomach. She touched the skin, still sticky with gel, and then pulled the tissue from her waistband and began to drag it across her skin in hard, savage movements. Red marks blossomed where she pressed too hard, but she didn't care. And then she fastened her jeans and pulled down her top, all the while fighting back tears. Her eyes felt swollen and sore already and her nose and throat were thick with snot; she must be a mess of mascara and eyeliner. But it didn't matter, because the only other person in the room couldn't bring himself to look at her.

Nessie swallowed as the lump in her throat grew hard and painful. Owen was hurting too; she could see it in the hunched stillness of his shoulders. She longed to wrap her arms around him – to feel him draw her near and for their sorrows to merge into one great pool of sadness that eventually, in time, might melt away. But the rigid set of his body stopped her from reaching out. His dark-eyed gaze was fixed on the floor and she wasn't even sure he knew she was there.

The minutes ticked by. Eventually, there was a light tap at the door, and Elspeth appeared again. She took her seat in front of the computer and turned her back to it, facing Nessie and Owen.

'I know this will be hard for you to think about now, but we have to consider your health,' she said, gazing at Nessie. 'Since your body doesn't seem to be miscarrying the foetus on its own, I strongly recommend you undergo a procedure to clear your womb as soon as possible.'

Nessie gripped the metal sides of the bed so hard her fingers hurt. 'But what if you're wrong?'

Elspeth's eyes were steady. 'I'm afraid there really isn't any doubt. And the sooner you undergo the procedure, the sooner we can get you back to full health. Then you can start to think about the future.'

The future, Nessie thought, and her head swam once more. An hour ago, she'd thought her future held a baby. Now it was just a yawning pit of nothing.

'How soon can it be done?' Owen asked, his voice raspy.

The sonographer consulted a sheet of paper she'd brought back in with her. 'We have an appointment in three days' time – on Friday. It involves a general anaesthetic, and you'll need to be gentle with yourself for a few days afterwards, but there shouldn't be any long-term effects.'

Nessie felt her fingers touch her stomach once more, protective and fearful at the same time. 'I don't know—'

'You don't need to decide today,' Elspeth said gently. 'I'll give you a number you can call when you've had time to think. But try not to leave it too long – it's you we're worried about now.'

Owen spoke then, but Nessie found it hard to focus on the words. How was she supposed to make a decision like this so soon after her world had been tipped upside down? She wasn't ready. She might never be ready.

'Nessie?' Owen had one hand on her shoulder and was shaking it gently. 'It's time to go.'

She stared at him numbly for a moment, then nodded.

'I'm sorry it was such sad news,' Elspeth said, squeezing Nessie's arm. 'But you're going to be fine. I promise.'

Again, Nessie nodded. And then she followed Owen out into the waiting room, where she didn't dare look up at the round-bellied women who weren't failures like her, and out to the car park. It was still raining and she let the raindrops fall onto her face like cooling kisses that soothed the heat and hurt from her swollen eyes. It was only when she was drenched to the skin and shivering from the cold that she got into the car beside Owen. They drove home in silence. Nessie rested her head against the window as the countryside flashed by, trying not to remember the way she'd felt only an hour or so before, the way she and Owen had been. Nothing would ever be the same again.

Chapter Fifteen

The knock on the bedroom door woke Nessie up.

Kathryn poked her head into the room, smiling. 'Oh good, you're awake. You've got a visitor.'

She pulled back the door to reveal Sam, who managed a watery smile. 'Hey, you. How are you feeling?'

It was a question Nessie wasn't sure she could answer. The general anaesthetic had left her woozier than she'd expected; there'd been a moment when she'd first come round when she could have sworn she'd seen their mother standing beside the bed. And now the after-effects of the medication had worn off, she felt tired and empty. Empty, as though something precious had been taken away from her.

'I'm okay,' she said, trying to smile back. 'Been better, you know.'

'You've certainly looked better,' Sam said, her voice warm.

This time, Nessie's smile was easier. 'Thanks. I love you too.'

'I'll go and put the kettle on,' Kathryn said and she closed the door as she left.

Sam stepped forwards to perch on the bed beside Nessie. 'I promise I won't stay long.' She reached into her bag and pulled out a box of Italian chocolates. 'These are from Franny and Henry. She wanted to deliver them herself – I don't think she trusted me not to eat them – but I managed to put her off.'

'Good,' Nessie said, feeling weak at the mere thought of having to entertain Franny from her sickbed. 'Will you thank her for me, though?'

'I will,' Sam said. She fixed Nessie with a look that radiated concern. 'But seriously, how are you? I've been so worried – you were like a wraith when you came back from the hospital on Tuesday and I've barely seen you since.'

Nessie's fingers fiddled with the edge of the duvet. 'I'm sorry. I didn't really feel like facing everyone.'

'Bloody hell, Ness, you don't have to apologise,' Sam exclaimed. 'I can't even imagine what you're going through – you and Owen. But you know I'm here for you, right? And don't even think about rushing back to work. We're coping perfectly well without you.'

It was something that had been worrying Nessie. The whole village knew what had happened and she wasn't sure she was ready to face their well-meaning sympathy yet. In fact, she wasn't sure she'd ever be ready, but that was a thought for another day. 'Thank you. I'm fine. Bearing up, you know.'

Sam studied her. 'I'm not sure I believe that, but okay. And how's Owen? Is he looking after you?'

Owen. Nessie resisted the urge to glance out of the window, to the forge where she knew Owen would be, taking out his suppressed pain and fury on white-hot iron and steel. She wished she could tell Sam the truth, that he'd become introverted and silent and almost someone she wasn't sure she knew, but it felt disloyal to talk about him behind his back when he'd suffered exactly the same loss she had. But the truth was she'd lain in bed beside him each night after that first visit to the antenatal department and she hadn't known how to reach him. It was as though he'd retreated into an inner castle and pulled up the draw-bridge. She knew he was grieving. But she didn't know how to help.

'He's doing his best,' she told Sam eventually. 'Kathryn says he was the same after Eliza died – quiet and withdrawn. But he took me back to the hospital today and waited while they did what needed to be done. And then he brought me home again.'

Sam's eyebrows shot up, as though she didn't think much of Owen's bedside manner. 'That sounds like the bare minimum he should be doing. How is he with you – emotionally, I mean.'

Nessie hesitated for a fraction of a second, then smiled. 'He's fine. Honestly.'

'Hmmm,' Sam said, clearly far from convinced. 'Are the two of you talking things through?'

Once again, Nessie thought of Owen lying sleepless beside her, his back turned. 'It's a bit soon. But we will.' She let out a yawn. 'Sorry. I'm a bit wiped out.'

'No problem,' Sam said. 'I should probably get back anyway, before Laurie and Gabe end up punching each other.'

'What?' Nessie said, suddenly alarmed. 'Why would they be punching each other? What's going on?'

'Nothing!' Sam said brightly. 'Just my little joke – forget I mentioned it. Get some rest – I'll see you soon, okay?'

She bent to plant a kiss on Nessie's cheek and then hurried out, leaving Nessie to wonder whether her sister had been joking at all. But her eyelids felt suddenly heavy and her limbs seemed to be made of lead. She turned her head towards the window, gazing at the forge for one last second before sleep came to claim her.

'Ho ho ho, Merry Christmas!'

The door of the Star and Sixpence slammed back and Micky Holiday stood there, silhouetted against the grey afternoon skies.

'Micky!' Ruby squealed, jumping from her usual seat by the fire and hurrying over to embrace him. 'How lovely to see you!'

The silver-haired rock star bent his head to kiss her and then beamed as he gazed around him. 'By god, it's good to be back.'

It was the Monday before Christmas Eve and the bar was quiet. By the evening, it would be busy, but for now, there were just a few regulars sitting around chatting or dozing. Laurie was behind the bar and Sam saw he wore an expression of astonishment and awe.

'Is that—'

'Micky Holiday, lead singer of the Flames,' Sam confirmed. 'And currently Ruby's boyfriend, although neither of them will admit it.'

'Blimey,' Laurie said, shaking his head in disbelief. 'She puts it about a bit, doesn't she?'

Sam gave him a sharp look. 'Hey. That's no way to talk about Ruby, or any of our customers for that matter. I know you two have had your differences in the past, but you put that to one side when you step behind this bar.'

Laurie had the grace to look embarrassed. 'Okay. Sorry.'

With a shake of her head, Sam hurried towards Micky to greet him.

'Sam,' he said, kissing both her cheeks. 'It's so good to see you.'

'And you,' she replied, taking in Ruby's flushed face and delighted eyes. 'What can I get you to drink?'

She saw his eyes stray to the pumps and, for a moment, she thought he would ask for a pint of Thirsty Bishop. But he simply smiled and said, 'You know, I'd sell my own granny for a flat white right now.'

'Ruby?' Sam asked, noticing her empty glass.

'Another Virgin Mary, please,' Ruby replied. 'Why don't you grab yourself a drink and join us?'

'Oh no,' Sam protested, 'you two have a lot of catching up to do. You don't want me cramping your style.'

'Nonsense, darling,' Ruby said. She lowered her voice to a stage whisper. 'Besides, it saves me having to listen to all Micky's boring stories about the good old days again.'

Micky grinned. 'You know you love it. But by all means join us, Sam. You know what they say – two's company and more's an orgy.'

Ruby's delighted peal of laughter followed Sam back across the floor to the bar, where she set about making the drinks. When she was done, she popped her head into the kitchen on impulse and found Gabe working on his laptop. 'There's someone here I think you'll know,' she said enigmatically.

As she'd anticipated, Gabe recognised Micky right away. 'It's such an honour to meet you,' he said, once Sam had introduced them and they were all seated in front of the flickering fire. 'I grew up listening to your songs – both my mother and my grandmother are big fans.'

'Glad to hear it,' Micky said easily. 'Ruby's told me a lot about you too, although she didn't say how good-looking you are.'

Ruby waved a dismissive hand. 'Didn't I? It must have slipped my mind.'

'I bet it did, you minx,' Micky said with a grin. He nodded at Gabe. 'Take care, mate. She's used to getting what she wants.'

'Are you touring at the moment?' Sam asked, to spare Gabe's blushes as much as anything else.

'Nope. I know it's not very rock and roll to say this, but that lifestyle all gets a bit much after a while.' He paused and

sipped his coffee. 'I'm tired of drink and drugs and debauch-
ery. What I'd like to do is grow a marrow that's bigger than
my own head.'

Sam blinked, unsure whether she'd heard correctly. Gabe
looked just as confused, but Ruby rolled her eyes. 'Not this
again. I've told you before, Micky, the day you retire is the
day I'll stop wearing make-up.'

Micky fixed her with his trademark twinkly-eyed look.
'Then I hope you're ready to go *au naturel* because I've got
news for you. As of last week, I am no longer the lead singer
of the Flames.'

Sam gasped. She'd heard Micky threaten to quit the band
more times than she could remember in her days on the PR
circuit, but she'd never once believed he'd go through with it.

Ruby looked similarly stunned. 'But—' she began and
then tried again. 'But why? What are you going to do with
yourself?'

'I told you,' Micky said patiently. 'I want to slow down,
take up gardening, that sort of thing. In a quintessential
English village, not unlike this one, in fact.'

Ruby's eyes narrowed. 'What aren't you telling me,
Micky Holiday? Have you been caught doing something you
shouldn't have been? Are you looking for a place to hide?'

Micky sighed. 'You're so suspicious.'

'With good reason,' Ruby said, her gaze narrowing still
further. 'What's going on?'

He took a swig of his coffee and lowered his voice. 'All
right, if you must know, I've had a spot of trouble with my

liver. The doctors say I need to change my lifestyle – stop drinking Jack Daniels and start exercising, that sort of thing. So I thought, where can I go that's perfect for slowing down?'

'And you decided on Little Monkham,' Sam said, with a sideways look at Ruby.

'That's right,' Micky said. 'It's got everything I need, plus a cracking little boozer to while away the hours in. Perfect.'

Ruby did not look convinced. 'Lola Swann said you'd got another woman.'

'Ruby,' Sam intervened sternly. 'That's not what Lola said. She said Micky wasn't being honest with you.'

The rock star spread his hands. 'And she was right. Thing is, the doctors have been telling me about the liver thing for years and I've always ignored them. Only now they're getting a bit insistent, a bit overdramatic – saying it's a matter of life and death. So I figure I've got to listen to them.'

Understanding dawned on Ruby's face. 'So that's what you lied about. When I asked you what all the pills were for and you said they were uppers and downers – what they're really for is your liver.'

For the first time ever, Sam thought Micky looked uncomfortable. 'It's not very rock and roll, is it? Taking pills for a dicky liver. I'd much rather you thought they were drugs.'

Ruby began to laugh. 'Only you, Micky Holiday. Only you.'

Sam and Gabe started to laugh too and eventually, Micky's tanned face crinkled into a smile.

'And I suppose you're going to want somewhere to live,' Ruby said, once her laughter had died down.

'Got somewhere,' he said, looking pleased with himself. 'I don't know whether you noticed that the cottage next door to yours has been sold?'

Ruby nodded and then her mouth gaped. 'You?'

He nodded. 'Me. You're looking at the owner of Lock Cottage. I can move in any time I like.' He leaned towards her with a wicked smile that Sam had seen seduce much younger women than Ruby. 'This way, we can have lots of late-night fun and you don't have to listen to me snore all night or trip over my dirty boxers the next morning. As long as you don't mind having a rock star for a neighbour.'

Sam couldn't quite believe what she was hearing and Ruby seemed to be struggling too.

'You mean it, then?' Ruby said, gazing into his eyes. 'You're moving here for good?'

He reached across and took her hand. 'I do,' he said, kissing her palm. 'I'm moving here for you, Ruby. So there can be an us.'

Ruby beamed in delight and jumped up to plant a kiss on Micky's lips.

Gabe leaned towards Sam. 'Do I sense another wedding in our future?'

Sam felt an unexpected thrill at the words 'our future' and squashed the sensation as firmly as she could before turning to look into Gabe's eyes. 'You know, I think you're probably right. But don't tell Franny – I think she's always held out hope that Micky might marry her.'

'Surely it's too late for that,' Gabe said, confused.

Sam winked. 'Have you met Franny? She's not the kind of woman to let an inconvenient husband stand between her and true love. I'm not sure Micky knows what he's let himself in for.'

Micky wiped the traces of Ruby's scarlet lipstick from his mouth, apparently unperturbed at the thought of Franny's potential wrath.

'You're not really going to stop wearing make-up, are you?' Sam asked, glancing at Ruby. 'I mean, you're beautiful either way, but—'

Micky reached across and took Ruby's hand. 'I think I can answer that. The only thing that will come between Ruby Cabernet and her mascara is death itself, right?'

Ruby smiled. 'Spoken like someone who's known me a very long time. So let's hope Franny doesn't decide to bump off the competition.'

Chapter Sixteen

'Have you got a minute, Sam?'

The question made Sam look up from her seat on the sofa to see Connor lurking in the living room doorway, an uncomfortable expression on his face. She frowned, discreetly checking the time and saw it wasn't even nine o'clock – Connor rarely ventured upstairs, especially not a full two hours before he was due to start work.

'Of course,' she told him, with a welcoming smile. 'We don't normally see you at this hour, especially on a Wednesday – is there a delivery I don't know about?'

He shuffled into the room and sat awkwardly on the recliner to her right. 'No delivery,' he said, looking even more wretched. 'I came in early so I could catch you before – well, before Laurie came in.'

'Laurie?' Sam repeated, puzzled.

Connor nodded. 'Normally, I'd speak to Nessie, but I know she needs her space and I didn't want to trouble her.'

He took a deep breath and ploughed on. 'I like to think I run a good cellar. I'm no Joss Felstead, of course, but our beer is still pretty good. We don't get many complaints.'

'We don't get *any* complaints,' Sam corrected him gently. 'And that's almost entirely thanks to you.'

The burly ex-fireman tipped his head, acknowledging the compliment. 'Well, like I said, I try to run a decent cellar. And you've always let me get on with it – you trust me.'

Sam felt her frown deepen. 'Of course we trust you. What's this about, Connor?'

He sighed. 'There's no easy way to say this, so I'm just going to come out with it. Just lately, I've noticed some odd stuff going on downstairs. Little things, like the cleaning products not being where I left them, or the barrels not quite being level. At first, I thought it was me – that I was losing the plot – but then stock levels started to fluctuate a bit. I'd think we had twelve bottles of Malbec, for example, and it'd turn out we only had ten.'

She stared at him, nonplussed. 'So there's a stock-control issue, is that what you're saying? Because mistakes like that happen all the time – someone rings through a Malbec as a Rioja on the till and we don't put two and two together until ages afterwards.'

'No, that's not what I'm saying,' he said, his gaze steady. 'Believe it or not, I keep a very close eye on the bottles we keep in the cellar and I can usually tell when there's been an honest mistake. But what I'm telling you now is that someone, for reasons best known to themselves, has been meddling with my system. And the only person I can think of who might do that is your brother.'

Sam opened her mouth to defend Laurie and then closed it again fast. Because it wouldn't be the first time he'd taken it upon himself to step in where he wasn't needed; there'd been the food order for Franny's wedding. That well-meaning interference had caused Gabe to threaten her with breach of contract. And although he'd steered well clear of anything to do with the kitchens since, Sam wouldn't be at all surprised to find Laurie overstepping his responsibilities in other places. Like the cellar . . .

'I'll talk to him,' she told Connor. 'And I'm sure I speak for Nessie when I say we're sorry you've had to bring this to our attention.'

Connor gave an embarrassed shrug. 'I don't like to throw my weight around and get all territorial, but looking after the cellar here is really a one-person job.' He seemed to replay the words in his head. 'Although any suggestions you and Nessie make are always welcome.'

'Relax, Connor,' Sam said, smiling in what she hoped was a reassuring way. 'I get what you're trying to say. I'll make sure Laurie knows to leave everything to you in the future.'

'Thank you,' Connor said, getting to his feet. 'I knew you'd understand.'

Sam waited until the mid-afternoon lull to tackle the problem. She left Tilly to cover the almost empty bar and asked Laurie to keep her company on a walk around the village.

'You know what it's like at this time of year,' she said, patting the waistband of a pair of skinny jeans that seemed to have become a good deal tighter in the last week. 'There's so much food and not enough willpower. I need all the help I can get.'

If he suspected she had an ulterior motive, he didn't show it. Instead, he nodded and went to get his coat. Five minutes later, they were trampling the wet grass of the green, heading in the direction of St Mary's.

'We haven't had time to catch up for ages,' she said, as they passed Martha's bakery. 'How are you finding life in Little Monkham?'

He took a moment to consider the question. 'If you're asking me whether I'm enjoying working at the pub, then the answer is yes. I love getting to know you and Nessie – you're the best sisters I could have hoped for – everything Dad said you'd be.'

'But?' Sam prompted when he fell silent. 'It sounds like there's a but.'

He fired a sideways look her way. 'But you and Nessie are quite terrifyingly good at running the Star and Sixpence. And I can't help wondering whether there's room for me, or whether I'm a bit of a spare part.'

'That's not—' Sam started to say and then stopped herself because she realised Laurie had hit the nail squarely on the head. 'Is that why you changed Gabe's order last month?'

Laurie nodded. 'I honestly didn't mean to make him angry. I just wanted to feel as though I was contributing something.'

'I can see that.' Sam took a deep breath. 'But, as you discovered, there are lots of good reasons why we do things the way we do. It's not always the cheapest, or the easiest option, but the chances are it's a tried-and-trusted business practice.'

Laurie said nothing.

'Take the cellar, for example,' she went on, pushing open the wooden gate that led to St Mary's churchyard. 'Connor keeps things running pretty tightly, to make sure our beer and lager are up to scratch. Nessie and I wouldn't dream of messing with his routine.'

Was it her imagination or did Laurie's cheeks turn the tiniest bit pink? 'No, I can see how that might cause an issue.'

He wasn't admitting anything, she thought, but in some ways, that made things easier. She mentally changed tack. 'In fact, we joke that the cellar is off limits to us mere mortals – only Connor is allowed to cross the magic portal.'

Again, he stayed silent, apparently pondering her words. There was a touch of petulance about the curve of his lip, a suggestion that he was having trouble keeping his temper, and she wasn't sure whether it was what she was saying or the fact that she was saying it at all. *Imagine how he'll react if I ask about the missing wine*, she thought, immediately deciding to let that go.

'So you see, there's method in our madness,' she said aloud, trying to lighten the conversation. 'It only looks like we don't know what we're doing.'

He glanced across at her then and she was relieved to see

he was smiling. 'I'm pretty sure you and Nessie know exactly what you're doing. Maybe one day you'll let me learn.'

'You're already learning,' Sam told him. 'And most of the time, you're doing a great job.'

'Thanks,' Laurie said. He glanced around at the rows of headstones. 'So, where's the old man buried then?'

'Over there,' Sam said, waving at the newest area of the graveyard. 'Do you want to go and see it?'

Laurie shook his head. 'Not really. Seen one grave, seen them all.'

It wasn't the response she'd been expecting, but here was something else she could understand; Laurie had been abandoned by their father just as Nessie and Sam had been. But when it came down to making a will, Andrew Chapman had declined to include his son. And that had to hurt Laurie more than anything, Sam thought.

'I'm glad you tracked us down,' she said, as they walked. 'I know Nessie agrees.'

There was a momentary pause, then Laurie smiled. 'Me too. And I'm sorry if anything I do upsets the apple cart. I'll try to do better.'

'That's all any of us can ask,' Sam said, linking her arm through his.

It took a week for Nessie's body to feel like her own again after her brief hospital stay. She spent most of the time in bed, reading or watching television shows she couldn't remember once they were over. Sometimes Luke crept in to join her and they huddled together, watching the same show on the too-small screen of her tablet. He'd taken the news hard at first, his blue eyes shimmering with tears the moment he understood what was being said, and he'd been subdued ever since. But he'd also become more affectionate with Nessie, offering unsolicited cuddles and an apparently inexhaustible supply of terrible jokes.

Kathryn was a great comfort too, supplying endless cups of tea and making herself available in case Nessie wanted to talk. And, of course, Sam was being brilliant – Ruby too. But the person Nessie needed the most was Owen, and his coping mechanism was to keep busy, locked away in the forge all day, every day. He came to bed late each night and slept beside her the same way he always had since she'd moved in. But the Owen she watched when insomnia struck in the early hours of the morning was not the same man he'd been before the scan had broken their hearts and their dreams. This Owen was distant and silent and Nessie had no idea how to talk to him.

On Friday, Nessie came downstairs to find Kathryn decorating a delicious-smelling chocolate cake in the shape of a log. 'Yuletide greetings,' she said in a sing-song voice. 'It's 21st December – the winter solstice.'

Of course it was, Nessie thought with a guilty glance at the calendar that hung on the kitchen wall. How could she have forgotten? But it didn't feel like four days until Christmas, despite the decorations everywhere she looked and Christmas music on a constant loop; she'd barely been out of Snowdrop Cottage for a week and had never felt less prepared for the festive season.

'Happy Yule to you, too,' she said, dredging up a smile for Kathryn. 'Are you doing anything to celebrate?'

'Owen and Luke have gone to find us a proper log,' the Welshwoman explained. 'I think they said something about getting one for the Star and Sixpence too.'

That answered her next question, Nessie realised, the one she hadn't even realised she'd been thinking. This time last year, Owen had brought an enormous log over to the pub and they'd watched it burn together, toasting the future and wishing each other happiness. *Look how that turned out*, she thought, blinking at the all-too-familiar sting behind her eyes. Was she ever going to stop crying?

'Are you sure you're ready to go back to work?' Kathryn asked, watching Nessie carefully. 'I know you feel bad about leaving them to it, especially at this time of year, but honestly, Sam seems to have things well under control.'

With a superhuman effort, Nessie managed something she hoped resembled a smile. 'I'm sure she has. But actually, I'm looking forward to going back. I've barely left the house for a week – I haven't even heard how Franny's honeymoon went.'

Kathryn pulled a face. 'You'll need a couple of hours for that. Maybe take some snacks. Establish an emergency escape route.'

'Sounds like a plan,' Nessie replied, and this time her smile wasn't forced.

'But seriously, Nessie, just take it easy, that's all I'm saying,'

Kathryn went on. She hesitated. 'I'm sure you know this, but I think Owen is struggling. The way he's acting now reminds me of the days after Eliza's death – all silent and scrunched up.'

It was a good description, Nessie thought, her heart aching at the thought of the long-healed pain this fresh loss must be causing. The Owen she knew and loved seemed far away, hidden behind miserable hunched shoulders and an impassive expression. What she needed – what they both needed – was a way to break down the distance between them so that they could comfort each other. Maybe the flames of the yule log would work their magic again and she and Owen might slowly start to talk as the wood burned.

'I don't know how to reach him,' she told Kathryn. 'It's like he's here, but not here.'

Kathryn put down her chocolate ganache icing bag and enveloped Nessie in a hug. 'Grief never goes away but it does get easier,' she said. 'And although you've suffered a heart-breaking loss, you do still have each other. Hold on to that.'

The words echoed in Nessie's head all morning: *you do still have each other.* She understood what Kathryn meant, but it didn't feel as though she had Owen; not really. In her worst moments, she'd felt so alone that it was almost as though she was grieving by herself. Those were the times when the little voice in her head reminded her that she only had herself to blame; if she'd only rested more, taken better care of the tiny life inside her, they wouldn't be in this situation. It was nonsense, of course, but Nessie found it difficult to remember that all the time. It was easier to forget when she was in the pub, at least for a short while. There was plenty to distract her.

The regulars were the same as they always were; perhaps a little more concerned than usual, yet mindful of her privacy. She thought Henry's brusqueness had been tempered by a gentler quality, and Father Goodluck had squeezed her fingers when he'd paid for his cappuccino. Sam hardly left her side throughout the morning, fussing around her with the kind of well-meaning concern that only made it harder for Nessie to settle. It wasn't until she asked Sam to give her some space that her sister realised she was overdoing the TLC.

'Sorry,' she said, a stricken look on her face. 'I thought you might not want to be left to your own devices.'

'You're great company,' Nessie said sincerely. 'But I feel like you're watching over my shoulder in case I make a mistake or something. And I'm really fine.'

'Good,' Sam said. 'And no one has stuck their nose in where it isn't wanted, have they? They've all behaved?'

'Impeccably,' Nessie replied. 'In fact, they've all treated me as though nothing has changed. It's easier that way.'

Sam touched her arm. 'I'm glad.'

Nessie looked around, taking in the decorations. 'It's gorgeously festive in here. I see you got a tree that fits this year.'

Her sister grinned. 'Yes, I made sure it was the right size. There shouldn't be any snarky comments from Franny.' She paused and gave Nessie a long look. 'Listen, I've been thinking about the next few days. I know you did the carol service last year, but I thought – well, maybe you wouldn't fancy it this time. So why don't I go instead?'

Nessie blinked in surprise. It was a long-standing village tradition that the licensee of the Star and Sixpence attended the Christmas Eve carol service at St Mary's; last year, it had been the moment Nessie had realised she was in love with Owen. The entire village would be there, unless they had a very good reason not to be, technically overseen by the twinkling gaze of Father Goodluck, but it was Franny whose displeasure everyone sought to avoid. Sam had the perfect excuse to stay away – there was a Christmas Fayre outside the pub each year and the wine needed to be mulled and chestnuts roasted – but she was now offering that to Nessie and the simple gesture meant more than she could convey.

'I hadn't really thought about it,' she said slowly, probing the idea of gathering with almost everyone she knew to celebrate the birth of a baby so many centuries earlier. 'Are you sure you're willing to step in?'

'For you, yes,' Sam said, without hesitation.

Nessie pressed her lips together, determined not to cry. 'Let me think about it,' she said, once she was certain her emotions weren't going to get the better of her. 'It's a lovely thing to offer, Sam. I know how much you hate the religious stuff.'

'I don't hate Christmas,' Sam said. 'But I do hate seeing you in pain. And I can go along and mumble to carols if it saves you some heartache.'

'Thank you,' Nessie said, digging her nails into her palms. 'I appreciate it.'

'No problem,' Sam replied, and a wistful look crept over her face. 'And hey – maybe I can sit at the back and have a cheeky snooze.'

Nessie thought back to the rousing candlelit service the year before and smiled. 'Maybe. Just make sure you don't set fire to the pew.'

It was late when Owen finally brought the yule log over to the Star and Sixpence. Nessie had given up expecting him, even though Kathryn had assured her over the dinner table that he and Luke had brought two logs home. But Owen himself had been absent, busy in the forge, and so Nessie had taken refuge of her own in the pub. She'd sent an exhausted-looking Sam to bed, waving away her objections, and got on with cleaning the bar ready for the following day. Anything was better than going back to an empty bed at Snowdrop Cottage.

So she was surprised when the door creaked open just after 11.20 p.m. and Owen pushed his way in with what looked like half a tree trunk in his arms.

'Hello,' he said, stopping when he saw her taken-aback expression. 'Didn't Kathryn tell you I had this for you?'

Nessie couldn't quite bring herself to look at him. He didn't seem to have any idea how painfully the distance between them cut into her. 'She did. But it's so late that I assumed you'd changed your mind. I've let the fire die down now.'

An awkward silence formed. Owen shifted his grip on the log and nodded towards the still glowing embers in the fireplace. 'There's plenty of life in it. All it needs is a little encouragement.'

'Don't we all?' Nessie muttered under her breath as he eased the log onto the rug in front of the fireplace. Was it wrong of her to feel a little resentful of his assumption that almost-midnight was a perfectly reasonable time to appear with a yule log to burn?

Seemingly oblivious, Owen reached into his pocket and pulled out a fragment of wood. 'I brought the piece of last year's log, so we can use it to light this one.'

It was a midwinter tradition that stretched back centuries, an ancient celebration of the longest night that meant the days would soon get shorter. Most people would recognise the log-shaped cakes that filled the shop shelves from the start of November but few would know what they represented, much less go to the trouble of acquiring exactly the right kind of log to burn. The fact that Owen took the little ceremony so seriously was one of the things that Nessie liked most about him.

Her mood softened a little. 'Can I get you something to drink?'

That was part of the tradition too; something warming to toast the year that had been and ask for blessings for the year to come. Owen had chosen whisky last time, smooth peaty Ardbeg that Nessie had tasted on his lips many times since then. She waited, trying not to place any significance on his choice this evening. It didn't mean anything, after all. But it wouldn't do her any harm to know he was also remembering how things had been twelve months ago.

Owen's gaze narrowed in thought as he scanned the shelves behind the bar. 'Perhaps a Merlot, if you've got a bottle open?' he said eventually.

'I'll join you,' she said, trying to ignore the crunch of disappointment. 'I can't think of a more perfect night for a glass of red.'

Neither spoke as Nessie poured the wine. The fire crackled and sparked as the wood caught, loud in the silence. Owen sat in one of the armchairs that faced the fireplace, his face ruddy in the flicker of the flames. She placed the brimming glasses on the table and perched on the chair opposite.

'Ready?' Owen asked.

When Nessie nodded, he positioned the yule log in the fireplace, sending a shower of sparks dancing in the air, and gripped the fragment of wood from the previous year in the tongs, thrusting it into the dying embers. Immediately, it caught light.

'Here,' he said, passing the tongs to Nessie. 'Hold it under the roots – they'll burn first.'

He wasn't wrong. Before long, greedy yellow flames were licking the roots and creeping along the mottled bark of the log. Owen watched for a few moments more, wanting to be sure that the new log was properly aflame, and then took the tongs back and motioned for Nessie to sit back. When they were both safely on their seats, and the log was starting to burn, he reached for his wine glass.

'To the year that's passed,' he said, his eyes fixed on the fire, and the sadness in his voice almost broke Nessie's heart. 'We had some good times.'

She held her breath, waiting for him to say something – anything – that might break the invisible barrier that had risen up between them. But he remained silent. And so she lifted her own glass. 'To the year ahead. I hope . . . I hope it brings—' Nessie stopped, unable to think of a way to express the need in her heart without causing Owen to feel worse than he did.

'Peace,' Owen said quietly, as the seconds ticked by. 'I hope it brings us peace.'

The word hung in the air, punctuated by the crackling flames. Nessie stared at Owen, who was staring at the fire as though it might reach out and grant his wish there and then; it wasn't what she would have asked for, but perhaps it wasn't a bad place to start. And perhaps once peace came, healing might start.

Clinging on to that thought, Nessie tapped her glass softly against Owen's and took a long slow mouthful of wine. 'To peace,' she said, once she'd swallowed.

And hearts that heal, she added silently, watching the flames flicker.

Chapter Seventeen

Christmas Eve dawned frosty and pale; the kind of wintry day that made Sam grateful for her fur-lined boots and thick coat as she hurried to Martha's for some last-minute mince pie supplies. Even the sky looked washed out – an insipid bluey-grey, instead of the biting brightness Sam usually associated with hoarfrost – and she doubted they would have snowfall the way they had the year before. Although she had to admit the village green looked almost as though it had snowed; the feathery white frost that covered the grass appeared, at first glance, as though a billion delicate flakes had settled there. The rooftops of the houses were glistening white too; the effect was like a living Christmas card and Sam couldn't help wishing Gabe had seen it before he left for Spain. Although he must have seen frost before, she reminded herself, feeling foolish. And even if he hadn't, he'd be back in time for the New Year's Eve party and the current cold snap was forecast to continue well into January. There would be plenty more frosty mornings to come and, judging from Gabe's cool manner as he'd said goodbye to her, not all of them would be outside the Star and Sixpence.

'The order for the New Year's Eve party menu will be arriving on the 29th,' he'd reminded her the day before as they'd stood in the bar, a small suitcase at his feet. 'Don't pack it away – I've arranged for Olivia to come in and inspect it. She'll put everything away, ready for New Year's Eve.'

There hadn't been a problem with the quality of the ingredients she'd ordered since his run-in with Laurie, but he obviously wasn't taking any chances if he was making one of his sous-chefs come in especially to check the delivery. But Sam had merely nodded. 'I understand.'

He reached for his case. 'I'll be back on the 30th, but you've got Olivia's number if there are any problems before then.'

'Have a good trip,' Sam said. '*Feliz Navidad*.'

He almost smiled then. 'Merry Christmas, Sam. I hope you get what you want.'

Unlikely, Sam thought as she watched him walk away. Christmas might be a time for miracles, but even Santa couldn't bring her the Gabe she'd known before Franny's wedding.

She shrugged the memory away as she pushed back the door of the bakery. A cloud of cinnamon-spiced warmth enveloped her and the warm voice of Michael Bublé singing 'White Christmas' lifted her mood.

Martha beamed at her from across the glass counter. 'And here she is – the very woman. We were just talking about you, Sam.'

'Really?' Sam said, glancing from the baker's smiling face to old Mrs Harris and even older Miss Hudson. 'All good things, I hope.'

Miss Hudson nodded. 'Of course, dear. We were just saying how very good you are at bringing attractive men to Little Monkham – first that lovely actor chap – what was his name again?'

'Nick Borrowdale,' Mrs Harris supplied promptly, her iron-grey curls bobbing with enthusiasm. 'The one from *Smuggler's Inn*.'

'That's him,' Miss Hudson agreed. 'And now Gabriel.'

'The angel Gabriel,' Martha said, with a distinctly unholy wink.

Mrs Harris sighed. 'I do love a man who can cook. What's your secret, dear? How do you tempt them here?'

Sam laughed. 'I don't have a secret. It's the Star and Sixpence they come for, not me.'

It wasn't strictly true; Nick had only ventured to Little Monkham because she'd asked him to, long before they'd become an item. But he'd still tirelessly given his time to support the pub, so Sam told herself it wasn't much of a lie.

'Well, we're very grateful,' Martha said. She paused in the act of wrapping up Sam's order. 'I don't suppose we'll be seeing much of either of them over Christmas.'

Sam shook her head. 'Gabe flew back to Seville yesterday, I'm afraid. And I don't actually know what Nick is doing at the moment – the last I heard, he was filming in Morocco. You'll have to make do with Micky Holiday.'

Now it was Miss Hudson who sighed. 'If only.'

'He's performing at the New Year's Eve party,' Sam said, lifting the boxes of mince pies from the counter top. 'Nessie and I will make sure there's plenty of mistletoe around if it helps?'

'Just make sure Ruby isn't looking,' Martha said. 'Now, I don't suppose we'll see you at the carol service this afternoon, will we?'

Sam shook her head. 'No, Nessie has decided she wants to go, so I'll be mulling the wine and warming the mince pies ready for you all afterwards.'

'Very important work,' Mrs Harris said approvingly. 'Christmas wouldn't be Christmas without the fayre on the green.'

'Very true,' Miss Hudson said. 'But don't let us keep you, dear. I'm sure you still have lots of preparation to do.'

'I have,' Sam said, wondering if anyone in Little Monkham thought she was capable of doing her job. She dredged up a cheery voice and smiled as she left the shop. 'See you later, ladies. Happy carolling!'

The carol service was every bit as festive as Nessie remembered. St Mary's was resplendent in red, gold and green, with wreaths of glorious many-berried holly wrapped around the tall candlesticks that flanked the nativity scene on the altar. Father Goodluck was in jolly form as he led the congregation through the readings and much-loved songs. Lit up by the glow of the candles all around her, it did Nessie's heart good to hear Owen and Luke singing 'Good King Wenceslas' and hers was not the only jaw to drop when Micky stood up and delivered a flawless first verse of 'Once in Royal David's City'. Who would have suspected that his raspy rock vocals hid a beautiful tenor voice that caused goosebumps, Nessie wondered as she listened in spellbound delight. Franny would be rubbing her hands with glee at the thought of recruiting him to the choir.

Eventually, the service wound its way to 'O Come All Ye Faithful'. Nessie had planned to sneak out early to help Sam, but she found herself wedged in between Henry and Martha's husband, Rob, and she didn't want to disturb them. So she held her candle high and tried not to worry whether she was hitting all the notes. It certainly didn't seem to be something that troubled Henry.

As the final organ notes died away, Henry blew out his candle and turned to Nessie. 'Merry Christmas, in case I miss you at the fayre,' he said, pressing his hands on hers and squeezing in a way that conveyed more than he ever could with words. 'See you on Boxing Day for a lunchtime pint.'

All Nessie's hopes of making a quick getaway were thwarted by the kindness of the people around her. Few of them mentioned the miscarriage directly, but the acknowledgement of her loss was present in every smile, every warm word, every hug. By the time the crowd had thinned enough for Nessie to think about making for the door, her throat ached and her eyes prickled with unshed tears. But they weren't tears of sadness; they were tears born from feeling supported, from being surrounded by good wishes and love.

Luke dashed past the end of Nessie's pew, his face alight as he chased one of his friends. She opened her mouth to remind him to take care on the well-worn flagstones, but he was gone before she could get the warning out. And then she saw Owen, head bowed in front of the altar, gazing down at the nativity scene with slumped shoulders.

'Go to him,' a soft voice urged, and Nessie turned to see Ruby hovering a few feet away, compassion etched across her elegant features. 'He needs you.'

'I don't think he does,' Nessie replied helplessly. 'He's shut me out – won't even talk to me.'

'Because he's trying to be strong,' Ruby said. 'Men aren't supposed to feel the loss of a baby as keenly as a woman – that's society's expectation, isn't it? But it's my experience that we all grieve when we lose something we love. Why should Owen Rhys be any different?'

The words caused a lump to form in Nessie's throat. She took a slow steadying breath and held on to the cool hard wood of the pew. 'Kathryn says he was like this when Eliza died too.'

'He was,' Ruby agreed. 'But that's the trouble with the deep ones. They retreat far inside when something hurts and they don't always see that others are hurting too.'

Nessie glanced across at Owen again. He didn't seem to have moved; she wasn't sure he was even aware that everyone around him had gone.

'The saddest thing is that neither of you needs to struggle alone,' Ruby went on. 'Go to him now. Join your pain with his. I promise you it helps.'

Nessie nodded, not trusting herself to speak.

'And don't worry about the fayre, or the pub,' Ruby finished, with the faintest hint of severity. 'We'll cope.'

But Nessie was already moving, slipping out of the row and making her way down the aisle to where Owen stood as though carved from wood. She waited at his shoulder for a moment, unsure what to do next, then she slid her hand into his and followed the line of his stare.

It shouldn't have been a surprise, but understanding hit her like a heavyweight punch when she realised what had him so transfixed: the small wooden cradle, which would remain empty until the Christmas Day service. The cradle she'd worked hard to avoid seeing until now.

They stood for a few moments, side by side, as the last of the congregation made for the exit. There was a solid thud as the door swung closed, shutting out the cheerful chatter of the crowd, and then the silence settled around them.

His breathing gave him away. At first, Nessie thought she had imagined the catch, the faint irregularity that reminded her of her own efforts to hold back tears. She forced her own breathing to slow and listened hard, her fingers clutching his. When the second barely audible sob came, she was sure and felt an answering call go out from her own sorrow. Her fingers tightened around his.

'It's okay, you know,' she whispered. 'It's all right to cry.'

Almost as though her words had released something, Owen's shoulders began to shake. Immediately, Nessie turned to wrap her arms around him. He sank his face into her shoulder and she felt him shudder with each indrawn breath. She bit her cheek, determined not to cry, determined to show him that she could be strong so he didn't have to be. He wept for a long time. But gradually, slowly, the shuddering became less and he raised his head to look at her through eyes that shone like wet coal.

'I'm sorry.'

'Don't be. There's nothing to be sorry for,' she said, daring to reach up and stroke his tear-stained cheek.

He let out a broken sigh. 'There is. But I don't know where to begin.'

Nessie glanced at the crib again. 'Today was always going to be hard. Maybe it's been harder for you than it has for me.'

Owen was quiet for a second or two, then shook his head. 'No. There's . . . there's something I need to tell you.'

Nessie's heart plummeted to her boots: this was it, the moment he told her she wasn't the woman he'd thought she was. The moment he said what she'd whispered to herself every night since they'd got the news – that he blamed her just as much as she blamed herself. She steeled herself, preparing for the blow. 'Go on.'

'You're right, these past few weeks have been hard. But not for the reason you might think.'

She blinked hard and waited, misery burrowing into her stomach. 'Why then?'

He ran a hand through his hair. 'I don't want you to think I'm not sad about the baby – of course I am. I know you are too, desperately sad. But that moment in the antenatal clinic isn't what gives me nightmares.' He looked her straight in the eyes. 'It's the thought of losing you. When they wheeled you away on that bed, to have your operation, I started to worry that I'd never see you again. That's what happened with Eliza, see – she was there one minute and gone the next. I thought I'd lose you the way I lost her.'

Nessie gasped. 'Oh, Owen.'

'I know it isn't rational,' Owen said wretchedly. 'But I can't control it. And once that thought spirals out of control, it eats away inside until it's all I can think about. I can cope with the loss of our baby, Nessie. I can't cope with the thought of losing you.'

Nessie wanted to sob for both of them. 'I'm fine,' she said quietly, taking both his hands in hers. 'Doing really well, all things considered. And I promise you, I'm not going anywhere.'

His gaze was dark and fearful as he stared at her. 'I hope not. Because I love you. And I need you. Luke needs you too.'

Tears spilled down Nessie's cheeks at the words. 'I love you too. Both of you.'

Owen let out a long breath and pulled her into his arms. 'Good,' he said, his lips against her hair. 'I'm sorry. I should have told you earlier.'

She managed the ghost of a smile, despite her tears. 'It's okay. You've told me now. That's all that matters.'

Nessie had no idea how long they stood together, whispering back and forth. She only knew that it felt so good to be in Owen's arms at last, listening to his voice as he talked. Their troubles weren't over – not by a long way – but this could be the start of their recovery. And Nessie allowed herself a tiny prayer of thanks to the yule log because perhaps now – finally – they might find peace together. Maybe now their hearts could begin to heal.

Chapter Eighteen

'You know what this Christmas Fayre needs?' Laurie gazed around the darkened village green, a thoughtful expression on his face. 'More fairy lights.'

Sam laughed as she took in the twinkling tree branches overhead, and Santa's grotto, bedecked with brilliant white icicles. She swirled the roasted chestnuts around the brazier, sending a shower of sparks into the night air. 'I'm sure you're right. We're not quite visible from space yet, after all.'

Laurie shook his head in admiration, evidently impressed by the crowd. 'It's all so great. I love the way the pub is at the centre of the village community.'

'It's always been this way,' Sam replied. 'Even when Dad was in charge. Or maybe especially then, because people rallied round to help.'

He turned to study the Star and Sixpence, picked out in amber light against the darkened sky. 'It sounds like you've really turned this place around. It's thriving.'

The praise gave Sam a quiet buzz of satisfaction. It was certainly true that she and Nessie had worked hard over the last two years, restoring the building bit by bit, trying new ventures like the bed and breakfast rooms and the restaurant. But they couldn't have done any of it without the support of the community. 'It's a team effort,' she said, suddenly recalling Gabe's words to her. 'There's a lot of love for the Star and Sixpence.'

'Love that you nurtured,' Laurie pointed out. 'Don't be so modest.'

Sam smiled at him. 'Well, Nessie and me. But thank you. It's nice to be appreciated.'

'Any time,' he replied. 'Actually, there's something I wanted to talk to you—'

'I hope you've saved some chestnuts for me?'

Sam's head jerked up. There was only one person she knew whose Irish accent could melt chocolate and that was Nick Borrowdale. She whirled around, all thoughts of Laurie forgotten, and saw him walking towards her with a broad grin on his famously handsome face. She dropped the spatula and ran towards him. 'Nick!' she cried, throwing her arms around him. 'Oh my god, I had no idea you were coming!'

'I know,' he said. 'It's what we in the acting business call a plot twist.'

Sam laughed. 'I thought you were filming in Morocco. When did you get back?'

'This morning,' he replied. 'Now, are you going to put me down at all? People are starting to stare.'

'Let them,' Sam said fiercely, startled to discover there were tears stinging the backs of her eyes. 'God, Nick, I am so pleased you're here.'

He raised one eyebrow. 'I know. Best Christmas present ever, am I right?'

His smug tone broke the spell. Sam stepped back far enough to hit him on the arm. 'Don't flatter yourself, Borrowdale. Obviously Michael Bublé is top of my Christmas list.'

Nick pulled out his phone. 'Want me to call him? I'm sure he'd be thrilled to fly over to serenade you over Christmas dinner tomorrow.'

Sam blinked up at him, not quite able to process his unexpected presence. 'No, you're more than enough. How long can you stay?'

'Only a few days,' Nick said, pulling a face. 'And I need to visit my family too. But I'm all yours until Boxing Day.'

Laurie cleared his throat, reminding Sam he was there.

'Sorry, how rude of me,' she said. 'Laurie, meet Nick.'

'Ah, the famous Laurie,' Nick said, shaking his hand. 'I've heard a lot about you.'

Sam watched as pleasure mingled with embarrassment crept over Laurie's face. She hid a smile; no one was immune to the Borrowdale charm.

'It's a real pleasure to meet you,' Laurie replied earnestly. 'I loved you in *The King of the North*.'

'Thanks,' Nick said. 'I dislocated my shoulder filming the leap from the helicopter, so it's always good to know someone actually watched it.'

'Oh, stop it,' Sam said fondly. 'Laurie, can you take over here? I need to let Nessie know there'll be another mouth to feed at Christmas dinner.'

'Sure,' Laurie said, lifting the spatula.

Sam slid her arm through Nick's. 'I imagine there'll be one or two village ladies who are very happy you're here,' she said, just as a screech of delight split the air and Martha came bustling towards them. 'I hope you're ready to see your number one fan.'

Nick smiled. 'That's a price I'll pay to hang out with you.'

Sam tried not to dwell on how much her mood had improved with Nick's arrival. It was like pulling on a favourite jumper and feeling warmth seep into her body; the kind of comfort that only someone who knew her inside and out could bring. And it didn't matter that they had history together – the months they'd spent as a couple had only deepened their friendship. There wasn't even a hint of regret or bitterness on Nick's part that Sam had chosen Joss over him; it had taken time, but things had gradually gone back to the same easy closeness they'd always had. And he'd been there for her when things ended with Joss, without so much as a hint of recrimination or blame. Perhaps it wasn't such a mystery that his unexpected presence had made her feel so much happier, Sam thought as she watched him charm Miss Hudson and Mrs Harris. Perhaps he was her reward for all the hard work she'd put in during Nessie's absence.

By ten o'clock, the last of the merry revellers had been sent on their way and the pub's doors were closed. Nessie excused herself as soon as the clearing up had been done.

'Owen and I have a lot of talking to do,' she said quietly.

Sam pulled her into a hug. 'About time. And don't rush over here in the morning – Nick and I will do all the preparations.'

Nessie gave her a quizzical look. 'Really? I'm pretty sure you once told me life was too short to peel a parsnip.'

'That was before Gabe,' Sam said. 'I'm a dab hand with a vegetable peeler now.'

'Okay,' Nessie said, flashing her a look of pure gratitude. 'I'm sure Nick will give you a hand.'

Sam shuddered. 'God, no. Have you ever seen him in a kitchen? He's even more clueless than I used to be. No, leave everything to me.'

'Thanks. I'll be over around eleven, if that's okay?'

'Fine,' Sam replied. 'Happy Christmas, Ness. I'm glad you and Owen are talking.'

Her sister smiled and Sam caught the glint of moisture in her eyes. 'Happy Christmas to you too. See you in the morning.'

And finally, it was just Sam and Nick. She poured two glasses of champagne and carried them over to the seats beside the fire, where Nick was waiting.

'So,' he said once she'd settled into an armchair. 'What's going on with you?'

For a second or two, Sam considered glossing over the truth, telling him everything was fine. But then she met his warm, knowing gaze and the wall she'd been using to keep her jumbled emotions at bay cracked and fell. Nick listened carefully, without interruption, his eyes never leaving hers as he sipped his champagne. And when she'd finished, he gave a rueful shake of his head and smiled.

'You have the most incredible talent for making life hard for yourself, Sam.'

'I know,' she groaned, putting her head in her hands. 'Believe me, if I could go back in time and change things, I would.'

'Too late for that,' Nick said practically. 'But if there's one thing I've learned from my affairs of the heart, it's that some people are worth fighting for. What you have to decide is whether Gabe is one of those people.'

'Yes.' The word was out of her mouth before she had time to think about it. 'I mean, probably—'

'Eh, I'm afraid I have to take your first answer,' Nick said, with mock-severity. 'And that being the case, I think you also need to decide what you're going to do about it.'

'What can I do?' Sam said, spreading her hands. 'He's made his feelings clear.'

Nick tipped his head. 'No, he's made his *hurt* feelings clear. And that in itself tells you something. Besides, you're forgetting how well I know you, Sam Chapman. You're the queen of hiding your emotions. I'm willing to bet Gabe has no idea he was anything more than a passing fancy for you.'

It was entirely possible, Sam realised. No, it was more than that; it was entirely probable. She'd never actually told Gabe how she felt, after all and—

An enormous yawn crept over her, bringing with it a wave of exhaustion so heavy that she had to fight an urge to close her eyes there and then.

'Am I keeping you up?' Nick said, studying her with some amusement.

'Sorry,' she said, flushing. 'It's been a long day.'

His eyes sparkled with mirth. 'You've changed. Ten-thirty used to be the start of the party, not the end!'

She felt the start of another yawn and covered her mouth. 'Sorry. I don't know why I'm so tired all of a sudden.'

'Don't apologise,' he said. 'Let's finish these drinks and call it a night. I'm pretty exhausted myself.'

He looked anything but tired, Sam thought, eyeing his bright gaze, gently mussed hair and stubble-covered chin; he looked ready to hit the town. But she appreciated his efforts to make her feel less like she was letting him down.

It wasn't until they were on their way up the stairs that Sam gave any thought to where Nick was going to sleep. 'Oh no,' she groaned, one hand passing wearily over her face. 'The beds are stripped in the guest rooms. I'll have to make one up for you.'

He shook his head. 'No, you won't. Just point me towards the sheets and I'll do it myself.'

'I can't let you do that,' Sam said, aghast at the thought. 'Nessie would kill me if she found out I'd let a guest any-where near the linen cupboard.'

'I'm not a guest,' he reminded her. 'I'm a friend. And friends don't expect special treatment.'

'But—'

'No buts,' he said, dipping his head to kiss the top of her head. 'Go to bed, Sam. I'll see you in the morning. And don't worry about the sheets – I'll find them. I might even put them on the bed – it'll be an adventure.'

Sam started to argue, but another yawn took the place of what she was going to say. 'Okay,' she conceded. 'Sleep well.'

He gave her a warm smile. 'You too.'

Sam knew she'd overslept the moment she opened her eyes. The sunlight slicing around the shutters was too bright, the angles all wrong, for it to be eight o'clock. Her phone told her it was nine-thirty; somehow, she'd slept right through both the alarms she'd set the night before.

'Crap,' she muttered, rolling sideways with a yawn and fumbling under the bed for her slippers. 'Nessie is going to kill me.'

Christmas carols greeted her as she opened her bedroom door. Frowning, she made her way to the kitchen, expecting to find Nessie had reneged on her promise and was elbow-deep in potato peelings. Instead, she saw Nick, wearing the red polka-dot apron Sam wore to prepare the guests' breakfasts and grinning at her with a vegetable knife in one hand. Was she dreaming?

'Morning,' he said. 'I thought I'd make a start, seeing as you apparently need more beauty sleep than Cruella de Vil these days.'

There wasn't much she could say to that, Sam thought; her hair certainly resembled a Disney villain's. 'I need coffee.'

He waved the knife towards the Nespresso machine, sending a fragment of carrot flying towards the window. 'I'll have a macchiato, if you're making one.'

By the time Nessie arrived, Sam and Nick had peeled everything that needed peeling and had set the long table in the bar for seven guests.

'I'm impressed,' Nessie said, gazing in astonishment at the brimming saucepans. 'You should visit more often, Nick.'

'Oi!' Sam said, pretending to be offended. 'I'll have you know this is all my own work.'

Nessie fixed Nick with a knowing look. 'How late did she sleep? You can tell me, it's fine.'

He shook his head in gallant fashion. 'Up with the lark, she was. I was the one who overslept.'

It certainly felt as though she'd been up for hours, Sam thought, pushing back another wave of weariness. At this rate she'd need an afternoon nap just to make it through to bedtime.

The day itself passed in a pleasant whirl of eating and drinking and laughter. Sam couldn't help noticing that both Nessie and Owen were a long way from their normal selves, but they weren't as far apart as they had been, either physically or emotionally. From time to time, she caught Kathryn watching them closely too and they exchanged a smile. Laurie was on good form, considering it was his first Christmas with them, and Luke was his usual chatterbox self, encouraging them all to have a go at the football game that had come with his new games console and pretending to be offended when Nick beat him in the very first game.

'Now we know what you do in between takes,' Sam teased.

He shrugged and concentrated on the screen. 'There's a lot of downtime in the movie industry. Oi, referee, that was never a foul!'

The afternoon passed gently into evening. Just as she'd expected, Sam found herself dozing as she listened to the family chatter around her. And she wondered what Gabe was doing right at that moment; was he full of food and surrounded by love too? She hoped he was.

And then it was late, and Sam found herself covering up her yawns again.

'Time for us to make a move,' Nessie said, once their traditional game of Monopoly ended with Laurie making every single one of them bankrupt. 'Busy day tomorrow.'

Sam nodded. 'Especially now the village ladies know Nick is in town.'

Owen reached out to shake his hand. 'Good to see you again, Nick. Catch you at the bar for a pint of Thirsty Bishop?'

'Never mind the ladies,' Kathryn said, rolling her eyes. 'They'll have to form an orderly queue behind the men.'

Sam did her best to keep Nick company once everyone had gone, but her body had other ideas. She woke up on the sofa, with a blanket draped over her, as the end credits of the film they'd been watching rolled across the screen.

'Sorry,' she mumbled, rubbing her eyes. 'I'm a terrible friend.'

Nick smiled from the armchair beside her. 'You are. The least you can do when I turn up unexpectedly and crash Christmas is entertain me. I'd like a refund, please.'

Now it was Sam's turn to smile. 'You'll need to contact the complaints department. Best of luck with finding it.'

He studied her for a moment, his good humour fading. 'Is everything all right, Sam?'

She sat up, trying to smooth her hair. 'Of course. I'm just tired. It's been a hectic few weeks, what with Ness needing some time to recover.' She pulled a wry face. 'Christmas isn't exactly quiet in the hospitality business, you know.'

'No, I know,' he said, his forehead creasing with concern. 'But you look a bit – well, you'll forgive me for saying this, but you look a bit less sparkling than usual. Are you coming down with something?'

Sam started to deny it and then hesitated. She had been more tired than usual over the last few days and there was a tingle in her nose that suggested a cold was on its way. 'Oh god, I can't be ill,' she said with a groan. 'Not before New Year's Eve. I've got way too much to do.'

'Berocca and rest, that's what you need,' Nick said wisely. 'Why don't you let me help out behind the bar tomorrow? That way you can fight off whatever it is that's bringing you down and be match fit for the big party.'

'I can't ask you to do that,' Sam said. 'You're a guest.'

'Like I keep telling you, I'm a friend,' he insisted. 'And

friends help each other out. No arguments, Sam. It's happening.'

Feeling too weary to argue, Sam conceded defeat with a grateful smile. 'Do you even know how to pull a pint?'

'Of course I do,' Nick said promptly. 'I'll have you know I've played a barman twice.'

'In that case, the job's yours,' Sam said, doing her best to smile. 'God help you if you mess up Henry's pint.'

Chapter Nineteen

The days between Christmas and New Year seemed to both drag and fly by. Nick managed to make his getaway, in spite of Martha's half-formed plan to imprison him in the bakery; Sam wished he'd been able to stay longer but accepted a promise that he'd be back as soon as his schedule allowed.

'As long as *you* promise you'll sort things out with this Gabe,' Nick had insisted as he'd said goodbye. 'Or I might be tempted to take matters into my own hands.'

The threatened cold had materialised on Boxing Day and Sam had spent the next few days coughing and sneezing. She kept a nervous eye on the calendar, hoping she'd be well again by New Year's Eve and was relieved when she started to feel better. If she was going to take Nick's advice and tell Gabe how she felt, the last thing she needed was a nose that was redder than Rudolph's.

She found herself almost sick with nerves the morning

Gabe was due to return. Her stomach roiled unpleasantly as she made up the guest rooms and she had to stop on more than one occasion to wait for the feeling to pass. By the time his car pulled up outside, she'd decided the best plan was to leave the Star and Sixpence and return to London, so their paths would never cross again.

'Get a grip, Sam,' she muttered under her breath as she splashed some water over her wrists and smoothed her hair into something that was vaguely presentable. 'It's just Gabe and he's seen you looking much worse than this.'

She wasn't prepared for the surge of attraction she felt when he walked into the bar. Her nerves tingled and there was a sharp burst of electricity deep inside her that made the breath catch in the back of her throat. His skin was more tanned than it had been before and he looked relaxed as he greeted Nessie and Connor. When his eyes met hers, she had to grip the bar.

'Hello, Sam. How are you?'

'Fine,' she replied, hoping her voice didn't sound as squeaky and tight as it felt. 'Did you have a lovely Christmas?'

'I did,' he said, his gaze fixed on her. 'But it is good to be back.'

It didn't mean anything, Sam told herself as she lay in bed later, listening to the sound of him moving around in the room next door. He loved his job and had never made any secret of the fact that he adored the quaint village feel of Little Monkham. But there was a large part of her that hoped he'd meant more than that. She couldn't help hoping that the reason Gabe was glad to be back had more to do with her than his job.

Sam struggled to get out of bed on Sunday morning. It was only the sound of Gabe's door opening that gave her the impetus to push back the covers and brave the early morning chill. But she was determined to clear the air between them and this was the only time of day when she could guarantee they would not be interrupted. Dragging a brush through her hair, she reached for her dressing gown and suppressed a sudden bubble of wild laughter when she caught sight of her flannel pyjamas and slipper-clad feet. It had to be the least glamorous chat-up outfit ever.

He was seated at the kitchen table, reading a battered copy of *Don Quixote*, when she forced herself to walk nervously inside.

'Good morning,' he said, looking up. 'Did you sleep well?'

Sam cleared her throat. 'Not bad. How about you?'

He placed his book face down on the table and stretched, revealing a sliver of taut, tanned stomach beneath his T-shirt. 'I slept very well, thank you. There is something about this place that is very restful, at least at night.' His mouth quirked. 'During the day, it is too busy to be restful.'

Sam nodded. 'Things will settle down in January. It'll be less hectic then.' She paused, then ploughed on. 'And was everything okay with the food order? Olivia didn't mention anything, so I assumed it was all okay. We can try and fix things if it isn't – I know it's Sunday, but a lot of places will be open, so if there's something you need to replace, all you need to do is let us – me – know.' She broke off, aware she was gabbling.

'The order was fine,' he said. 'All exactly as I requested, thank you.'

She nodded again and steeled herself. It was better to come right out with it, she decided as she tried to quell a rising tide of panic. No sense in waiting.

But Gabe beat her to it. 'There is something I need to say to you, Sam,' he said, his brown eyes suddenly intense. 'I have not been very fair to you. The mistake with the order for the wedding was not your fault, but I allowed myself to blame you.'

Sam stared at him, mouth open. 'But—'

He held up a hand. 'No, you must allow me to say this. It has been troubling me for some time and when I am wrong, I admit it.'

She sat at the table, unable to believe what she was hearing. 'Go on.'

'But more than blaming you for Laurie's interference in the days that followed the wedding, I am not proud to say I punished you.' Gabe sighed, but his eyes did not leave Sam's. 'I was not thinking straight. Jealousy was clouding my mind.'

The word hit Sam hard. 'Jealousy?'

Gabe nodded. 'Over your night with Joss. I knew I had no right to tell you what you could and could not do – on the surface we had only shared one or two kisses – but I also knew I wanted more than that.' He paused. 'I foolishly hoped you felt the same. And then Joss appeared and I was jealous of him and the easy way he came back into your life.'

Once again, Sam tried to interrupt, her stomach tied up in an agony of anguish, but Gabe would not let her.

'No, I must finish this now.' He glanced away in obvious embarrassment. 'I allowed my feelings for you to affect my professional judgement and I am truly sorry. It will never happen again.'

Sam's heart hammered in her chest. Had he ... had he really just admitted he had feelings for her? Or had she hallucinated that part of his speech?

She swallowed hard. 'What if I did feel the same?'

His head jerked up, wide-eyed. 'What?'

'What if I wanted more than a few kisses from you too?' Sam said, fighting to keep her voice steady. 'What if I had feelings for you?'

He stared at her wordlessly. 'Are you telling me this is true?' he said eventually. 'What about Joss?'

Sam shook her head impatiently. 'I told you at the time, it wasn't what you thought. Yes, we spent the night together, but we both agreed it was a mistake. I haven't seen Joss since. We haven't even messaged each other.'

Slowly, Gabe got to his feet and rounded the table to kneel before her. 'So what would happen if I kissed you now?'

Heart hammering in her chest, Sam gazed into his eyes. 'I'd kiss you back.'

Without a moment's hesitation, Gabe cupped her cheek

and pulled her face towards him. His lips brushed hers, soft and tentative at first, as though he wasn't sure how she might react. A burst of heat ignited within Sam and she leaned forwards, pressing against him, deepening the kiss. One hand tangled in his hair and the other caressed the back of his neck. There would be no misunderstandings this time, she decided with the only part of her brain that wasn't distracted. She'd make sure he knew what she wanted.

When the kiss ended, they were both breathless and dazed. Sam blinked in the sunlight, looking at Gabe as though she was seeing him properly for the first time. 'Just so we're clear,' she said, her voice low and husky. 'It's you I want, Gabe. No one else.'

He answered by kissing her again. And she gave up trying to think.

'Great party, Sam!' Rob beamed at her and raised a half-empty glass of Thirsty Bishop in salute. 'Micky's a bit of a legend, isn't he?'

Sam turned to watch Micky strut across the stage, crooning into his microphone. No one could say he didn't know how to entertain, she thought, shaking her head at his energy. She felt tired just watching him.

'He's rock 'n' roll royalty,' she said to Rob. 'We're so lucky to have him here.'

Rob raised an eyebrow. 'If you ask me, it's you we're lucky to have. What you and Nessie have done for this place—' He waved an arm and was in serious danger of losing the remainder of his pint. 'What you've done is nothing short of brilliant. And we're all grateful. Especially Martha.'

Sam smiled. Martha might go on about fancying Nick and Gabe, but she was devoted to Rob, just as he was to her. But they were both Star and Sixpence stalwarts; Sam couldn't imagine the pub without them. 'Thank you. Believe me, it's our pleasure.'

Gabe came to find her just after eleven-thirty. 'I'm not taking any chances,' he said, snaking an arm around her waist. 'There's only one person I want to welcome the new year with and that's you.'

Sam reached up to kiss him. 'Hold that thought. We need to pour the champagne – everyone needs a glass in their hand when the clock strikes midnight.'

The last thirty minutes of the year whizzed by in a blur of bubbles. At last, everyone was ready and they gathered on the village green to bring in the new year. Sam caught sight of Nessie, hand in hand with Owen, and smiled. She knew it hadn't been easy, but they seemed to be getting stronger with each day that passed.

Leaning into Gabe, Sam tipped her head back to gaze at the stars overhead as the thirty-second countdown began. A rush of light-headedness assailed her, causing her vision to waver. Sam shook her head to clear the fuzziness and tiny pinpricks of light danced across her eyes, shadowed by grey. Maybe she should lay off the champagne, she thought muzzily.

'Sam?' Gabe said, but his voice seemed to be coming from a long way away.

'I'm okay,' she started to say, but her lips wouldn't form the words.

Her legs began to buckle. She heard the countdown from ten begin and then the darkness claimed her.

When she came to, she was lying on one of the oversized sofas inside the pub with a sea of anxious faces around her.

'She's awake,' Nessie said, and the relief in her voice was unmistakable. 'Can you hear me, Sam?'

'Yeah,' Sam said, still confused. 'What happened?'

Gabe's face swam into view. 'You fainted, out on the green. I caught you before you hit the ground and carried you in here.'

Fainted? Sam tried to sit up, horrified.

'No you don't,' Nessie said, placing a hand on her shoulder to ease her back onto the sofa. 'Not until I know you're okay.'

'Is there some water?' Sam asked, still trying to understand what had happened. The last thing she remembered was standing on the green with Gabe, waiting for the countdown to begin. She didn't remember feeling unwell.

A glass was thrust into her hand. Gabe and Nessie helped her upright. She took a long drink and felt a burst of anguish at the worried expressions around her.

'Oh god, I've totally ruined New Year's Eve, haven't I?'

'Of course not,' Nessie reassured her. 'You can't help it if you're not well.'

'But I'm fine now,' Sam said, feeling her cheeks start to burn. 'Really I am. Go and have a drink, everyone. I'm sorry.'

Once the crowd had dispersed a little, Nessie fixed Sam with a stern look. 'You've been poorly for over a week now. I think it's time you visited the doctor, don't you?'

Sam shook her head. 'It's New Year's Day. I won't get an appointment for ages, by which time I'll be totally fine.'

'No arguments,' Nessie said, in a voice that Sam knew better than to argue with. 'Ring the surgery tomorrow and get the first available appointment. Do you hear me?'

'Yes, Nessie,' Sam said meekly.

'Good,' Nessie said. She glanced at Gabe, who was hovering beside her, looking troubled. 'Can I leave her with you for a while? I need to help out behind the bar – poor Laurie is rushed off his feet.'

'Of course,' Gabe said, sitting next to Sam. 'I'll look after her.'

Sam waited until Nessie had gone before turning to Gabe. 'Honestly, I'm fine. I probably haven't eaten properly, that's all.'

'Again?' Gabe growled. 'I can see I am going to have to cook for you, if you won't do it for yourself.'

Sam smiled. She could think of worse things. 'I bet I spilled my champagne, didn't I?'

He rubbed at his trouser leg. 'You did.'

'Oh. Sorry.' She hesitated and looked up at him through her eyelashes. 'I don't suppose there's any chance of another glass, is there? Purely for medicinal purposes. It is New Year's Day, after all.'

For a moment, she thought he might refuse. Then he smiled. 'Only if you let me feed you some canapés first.'

Sam let out a long-suffering sigh. 'If you must, Gabe. If you must.'

Dr Arnold smiled, her hands folded on the desk in front of her as she studied Sam. 'What can I do for you today?'

Sam shook her head, embarrassed, and wondered for the hundredth time why she'd allowed Nessie to talk her into this when she was perfectly fine. 'It's probably nothing. My sister insisted I come.'

She explained her symptoms, downplaying the fainting episode as much as she could. When she'd finished, the GP nodded. 'Well, it doesn't sound too serious. Where are you in your cycle?'

Sam blinked. 'My what?'

'Your cycle,' Dr Arnold repeated patiently. 'When was your last period?'

The question caught Sam by surprise. 'I don't actually know,' she said slowly. 'They've always been a bit erratic. Um . . . let's see. I didn't have one in the run-up to Christmas so that's a good few weeks now – in fact, I don't remember having one in December at all. So probably November.'

Dr Arnold nodded. 'So four to five weeks ago, yes?'

Unease stirred in the pit of Sam's stomach. 'Yes.'

'And is there a chance you might be pregnant?'

Sam felt the blood drain from her face. It couldn't be that. 'No, of course not.' Her mind started to whirl as she tried to do the maths. 'I can't be – I've had no morning sickness. My sister started to suffer with that almost right away.'

'All women experience pregnancy differently,' Dr Arnold said in a matter-of-fact tone. She reached into a drawer. 'Take this card and pee on it, please. There's a toilet just outside this room.'

Sam shook as she locked the toilet door and did as the doctor had instructed. It was obviously just a precaution, she told herself. Her symptoms didn't fit with pregnancy; she'd had a cold and been a bit run-down, that was all.

Dr Arnold took one look at the card and gave Sam a small, practised smile. 'The test is positive. You're pregnant. You might want to do a home pregnancy test to confirm how many weeks along you are, since you're not sure when your last period was.' She paused. 'And if you're not sure whether you'd like to keep the baby, I can give you some information about that too.'

Sam knew she was gaping, but she couldn't seem to control the muscles in her face. 'But I can't be pregnant,' she managed eventually. 'My sister just ... she just lost her baby.'

The GP's face clouded with sympathy. 'I see. That's a shame. But there's no reason to think you'll do the same – as I said, every woman is different.'

She continued to talk but Sam stopped listening. She was imagining Nessie's face when she told her the news. Picturing the way her expression would crumple when she found out Sam would be having a baby when she wasn't. She'd have to tell Joss too; how would he react? Oh god, it was all too much to think about.

'Sam?' Dr Arnold said. 'Are you all right? Is there someone I can call?'

Picking up her bag, Sam got quickly to her feet. 'No, I'll be fine. Thank you, Dr Arnold. You've given me a lot to think about.'

Nessie had parked on the opposite side of the road. She gave a cheery wave when she saw Sam, and Sam considered turning around and hiding in the surgery. But she couldn't do that for the next seven months. Mouth dry, she crossed the road and got into the car.

'All okay?' Nessie asked. 'Did they get to the bottom of it?'

Sam hid her hands in her coat so her sister wouldn't see them shaking. 'The doctor thinks I might be a bit anaemic,' she said, trying to keep her tone level. 'I have to go for some blood tests.'

Nessie started the engine and pulled out into the traffic. 'That's easily sorted. We'll stock up on spinach on the way home, maybe pick up a multivitamin.' She glanced across at Sam and smiled. 'No big deal.'

'No,' Sam echoed, looking out of the window and catching a glimpse of her pale, clammy reflection. 'No big deal.'

Except that it was, she thought as the car carried her back to the Star and Sixpence. It didn't get much bigger, in fact. She closed her eyes and rested her forehead against the cool glass. What the hell was she going to do?

PART THREE

Cosy Nights
at the Star and Sixpence

Chapter Twenty

YOU ARE INVITED TO AN

EASTER EGGSTRAVAGANZA

at the Star and Sixpence,

Little Monkham.

Easter Egg Hunt, Easter Bonnet Parade,

Guess the Weight of the Cake

and much more!

Easter Sunday

12 p.m. until 5 p.m.

The cold was biting, even for the middle of February. Sam wrapped her arms around her body and put her head down as she crossed the hospital car park, wishing she'd thought to wear a hat. She glanced sideways at Ruby Cabernet, who *was* wearing a hat: an adorable green cloche that set off her loose wave of red hair beautifully. The nursing staff in the maternity wing had seemed a bit star-struck and even the sonographer undertaking Sam's twelve-week scan had seemed slightly distracted by the impossibly glamorous woman sitting opposite her.

'Not far now,' Ruby said, slipping her arm through Sam's and nodding towards a suspiciously dark patch of tarmac. 'Watch out for that patch of ice.'

Sam felt her chilled features crack into a half-hearted smile. 'Thank you for coming,' she said, after a few seconds had ticked by. 'I'm not sure I could have gone on my own.'

'Of course you could,' the older woman said, her tone warm but dismissive. 'You're stronger than you think. But I'm thrilled you asked me – what an honour, to be one of the first to meet your baby. You know that means I get cuddle priority when he or she is born?'

Sam's smile widened in spite of the hollow feeling in her chest. As much as she loved Ruby, she hadn't been her first choice to come along today. But her sister Nessie had made it clear she wouldn't be joining Sam – for reasons that were heartbreakingly understandable – and Joss, the baby's father, had no idea his ex-girlfriend was even pregnant. So it had been Ruby or no one …

'You're going to be his or her grandmother,' Sam said, squeezing Ruby's arm with a gloved hand. 'Of course you get first cuddles.'

Ruby beamed for a moment, then sighed. 'I know this has all come as something of a shock, darling, and you're still reeling, but I promise everything will work out.' She stopped walking to gaze into Sam's eyes. 'You are going to be absolutely fine. Both of you.'

Sam thought back to the moment she'd heard her baby's heart beating for the first time and seen its tiny head and arms outlined in white on the grey screen. Just for a moment, she'd forgotten all of the fear and anguish she'd felt since discovering she was pregnant just after New Year's Day and had felt a storm of love and protectiveness for the baby who'd caught her so utterly by surprise ... And then the fear had roared back stronger than ever, because what did she know about babies? She had no right to be bringing one into the world when she was so poorly equipped to look after it.

'I wish I could believe that,' she whispered to Ruby as the icy wind took her words and whistled them away.

'You can,' Ruby replied, a fierce expression on her face. 'And I'm going to be beside you every step of the way.'

Sam stared at her for a moment, wishing she had a fraction of Ruby's confidence. Then she nodded. 'Okay, I believe you.'

'Good,' Ruby said in satisfaction. 'Now, can we get out of this bloody subarctic weather and back to Little Monkham? I actually think my eyelashes have frozen together.'

Laughing in spite of herself, Sam reached into her coat pocket for the car keys. 'Yes. I'm ready to go home.'

Except that there wasn't much at home for Sam at the moment, she reflected as she settled into the driver's seat and started the engine. But maybe if she said it enough, she might actually convince herself it was true.

Chapter Twenty-one

Spring was taking its time to arrive in Little Monkham. The trees on the village green were stubbornly refusing to do more than hint at bursting out of their winter hibernation. Nessie Chapman glanced up at the green-tipped branches as she crossed the grass and thought they seemed to be holding their breath, waiting for the last frosts to loosen their grip on the chilly March mornings before allowing their buds to unfurl. There had been a dusting of snow on the rooftops that morning, and the sky looked leaden, so maybe the trees were wise to keep their leaves tucked away. In fact, the heavy sky matched Nessie's mood perfectly: grey and dull. But she couldn't blame her mood on the weather – she'd felt that way for months, since the day she and Owen had been told their unborn baby had no heartbeat. Christmas had helped distract her, with all its accompanying bustle and sparkle, but January had been hard. And it was made all the harder by her sister's bombshell, two weeks into the new year: Sam was pregnant.

Nessie still remembered the numbness that had settled over her as Sam had said the words. She hadn't replied, her brain able to comprehend what Sam was telling her but not managing to process it. Her chest had felt tight; she'd fought for breath as the walls of the small kitchen had seemed to close in on her. And, all the time, her sister had watched her, green eyes glistening with unshed tears.

'Say something, Ness,' Sam had pleaded, when the silent seconds turned into minutes. 'I'm sorry – I didn't mean for this to happen.'

And that made it worse, somehow, Nessie had thought dimly as she'd stared into her half-drunk cup of tea; Sam didn't even want a baby. 'Then how did it happen?'

Sam had let out a long shuddering breath. 'I don't know. We were drunk – maybe we weren't as careful as we should have been. You'd think by the age of thirty-one I'd know how to use a condom, but apparently not.'

And that had forced Nessie to consider that it took two people to make a baby; how did Sam's ex-boyfriend feel about unexpected parenthood?

'I haven't told him yet,' Sam had admitted, when Nessie asked the question.

'Sam!' Nessie had exclaimed, incredulity making her tone shrill.

'I wanted to tell you first,' Sam had said, holding her hands up in defence. 'And I wanted to get things straight in my own head. To decide ... well, to decide what the best course of action might be.'

It had taken a moment for Nessie to understand what she was saying. When the meaning behind the words became clear, a shiver had shaken Nessie's whole body. Surely Sam couldn't be talking about . . .

Nessie hadn't been able to stop the sob that had escaped her then. She'd wanted her baby so desperately, and it hadn't survived. Now she was having to listen to her own sister talk about voluntarily ending her pregnancy, and it was all too much to bear. She'd shaken her head, sending a torrent of tears cascading down her cheeks.

Sam had given her a wretched look. 'I'm sorry, Nessie. I know this must be impossibly hard for you—'

Nessie had stumbled to her feet, barely noticing that the sudden movement tipped her tea all over the kitchen table. 'I can't do this.'

'I'm so—'

'Stop!' Nessie cried, clamping her hands over her ears. 'Stop saying you're sorry. Can't you see it's too late for that?'

Sam had started to cry too, and part of Nessie ached for her, because she could imagine the turmoil her sister was going through. But that tiny spark of compassion had been swept away by the tide of Nessie's own pain.

She'd taken a shuddering breath. 'If you're going to have an abortion then why tell me at all? Why not just go and do it?'

Hurt had flashed across Sam's tear-stained face. 'Because I – I can't imagine anything worse than having to go through that on my own, in secret. Because you're my sister and I

thought you might want to know, in spite of what happened to you. Because—'

Nessie couldn't bear to hear any more. Turning her back, she'd walked to the door on legs that felt as though they were made of wood. 'How could you let this happen, Sam? How could you be so stupid?'

She was at the top of the stairs that led to the bar before she heard her sister's reply.

'I'm keeping the baby. In case you care.'

Nessie had frozen, one hand on the banister, and closed her eyes as a deluge of fresh anguish washed over her. There was no good outcome here; whatever Sam chose to do, it would feel like a knife to her heart. And right then, all Nessie had wanted to do was get away, to pretend it wasn't true. Opening her eyes, she'd trudged down the stairs and into the Star and Sixpence.

Even now, almost two months later, Nessie found it hard to believe there was a new life growing inside Sam. She looked the same as she always did – slim and beautiful, without much of a bump or a hint of the morning sickness that had wiped Nessie out. It was easy to wonder whether there had been some terrible mix-up. Except that she knew Sam had been for a scan – maybe even lain on the same bed she had when she'd learned her baby had gone – and everything had been fine. Unsurprisingly, Sam hadn't asked Nessie to accompany her; she'd taken Ruby Cabernet, their late father's girlfriend. Nessie only knew it had happened because Ruby had thought she ought to know.

'I don't expect you to fall over yourself to congratulate Sam, but I imagine it's been weighing on your mind,' Ruby had said, her voice gentle but her eyes sharp. 'And perhaps now you can both begin to accept that it's real.'

But acceptance was easier said than done, Nessie thought as she juggled the parcel in her hands to reach for the post office door handle. It didn't help that no one else in Little Monkham knew; Sam had sworn both Nessie and Ruby to utter secrecy, claiming she wanted to get the scan out of the way first. And then she'd said Joss had a right to know before it became common knowledge, which meant a trip to Chester to see him – a trip Sam didn't seem in a hurry to make. She'd have to make it soon, Nessie decided, meeting the eagle-eyed gaze of the village postmistress, Franny Fitzsimmons. If she didn't, someone else was certain to put two and two together and break the news to Joss first.

'Good morning, Vanessa,' Franny said, frowning from behind the cash register. 'You look like you have the weight of the world on your shoulders. I do hope everything is all right.'

'Fine,' Nessie said, hoping Franny wouldn't notice her fractional hesitation. 'Just the usual work stress. Laurie is away on holiday this week – I don't think we realised how much responsibility he's taken on over the last few months. We're missing him – or at least I am.'

She stopped, worried her gabbling would set off Franny's unerring instinct for intrigue, but the older woman simply nodded.

'Yes, he's certainly made himself useful. Now, what can

241

I help you with today?' Franny gestured to the post office window at the back of the shop and Nessie made her way past the shelves lined with jars and packets.

It was the only grocery store in the village and enjoyed all the supply-and-demand benefits to be had from cornering the market. Sam and Nessie had speculated more than once whether other shops had tried to move in, without success; Franny was also Chairwoman of the Village Preservation Society and ran things with an iron fist. Nessie was fairly sure any competing business would meet with a firm refusal if they dared enquire about opening a shop. It also meant that almost every person in Little Monkham found themselves under Franny's gimlet gaze at some point, a situation Nessie had no doubt helped the postmistress poke her nose into everyone else's business.

'How's Henry?' she asked as Franny weighed the parcel. 'Is married life agreeing with him?'

Franny gave her a serene smile. 'I don't think he'd dare say if it wasn't. But we are both very happy. Never been happier, in fact.'

She certainly looked contented, Nessie decided. Softer, somehow, as though she'd let go of some inner bitterness ̶ ̶ ̶ ̶ ̶ ̶ ̶ ̶ ̶ winter wedding just before Christmas. Maybe that was why Franny had taken Nessie's explanation of her own tension at face value; maybe she was so pleased with her own lot that she couldn't fathom why the rest of the world wasn't happy too.

'I'm very glad to hear that,' Nessie said. 'Good for you.'

Sixpence then the owners of the Speckled Goose would be delighted, Nessie thought, picturing the delicate but sturdy fleur-de-lys grate that sat in the hearth of the pub's grand fireplace. Owen was well recognised as a master blacksmith and his list of prospective and satisfied clients was growing almost faster than he could handle.

'That's good news.'

'It is,' he agreed, then glanced around the kitchen. 'Where's Luke?'

'Upstairs,' Nessie said, her eyes drawn to the ceiling. 'Doing his homework.'

Luke was Owen's nine-year-old son, the only child from his marriage to Eliza. If Nessie had been worried about how he would feel about her moving into Snowdrop Cottage, any concerns had soon melted away; Luke had taken the new arrangement easily in his stride, especially once he'd tasted her chocolate fudge cake.

'Homework,' Owen said, raising his dark eyebrows in undisguised scepticism. 'Playing that online game with his mates, more like.'

Nessie smiled at the often-heard grumble. 'I told him he had to do his homework first. He promised me faithfully he would.'

Owen flicked the kettle switch and reached for his favourite mug. 'Maybe I'll sneak up the stairs and surprise him in a while, see how well he's sticking to that promise.' He waved the cup around. 'Tea?'

'I'd better not,' Nessie said, even though she'd like nothing more than to sink into the squashy living-room sofa with a cuppa and hear more about his day. 'I need to get back to the pub for the evening shift.'

A crease lined Owen's forehead. 'But it's Wednesday. Your night off.'

She steeled herself for yet another white lie. 'Sam's been covering for Laurie. She's a bit tired, so I said I'd cover for her this evening. I hope you don't mind – I left you a lasagne in the oven.'

He was silent for a moment. 'Of course I don't mind, but it's not the first time you've covered for her lately. Is everything okay?'

'Of course,' Nessie said, a little too fast, and she cursed herself when she saw his frown deepen. 'It's just a bit full on at the moment, that's all. The restaurant brings in lots of thirsty customers and we're short-staffed while Laurie's away.'

Owen considered her. 'As long as that's all it is. Both you and Sam have seemed more stressed than usual over the last few weeks – you'd tell me if there was a problem, wouldn't you?'

A few seconds ticked by, during which Nessie battled a treacherous urge to spill her sister's secret. But Sam had made her promise not to tell and Nessie could never break that confidence, no matter how wretched it made her feel. 'Yes,' she said, crossing her fingers and reminding herself that one more lie didn't matter. 'I'd tell you.'

'All right then,' Owen said, although he looked far from satisfied. 'Shall I save you some lasagne?'

Nessie shook her head as she reached for her coat. 'No, I'll grab something from the kitchen during the evening.'

Owen smiled. 'So that's the real reason you're working tonight – you want whatever Gabe is serving up to the good and the great of Little Monkham.'

'What a thing to suggest,' Nessie said in mock-outrage. 'I'll have you know my lasagne matches up to anything our star chef could whip up.'

'You'll get no argument from me,' Owen said. 'Although that mouth-watering steak and ale pie of his makes a strong case.'

'I might have known your favourite dish would involve Thirsty Bishop,' Nessie replied fondly. 'Maybe I should stay here while you go over to the pub.'

He laughed. 'I wouldn't dream of getting between you and whatever's on the menu. See you when you get back.'

It wasn't an entirely unfair accusation, Nessie reflected later, when dish after delicious dish came out of the Star and Sixpence kitchen to land on the tables of the lucky diners; the possibility of leftovers was a bonus on the evenings when the restaurant was open. But Nessie would much rather be with Owen, eating her own cooking, than forcing herself to be jolly behind the bar of the pub. There wasn't much she could do about it, however; Sam had looked exhausted when Nessie had walked in. The conversation had remained stiffly business-like as Sam had passed on a few minor quibbles from the day, before escaping upstairs without quite meeting Nessie's eyes.

'She looked peaky,' Ruby Cabernet observed, tilting her glorious red head as she perched at the bar. 'Then again, so do you.'

Nessie smiled and refilled Ruby's glass with grapefruit juice. 'No need to worry about me. I'm just—'

'Tired?' Ruby cut in, arching one of her perfect eyebrows. 'Heartsick, disappointed, sad and wondering why it's not you?'

Nessie's face grew suddenly hot. 'That's not fair, Ruby.'

'Maybe not, but it is true,' the older woman said. 'What I'm getting at is that it's only natural you feel all of those things, darling. Given the circumstances.'

'I'm not jealous of Sam,' Nessie replied, fighting to keep her composure as she noticed Henry leaning in to hear better. 'No matter what she has that I don't.'

Ruby had obviously noticed the eavesdropper too because she lowered her voice to a whisper. 'I can only imagine how hard this is for you, Nessie. I hope you know that my door is always open if you need to talk.'

Nessie swallowed hard and managed a brittle smile. As in the days that had followed the miscarriage, she found sympathy much harder to cope with than silence. 'Thank you. Would you excuse me for a moment? I need to go and check something with Gabe.'

She made her way to the kitchen, grateful to escape from Ruby's well-meaning but pointed observations. As kind as the offer was, she had no intention of opening up about how Sam's pregnancy was making her feel. Because if she began down that road, she was very much afraid she might not be able to stop.

'Just checking in,' she called to Gabe as she poked her head through the kitchen door. 'Everything going well?'

The dark-eyed Spanish chef nodded and glanced around at his team of hard-working chefs. 'Perfect, thank you.'

Nessie smiled as she stepped back to hold the door, her eyes drawn to the large platter of creamy seafood linguine that Charlotte, the waitress, carried.

Gabe threw her an amused look. 'And in answer to your unspoken question, yes, I expect there will be some of that left over tonight. Perhaps even enough for two, if you want to take some home for Owen.'

'Am I that transparent?' she asked, her mouth twisting in wry self-deprecation. 'But none for Owen. He's had to settle for my cooking tonight.'

'Then he has already dined like a king,' Gabe said gravely. 'I'll just save one portion for you. I tried to offer some to Sam but she refused.'

'No, not seafood.' The words were out before Nessie could stop them. She waved a flustered hand. 'She can't.'

Gabe eyed her quizzically. 'But she's eaten it before – she's not allergic.'

'No,' Nessie said, casting desperately round for something to cover her mistake. 'I think she's ... just gone off it.'

His lips quirked as he shrugged. 'It happens, I suppose, even where my recipes are concerned. I'll put some in the fridge for you, ready for a not-quite-midnight feast.'

'Thank you,' Nessie said, her panic subsiding a little at the thought. 'That's definitely something to look forward to.'

'And I'll find something else to tempt Sam,' Gabe said. 'She needs to keep her strength up.'

Nessie eyed him sharply, wondering whether he knew more than he was telling. He and Sam shared the pub's first-floor accommodation; it was entirely possible he'd figured things out. But Nessie discounted the idea almost immediately. He and Sam had been on the brink of turning their will-they-won't-they flirtation into something more at the start of the new year, but Nessie knew Sam had pulled back, using her health as an excuse. Gabe couldn't know the truth . . . could he?

'I'm sure she'd appreciate it,' Nessie replied, hoping her brisk smile gave nothing away. 'Thanks, Gabe.'

Chapter Twenty-two

Sam was dozing on the sofa, the TV playing unheeded, when she heard the tread of feet on the stairs that led up from the bar. Passing a groggy hand over her eyes, she sat up and peered out at the landing, wondering whether it would be Nessie or Gabe. She wasn't sure who she'd prefer to see; as much as she loved her sister, there was no denying things had been strained between them ever since Sam had revealed her pregnancy. And she wasn't proud to admit there'd been more than one occasion when she'd avoided Nessie lately, unable to bear the unspoken hurt and reproof behind her eyes. Things with Gabe were simpler, but only because she hadn't been as honest with him; she hadn't exactly lied when she'd told him she needed to cool things off between them to focus on her health – technically, a baby was a health risk – but she wasn't at all sure he'd be as sympathetic when she revealed her one-night-stand with Joss had had greater consequences than any of them had realised. At least for the moment, Gabe was on her side, which gave him a slight edge in whom Sam would prefer her visitor to be.

Her insides lurched in familiar treachery when he appeared in the doorway; her brain might have decided there couldn't be anything between them, but her body did not agree. And then she saw he was carrying a tray laden with a silver cloche and her resolve weakened a little more. How was she supposed to resist a man who took the trouble to do this?

'You look like a little mouse, tucked away in her nest,' he said when he saw the duvet she'd wrapped around herself. 'Are you cold?'

'I was,' she admitted. 'But I've never been a fan of winter. I much prefer the summer – lighter evenings, cocktails outside, pretty dresses.'

Except that by the time summer rolled around, she'd be too big for floaty dresses, Sam thought with an inward sigh. She hadn't brought herself to look at maternity clothes yet, but she didn't hold out much hope for anything stylish. And cocktails were off limits for the foreseeable future, whether indoors or out.

Gabe placed the tray on the coffee table and lifted the cover. 'Salmon with minted new potatoes, and creamed spinach with toasted pine nuts.' He looked up. 'Healthy food to help you feel better.'

Sam inhaled the aroma of mint mingled with butter and gazed at the plate. 'Thank you. But this wasn't on the menu.'

He shrugged. 'No, but you made it clear you didn't want

what was on offer. So I cooked something simple but nutritious. For you.'

Sam's stomach rumbled loudly, as it seemed to do all the time these days. She reached for the tray. 'Well, thank you. I really appreciate it, Gabe.'

He helped arrange the food on her lap and then settled back into an armchair.

'Shouldn't you be getting back?' Sam asked, around a mouthful of deliciously buttery potato.

'Back?' Gabe said, frowning quizzically. 'It's ten-forty – the kitchens are closed.'

She swallowed fast. 'Ten-forty? But that means I've been asleep for ...'

'Over three hours,' he said. 'I came up to ask what you'd like to eat over an hour ago, but you looked so peaceful that I decided not to wake you.'

Sam ate in silence, keeping her eyes fixed on her plate so that she didn't have to meet Gabe's undoubtedly curious gaze. He'd never pressed her for details about the health issue that had caused her to take a step back from their burgeoning relationship, but she was sure he must have wondered.

'Your sister says you are not able to eat seafood,' Gabe went on. 'That's a new thing, isn't it?'

Again, Sam took refuge behind her food, chewing longer than she needed to in order to buy thinking time. 'New-ish,' she said evasively. 'It's not unheard of for people's tastes to change, is it?'

'No, it's not,' he agreed. 'Although there is usually some

kind of reason for the change. If you told me you were bored of it, that would be different, but both you and Nessie speak as though you cannot eat it. And that makes me wonder why.'

She forced herself to take another forkful of salmon, hoping Gabe would suddenly remember some kind of pressing reason to go back to the kitchen. Instead, he glanced at the floor beside the sofa.

'No wine?'

'No,' Sam replied, trying not to grind her teeth in frustration. 'Not tonight.

He nodded and then, apparently satisfied, lapsed into silence.

Relieved, Sam continued to eat, feeling her weariness start to subside as the food reached her stomach. It wasn't until she'd finished and laid her cutlery side by side on the white plate that Gabe spoke again.

'When were you going to tell me, Sam?'

She froze. 'What?'

Gabe sighed. 'When were you going to tell me about the baby?'

A rush of hot panic flooded Sam's chest. She opened her mouth and closed it again, flustered. How could he *know*? She'd been so careful . . .

'Don't try to deny it,' Gabe said, his tone gentle. 'It's written all over you. I've observed my cousins during their pregnancies and they have a certain look about them – sort of a glow from inside and a new roundness to their features, like everything is softening for the new life they are making.'

His gaze was steady and suddenly Sam didn't want to hide any more; at least not from him. She took a long sip from her water bottle and gathered her thoughts.

'I haven't told anyone, apart from Nessie and Ruby. I – I didn't know how to say it, Gabe. "Sorry we can't get it together – I'm having another man's baby" . . .'

Gabe stared at her. 'Doesn't the father know?'

A warm flush of embarrassment washed over Sam's face. 'No. Not yet.'

She hoped he knew she meant Joss; there was hardly a list of potential candidates. But Gabe's frown told her he didn't approve of the fact that she'd kept her pregnancy even from the baby's father.

'Sam—' he began, but she cut him off.

'That's why I didn't tell you, or anyone. It didn't feel right telling people before I'd had a chance to speak to Joss.' She passed a weary hand across her face. 'And then I was so tired that a trip to Chester seemed beyond me, so I thought I'd wait until I was feeling stronger. More like myself.'

Gabe studied her for a moment, his dark eyes unreadable. Then he sat back, with a shake of his head. 'I can't believe I didn't see it earlier. It certainly explains a few things.'

'Like why I fainted on New Year's Eve?' Sam said, managing a rueful smile. 'Yes, that little mystery was cleared up by the GP a few days later.'

'And why you are still so exhausted, despite my best efforts to nourish you,' Gabe said, glancing at the empty plate. 'It's actually a relief – I was starting to worry.'

His concern made her heart melt. 'No need,' she said wryly. 'Just a life-changing event on the horizon.'

He smiled. 'But it also explains why you brushed me off with no real explanation.'

Sam bowed her head. 'I'm sorry. I didn't want to – it just seemed best, that was all. Less complicated.'

'I can see that,' he replied, and his tone was kind. 'But you won't be able to hide this for much longer. When do you plan to tell Joss?'

It was a good question; one Sam didn't really have an answer to. The truth was, every time she tried to visualise telling Joss that he was going to be a father, her courage failed her. He wouldn't be interested, she told herself; his face would twist in shock and he'd throw her out, demanding that she never contact him again. Except ... except wasn't that a lie she was telling herself, to justify not telling him?

Gabe seemed to know what she was thinking because he leaned forwards, his expression intent. 'If you want my advice, the sooner you tell him, the better. Obviously, I don't know Joss, but everything I've heard about him suggests he's a good man. He deserves the chance to be a good father.'

His compassion made Sam swallow hard before she answered. 'It's going to be a shock.'

'But one he will adjust to.'

Sam's eyes found his. 'You weren't shocked.'

'No,' he conceded. 'But I see you every day – perhaps on some level I knew long before now. It just took a little while to connect the dots.'

Anxiety swelled in her chest. 'I'm scared, Gabe. What if he doesn't want anything to do with us?'

'Then that will be his loss,' Gabe replied. 'But you will be fine – you are a strong woman, Sam – like our own mothers, who raised us without needing a man. And you'll have help – I am sure Nessie will support you.'

Sam's gaze moistened. 'I don't think she will.'

Gabe got up and knelt beside her. 'Of course she will. This must be hard for her too, but give her time.' He hesitated, then took her hand. 'And I will be here too, as a friend.'

It was too much for Sam; her throat ached with the effort of holding back her tears. She let out a sob. 'Thank you.'

He squeezed her fingers and offered her a napkin. 'No problem. And, mark my words, you are going to be the best-fed mother-to-be this side of Seville.'

An involuntary smile tugged at Sam's lips. 'But no seafood linguine.'

'Noted,' he said. 'Don't cry. Everything is going to work out.'

And for the first time in months, Sam started to feel it might be true.

Sam walked past the entrance to Castle Court three times before she spotted it, tucked away between a pub and a clothes shop. It was her first visit to Chester; another time, she might have admired the quirky multi-levelled black-and-white buildings that lined the streets, but her heart was thudding so hard that it was almost all she could focus on.

She paused and stared down the alleyway that led to Joss's workplace. He'd be surprised to see her – she hadn't told him she was coming, because that would have made him ask why – but hopefully he'd be able to make time to talk; surely the bar he worked in couldn't be that busy at eleven o'clock on a Monday morning. But if it was, she'd have to wait until he did have time for her. It wasn't as though she had anything else to do.

When she stepped into Castle Court itself, the prettiness of the scene took the edge off her anxiety. Three storeys of shops overlooked a courtyard dominated by a tall tree at its heart. Sam knew without entering that the shops were the kind that would magically soothe her troubles away, albeit temporarily: a patisserie, a chocolatier's, an exquisitely decorated biscuit shop and a Dutch pancake restaurant that was filling the air with the most delicious smell. There was no doubt about it, she decided as she turned her gaze towards the second and third floors, this was foodie heaven. Gabe would love it, she thought, and then felt her insides tighten again as she remembered why she was there.

Squaring her shoulders, she set her sights on the top floor and started to make her way towards Seb's cocktail bar.

The man who greeted her was tall and good-looking. 'Welcome to Seb's,' he said with an easy smile, and his words were coloured by more than a hint of a South African accent. 'How can I help you today – coffee? Brunch?'

Sam glanced around; the bar wasn't busy, but several tables were occupied and there was a couple deep in conversation on one of the inviting-looking sofas. 'Actually, I'm looking for Joss Felstead. Is he working today?'

The man lifted one eyebrow and studied her with more interest. 'Sure, he's out the back. Let me give him a call for you – why don't you take a seat?'

Sam's heart began to thud again as she waited, her nerves prickling with pins and needles. She took several deliberate deep breaths and willed herself to calm down. It wouldn't do to pass out before she'd even said hello.

When Joss appeared, he almost did a double take. 'Sam? Is everything okay?'

She stood up, hoping her tingling legs would support her weight. 'Hi. Sorry to bother you at work but ...' she trailed off as another wave of anxiety washed over her. 'We need to talk.'

Frowning, Joss glanced at the South African man, who was watching curiously from behind the bar. 'Seb, do you mind?'

'Not at all,' Seb replied. 'Take all the time you need.'

Joss nodded his thanks and turned his attention back to Sam. 'Here?'

She hesitated, noting the way Seb continued to observe them. 'Is there somewhere else we can go? Somewhere more private?'

Something that looked a lot like understanding settled over Joss's features. He nodded. 'My place is just upstairs. Come on.'

Sam followed as he made his way along the passage, past the shops to a small staircase that led to a narrow landing with several brightly-coloured front doors.

'These are the garret rooms. A few of us live up here.'

He thrust a key into one of the locks and ushered her inside. Sam looked around – the living room was small, with a kitchen-diner and two other doors that Sam assumed led to a bedroom and bathroom.

'This is nice,' she managed, hoping her voice wouldn't crack. 'Handy for work.'

Joss nodded. 'It's good enough for now.' He paused and cleared his throat. 'Do you want a cup of tea?'

Sam shook her head; as much as she'd love the soothing warmth of tea, she wasn't sure she could take much more of the adrenaline that was coursing through her body. 'No thanks. I need to say what I've come to say.'

Joss's expression grew ever more watchful as he nodded again. 'At least take your coat off and sit down. And try to remember to breathe, Sam. Whatever you've got to say, I'm not going to bite.'

The brief flash of wryness allowed a little of the tension to slide from Sam's shoulders. She sat on a hard oak chair that stood beside a small dining table and sighed. 'No, I know. It's just ... you're in for a bit of a shock and there's no easy way to break this to you.' She reached into her handbag and slid the black-and-white photograph from a side pocket. 'I'm pregnant, Joss. You're going to be a father.'

Joss said nothing, his blue eyes wide as he stared first at her and then at the photograph in her hands.

'I – *we* – don't expect anything from you – obviously, you've got a life here now and I'm not telling you this because

I expect us to get back together or play happy families or anything like that.' Sam took a deep breath as her heart rate started to return to normal. 'But it's your baby too and I thought you had a right to know.'

Joss remained silent and still, then ran a hand through his fair hair. 'How long have you ... I mean, how far along are you?' he asked, his tone wooden.

'Sixteen weeks,' she said, willing him to take the picture. 'Obviously, I don't need to explain how it happened.'

'Franny's wedding,' he said unnecessarily. He licked his lips. 'And you're ... it's ... everything is all right?'

Sam fought off a hysterical laugh. 'No. I'm pregnant, Joss. My sister hates me, I feel like death and I'm scared out of my wits. *Nothing* is all right.'

He looked at the floor. 'No, I don't suppose it is.'

The urge to laugh melted away; none of this was his fault, any more than it was hers. 'But everything is fine with the baby,' she said, softening her voice. 'Look – two arms, two legs and one head.'

For a moment, Joss didn't move, didn't reach out to take the photograph she held towards him. And then, slowly, he closed the space between them. His hand shook as he touched the monochrome square.

'He has my nose,' he said, after almost a minute had passed. 'Don't you think?'

Sam nearly smiled. 'I hope not. Mine is better. But I won't know whether it's a boy or a girl until after the next scan.'

Joss nodded, his gaze fixed on the picture. 'We.'

'Sorry?' Sam said, the breath catching in her throat.

'*We* won't know,' he said. 'I don't know what kind of a response you expected, Sam – clearly you've been dreading telling me – but I hope you know I'm not the kind of man who'd shirk his responsibilities. And I admit it's going to take a while to get my head round this, but there's no way I'm letting you deal with it on your own.' He fixed her with a determined gaze. 'I'm going to be there. For everything.'

It took a few seconds for the words to sink in. 'But your work—'

'It's a bar job,' he interrupted gently. 'And yes, I like it here, but I liked it in Little Monkham too. I only left because there wasn't anything there for me. And in a few months' time, there will be.'

He meant it, Sam realised, taking in his resolute expression. 'You don't have to move back to the village.' She placed a hand on her stomach. 'Not just for us.'

'But I want to,' he said. 'I'll admit I haven't given much thought to the kind of dad I want to be, but I do know I don't want to be the sort who only sees their kid once a month. So I'll need to be near you. Not right away, and maybe not in Little Monkham itself, but somewhere nearby.'

Sam let out a long slow breath. She wasn't sure how she felt about Joss moving back to the Little Monkham area or about how much he'd be part of her life in the months to come, but it was something she'd have to get used to. 'Okay. I've got another scan in the middle of April – shall I send you the date?'

'Yeah,' he said, lapsing into silence as he looked down at the photograph once more. 'My mother is going to be over the moon.'

The idea that someone might be thrilled with the new life growing inside her made Sam's eyes swim; it wasn't the baby's fault that its parents were woefully unprepared for their new roles. And, as Joss said, the thought of having a baby took a lot of getting used to, but hadn't she started that process the moment she'd decided to go through with the pregnancy?

'Sam?' Joss's voice cut into her thoughts.

'Yes?'

He knelt down to take her hand. 'Thanks for coming here today. I know it wasn't easy.'

She dredged up a smile. 'No, it wasn't. But I feel so much better, like a big grey cloud has lifted. Thanks for not kicking me out.'

Joss half-laughed. 'Is that what you thought I'd do?' He took her other hand and helped her up, then pulled her carefully into a hug. 'Has anyone ever told you you're an idiot, Sam Chapman?'

'No,' Sam said, and she closed her eyes and leaned into him. 'Not today, anyway.'

It was Saturday evening and the Star and Sixpence was pleasingly full. Sam paused beside the last-orders bell and took a deep, fortifying breath before ringing it.

'Ladies and gentlemen,' she called, as heads turned her way

and conversations grew hushed. 'Friends and neighbours. I have a small announcement to make.'

An expectant silence filled the bar.

Sam met Ruby's encouraging gaze and swallowed hard. 'Most of you know that Joss Felstead and I broke up last year. But, as Shakespeare almost once said, the slings and arrows of outrageous fortune never did run smooth—'

A rumble of laughter floated towards her.

'—And I'm delighted to reveal that there will be the pitter-patter of tiny feet behind the bar very soon. Joss and I are expecting a baby.'

There were several sharp intakes of breath and several whispered conversations. But Ruby was ready, a glass in her hand.

'Congratulations, darling!' she called, lifting her cranberry juice in a toast. 'What wonderful news!'

And then everyone was calling out their good wishes, and Sam found herself being enveloped in warm hugs. There was one face she didn't spot, not until she looked over the sea of customers to the door, and that was Nessie's. When their eyes eventually met, she gave Sam a stricken look and then vanished into the darkness outside.

'Give her time,' Ruby murmured, maintaining her position at Sam's side. 'She'll come round.'

I hope so, Sam thought, struggling to keep her face from crumpling. *Because I don't think I can do this without her.*

Chapter Twenty-three

Nessie's phone pinged early on Sunday morning, not long after Owen and Luke had left for football. She reached across to the bedside table and saw Kathryn's name on the screen. Her heart sank. It wasn't unusual for Owen's sister to message, but not first thing on a Sunday, when she'd probably had a late gig with her folk band the night before. The tour they were on was punishing; Nessie didn't even know where in the country Kathryn was. So there was probably only one reason she'd make the effort to get in touch now, Nessie reasoned. And she wasn't sure she felt strong enough to cope with either Kathryn's curiosity or her well-meaning sympathy.

It took her a few minutes of staring at the ceiling to summon up the strength to read the message.

Owen told me the news. How are you? X

It was a fair question, Nessie thought, dropping her phone onto the duvet and closing her eyes. How was she? Part of her wished Sam had warned her what she'd planned to do but, in her heart, she couldn't really blame her sister for wanting to tell as many people as possible in one go. And what would Nessie have done if she'd known – hidden away and pretended it wasn't happening? That seemed like a cowardly way to act. No, the only thing she might have done would be to warn Owen; he'd been understandably hurt that he hadn't heard the news from Nessie herself.

'How long have you known?' he'd asked her quietly, as they'd got ready for bed the night before.

'Since January,' she'd admitted, bracing herself for his anger.

It didn't come. Instead, he'd wrapped his arms around her and held her close. 'That must have been so hard for you. Why didn't you tell me?'

'Sam asked me not to tell anyone,' she'd mumbled, determined not to cry again. It felt as though all she'd done over the last five months was battle tears.

Owen had stroked her hair in silence for a few seconds. 'That's not very fair. Didn't she think how you might be feeling?'

'Don't blame her,' Nessie had said, instinctively defending Sam in spite of the wretched ache in her chest. 'She's had a tough time too.'

'I don't doubt it,' Owen had replied. 'But swearing you to secrecy when she must have known you'd be upset seems a little thoughtless.'

An image of Sam in the bar, surrounded by friends

congratulating her on the news, had popped into Nessie's head. It wasn't fair, she'd thought, closing her eyes against a hot rush of misery. It should have been her. And Owen was right; removing the comfort of talking to him about her pain had made everything more difficult. But that was how Sam had always been – impulsive and daring and just the tiniest bit self-centred.

'And I wish you'd told me,' Owen had continued, but there was no accusation in his words. 'I understand why you didn't, but it was something of a shock hearing the announcement.'

She'd blinked hard. 'I know. I'm sorry.'

Sighing, he'd scratched his stubble-covered chin. 'I'll tell Luke in the morning, on the way home from football practice.'

Nessie shifted in bed and checked the time – it was after nine-thirty, football would be over by now. Knowing Luke, he'd have bombarded Owen with questions and would still have more to ask when he arrived home. But she also knew Owen would have warned him to tread carefully around her, not to seem too excited and keen, for fear of upsetting her.

She passed a weary hand over her face and pressed her lips together; she ought to be fine by now. Miscarriages were hardly rare – women all over the world had the same experience every day, picking themselves up and getting on with their lives, sad but accepting of their loss. What kind of sister was Nessie if she couldn't put her own sorrow to one side long enough to be happy for Sam?

All too soon, she would be visibly pregnant, Nessie thought tremulously, and that would make everything incontrovertibly real. She had to get herself together before then, for all their sakes. It wasn't fair on anyone to go on like this.

She reached for her phone and read Kathryn's message again. Taking a deep breath, she typed a reply.

It's been a bit of a shock. Lots of change ahead! X

Kathryn's response was almost immediate.

Yes, but how are you? Don't dodge the question. X

The stern instruction made Nessie smile.

I'm OK, she replied. *Or at least I will be.* X

She put down her phone and got out of bed. It made what she'd written feel like less of a lie.

Nessie was in the kitchen when Owen and Luke arrived home. She heard them long before she saw them; the old Land Rover did not have the quietest of engines and its big tyres crunched on the gravel as Owen steered it through the gates and into the yard. Then there was Luke's excited chattering, although Nessie couldn't make out the exact words, and Owen's good-natured but repeated reminders to leave his muddy football boots outside. All of which gave Nessie plenty of time to gather her defences against Luke's reaction to the news. And yet she still wasn't ready when he finally barrelled through the back door and into the kitchen.

She'd expected him to hang back, cautioned by Owen,

but he surprised her by rushing forward to throw his arms around her in a hug that made the air huff from her lungs.

They stood there in silence for a moment, then Luke spoke. 'Dad told me about Sam's baby,' he said, his voice muffled against her jumper. 'And I wanted you to know that I know it's not the same and I'm not actually your son, but I'd really like it if you were my mum.'

The words tumbled out so fast that Nessie wasn't sure she'd heard him right. It wasn't until he lifted his head to smile at her and she saw the love in his summer-blue gaze that she understood what he was saying. Tears sprang into her own eyes then, and she couldn't prevent the ragged gasp that tore from her throat. She placed a hand on his sandy hair, unable to speak.

Owen pushed open the door and stopped still at the sight of them, his face falling as he saw the tears on Nessie's cheeks. 'Luke—' he began, but Nessie shook her head.

'It's okay,' she said, amazed that her voice sounded almost normal. 'Luke was just asking if I'd like to be his mum.'

Owen did not gasp or cry. Instead, Nessie saw the muscles in his jaw tighten and she knew he was fighting for control of his emotions just as much as she was.

'And I think,' Nessie went on, managing a smile, 'that I'd like to be his mum very much indeed.'

Luke's freckled face split into a grin. 'Awesome!' He paused and his expression lit up, as though something amazing had just occurred to him. 'And maybe my mum could look after your baby. In heaven, or wherever they are. So it's like a trade.'

Nessie sucked in a great big breath, determined not to give in to the wave of grief that suddenly threatened to overwhelm her. She met Owen's gaze and saw that he'd given up trying not to cry; his dark brown eyes were brimming with tears. Holding out an arm, she summoned him close so that the three of them were wrapped around each other.

'That's a lovely thought, Luke,' she replied, the moment she felt she could speak without making the boy worry he'd said something wrong. 'Thank you very much for suggesting it.'

He submitted to the indignity of the hug for a few more seconds, then began to squirm. Nessie and Owen smiled at each other and parted to let him escape.

'Now, why don't you go and get that muddy football kit off?' Nessie said, as he danced towards the door that led to the living room. 'Before you switch on that wretched games console, if you don't mind.'

Luke stopped halfway across the room, turning to frown his objection. But then his expression lightened and he flashed her a suspiciously obedient grin. 'Yes, Mum,' he said. 'Whatever you say.'

'Nessie, darling. How are you?'

Nessie paused in the act of getting into the car and glanced in the wing mirror to see Ruby heading towards her, snugly wrapped in a glorious faux-fur leopard-print coat that looked as though it belonged in a Grace Kelly photo shoot. For half a second, she thought about pretending she hadn't heard, but

Ruby's high heels had begun to crunch across the gravel and she knew there was no escape.

'Hi, Ruby,' she called, forcing herself to sound cheery. 'I'm fine. How are you?'

The other woman waved a hand at the mid-morning blue sky overhead. 'I feel like breaking out my old Dame Vera Lynn records and singing at the top of my lungs. Do you think spring might finally be on the way?'

'Quite possibly,' Nessie said, smiling in spite of herself. 'Let's hope so – we need good weather for the Easter Extravaganza next month. I don't suppose it would be nearly as much fun hunting for eggs in the snow.'

Ruby nodded. 'No, we definitely need sunshine and spring freshness for that.' She paused and lowered her voice, 'And how are things with you?'

'Everything is fine,' Nessie repeated, determined not to get sucked into another conversation about Sam's pregnancy. 'I'm just off to the wholesalers to pick up a few things for Gabe.'

'Would you like some company?' Ruby asked. 'I'm not busy.'

Nessie hesitated. It was only natural that Ruby was concerned – she often said that she considered both Sam and Nessie to be the daughters she'd never had – but her well-meaning questions would almost certainly upset the precarious sense of peace Nessie had carved out for herself in the few days since her sister's announcement. There were still more downs than ups, but Nessie thought she could feel herself starting to heal. The last thing she wanted to do was pick at the wound. 'It's only a lightning visit,' she told Ruby. 'Another time, maybe?'

Ruby accepted the rejection with her usual good grace. 'I'd like that. But don't let me keep you – I was popping in to beg a recipe from Gabe and thought I'd say hello to you first.'

'Gabe's in the kitchen,' Nessie said, swinging into the driver's seat. 'If you're really lucky, you might even get some of the brunch he was rustling up for Sam.'

'Lucky me,' Ruby replied. 'Drive carefully, darling. See you later.'

Nessie swung the car door shut. 'I will. See you.'

She started the engine and waited until Ruby had disappeared inside the pub before taking out her phone to check the traffic. As she opened the app, she noticed an unread email and clicked on the icon.

To: Nessiechapman@starandsixpence.co.uk
From: Anne.Coutts@McBrideBreweries.com
Subject: Management Opportunity

Dear Miss Chapman

I hope this email finds you well.

We've never met in person but I know you by reputation and I'm well aware of your excellent work at the Star and Sixpence. I'm writing because I'd like to discuss a position at McBride Breweries that I think might interest you. Please do drop me a line or ring me if you'd like to meet for coffee and a chat about the very generous offer we have in mind for you – we have offices across the country and I am very happy to travel to wherever suits you best.

I look forward to hearing from you.

Kindest regards,

Anne Coutts

Managing Director, McBride Breweries Ltd

Nessie sat for several minutes after she'd read the message, frowning at her screen. Of course she'd heard of Anne Coutts – anyone in the hospitality business knew the high-flying MD of one of the most successful breweries in the country – but she had no idea why Anne might have heard of her, much less why she'd felt the need to send such an astonishing email.

There must be a mistake, Nessie thought, opening the message again to check the name at the top; maybe it was meant for Sam. But it was definitely her email address – not the generic one they published on the Star and Sixpence website; enquiries came into the general shared address, not to Sam or Nessie themselves. In fact, the only people who messaged Nessie's named account were the ones she'd expressly given the address to. And she would definitely know if she'd given it to Anne Coutts . . .

Deep in thought, she shut down the message and switched to Maps.

It didn't really matter how Anne had got her email, she decided, reversing out of the car park and setting off along Star Lane – she wasn't looking for a new job, generous offer or not. She'd send a reply once she'd been to the wholesaler, thanking Anne for thinking of her and politely declining her offer of coffee.

She glanced in the rear-view mirror at the rapidly receding Star and Sixpence, outlined against the cloudless blue sky. As refreshing as it was to be heading away from the pub and all its complications right now, she couldn't imagine working anywhere else. Anne Coutts was going to be disappointed.

The weather continued to brighten over the weeks that followed, much to Nessie's relief. The trees on the village green finally burst into leaf and the mornings were damp and dewy, rather than brittle with frost. Things had thawed a little with Sam, too; without ever discussing it, both sisters seemed to be making a concerted effort to close the distance that yawned between them. Nessie did not find it easy; she tried to avoid looking at Sam's softly swelling stomach, but at least the knowledge of what caused it no longer made her want to weep. It helped that Sam never mentioned her changing figure or complained about any of the aches and pains and problems that pregnancy brought – at least not within Nessie's hearing. At some point, Nessie knew she would have to face up to reality, preferably before the baby was born, but, for now, it helped not to think too much.

Laurie turned out to be an unexpectedly handy go-between. Nessie had lost count of the number of times she'd turned to him for something she might otherwise have had to ask Sam for, and she suspected Sam had used him in the same way. He seemed to enjoy the role; there'd been one or two occasions in the past where he'd overstepped his responsibilities in the day-to-day running of the pub, but he'd been a model member of the team since Christmas and Nessie thought it would do no harm for him to glean some insight into the way she and Sam managed the business.

'I don't know how you find the time for all this,' he said admiringly one Tuesday morning as they sat in the downstairs office and she explained how the bed and breakfast booking system worked. 'Between the restaurant, the guest rooms and the awards, you've turned this place into a real gold mine. It's pretty incredible, Nessie.'

The praise made her feel warm inside. It'd been hard work – had taken months and months – but it finally felt as though everything was coming together. They had a brilliant chef running the restaurant and the guest rooms were booked out months in advance. All they needed now was to bag the national Pub of the Year award to go alongside the regional prize they'd won a year or so ago and Nessie would be over the moon.

'It's a shame Sam is breaking up the dream team, though,' Laurie went on, with a regretful look. 'I can't see her keeping that white-hot focus with a baby to care for.'

It was a thought that had occurred to Nessie too, although she was uncomfortably aware that she'd have been doing the same thing had she not lost her own baby. 'I don't think she should try to,' she said, hating the stiffness in her voice. 'It's understandable that her priorities will change – we'll cope.'

Laurie didn't appear convinced. 'Poor Sam. It can't be easy, knowing she's going to be bringing the baby up on her own.' He paused. 'Especially when she knows so well what it's like to grow up without a father.'

His underlying bitterness made Nessie wince; he made no secret of his anger with their own father, who had abandoned him and his mother all those years ago.

'But Sam says Joss is moving back to the village. He'll be part of the baby's life.'

Now it was Laurie's turn to look uncomfortable. 'If he's the father.'

Nessie felt incredulity wash over her. 'What?'

Laurie shook his head. 'I'm probably wrong. Forget I said anything.'

'You can't say something like that and then tell me to forget it,' Nessie said, feeling her cheeks grow warm with indignation. 'What are you suggesting, Laurie?'

'Nothing, really,' Laurie replied, fiddling with the computer mouse. 'It's just – well, I wondered how sure Sam can be that Joss is the dad, given that she was also sleeping with Gabe.'

Nessie stared at him, open-mouthed. 'But—that's not—'

He spread his hands. 'Maybe she thinks Joss is a safer bet to stick around. Let's be honest, Gabe is only here because we pay him a lot of money. He'd be off like a shot if he got a better offer. And I don't think he's the marrying type, either.'

A sudden clatter outside the door snapped Nessie out

of her confusion. She looked up to see Gabe looming in the doorway, a thunderous expression twisting his handsome features.

'Liar!' he snarled. 'None of what you just said is true.'

Laurie looked momentarily caught out, then raised his chin in challenge. 'So you're not here because we pay you?'

'Of course I am,' Gabe said, scowling. 'I work here. Do I need to explain the nature of having a job?'

Nessie buried a shudder of embarrassment. 'Laurie, I think—'

'Don't take his side!' Laurie snapped. 'He's the one eavesdropping on our conversation.'

'Eavesdropping on your lies,' Gabe said. 'I don't know what game it is you are playing, Laurie, but I will not stand by while you try to stir up ugly rumours about me or Sam. I'm not the father of her baby. Joss is.'

'So you say,' Laurie muttered, his face an unattractive shade of red.

'I do say,' Gabe growled. His gaze flickered to Nessie, then back to Laurie. 'But I can assure you that if the baby was mine, I would not be looking for the quickest way to abandon them. No matter how badly you think of me.'

Nessie wished the ground at her feet would open up and swallow her. 'Stop it, both of you. Sam is only upstairs, she'll hear you.'

Laurie gave her a mutinous glare and she thought for a heartbeat that he might ignore her. But then he lowered his eyes and glowered at the carpet instead.

'Laurie, you need to apologise to Gabe,' Nessie continued,

hoping her voice was steadier than she felt. 'I don't want to hear about this again.'

A few excruciating seconds rolled by. 'Sorry,' Laurie mumbled, with only a cursory glance in Gabe's direction.

The chef said nothing.

Nessie threw him an exasperated look. 'And, Gabe, I hope you don't skulk around outside the office all day, on the off-chance that you might hear us talking about you.'

His dark eyes flashed. 'I do not. But—'

'But nothing,' Nessie insisted. 'Didn't your mother ever tell you eavesdroppers never hear good of themselves?'

'No,' Gabe said. 'She was too busy bringing me up alone after my father left. So please don't suggest that I would be the kind of man to do the same thing.'

Laurie had the grace to look a little ashamed, but Nessie wasn't about to let him say anything that might make a bad situation worse. She gave a single unsmiling nod, which she hoped would serve as a warning to both men. 'Enough, then,' she said, her stomach roiling with a mixture of crossness and mortification. 'I'm sure we all have better things to be doing, anyway.'

Gabe nodded once. 'If anyone needs me, I'll be in the kitchen.' He stopped to glare at Laurie. 'Working.'

Laurie opened his mouth to speak and Nessie knew he was going to say something else inflammatory. She jumped in, before he could fan the flames.

'Thanks, Gabe.'

She waited until she was certain he'd gone before rounding on Laurie.

'How could you say such a thing?'

He shrugged, as though he didn't care, and then seemed to register the depth of her anger. 'Sorry,' he said again, with more conviction. 'I didn't mean to get you involved there.'

'Involved?' Nessie repeated in disbelief. 'Of course I'm involved. Sam is my sister – I'm hardly going to stand by while you throw around accusations like that.'

Laurie's face fell. 'It wasn't an accusation,' he said quietly, getting to his feet. 'Just a thought I'd had. And Sam is my sister too – I just thought you ought to know the situation, that's all. In case you end up holding the baby.'

He left the room. Nessie stared after him, nonplussed. Where on earth had he got the idea that Gabe might be the baby's father? Her frown deepened as she considered something else: what exactly had he hoped to achieve by sharing his suspicion?

Chapter Twenty-four

Sam had no real idea how Joss would react to seeing his child on the monitor. He'd arrived from Chester on Thursday morning, looking nervous but unwavering, and hadn't said much as they drove to the hospital. The sight of so many pregnant women seemed to sober him further; when the sonographer had summoned them, Joss had gripped Sam's fingers and she hadn't pulled away.

His expression when he saw the baby almost melted Sam's heart. The sonographer – a woman who'd introduced herself as Mel – had seemed to sense this was his first time, because she took the time to explain exactly what they were seeing.

'There's a hand,' she said, pointing at the screen. 'And those are the feet, although they're tucked away so neatly that it looks as though he or she is doing yoga.'

Joss stared in obvious fascination. 'I still think that's my nose.'

'Will you stop going on about the nose?' Sam said with

wry exasperation, as Mel made some notes on her file. 'Is everything okay?'

'Things look fine,' Mel replied, nodding with brisk reassurance as she clicked at the screen. 'Your baby is a good size and the heartbeat is strong. Did you want to know the sex? I can try to find out, although it's never an exact science.'

Sam hesitated as her eyes met Joss's. They hadn't discussed the question of finding out the sex of the baby, although she'd thought about it a lot in the days leading up to the scan and had privately decided she would rather not know. But would Joss feel the same?

'Well?' she asked. 'What do you think?'

A faint smile tugged at his lips. 'This baby has surprised us both once already. I think we should probably let him or her surprise us again.'

Sam felt an answering smile cross her own face. 'Okay,' she said and turned to Mel. 'We don't want to know the sex, thank you.'

The sonographer nodded. 'No problem. I'll just take a few more measurements and then we'll be done.'

Joss was a different person on the way home. 'Fancy heading over to Great Bardham for lunch?' he asked as Sam navigated the country roads. 'There's a good old-fashioned pub that does brilliant food.'

She risked a sideways glance. 'Really? Don't you have to get back for work this evening?'

'No, Seb gave me the whole day off. So I'm in no rush, unless you are?'

Sam considered the question. She had a mountain of PR and marketing work for the Easter Extravaganza to get through, not to mention going through Gabe's food order for the following week. But it was good to see Joss again, and there were probably things they needed to discuss. Surely a quick pub lunch wouldn't do any harm?

'No,' she said, seeing the sign for the village of Great Bardham up ahead. 'No rush.'

The pub was exactly as Joss had described: an old, red-brick building that probably had its roots in the sixteenth century, just as the Star and Sixpence did. The inside had been tastefully modernised, Sam noted with approval, but had retained the charm of the original building.

'It's a McBride pub,' Joss said, as a waitress showed them to a table in the half-full restaurant section. 'They're really good at restoring these old places and the beer they brew isn't bad, either.'

He ordered a pint of Black Badger from the waitress, along with Sam's water, and sat watching her study the menu.

'The burgers are amazing,' he said. 'I recommend the one that comes with melted Stilton on top.'

Sam grimaced. 'No blue cheese for me, sadly.'

Understanding dawned in Joss's eyes. 'I feel like I should apologise. Are you finding it very hard?'

She wondered how he would react if she gave an honest answer: that yes, she found having to forgo some of her favourite foods difficult, and yes, she held him partly responsible. That she sometimes woke up in the night panicking about what the future held: how would she cope with a newborn baby, would Nessie ever forgive her, was she going to make a good mother or would she totally balls things up? And, most of shallow of all, how much worse would Joss feel if she confessed that she was terrified of the way her body was changing?

Even just a few weeks earlier, it had seemed impossible that there was a whole new person growing inside her; then she'd felt the first flutter of movement and it had all become real. Now there were regular flurries that she recognised as kicks – soon, other people would be able to place their hands on her stomach and feel them too. And now that she couldn't ignore reality, Sam had started to worry that her body would somehow not know what to do to keep this little person alive and deliver them safely when the time came. Things had gone wrong for Nessie. They could go wrong for Sam too.

But she knew as she gazed into Joss's questioning blue eyes that she wouldn't burden him with any of her secret fears. It wasn't fair – there was nothing he could do to help, especially not from Chester. 'Oh, you know,' she said, forcing herself to sound carefree. 'Swings and roundabouts. I haven't had a hangover for months.'

The waitress arrived to take their food order. Sam tried not to mind when Joss ordered a medium-rare blue cheese burger and focused instead on how good her spinach and ricotta ravioli would taste. If she was very lucky, she might even have room for the sticky toffee pudding she'd spotted on the dessert list.

'So, I've been thinking,' Joss said, after a long and evidently satisfying draught of Black Badger. 'And it seems to me that we've got some decisions to make.'

Sam took a sip of her own drink and tipped her head. 'What kind of decisions?'

He fixed her with an unblinking stare and cleared his throat. 'Big ones.'

She swallowed. Joss wasn't wrong, but now that it came down to it, she wasn't sure she was ready for a heavy conversation about their undoubtedly complicated future. 'I'm not sure I want—'

'Hear me out,' he said. 'If I remember rightly, you and me were pretty good together, right?'

'Apart from the rows and the petty jealousies and the epic sulking,' Sam replied dryly.

'Apart from those,' Joss agreed, waving the objections away. 'What I'm getting at is that we made a good couple, but we let stupid things come between us.'

Sam studied him, her sense of foreboding growing. 'They didn't seem stupid at the time. They seemed insurmountable, which is why we split up.'

He frowned. 'Were they really insurmountable? Or did we give up too easily because we didn't have a good enough reason to work things out?'

So that's where he's going, Sam thought with a silent groan. 'Joss—'

'And now we do have a reason.' He carried on as though he hadn't heard the warning tone in her voice. 'The best reason, I'd say. Because we loved each other once, Sam. Why can't we fall back in love for the sake of our baby?'

She opened and closed her mouth more than once but couldn't find the words. He wasn't wrong – they had been in love. She'd thought they might even spend the rest of their lives together. And it hadn't been easy to let go of that dream; a tiny part of her still clung to it, in fact, because on some level she still loved him. But a baby wasn't a good enough reason to get back together – surely he had to see that? No matter how much easier it might make things seem.

Sam shook her head gently. 'I'm sorry, Joss. I don't think it's a good idea.'

He took another sip of his beer. 'I think you do. But you don't want to admit I'm right.'

Exasperation flared across Sam's nerves; this was one of the reasons why they'd split up, because of his cocky arrogance that he knew better than her. 'That's not it, actually.' She took a deep breath and met his gaze head-on, determined to make him understand. 'We're having a baby together, but that doesn't mean we have to *be* together. When I came to see you in Chester, it wasn't to rekindle our relationship, it was to give you a chance to be part of our baby's life. But . . . that doesn't mean you get to be part of my life too.'

Joss was silent for a long time, making her worry she'd been too harsh. 'Right,' he said finally and she could almost feel his disappointment.

'Think it through,' Sam urged, squashing her guilt before it could derail her argument. 'All right, maybe we could make it work at first, for the sake of the baby. But how long would it be before you started to feel that I'd trapped you, or I began to resent you? And don't tell me it wouldn't happen – that's exactly what happens in loveless relationships, Joss.'

'But it wouldn't be loveless,' he said, his blue eyes almost pleading. 'I love you, Sam. I love our baby, even though we've only just met.'

She wavered then. 'Don't do this.'

'It's true,' Joss insisted, as though sensing her uncertainty. 'And I think you love me too.'

The trouble was that she did love him. But not the way she needed to. 'I'm sorry, Joss. I – I don't think I do. And I don't think you really love me – not deep down.'

His gaze dipped and several moments passed before he spoke again. 'Okay, I understand.'

Tears pricked at the back of Sam's eyes as she watched him. 'I'm sorry.'

'Don't be,' he said, looking up with a brittle smile. 'I should have known I wouldn't be able to change your mind. It was hard enough when we were together.'

'You'll thank me one day,' she said, swallowing hard.

He managed a half-laugh then. 'Let's not go that far, Sam.'

The training course was over.

Nessie yawned and stretched as the last of her fellow delegates departed; she was surprised there wasn't more she hadn't already known. It had been a risk, spending a day away from the Star and Sixpence when the Easter Extravaganza was in less than a week, and Nessie suspected the course might have proved to be a waste of her precious time if it hadn't felt so good to get out of the confines of Little Monkham. She loved the village, but it was definitely good to get away every now and then, and the bustle of Birmingham's crowded streets had made a pleasing change on her walk from the station that morning.

'Nessie Chapman?'

She looked up from her seat, startled; she was sure there hadn't been anyone she knew on the course. But the woman standing in front of Nessie hadn't been a delegate. She was older, dressed in a pin-sharp grey suit, with platinum blonde hair, and she wore the kind of confident smile that suggested she was used to being listened to.

'Hi,' Nessie said, smiling back. 'Do I know you?'

'No, we've never met,' the woman said. 'Although I did email you several weeks ago. My name is Anne Coutts and I'm here to offer you a job.'

Nessie felt her smile slip a little. 'It's lovely to meet you and I'm very flattered by your interest, but I'm not actually looking for a new job. There's no way I'd consider leaving the Star and Sixpence.'

Anne took a seat at the table. 'I thought you might say that but just hear me out, that's all I ask. And if you're still not interested, then I'll leave you in peace.'

'Okay,' Nessie replied, hoping she didn't sound as reluctant as she felt. She wished she'd been quicker off the mark in packing up her things, but perhaps Anne would have simply caught her somewhere else.

'As I said in my email, your reputation is quite something,' Anne said. 'Success stories like the Star and Sixpence are exactly what the industry needs right now and I'd like some of your magic to rub off on our McBride pubs.'

'It's not just me,' Nessie said, uncomfortably aware that it was mostly Sam's PR genius that had made the Star and Sixpence what it was. 'My sister is probably the one you want.'

Anne tipped her head. 'No, I'm fairly certain it's you, Nessie. I'm not sure how much you know about McBride, but we have over a hundred pubs spread across the country and we have a pretty effective PR team in place already. What I need is someone who can bring a fresh perspective to the table – someone who has experience of re-engaging with the local community and putting the pub right back at the heart of it.' She paused and looked Nessie in the eye. 'And I hope that someone is you.'

Nessie swallowed. 'Honestly, I don't have that much—'

'Here's what we're offering,' Anne continued, as though Nessie hadn't spoken. 'I don't want to overwhelm you, so we'll start small – perhaps with a portfolio of five pubs that need your magic touch. Once you've got your feet under the table, as it were, we'll increase the number. You'll have a team to support you, of course, and all the weight of McBride Breweries behind you.' She pulled out a sheet of headed paper and pushed it across the table. 'This is our starting offer – it might seem generous, but I believe it only reflects your experience and talent.'

Almost involuntarily, Nessie glanced down. She had to swallow a gasp as the six-figure number danced before her eyes. Surely there was a mistake, she thought, blinking as though the numbers might vanish. But they stayed there, solidly black and white. Her gaze moved down the page, taking in words like 'performance bonus' and 'flexible working arrangements'.

'Are – are you serious?' she asked, looking into Anne's eyes.

'Of course,' the older woman replied, smiling warmly. 'We want you, Nessie. I think you're the perfect woman for the job.'

Dazed, Nessie read the details once more. It was more money than she'd ever dreamed of commanding and the role sounded amazing, in spite of her conviction that she couldn't do any of it. The title alone – Head of Community Spirit – sounded so far beyond her that she wanted to laugh. And yet there was a faint whisper in the back of her mind, struggling to be heard over the doubts, that said maybe she *was* perfect for the job. Because Anne was right; she'd done it once already, albeit in partnership with Sam. Could she take what she'd learned at the Star and Sixpence and apply it somewhere else? It would be a challenge, but the opportunity to spread her wings might be exactly what she needed to restore her bruised heart.

'Think it over,' Anne urged, as though reading Nessie's mind. 'From what I've heard of your sister, she's more than capable of taking over the reins at the Star and Sixpence.'

And that was all it took to bring reality crashing back

in. Because of course Nessie couldn't abandon the Star and Sixpence; Sam was going to have more important things to look after than the pub. And Laurie might be keen, but he was also hot-tempered and inexperienced. There was no way they could delegate management of the business to him.

'It's very kind of you—' she began, but Anne interrupted again.

'Take some time,' she instructed, handing Nessie a business card. 'This is a fantastic opportunity for McBride's and for you, and I'd love to work together.'

Nessie didn't know what to say; the other woman seemed determined not to take no for an answer. 'Thank you,' she managed after a few seconds.

Anne smiled as she stood up. 'Great to meet you at last, Nessie. I look forward to hearing from you once you've given it some thought.'

In a waft of expensive perfume, she was gone, leaving Nessie to stare at the offer on the table once more. Slowly, she folded the paper in three and slipped it inside her notebook. Then she sat for a few moments, staring at nothing, trying to process what had just happened; being headhunted seemed like the kind of thing that might happen to Sam, not her. And yet Anne had been very clear it was Nessie she wanted . . .

Eventually, she roused herself and got to her feet to start the journey back to Little Monkham, trying to ignore the sinking feeling that settled in her stomach when she thought of walking into the Star and Sixpence. For the first time ever, Nessie was reluctant to go back.

Chapter Twenty-five

'Ness, where's the list of stalls for Sunday?'

Laurie leaned over the office desk, lifting up Nessie's neat piles of invoices and riffling through them.

Nessie looked up from the filing cabinet and frowned. 'Don't mess those up – they're in date order. The list is in my notebook – look, it's on the chair.'

Laurie shook his head in amusement as he replaced the bills and reached for the notebook. 'You're the most organised person I know.'

'That's how everything gets done,' Nessie said, concentrating on the open filing cabinet drawer once more. 'Organisation equals productivity, at least in my book.'

Laurie didn't respond. At first Nessie didn't notice, but he was silent for so long that she finished slotting her paperwork into the drawer and the uncharacteristic silence caught her attention.

'Have you got it?' she asked, glancing across the office.

He was staring at an unfolded sheet of paper and Nessie knew in a cold rush of certainty that it was the job offer from Anne Coutts. She'd put it back in her notebook after showing it to Owen when she'd got home on Monday, and there it had stayed for three days while she wrestled with the fantasy of accepting it.

'What's this?' Laurie asked.

There was no point in lying, Nessie thought as dread squeezed at her gut. It was so obviously an offer of employment that Anne might as well be standing in front of them.

'McBride Breweries want me to go and work for them,' she said, forcing her voice to remain steady.

He raised his eyebrows. 'So I see. Wow. They really want you to, don't they?'

Nessie shrugged uncomfortably. 'It's too much.'

'Clearly they don't think so,' Laurie said, fixing her with an interested gaze. 'Are you going to accept?'

'No,' Nessie replied instantly. 'How could I? And anyway, this is where I belong. At the Star and Sixpence.'

Laurie puffed out his cheeks. 'I don't know. It's a lot of money to turn down.' He stopped, his face brightening. 'But it could be the perfect time for you to go – Sam can look after things until the baby arrives and then she can leave everything to me!'

His eagerness tore at Nessie's heart. 'Laurie, I don't think that's a very good—'

'Of course it is,' he cut in. 'It's brilliant. I know loads about how everything works now, and there's plenty of time for

Sam to teach me the rest. It means you get to take your dream job, Sam gets to focus on the baby and I get to be the boss.'

The thought of leaving Laurie in charge of the pub caused a spike of anxiety. 'No,' Nessie said, as gently as she could. 'It's not going to happen because I'm not taking the job. I've spoken to Owen and we agree that it's best for everyone if I stay here.'

Laurie's expression grew mulish. 'But it's such a good plan.'

His disappointment was almost palpable. Nessie took pity on him. 'It is a good plan. And maybe in the future that's exactly how things will work out.' She took a deep breath. 'But right now, you don't have quite the right level of experience to take over the business.'

His expression darkened again and, for a moment, Nessie thought he would argue. But then he sighed and shook his head. 'I suppose you're right.'

'I'm sorry,' Nessie said. 'I know you want to help. And I'm not saying never – just not now. Okay?'

Laurie folded the paper up and slipped it back inside Nessie's notebook. 'Okay. I understand.'

'And . . .' Nessie hesitated, then plunged on. 'I'd appreciate it if you didn't tell Sam about this. I don't want to upset her.'

'Of course,' he replied, his tone slightly wounded. 'I won't breathe a word.'

'Thank you,' she said, letting out the breath she hadn't known she was holding. 'Now, did you find the list of stall-holders? We'd better start ringing round to make sure they're all still coming.'

*

293

Sam awoke on Easter Sunday with worry twisting like a viper inside her. She lay there for a moment trying to work out what was causing it and then she remembered: the Easter Extravaganza. There were eggs to be hidden, a marquee and stalls to set up and the Little Monkham Bake Off to manage, not to mention Gabe's special Easter menu bookings to oversee and around a million other things that she'd forgotten about. She turned over to check her phone and groaned, her bump pressing against the mattress; it was time to get up, but she'd never felt less like leaving the cocoon of her bed.

A few minutes later, there was a knock at the door. Gabe's muffled voice floated through the wood. 'Breakfast is ready.'

The thought eased Sam's reluctance to face the day. If there was one perk to being pregnant, it was not having to think about her weight, which was very handy when Gabe insisted on feeding her at every given opportunity. He'd been true to his promise, looking after her as though she was a child herself, and she knew she'd be forever grateful for his care and support. In fact, she didn't know how she'd manage without him. There had been times when they'd been sitting together on the sofa, watching a film or discussing their day, that she'd fantasised about leaning over and planting a kiss on his lips. She would never do it, of course; Gabe was so honourable that he'd undoubtedly be horrified at the thought of kissing her while she was pregnant with someone else's baby. But the fantasy showed no signs of fading away, which she supposed was a more frustrating side effect of her situation; raging hormones with nowhere to go.

'Coming,' she called and levered herself out of bed to pull back the wooden shutters that lined the windows. She'd spent the whole week watching the Met Office website like a hawk; the forecast had been unsettled for days and she had a deep foreboding that the weather was going to ruin all their plans.

She could have cried when the first rays of beaming sunshine sliced through the leaded window. The sky was blue, without a cloud in sight, and she knew without checking that the air would already have a hint of spring warmth. It was perfect, she thought, throwing a quick prayer to the PR gods that the dark clouds would stay away all day. She yanked on her dressing gown and hurried along the landing to see what treats awaited her.

Gabe was sitting at the kitchen table, his dark hair tousled and a thicker than normal layer of stubble masking his jaw. He'd already begun to eat, his eggs Benedict more than halfway gone. Sam didn't blame him – she'd never been fast at dragging herself out of bed in the mornings and now she could give sloths a run for their money in the slowness stakes. It was something else that would need to change when she had a newborn to look after.

'Good morning,' Gabe said, pushing a plate piled high with eggs and spinach and a toasted muffin across the table. 'I see you managed to fix the weather for today.'

She sat down and picked up her fork. 'It's such a relief. Imagine if we'd had to hide the eggs inside the pub – there'd be kids everywhere. Total nightmare.'

His eyes slid to her stomach in amusement. 'Someday you might not mind kids so much.'

'I don't mind them now,' she said, around a mouthful of spinach and pine nuts. 'But I don't want them all running amok in my pub. Thankfully, we can hold the egg hunt outside. Laurie's in charge of that.'

Was it her imagination or did a frown of uneasiness flicker across Gabe's face at the mention of her brother's name?

'What?' she asked, lowering her fork.

'How much do you know about Laurie?' Gabe asked, after a few seconds of silence. 'I mean really know, other than what he's told you?'

Now it was Sam's turn to frown. 'I know we share a father. Why?'

Gabe's expression was brooding as he pushed the last few scraps of ham around his plate. 'Just a feeling I have. A hunch that something is not quite right.'

She stared at him. 'What on earth do you mean? I know you don't always see eye-to-eye, but, as I've said to you before, he's still family. If there's something going on, I need to know.'

He avoided her gaze, concentrating instead on loading his fork. 'It's nothing. Forget I spoke.'

'What's happened?' Sam demanded, her suspicions rising. She'd known Gabe still bore a grudge over Laurie's interference in his food orders, but she'd assumed he was professional enough not to let it affect their working relationship. 'Tell me.'

There was a long silence, then Gabe sighed. 'Like I said, nothing.' He gestured to the clock on the wall. 'Hadn't you better hurry up? The marquee people will be arriving soon.'

Much to her annoyance, Sam saw he was right. 'We'll come back to this,' she told him, scooping up as much food as her fork could hold. 'I won't forget.'

Gabe nodded thoughtfully. 'That's fine. Maybe I'll have something to tell you then.'

He stood up and loaded his plate into the slender dish-washer before escaping downstairs, and Sam didn't have time to dwell on the mystery as she was swept up into the hurly-burly of organising the Extravaganza.

She barely saw Nessie, other than to share a harried look with her as they passed each other from time to time, and Laurie was nowhere to be seen; Sam assumed he was out in the village, dreaming up places to hide the chocolate eggs.

'Where do you want this?' Martha from the village bakery asked, her arms laden with the biggest simnel cake Sam had ever seen.

'In the marquee, next to the Bake Off table,' Sam replied, pointing to the bunting-festooned tent in the centre of the village green.

Martha winked. 'Maybe I'll enter it into the Bake Off instead. I know Franny's got her eye on the Star Baker award again this year.'

Sam laughed. 'You know you're not eligible. Amateur bakers only – definitely not people who own a bakery. And certainly not the head judge!'

'Spoilsport,' Martha said, half-pouting. 'It'd be worth it to see the look on Franny's face when she realises she hasn't won.'

'But what would we put on the Guess the Weight of the Cake stall?' Sam asked.

'True,' Martha sighed. 'Ah well, I suppose I'll just have to hope someone else bakes up a storm. It's too bad Gabe isn't eligible, either – I wouldn't mind sampling his profiteroles, if you know what I mean.'

Sam didn't trust herself to respond to the blatant innuendo. 'See you later for the judging.'

The morning passed in a blur of activity, driving Sam from one job to the next and leaving her no time to feel tired. But by the time midday arrived, her aching calf muscles and tender back were telling her she'd done a full day's work already; even so, she couldn't relax until retired rocker Micky Holiday had cut the bright yellow ribbon and declared the Extravaganza open.

Sam crossed the green to where Nessie stood watching proceedings with an air of worried preoccupation. 'Come on. I think we've earned a coffee, don't you?'

The momentary hesitation on her sister's face hurt Sam's heart.

'Only if you want to,' she added. 'I'm sure we've both got plenty to be getting on with.'

'No,' Nessie said quickly. 'No, I could use a break. I'm sure you could too.'

Sam couldn't help noticing the way Nessie's eyes stayed

glued to her face, never straying down to her belly. She swallowed the sudden lump that formed in her throat. It was only natural that Nessie would be wounded by the pregnancy, but surely by now she should have accepted the reality of the situation? How much longer could they go on tiptoeing around, pretending everything was fine when it so clearly was not?

Sam forced herself to smile. 'Let's do it later. I should probably check that Laurie hasn't been mugged by chocolate-crazed kids anyway.'

She walked away before Nessie could argue and took a deep lungful of fresh spring air to calm her jangling nerves. She wasn't angry with her sister; how could she be? But she couldn't help wondering how Nessie was going to cope when the baby arrived. Would she refuse to look at it then too?

Sam found Laurie herding a cluster of village children around the green, searching out the eggs he'd hidden. Most of them were stood around the tree at the far end, gazing up at what looked a lot like a nest in the upper branches.

'Really?' Luke said as she approached, his freckled face perplexed. 'Up there?'

Laurie nodded. 'Yep. The Easter Bunny left a whole bag of chocolate in those branches.'

The reminder of the prize made Luke grin and he immediately started to look for a way up. 'Challenge accepted!'

'Oh no you don't,' Sam said, catching his arm as he stepped forward. 'No trips to A&E today, thank you very much. If there are any eggs up there, they can stay there for the birds.'

A chorus of disappointment rose from the assembled children.

Sam gave Laurie a hard look. 'Please tell me you didn't.'

He shrugged in a way that suggested he was bored. 'Of course not. I was only messing with their heads.'

But you were willing to let Luke climb up anyway, Sam thought, and something about his attitude reminded her of Gabe's question earlier that morning: *How much do you know about Laurie?*

'Connor could do with a hand in the cellar,' she said, reaching a snap decision and offering a silent apology to her aching legs. 'I'll take over here.'

If Laurie was surprised, he didn't show it. 'Yes, boss.'

Sam watched him amble towards the Star and Sixpence, then turned her attention to the children, who stood with their baskets in hand, awaiting directions. 'I don't know why you're all staring at me,' she said, grinning at their expectant faces. 'I've got no idea where the eggs are. You'll have to sniff them out!'

Luke's face lit up. 'I bet I know where we can look. Follow me!'

'Stay on the ground!' Sam called as they scattered towards the war memorial. 'No climbing!'

Luke waved an arm to show he'd heard and led his hunters on the charge.

Sam checked her watch; it was almost time for the Bake

Off judging. With an inward sigh, she rubbed the small of her back and trudged towards the marquee. At least there was the promise of cake in her immediate future.

Martha and Father Goodluck were already there, studying the entries and having whispered conversations behind their hands. Sam grinned as she noticed a number of tense-looking bakers hovering nearby; the Bake Off was a hotly contested competition, although Franny had won for the two years Sam had been involved. The postmistress was also standing near the table, but Sam knew from experience that she was watching out for foul play.

'How's it looking?' Sam asked Martha and the vicar. 'Any early front-runners?'

Father Goodluck smiled. 'There is one shaped like St Mary's – if I was a cynical man, I'd suggest that was a shame- less attempt to sway me.'

Sam glanced at the table – there was an exquisite replica of the village church, complete with a towering steeple, gingerbread vicar and several sugar paste gravestones dotted around the base. 'It's perfect,' she said.

'It's not all about presentation,' Martha reminded her. 'It has to taste good too. Many is the time I've bitten into an overbaked sponge that was drier than my Rob's beard.'

'That one looks delicious,' Sam said, pointing to a compar- atively modest cake covered in white icing and glacé cherries. 'I wonder what it is.'

Martha peered at the label beside the plate. 'Cherry Bakewell cake.'

Sam's stomach rumbled, reminding her that breakfast had been a long time ago.

Father Goodluck gave her a look of amused sympathy. 'Shall we start tasting?'

An anxious hush settled over the marquee as Martha began to cut into the cakes. One by one, Sam and her fellow judges sampled each slice, commenting in undertones on the texture and flavour and deciding which cakes weren't quite up to standard. By the end, they agreed on third place, but there was some debate over the winning entry.

'It has to be the church,' Sam said, glancing over at the now partially destroyed cake. There had been chocolate sponge inside the grey icing, with a secret surprise of tiny Tom Thumb drops that glistened like jewels.

'It was clever,' Martha conceded grudgingly. 'And the sponge was very light and moist – not overloaded by the buttercream on the outside.'

Father Goodluck reached out to pluck a morsel of the cherry Bakewell cake from his plate. 'But this one was a little slice of heaven. An almond sponge, cherry jam in the middle and fondant icing on the top – it's better than even Mr Kipling could manage.'

Sam gave the cake a curious glance; Father Goodluck was right – it was exceptionally good. And there was definitely something to be said for a simpler idea, baked to total perfection. The church ticked all the right boxes for aesthetics and cleverness, but the cherry Bakewell just edged it in the taste tests.

'Okay,' she conceded to Martha. 'I give in. The cherry Bakewell is the winner.'

The other woman grinned. 'You know it makes sense,' she said, reaching into her folder for the winners' labels. 'And I'm pretty sure that means there's an upset on the cards . . .'

She turned to the assembled crowd and raised her voice. 'Ladies and gentlemen, boys and girls, as always, the standard was exceptionally high in this year's Little Monkham Bake Off. But the judges and I have reached a decision. In third place, we have this fantastic coffee and walnut cake.'

There was a delighted shriek from Mrs Harris as Father Goodluck stood the third-place label beside her cake. Martha smiled and beckoned the grey-haired old woman forwards to stand next to the table.

'In second place, we have this truly magnificent reconstruction of St Mary's Church.'

But there was no happy shout this time. Muffled whispering broke out and Sam felt her heart sink as she realised what that must mean: the church cake was Franny's entry.

'Could the baker who made this cake make themselves known?' Martha called, in a tone so cheerful that Sam suspected she'd known all along who had baked that particular entry.

Grudgingly, Franny stepped forwards and joined Mrs Harris, ignoring the other woman's excitedly proffered handshake. Father Goodluck's smile slipped a little as he slotted the second-place label onto the table.

'And in first place, we have this delicious cherry Bakewell

cake,' Martha went on. 'All the judges agreed that it tasted as wonderful as it looked.'

There was an excited squeak that made Sam's jaw drop; Ruby was the last person she'd expect to produce a cake like that, especially since she'd always maintained life was too short to bake when the delights of Martha's shop were only a few minutes' walk from home. But then Ruby stepped aside and Sam saw the look of pink-cheeked pride on the face of Micky Holiday and the penny dropped. Ruby hadn't baked the cake; her rock star boyfriend had.

A shout of laughter beside her told Sam that Martha had worked out the truth too. 'Congratulations, Micky!' she called, stepping forwards to shake his hand. 'Who knew that the lead singer of the Flames was also a star baker?'

Beaming with pleasure, Micky took his place beside Franny and Mrs Harris. And Sam was entertained to see that Franny seemed to be having some kind of internal battle; on one hand, she was furious at coming second, but, on the other, she was a besotted fan of Micky's. It must be hard for her to decide which emotion came out on top. And then she seemed to reach some kind of conclusion, because she threw her arms around Micky and planted a big kiss full on his lips.

Grinning, Sam joined the three winners. 'The local paper will want to take a photo,' she murmured to Micky. 'Especially now you've come out as being a bit handy with a spatula. Would you rather I made an excuse? I don't mind.'

Micky laughed. 'Once a PR, always a PR, eh, Sam?'

'I always look after my clients,' she replied, patting his arm. 'Even when they've retired.'

'Did you like the cake?' he asked, and Sam thought she detected the faintest hint of nervousness behind the words.

'Loved it,' Sam said, without hesitation. 'Although I can't imagine where you got the recipe. Did you win it in a poker match or something?'

'Nah,' Micky replied. 'I stayed at this old house in Yorkshire last year – Ponden Hall – and the owner served that cake up for tea. I knew by then that I wanted to slow down a bit, stop touring and find somewhere to settle down, so I figured I'd get the recipe and give it a whirl when I had more time.'

'You certainly did that,' Sam said, with a laugh that was both incredulous and admiring. From the corner of her eye, she saw the photographer hovering. 'So how do you feel about the world knowing you're a master baker?'

Micky dropped her a knowing wink. 'Believe me, I've been called a lot worse.'

It was much later. The village green was clear once more, both of chocolate eggs and the family of stalls and tents that had sprung up earlier in the day. The cakes were long gone, devoured by appreciative friends and neighbours, and the weight of Martha's monster simnel cake had been more or less guessed. A few stalwart villagers, including Franny, Henry, Ruby and Micky, were sitting in front of the Star and Sixpence fireplace, which neither Sam nor Nessie had found the time to light. Gabe had left the kitchens to join them and Laurie was sitting off to one side, nursing a pint of Thirsty Bishop. The conversation was gentle and warm; Franny seemed to have forgotten her disappointment in not winning the Bake Off and was cheerfully sharing culinary tips with Micky.

Sam let the chatter flow over her, stifling a yawn as she leaned very slightly into Gabe beside her. He looked tired too, although she suspected he wore his exhaustion much better than she did; he'd worked flat out all day to ensure the pub's diners left full and satisfied and yet she could still picture him heading out for a night on the town. Whereas all Sam could think of was her bed.

'I think we can chalk today down as a success,' Nessie said, swirling her red wine around her glass and smiling. 'None of the children overdosed on chocolate, at least.'

Laurie let out a barely concealed snort. 'No thanks to Sam.'

Ruby stopped listening to Franny's conversation with Micky and turned her head to stare at Laurie.

Sam blinked in confusion. 'What's that supposed to mean?' she asked.

'Don't pretend you don't know,' he said. 'I had the kids running all over the village on wild goose chases, looking for eggs where there weren't any. But then Sam came along and basically gave the whole game away.'

'Because you were encouraging them to climb trees and disturb birds' nests,' she pointed out. 'Neither of which is safe or kind behaviour.'

'Is that true?' Nessie asked Laurie, frowning.

He shrugged. 'I might have suggested there were eggs in the trees, but I wasn't actually going to let them climb up to check. Sam totally overreacted.'

Franny was listening now too. 'There are some rare breeds of birds who nest in those trees. I would have been very upset if they'd been damaged as part of a game.'

Laurie's eyes narrowed. 'Like I said, I wasn't going to let the kids go up to check. It was just a bit of fun.'

'But it's not the kind of behaviour we like to encourage in Little Monkham,' she said severely, in a tone that made Sam want to wince.

'Of course it isn't,' Laurie muttered. 'Because that might involve fun.'

A deep frown of displeasure creased Franny's forehead; clearly she wasn't going to let the matter go without making her outrage clear. 'Samantha was quite right to stop you, Laurence. Someone could have been hurt.'

'But no one was,' he said, his voice growing louder.

'Thanks to Samantha,' Franny insisted. She fanned her face with one hand and Sam noticed a fine layer of sweat had started to bead on her upper lip.

'Are you too warm, Franny?' Sam asked. 'Can I get you some water?'

'I'm fine,' Franny snapped, glaring at Laurie. 'If some people would stop throwing toddler tantrums when they get told off then I'd be a lot better.'

Laurie let out an incredulous laugh. 'Tantrums? You've got

a nerve, after the way you acted when you didn't win first prize earlier. All the toys came out of the pram – I thought you were going to punch poor Micky here.'

'That's enough, Laurie,' Nessie said firmly. 'Let's not ruin a lovely day with an argument.'

His gaze whipped around to her, and Sam saw the flash of something cross his face. 'I don't know why you're pretending to care so much – you're leaving!'

Ruby gasped and Sam felt as if she'd been punched in the chest. She twisted around to stare at Nessie. 'What?'

'I'm not,' Nessie said, but her suddenly rosy cheeks told a different story. 'It's just—'

'She's been headhunted by McBride Breweries,' Laurie went on, spreading his hands. 'She made me promise not to tell you, but I've seen the letter and it's all there in black and white. They're offering her a fortune to go and work for them.'

Franny made an odd wheezing sound and Sam thought she knew exactly how she felt. 'Nessie, is this true?'

'Partly,' her sister admitted, with a wretched look at the stunned faces around her. 'But I wasn't going to take the job. I mean, how could I?'

Her gaze came to rest on Sam's bump for the first time and Sam understood.

'But you want to,' she said quietly. 'You want to take the job, right?'

To her left, Franny let out another wheezing huff.

Henry turned to her in concern. 'Are you all right, my love? You look a little peaky.'

There was a thick sheen of sweat on her face and she was paler than Sam had ever seen her. 'I feel ... a little strange,' she said, gasping slightly in between the words. 'Light-headed ... can't breathe ...'

Gabe jumped to his feet. 'Get her some water,' he barked at Laurie. 'Loosen her clothing.'

Franny clutched at the buttons of her blouse. 'You'll do ... no such thing ...'

'Just until you feel better,' Sam soothed, trying to ignore her alarm at the clammy whiteness of the other woman's skin. 'Henry, why don't you do it?'

But as he reached for the buttons, Franny let out a stifled moan. Her hand convulsed on her chest, turning into a claw that tore at the material of her blouse. Her eyes flew wide as the moan became a guttural croak that died in her throat.

'Franny!' Henry shouted, his voice rough with sudden panic. 'Dear god, what's happening?'

Nessie reached for her phone. 'It's a heart attack,' she said, stabbing at the keypad. 'Check her pulse someone.'

Sam saw Gabe take Franny's rigid wrist and feel for the pulse. But at that moment, her eyes fluttered shut and she slumped back against the sofa.

'Get her onto the ground, start CPR,' Nessie shouted, then spoke urgently into her phone. 'Ambulance, please.'

Sam watched with a sense of horrified unreality as Gabe and Micky laid Franny out and began chest compressions. Beside them, Henry's hands fluttered helplessly and his face was wet with tears.

'She's so still. Is she – is she going to be all right?'

Her own heart pounding, Sam stood up and guided him into her seat. 'I'm sure she's going to be fine,' she said, doing her best to sound reassuring. 'The ambulance will be here soon.'

Her eyes met Ruby's, wide with shock and grief and a terrible finality, and she knew without a single glance at the postmistress that the words she'd said to Henry were a lie. Franny was not going to be fine. Franny was gone.

Chapter Twenty-six

'I can't believe she's dead.'

Nessie stared into the glowing embers of the wood burner in the living room of Snowdrop Cottage and shook her head for what felt like the hundredth time. It didn't seem real, but, at the same time, she saw Franny's waxen, lifeless face every time she closed her eyes and knew that it was.

On the sofa beside her, Owen sighed and took her hand. 'I know. It's such a shock. Poor Henry.'

Across the room, Sam shifted on the armchair. 'Poor Henry,' she echoed. 'Did you see him stagger when the paramedics said there was nothing they could do? He looked like he was going to keel over too.'

Gabe tipped his head. 'Is it any wonder? He'd just watched his wife pass away without being able to do a thing to stop it.'

The thought made Nessie want to cry again and she'd done too much of that already. She squeezed her eyes shut and tried not to imagine the pain Henry must be feeling.

'I'm glad he's not on his own tonight,' she said, remembering how Micky had insisted he spend the night at his cottage next door to Ruby's. 'I can't think of anything worse than having to go home and be surrounded by all Franny's things, knowing she wasn't ever going to use them again.'

Owen squeezed her hand and she reached up to plant a small kiss on his cheek, because he knew better than anyone how it felt to return home after the loss of a spouse.

'Micky and Ruby will look after him,' Sam said. 'And tomorrow, someone can go and get whatever he needs from home, if he doesn't feel strong enough to go himself. The village will rally round.'

'It always does,' Owen said simply. 'We do what we can.'

There was no possibility that word hadn't spread; ambulances and police cars were such rare sights in the village that the appearance of both on the doorstep of the Star and Sixpence had attracted a cluster of worried onlookers, despite the late hour. By the time the paramedics had made their way back to the ambulance, with no patient on a stretcher to give hope that everything might still be okay, there was a crowd outside the pub. Nessie hadn't felt able to go out and give them the news, but she and Sam had distributed endless cups of tea. Eventually, once the local GP had been in to issue the medical certificate, one of the police officers had shared what had happened and the shock waves had been almost tangible as they'd rippled through Little Monkham. No one had been able to believe it; Franny had been an integral part of the village for so long that most people seemed to find it impossible to accept that she was gone.

'And she had no history of heart disease?' Gabe asked. 'No warning signs that we all somehow missed?'

'No, nothing,' Nessie said. 'The paramedics said it was a pulmonary embolism – she could have had it for weeks with hardly any symptoms. Until it reached her heart, of course.'

Sam let out a sudden yawn. 'Oh god, I'm sorry,' she mumbled, covering her mouth in embarrassment. 'It's been a really long day.'

'I know,' Nessie said, and for the first time since January, she didn't have to remind herself to be kind to her sister. 'Why don't you try to get some rest? You can stay here if you don't want to sleep in the pub – Kathryn's room is empty.'

'You can have the sofa if you like, Gabe,' Owen offered.

Nessie watched conflicting emotions chase each other across Sam's face. She turned to look at Gabe and something unspoken passed between them. 'No, I'd like to sleep in my own bed. I'm going to have to go back at some point – might as well get it over with. And Gabe will be right next door if I need him.'

There was something about the way she said it that made the memory of Laurie's insinuation about the baby's father resurface in Nessie's mind. She pushed the idea away; Gabe had flatly denied that it was possible and it seemed as unbelievable now as it had then. But that didn't mean Sam wasn't harbouring feelings for Gabe; he was taking such good care of her that Nessie found it easy to imagine her sister translating that tenderness into something more. And that made the situation with Joss even more complicated; the time was coming when Sam might have to decide which man she wanted in her life the most.

Nessie gave herself a brisk mental shake; it was none of her business who Sam had feelings for. And besides, her sister had rarely taken her advice in the past; she was hardly likely to start now.

'Promise me you won't try to clean up,' Nessie said, thinking of the empty glasses that must still be littering the tables. 'I'll come over first thing to do anything that needs to be done.'

Sam yawned again and got to her feet. 'Not much chance of me cleaning up tonight – I'm not sure I could keep my eyes open long enough.'

Nessie stood up too and smiled. 'Then don't.' On impulse, she closed the distance between her and Sam and pulled her into the briefest of hugs. 'Sleep as well as you can.'

'You too,' Sam said, her gaze searching as she stepped back. 'See you in the morning.'

Owen showed them out. When he returned, he didn't say a word but wrapped his arms around Nessie and buried his face in her hair. Nessie closed her eyes, breathing in his familiar scent and felt some of the misery that weighed on her spirits lift.

'Do you think you will sleep?' Owen asked, after a few minutes had gone by.

Nessie looked up at him. 'I hope so. You?'

He gazed down at her in concern. 'I'm not the one who just witnessed a traumatic event. But I hate to think of you lying there awake while I snore. You can wake me up if you want to talk.'

A wave of exhausted gratitude washed over Nessie. 'Thanks. I might just take you up on that.'

'Will Sam be okay?' he whispered as they climbed the stairs and tiptoed past Luke's room.

Nessie pictured the look that had passed between her sister and Gabe, and nodded. 'She'll be all right tonight. But tomorrow is going to be another story altogether.'

Sam didn't want to go into the bar; she forced herself to hurry past the fireplace and couldn't bring herself to even look at the spot where Franny had lain. Instead, she snapped off the lights as soon as she and Gabe reached the stairs that led up to the first floor, reminding herself that things would be easier to deal with in the sunlight of the next day.

At the top of the stairs, Gabe paused. 'Is there anything you want?'

Sam sighed. 'Apart from a time machine so I can go back to this afternoon and make Franny go to hospital, you mean?'

He managed a cheerless smile. 'Yes. Apart from that.'

'No,' Sam said, with a dispirited shake of her head. 'Nothing.'

'I am sorry for your loss,' Gabe said. 'I didn't know Franny as well as you did, but she seemed like a strong and principled woman who will be missed.'

'That pretty much sums her up,' Sam agreed, her voice catching. 'I'm going to miss her a lot.'

Gabe's dark eyes were filled with compassion. 'Goodnight, Sam,' he said, moving along the landing towards his bedroom door. 'You know where to find me if there's anything you need.'

She took a deep, calming breath and watched him go. Beneath her shock and sorrow, she was uncomfortably aware of the highly inappropriate stir his words had caused inside. The old Sam would definitely have read something flirtatious into the suggestion that she might need him; even yesterday's Sam might have wondered a little. But today's Sam knew Gabe was simply being kind in the wake of Franny's death.

Ten minutes later, she was lying in bed surrounded by darkness, listening to the creaks of the old building as it settled for the night. Minutes ticked by but sleep did not come. She shifted around and imagined Gabe on the other side of the bedroom wall; was he awake? Was he fidgeting and restless too, wondering the same thing about her? There was only one way to be certain, but she wasn't ready for the complications that would almost certainly follow. And the last thing she needed right now was extra complications.

In the end, her heart overrode her head. She stood on the landing for a moment, summoning up the courage to knock on his door. He must have heard the floorboards creak, because he came to the door before she could rap on the wood.

'You cannot sleep?' he asked when he saw her.

'Not a wink,' she admitted. 'And I think it's because ...
because I don't want to be on my own. Do you think you
can put up with me for a little while longer?'

Gabe pulled back the door. 'Of course. Shall I make you
some hot milk?'

'No, thank you.' She felt her cheeks grow warm at the
sight of his bare chest beneath his dressing gown. 'And I
thought maybe – if you don't mind – maybe I could ...'

He waited, his eyes never leaving hers, his expression steady.

Sam gave up trying to be coy. 'Look, there's no easy way
to ask this, so I'm just going to come out with it – can I sleep
in your room tonight? I want to know I'm not alone, to hear
the sound of someone else breathing next to me.' She paused
and mentally replayed the sentence. 'Oh god, that sounds
creepy, doesn't it?'

Gabe shook his head. 'No. It sounds like a perfectly
normal reaction to a terrible event.'

Sam found her gaze settling on the smooth brown skin of
his chest again. She looked away, suddenly afraid he'd get the
wrong idea. 'I promise to stay on my side of the bed.'

His mouth quirked, as though he was on the verge of
laughter, and she supposed it was a ridiculous idea; she was
five months pregnant, after all. 'Thank goodness for that,'
Gabe said, managing to keep a straight face. 'Of course you
can sleep here. Come in.'

There was no denying it felt odd to slip between the cool

317

covers and lie beside him. Sam tucked the duvet underneath her chin and gazed silently at his profile. He had a strong nose, she decided, maybe even noble, if men even had noble noses any more. His chin was covered by the usual dark stubble, but she could see the tip of a faint scar poking out of the hair. She wanted to ask him how he'd got it, but the question seemed far too intimate, given that they were in bed together.

'Comfortable?' he asked, turning suddenly and catching her staring. 'Shall I switch off the lamp?'

Sam nodded, her stomach clenching with the embarrassment of being caught watching him. But her tension relaxed a little in the darkness and she lay still, listening to his steady breathing.

'Say something to me in Spanish,' she said, after a few more seconds of almost-silence had passed. 'I don't mind what you say – I just want to hear your voice.'

He began to talk, his tone rising and falling with the unfamiliar sounds and words in a way that Sam found vastly soothing. After a few minutes, she felt her shoulders start to loosen as the toll of the day let go. Was it a story he was telling her, she wondered, or a recipe for paella; she couldn't tell. But before long, her eyes drifted shut and the words seemed to be coming from further away. Soon she couldn't hear him at all.

Sam awoke the following morning tangled in the sheets, with no sign of Gabe. The bedroom door was ajar, however, and she could smell bacon, which strongly suggested breakfast was on its way. Savouring the mouth-watering aroma, she padded to her own room and pulled on the dressing gown that barely fastened around her stomach; she really was going to have to buy some proper maternity clothes soon, she decided. Especially since Gabe showed no sign of relaxing his insistence that she eat everything he put before her.

'Nessie's downstairs already,' he explained when Sam entered the kitchen. 'I've invited her for breakfast – I hope that's okay? It seemed rude not to.'

Sam waited for the lurch of anxiety that usually occurred whenever she thought about seeing Nessie; it didn't come. 'It's a nice idea,' she told Gabe, surprised to discover she meant it. 'I suppose she's started cleaning up without me? Typical Ness.'

Gabe smiled. 'I am certain she has. Go and help her if you like – I'll call you when your food is ready.'

Predictably, the bar was almost spotless by the time Sam had pulled on some clothes and arrived downstairs. 'Bloody hell, what time did you get here? Did you even go to sleep?'

Nessie stopped wiping down the tables and shook her head. 'I tried – not sure how successful I was. How about you? Did you get much rest?'

'Went out like a light,' Sam admitted, remembering the way Gabe had lulled her to sleep in Spanish. 'Sorry.'

Her sister laughed. 'Don't be. Owen slept well too.'

Keen to do something to help, Sam moved behind the bar and started to unscrew the sparklers on the pumps.

'Leave those for now,' Nessie said with an unsettled frown. 'Connor or Tilly can do them when they come in. I – I want to talk to you.'

Dread steamrollered across Sam's heart. Was Nessie about to confess that she'd taken the job with McBride Breweries? Or was there something even worse? 'Okay, I guess,' she said, fear needling her insides. 'Go ahead.'

Nessie took a deep breath. 'I owe you an apology, Sam. I don't think I've been very kind or supportive to you. At the very least, I've been a rubbish sister, but what's worse than that is I haven't been much of a friend, at a time when you really needed one. And I'm sorry I haven't coped better with – with your pregnancy; I feel like I've let you down.'

She looked so miserable that Sam felt her eyes start to well with tears. 'You haven't let me down. I promise.'

'But I have,' Nessie insisted, with a stubborn half-shake of her head. 'I let my own sadness stop me from seeing how scared and alone you were. And I know you probably understand why I held back, but that doesn't excuse how I behaved.'

Sam could hardly believe what she was hearing – was Nessie really beating herself up for her own grief? 'You don't need to be excused,' she said. 'God knows I put you in a horrible position – who wouldn't have struggled with it?'

Nessie sighed. 'Let's just agree it hasn't been easy for either of us. But I did a lot of thinking in the night and one of the conclusions I reached is that life is too short to fall out over things we can't change. You're going to have a baby and – well – I couldn't be happier for you.'

'Oh, Ness,' Sam said, blinking hard in a futile attempt to prevent the flood of tears that threatened to swamp her. 'Do you really mean it?'

Her sister offered a watery smile. 'I really do. I can't wait to be an auntie.'

Sam sniffed hard and dabbed at her eyes with the sleeve of her dressing gown. 'You've got no idea how much better that makes me feel. But please tell me you're not taking that job – I know it's horribly selfish, but I couldn't bear for you to go.' She hesitated, then rushed on, 'I don't think I can have this baby without you.'

Nessie's smile melted away. 'I don't know if I can promise that, Sam. The money is amazing – six figures – and it would be a fresh start, as well as a new challenge.' She looked down at the floor. 'But I'm not sure I'm ready for it.'

And that was typical Nessie too, Sam thought, always doubting herself and her abilities. 'Of course you are,' she said, even though it hurt to say the words. 'You'll be brilliant. And ignore me – if it's what you really want then you should go for it.'

'That's the thing,' Nessie said, her tone despairing. 'I don't actually know what I want. What if I take the job and hate it?'

'You don't have to decide now,' Sam pointed out. She took a breath and did her best to smile. 'But whatever you choose to do, the Star and Sixpence will always be here for you. I'll always be here for you.'

Nessie wrapped her arms around Sam in a hug that gave

her a sense of peace she hadn't even realised she'd been missing. When Nessie stepped back, she laid one hand on Sam's bump and gazed solemnly into her eyes. 'And whatever happens, I'll be here for you too. For both of you, if you need me.'

The words were enough to break what was left of Sam's fragile self-control. She burst into tears. 'Of course I'm going to need you. I told you, I can't do this without you.'

'You're stronger than you think,' Nessie said soothingly. 'And you'll have Joss to support you. Plus Gabe, if he's got anything to do with it.'

Sam dabbed at her cheeks, the thought of Gabe's kindness setting off another torrent. 'Poor Gabe. I bet he wishes he'd never set foot in the Star and Sixpence.'

The look Nessie gave her was level. 'I'd be very surprised if that's what he thinks. In fact—'

But whatever she was about to say was interrupted by a faint shout from upstairs. 'Sam? Nessie? Breakfast is ready.'

'In fact what?' Sam asked, using her sleeve to wipe her face again.

Nessie let out a half-laugh. 'Forget it. I think it might be better if you work it out for yourself.'

'Ness!'

'Sorry,' Nessie said, not sounding sorry at all. 'Now, let's go and get our breakfast. All this emotional vulnerability is making me hungry.'

Sam sighed and patted her baby bump. 'I'm always hungry these days.'

Her sister was silent for a moment, and Sam had the horrible feeling she'd overstepped the line. But then Nessie reached out to squeeze her hand. 'I'm proud of you, Sam. You're going to be an amazing mum.'

Sam smiled. It felt good to be back on friendly terms with Nessie. 'Just like you'd be a great – what's that new job title?'

'Head of Community Spirit,' Nessie replied, after a slightly embarrassed pause.

Sam tried her hardest to maintain a straight face, but she knew she was fighting a losing battle. 'Right. Well, like I said, you'd be a great Head of Community Spirit.'

'Thanks,' Nessie said dryly, as her sister convulsed with laughter. 'That is actually the job title – I haven't made it up.'

'No, I know,' Sam replied, trying once more to be serious. 'But you've got to admit it sounds a bit like a cross between the WI and some hipster start-up. Hey, I've just thought of what your mission statement could be – "Raising spirits with spirits"!'

Nessie gave her a wry stare. 'I thought you said you were hungry.'

'I am,' Sam replied in a cheery voice. 'And the good thing about Gabe is that his spirits are easily raised. All you need to do is eat everything he puts in front of you.'

Chapter Twenty-seven

Nessie had barely finished knocking on the door of Henry's cottage when Ruby answered.

'Hello. How was the afternoon shift?' she murmured, casting a worried look past the older woman to the dimly lit hallway behind her. 'Did you manage to get him to eat lunch?'

Ruby sighed. 'Nothing.' She glanced at the tray in Nessie's hands, snugly wrapped in pristine white cloth. 'Although you might have more luck, if that's from Gabe.'

'Chicken in white wine sauce and new potatoes, fresh from the oven, and some Thirsty Bishop to wash it down,' Nessie said. 'If this can't tempt him, nothing will.'

Four days had passed since Franny's death and the repercussions were still being felt all around Little Monkham and the surrounding area. The Star and Sixpence had become an unofficial drop-in centre for those coming to pay their respects; Franny might have had a fearsome reputation, but there was no doubt she'd been admired and loved too, and there was a steady stream of visitors. At first, conversations had been shocked and sorrowful, but now it seemed that everywhere Nessie turned, she heard fond memories of the postmistress and her many years of service to the village. If Nessie had needed a lesson on what community spirit was, she knew she could do worse than be inspired by Franny's legacy.

It was no surprise that Henry had not set foot in the Star and Sixpence. He'd left Micky's cottage the morning after Franny had died and shut himself away, refusing to answer the door to anyone. Eventually, his worried next-door neighbour had surrendered the spare key to Father Goodluck and he had gone in with Owen to find a distraught Henry still in the clothes he'd worn the night of Franny's heart attack, sat in an armchair and gazing at wedding photographs. He didn't appear to have eaten; a plate of burned toast sat untouched in the kitchen and several cups of cold tea were dotted around the cottage, including one that had been knocked over and left to sink into the carpet. That was when the rota had been drawn up; the villagers agreed to take it in turns to sit with Henry – talking, listening or even in silence, letting him know he wasn't alone. But, as yet, no one had been able to persuade him to eat.

'It's like he's pining away,' Ruby said, shaking her head in despair as she stepped back to let Nessie in. 'I've never seen anyone so devastated. He's – well, you'll see how he is.'

'It's all been such a shock,' Nessie said, her heart starting to ache the way it had so many times since Sunday evening. 'But you must be exhausted. Why don't you go and get some rest? I'll take over here.'

Ruby didn't protest as she slipped out of the door. 'Thank you. Micky's got the late shift – I'll send him your way in a few hours. Good luck.'

'Thanks,' Nessie replied, hoping the delicious aroma of Gabe's cooking would make her task easier. Straightening her shoulders, she nudged the front door shut and made her way into the small living room. 'Hello, Henry. How are you?'

He turned his white-haired head towards her and Nessie almost dropped the tray in shock: his normally ruddy cheeks were waxy and pale and his eyes – usually so full of blustering self-importance – were sunken and dull. He smelled as though he hadn't washed for days. 'Oh, hello, Nessie,' he said, in a voice that was dry and cracked and entirely unlike him. 'Is it your turn to do the deathwatch?'

Nessie concentrated on sliding the tray onto a side table, taking the opportunity to compose herself before she replied. 'No, it's my turn to comfort a friend who has suffered a terrible loss.'

Henry grunted. 'And I suppose you expect me to eat that? I'm not hungry.'

The stubborn undertone warned Nessie she had a battle ahead. She thought fast. What was that old sales saying – *sell the sizzle, not the sausage.* Maybe there was another way to tempt Henry into breaking his fast.

'No, this is my dinner,' she said cheerfully. 'I hope you don't mind me eating it in front of you?'

A flicker of surprise crossed his face, quickly dissolving into apathy. 'I don't care.'

Settling into the armchair opposite, Nessie untucked the white cloth and examined the contents of the tray. Gabe had pulled out all the stops – beneath the silver plate cover there was a succulent chicken breast marinated in a creamy white-wine sauce, buttery new potatoes and honey-roasted carrots that Nessie knew would fall apart the moment a fork touched them. A gooey salted caramel brownie finished off Gabe's contribution and Connor had carefully laid two bottles of Thirsty Bishop beside each other, with a gleaming pint glass.

Nessie placed the cover to one side, allowing the lip-smacking smell of the food to float across the room. She took a deep breath, savouring the delicious scent and wondered if Henry was doing the same. Right on cue, his stomach rumbled.

'I'm starving,' Nessie said, hiding a smile as she unwrapped the cutlery. 'Haven't eaten since breakfast. I can't wait to tuck in – it smells so good.'

She didn't look up. Instead, she cut a sliver of chicken and slowly raised it to her mouth.

'Mmmm,' she said, after a few moments of chewing. 'I don't know how Gabe does it.'

Henry didn't answer, so Nessie moved on to the potatoes. The smell from the food filled the air; she had no idea how Henry was still resisting. Maybe it was time to wheel out the big guns, she decided, and picked up the bottle opener Connor had thoughtfully placed on the tray.

'Is that Bishop?' Henry asked in a sharp voice, when she lifted a bottle and expertly levered off the lid.

'That's right,' she said. 'I wouldn't have thought it would go with the chicken, but Gabe said the flavour complements the sauce.' She angled the glass and emptied the bottle into it, bringing the liquid to a perfect head at the end. 'I'd let you have a sip, but it's probably not a good idea on an empty stomach.'

Instantly, Henry scowled. 'Don't think I'm not wise to you, Nessie Chapman. I know what your game is.'

Nessie took another mouthful of food and raised her eyebrows. 'I don't know what you mean, Henry. I'm just eating my very delicious dinner and drinking an award-winning bitter.'

She took a long sip of Thirsty Bishop, trying hard not to show how much she disliked it. Give her a glass of Prosecco or a Bellini any day, she thought longingly.

Henry watched her in accusatory silence until, finally, it seemed he couldn't take it any more.

'I suppose I wouldn't mind a bit of that chicken,' he said, his tone grudging. 'If there's some to spare.'

Nessie glanced down at the plate, wondering how far to take the pretence that this was her dinner. She couldn't help feeling there was a fine line between selling the sizzle and accidentally eating the sausage. 'I could always ask Gabe to rustle me up another plate when I get back,' she said, colouring the words with as much reluctance as she dared. 'If you're hungry.'

His dark-ringed eyes regarded her suspiciously for a few seconds, then his stomach gurgled loudly in the silence. He waved an impatient hand. 'Pass it over, then. And don't drink all the Bishop, or you'll be running back to the pub for more.'

She half-expected him to wolf the meal down, but he took the time to tuck the crisp white napkin into the grimy collar of his well-worn shirt and ate slowly, chewing each small mouthful much longer than Nessie thought necessary.

When his plate was clean, he rested his head against the armchair and closed his eyes. 'And now the drink, please.'

The brownie lay untouched on the tray, but Nessie didn't argue. *One step at a time*, she told herself.

Henry took two long draughts, draining almost half the glass, then lowered his eyelids and sighed. 'She would have enjoyed that meal.'

The backs of Nessie's eyes prickled. 'I know.'

He was quiet for a heartbeat. 'She loved food, you see. When we first got married, she was always in the kitchen, experimenting with this and that, trying to be the per-fect wife.'

Nessie nodded but didn't interrupt; of course Franny must have been a good cook. Her cakes had been legendary, after all.

Henry opened his eyes. 'Tasted bloody awful. She was good at baking but couldn't get the hang of anything else.' He stared at Nessie. 'Made no sense to either of us, but I turned out to be the better cook. And that might have bothered some women – that the traditional roles were reversed – but she just told me we should play to our strengths and accepted it.'

It was exactly the kind of thing Nessie could imagine Franny saying, she thought, as a sad smile tugged at the corner of her mouth. 'I suppose she knew her limitations.'

He let out a derisive snort. 'I don't think she had any, apart from being a dreadful cook. She was the most extraordinary woman I've ever met.' His expression softened and he passed a quivering hand over his face. 'I don't know how I'm going to cope without her.'

'We'll help,' Nessie said thickly, her throat suddenly aching and hot. 'You're not going to be alone.'

Swallowing hard, Henry did his best to nod. 'I know. You're all very kind.' Lapsing into silence, he took several more sips of beer, then glanced over at Nessie. 'Have people been coming to the village?'

'Yes,' Nessie replied. 'The pub is full of them right now, in fact.'

Something akin to panic crossed his pallid features. 'I'm not ready to see them yet.'

'Of course not,' Nessie said. 'You need to get your strength back first, get back on your feet. There's no rush.'

He looked down at the tray on his lap. 'I need to arrange the funeral. People will want to come.'

'Don't worry about that tonight. Father Goodluck can help when you're ready.'

'She'd want me to do it properly,' he said, almost to himself. 'Make it a celebration as well as – as a goodbye.'

He struggled again, clearly trying to fight back a wave of emotion.

Nessie gave up her own battle and let tears fall unchecked onto her lap. 'It's okay to cry,' she told him. 'I found it helped, as long as you remember to stop eventually.'

'I know,' Henry said, and she saw his cheeks were wet. 'It's the stopping part that worries me.'

Nessie managed a tremulous smile. 'It gets easier.'

Pressing his lips together, he nodded, sending tears cascading downwards. Nessie didn't move, simply let him cry until, at last, he took the napkin that was still tucked into his shirt and dabbed at his face.

'Thank you,' he said, once he'd regained control. 'I know you understand.'

'I do,' Nessie murmured.

He let out a long shuddering sigh and sniffed hard. His nose wrinkled. 'And now, do you think you might take this tray? Something tells me I'm long overdue a shower.'

Relief coursed through Nessie as she swallowed a laugh and got to her feet. 'I didn't like to say.'

'Franny wouldn't have been so delicate,' Henry said. 'She'd have told me straight.'

She would, Nessie thought; tact was never Franny's strong point. But she'd usually meant well. 'Shall I leave you in peace for a while? Micky's due to pop in later.'

Henry looked around, seeming to see the mess for the

first time. 'That would be useful, yes. I seem to have some housekeeping to do as well.'

'I can do that,' Nessie offered.

'No, no. Franny would have my guts for garters if I let you clean up my mess.' He paused and gave her a grateful look. 'Thank you, Nessie. She always said you were a good girl.'

A bittersweet shiver swept down Nessie's back; the words were high praise coming from Franny. 'Thanks, Henry, that means a lot. Perhaps I'll see you tomorrow – with another little something from Gabe?'

He gave the question some thought, then nodded. 'Perhaps.'

Satisfied that progress had been made, Nessie took a moment to load up the tray and headed for the door.

'Oh, and Nessie?' Henry called, just as she reached the front door. 'Leave the second bottle of Bishop, will you?'

She grinned and balanced the bottle on the hallway table. Yes, progress had definitely been made.

The church was warm, but Sam still felt a chill as she gazed over the packed pews towards the flower-strewn coffin in front of the altar. She found it impossible to believe Franny was inside; it seemed too small to contain everything she had been. Father Goodluck clearly felt the same way, because his sermon had been full of fond anecdotes and tales of Franny's influence around Little Monkham and beyond. He described her as a force of great good, whose passing left a void that would take some considerable time to fill. By the time he had finished speaking, there was not a dry eye to be seen, but Sam saw plenty of smiles too.

'Beautiful,' Nessie whispered beside her. 'Franny would have loved that.'

She would have loved all of it, Sam thought, as the choir's voices soared in the final hymn and the pallbearers began their solemn procession down the aisle and out to the graveyard. There was no question that Franny would be buried anywhere other than St Mary's, where she could continue to keep an eye on the village; Sam imagined she'd come back and haunt them all if they laid her to rest anywhere else.

She'd known Joss was among the mourners; they'd exchanged several messages in the days following Franny's death and she'd seen him several times during the ceremony. But it wasn't until the black-clad crowds began to make their way back to the Star and Sixpence that she found herself near enough to speak to him.

'Hello,' she said, as he fell into step beside her. 'How are you?'

He shrugged. 'Still a bit shell-shocked, to be honest. I'd always assumed Franny was immortal.'

Sam smiled in spite of herself. 'I know what you mean. I don't think anyone can believe she's gone.'

His gaze travelled down to her coat, beneath which her baby bump could be clearly seen. 'You're looking well. How are things going?'

'Better,' she replied, tipping her head. 'Nessie and I have sorted out a few things. Did you hear she's been headhunted by McBride?'

Joss's blue eyes widened in surprise. 'No! Has she said yes?'

Sam sighed, conscious of another thing in her life that was both terrifyingly real and unimaginably distant at the same time. 'I think she's going to.'

'But where does that leave you?' Joss asked, his eyes flitting downwards again. 'You're in no position to take over running the Star and Sixpence.'

'That's true,' she conceded, although the observation still rankled. 'But I'll have lots of help. Gabe will be around and Laurie is keen to step up his responsibilities.'

'I bet he is,' Joss said, frowning. 'Look, not to be rude, but Gabe is a chef. What does he know about managing a pub?'

'He founded his own restaurant, Joss,' Sam said, trying not to sound defensive. 'I think he's got a handle on what it takes to run a business.'

Joss's frown deepened. 'Laurie, then – he's got no experience at all, except for working behind the bar.' He rubbed his beard and gave her a concerned stare. 'I'm worried it'll be too much, Sam. The last thing you need is work pressure on top of a new baby. Maybe I should come back and take over the reins.'

Sam felt her jaw drop. Who did he think he was, Sir Joss of the Shire, galloping in to save the day? 'I don't need rescuing.'

He waved an impatient hand. 'Of course you don't. But be realistic, Sam. You can't run the pub and look after a baby at the same time. You must know that.' His voice softened. 'Look, I know the Star and Sixpence like it was my own business. Which it practically was for several years, when

334

your dad's drinking got worse. And since I'm going to be moving back to Little Monkham soon anyway, why don't you let me help?'

The trouble was, it wasn't a bad idea, Sam realised as they rounded the corner and the pub came into view. Joss was a very capable pair of hands; she could trust him implicitly. Everything would be so much easier with him around . . .

'And,' he said, a sudden determination creeping into his voice, 'it would mean I could take care of you, too. I know you said no the last time I asked, but I'm not going anywhere, Sam. I still love you and I want us to be a proper family.'

Sam's shoulders sagged as she pictured a future with Joss. It wasn't an unpleasant image, and it would almost certainly help to solve her fear of being left alone with a baby she didn't know how to look after.

Joss seemed to sense her hesitation, because he reached for her hand and plunged on. 'You know we made a great team before. Why not give us a chance to be great together again?'

'I—' Sam wavered, her gaze fixed on the Star and Sixpence. 'I don't know . . .'

Up ahead, she saw Gabe turn round and scan the crowd, as though he was looking for someone. When his eyes found her, something that looked a lot like relief passed across his face and he smiled. And, remembering his assurances that he would be there to help, and how it had felt to fall asleep beside him, Sam knew what her response to Joss had to be.

'I'll think about your offer to help manage the pub,' she said carefully, fighting to ensure her voice didn't betray the emotion she felt surging inside. 'But *I'm* not part of the deal. Sorry.'

The last word came out as a whisper but Joss heard. For a moment, she saw a wounded look in his eyes, then a rueful smile crossed his face. 'I understand. But you can't blame a guy for trying again, right?'

She squeezed his fingers and let them go. 'No. I don't blame you at all.'

Chapter Twenty-eight

It was almost midnight when the last of the mourners left the Star and Sixpence.

Nessie closed the door with a weary sigh. 'I think that went as well as could be expected.'

Her sister placed a hand on her back and stretched, wincing a little as she did so. 'It did. I'm not sure I've ever seen Henry quite so drunk – I hope Owen and Gabe manage to get him home okay.'

'He did Franny proud today,' Nessie said, smiling at the thought of Henry holding court beside the bar, regaling everyone with stories about his wonderful wife. 'I think she'd forgive him for being slightly the worse for wear.'

'Probably,' Sam replied wryly. She looked round the untidy bar and groaned. 'Do we have to do all this tonight? My ankles feel like tree trunks.'

Nessie took pity on her. 'No. Let's do it in the morning – it's not as though anyone is going to be clamouring for a drink at opening time, after all.'

'That's true. Thanks,' Sam said, with a grateful smile. 'But wait for me to help this time, okay?'

'Okay,' Nessie promised, then paused. 'Joss looked well. It was good to see him.'

'Yeah,' Sam replied. She pulled a face. 'He had a suggestion to make, actually. In case you do decide to leave.'

'Oh?' Nessie said, going suddenly still. 'What kind of suggestion?'

Sam shrugged. 'Quite a good one. He wants to come back to work here – take over the management of the pub while I'm on maternity leave.'

'And how do you feel about that?' Nessie asked carefully, her voice as even as she could make it over the thudding of her heart.

'I think he's the obvious choice,' Sam said, her tone neutral. 'It means Gabe can focus on the restaurant side of things and I'll know the pub is in good hands.'

Nessie studied her sister's face closely. There was more to it than that, she could tell. Could it be that Sam was considering more than a business partnership with Joss? 'And?'

'And nothing,' Sam said. 'Oh, he wanted us to get back together, but I told him that wasn't happening.'

Relief coursed through Nessie so fast that she almost sagged. 'Oh. Good. Because there's something I wanted to tell you.' She took a deep breath and met Sam's eyes. 'Owen and I have talked it through and I've decided I'm not taking the job with McBride.'

'What?' Sam gave her a stunned look. 'But it's perfect for you. And the money ... the fresh challenge – I thought it was everything you wanted.'

'I won't say I wasn't tempted,' Nessie said. 'They were offering a lot. But I realised that none of that matters to me – there's a lot on offer here, too, and plenty of challenges. The truth is, I belong at the Star and Sixpence. With you.'

Sam's eyes filled with tears. 'But—'

'But nothing,' Nessie said, smiling. 'I want to be here, to watch you become the wonderful mother I know you'll be. And I want to see my niece or nephew grow up. I can't do that if I'm off raising spirits elsewhere.'

Sam dabbed beneath her eyelashes and sniffed. 'Raising community spirits,' she corrected. 'Raising spirits is an entirely different job.'

Nessie laughed. 'Okay, but my point is that I'm staying here. And if Joss wants to come back to help, we'll make it work somehow. Whatever the coming months and years bring us, we'll face it together.'

'That would be wonderful,' Sam said, opening her arms to hug Nessie. 'See? You've raised my spirits already.'

'Good,' Nessie whispered as she pulled her sister close. 'Mine too.'

PART FOUR

Last Words
at the Star and Sixpence

Chapter Twenty-nine

THE STAR AND SIXPENCE PROUDLY PRESENTS

Midsummer Merriment!

Join us for a festival of sunshine, cider and song.

Featuring:

Local and national ciders

Farmer's Market – Sausage Fest

Music from Sonic Folk, Sax Appeal and The Beasties

Plus, special guest star Micky Holiday.

On the Village Green, Little Monkham

Friday 21st June – Sunday 23rd June

There was a dog in the beer garden.

Sam frowned and paused in the back door of the Star and Sixpence, watching as the animal cocked its black-and-white head to gaze at her, as though hoping she might be carrying a sausage or two. 'I'm sorry to disappoint you, but this is all baby,' she said, patting the rounded bump beneath her jumper. 'Where's your owner?'

Taking a few steps to the left, she glanced over the low wooden fence towards the village green, squinting in the May sunlight and expecting to see an early-morning dog walker peering frantically around, but there was no sign of anyone. The dog wasn't wearing a collar, either, and when Sam looked more closely, she could see its body was thin and the fur matted.

'I think you're a stray,' she murmured. The dog whined and wagged its tail but stayed seated on the dew-covered grass by the wooden tables, keeping its distance. Sam bit her lip, wondering what to do. There must be someone she could call – the local council or maybe even an animal shelter – who would be able to find out quickly and easily if the dog had been reported lost. A month earlier, Sam would have known exactly who to ask: Franny Fitzsimmons, who had run the Little Monkham post office and knew everything about everyone. But Franny had passed away suddenly on Easter Sunday, leaving a hole in the hearts and minds of those who'd known her that was proving impossible to fill.

Sam sighed and pulled her phone from the back pocket of

her jeans. It was seven-thirty, too early to call for professional help, so she rang the pub's chef, Gabe.

'Sam?' he said, answering on the second ring. 'Is everything okay?'

'Fine,' she assured him, momentarily touched by the concern in his voice. 'I'm downstairs in the beer garden. I don't suppose you've got any spare sausages in the fridge, have you?'

Gabe let out an incredulous laugh. 'We just had breakfast, Sam. Surely you can't be hungry again already?'

'They're not for me,' she said. 'We've got an unexpected guest. Bring the sausages here and you'll see what I mean.'

He arrived a few minutes later, his dark hair damp from the shower and his stubble still glistening, with a plate of cold chipolatas from the restaurant kitchen balanced in one hand. 'Oh, I see,' he said in a low voice as the dog sniffed the air and pushed itself onto all fours. 'Now it makes sense.'

'I don't know who to contact, but I don't suppose anywhere is open yet,' Sam said, her own voice soft. 'So I thought if we could tempt him into the bar, we could keep him safe until we can find someone to help.'

The dog took several steps forward, its brown eyes fixed on the plate in Gabe's hand. It let out another whine. Gabe broke a chipolata in half and tossed it onto the grass. In a flash, it was gone. He threw another chunk, which vanished as fast as the first, and then glanced at Sam.

'Go inside and wait behind the bar,' he said. 'I'll bring him in.'

She opened her mouth to argue, but the set look in Gabe's eyes made her close it again. And she supposed he was right to be cautious; the dog seemed friendly and docile, but they had no idea of its actual temperament or what diseases it might be carrying. She couldn't take any chances, not when she was nearly seven months pregnant.

She watched from the safety of the bar a few moments later as Gabe encouraged the dog to settle by the grey, unlit fireplace. Its tail thumped the carpet with each piece of sausage; Gabe reached out to scratch behind the scruffy ears and Sam felt her heart melt as the wagging tail sped up to a frenzy. This wasn't a feral dog – it was used to being stroked and loved. This was – or had been – someone's pet.

'You're a hungry boy,' she heard Gabe say as he knelt down to caress the animal's head. 'Wait here and I'll see what else I can find for you.'

The dog seemed to understand because it lay down flat and placed its head on its paws.

Sam moved from behind the bar. 'I don't think we need to worry about him turning into Cujo,' she said. 'He's a total softie.'

Gabe stood up. 'I'm sure you're right. He's very thin, though. I think he's been missing for some time.'

Sam eyed the dog's bony haunches. 'Maybe we should hold off giving him too much rich food. It might be a while since he's eaten.'

'I could boil a chicken breast with some rice?' Gabe suggested, rubbing his chin. 'That's pretty bland.'

'Sounds perfect,' Sam said. 'I'll give him some water and see if Nessie knows who we should call.'

The dog's eyes followed Gabe as he crossed the room and it let out a soft whine when he disappeared through the kitchen door.

Sam gave the animal a commiserating look. 'I know the feeling.'

She called Nessie's number. Her sister answered almost as fast as Gabe had. 'Hi, Sam. Everything okay?'

Sam allowed herself a smile. 'Yes, everything is fine. I just need to pick your brains – or maybe Owen's . . .'

A minute or so later, Sam had the number of the local vet and a dog shelter based around fifteen miles away. 'But I'll be coming over shortly,' Nessie said once she'd relayed the information. 'If we ever find Luke's school shoes, that is.'

The comment made Sam grin; she could imagine sandy-haired Luke tearing through the rooms of Snowdrop Cottage in search of the missing footwear. Equally, she could picture his father, Owen, exhorting him to slow down and remember where he left them. And she'd be willing to bet it was Nessie who found the shoes first.

'Good luck,' she said into the phone, her tone wry. 'See you soon, hopefully.'

Moving with exaggerated care, she filled a bowl with water and eased out from behind the bar, trying not to startle the dog. It watched her actions with interest, muzzle resting on its salt-and-pepper paws, but seemed otherwise relaxed.

Sam placed the bowl of water on the floor and stepped back. 'Almost our finest brew,' she said. 'Cheers.'

The dog got to its feet and began to slurp noisily from the bowl.

Sam watched in sympathy. 'Thirsty as well as hungry. You've had a tough time, boy.'

Reaching for her phone once more, she left a message at the vet's practice; Owen had suggested trying there first, in case someone in the surrounding villages had reported their pet missing. Failing that, they'd also be able to check for a microchip, which might result in a happy reunion and had the added bonus of giving the dog a quick medical once-over. The dog shelter was a last resort, Sam decided, to be contacted in the event that the owner couldn't be found.

The dog lay down once more and seemed content to watch Sam potter around the bar, undertaking the various tasks that needed to be done before opening time. Nessie's arrival caused a flicker of interest; it raised its head as she pushed open the door and took a few measured steps towards the fireplace.

'Oh, he's a Border collie,' she said and held out one hand for the dog to sniff. 'Hello, I'm Nessie. Welcome to the Star and Sixpence.'

The animal eyed her for a moment, then the reappearance of Gabe caused it to turn away. The scent of warm chicken filled the air.

'Just a small portion for now,' he said, placing the plate on the floor beside the water. 'We don't want to overload you.'

'No collar?' Nessie asked, once the dog had started to wolf down the rice and chicken.

'No sign of one,' Sam replied with a sigh. 'It might have fallen off or got caught on something, if he's been missing for a while.'

Nessie frowned. 'He can't belong to anyone in Little Monkham – we'd know.'

'We'd certainly know if he'd been lost,' Sam said. 'So I'm thinking one of the other villages. Hopefully the vet will be able to help, once they open. I've left a message.'

'I wonder what his name is,' Nessie said. 'Something bouncy and fun, I think. Although I suppose there's always a chance he's a working dog, from one of the farms.'

'Maybe,' Sam replied. 'We won't know until the vet gets in touch.'

Gabe smiled as the dog gave the now spotless plate one final lick and then ambled underneath the table in front of the fireplace, sinking to the carpet with a huff of apparent contentment. 'Another satisfied customer.'

'He seems happy enough under there,' Nessie observed. 'Why don't we let him sleep? Gives me a good excuse to leave the hoovering until later.'

It was another hour before Sam's phone rang. She recognised the number on the screen as belonging to the vet and reached across the kitchen table to snatch up the handset eagerly. 'Hello?'

349

'Emily Bell here,' a female voice said, with a cheerful Australian twang. 'I got a message to give you a call – I hear you've found a stray dog.'

Sam relayed what little she knew.

'I can stop by after the morning surgery,' Emily offered. 'Around one o'clock?'

'Nothing sooner?' Sam asked, wondering where she might put the dog once it was time for the Star and Sixpence to open its doors.

'I'm afraid not,' the vet said. 'There's just me and the practice nurse here this morning and we've got a full appointment book. Sorry.'

Sam was just about to reluctantly accept the visit when she heard a volley of excited barks from the bar below. She reeled off the pub's address and told Emily she'd see her after lunch, then heaved herself to her feet and made her way downstairs to investigate. She found her brother, Laurie, with his back pinned to the main pub door, his face white with fear. The dog stood growling, hackles raised as it stared at Laurie with an unwavering gaze.

'What the hell is this?' Laurie said, his voice tight.

Sam edged forwards. 'I found him in the garden this morning. He's been really friendly, up until now.'

Laurie's eyes flashed. 'Yeah, looks friendly. Call it off.'

Sam puffed out a breath. She and Nessie had never had a dog as kids, or any kind of pet; their mother had always insisted it was enough work looking after the two of them, let alone throwing an animal into the mix. But even though the stray was growling and fierce, she wasn't afraid. Perplexed at the sudden shift in attitude, but not alarmed – not the way Laurie was. Then again, she wasn't the one being growled at.

'Here, boy,' she called, taking a few more steps and holding out a hand. 'Come on, that's enough now.'

The dog's head swivelled briefly her way, as though checking it had heard correctly, then resumed its narrow-eyed surveillance of Laurie.

'Here,' Sam repeated, a little more forcefully. 'Now.'

This time, the dog whined but did as she commanded. Ears flattened to its black-and-white head, it slunk to her side and sat down, although Sam noticed it kept a suspicious gaze trained on Laurie.

'Sorry,' she said. 'You must have scared him.'

Some of the colour had returned to Laurie's cheeks, but he looked far from happy. '*Seriously* – I scared him? I thought he was going to take a chunk out of me.'

She glanced down at the dog, docile but wary. Maybe it wasn't such a good idea to leave him in the bar once the pub opened. 'I'll take him upstairs,' she said, making up her mind. 'Are you okay to open up?'

Laurie cast a mistrustful look in the stray's direction. 'Yes. As long as you keep the Hound of the Baskervilles away from me.'

Sam couldn't help smiling. 'The vet is coming after lunch. Hopefully, she'll be able to identify the owner and they can collect him.'

Her brother grunted but didn't move. It wasn't until Sam

reached the foot of the stairs, the dog at her heels, that she heard Laurie start to cross the room.

'You'll probably have to fumigate,' he called, as she made her way to the first floor. 'I bet it's got fleas and god knows what else.'

Recalling the bony body beneath the matted fur, Sam swallowed a sigh; Laurie was almost certainly right. She glanced at the dog and made a decision. 'How would you feel about a bath?' she asked brightly.

'Physically, he's not in bad shape.' Emily Bell finished her examination and stepped back to lean against the kitchen counter. 'Thin, obviously, and his muscle mass is a bit less than I'd expect for a dog his age. But considering he's probably been lost for at least a week, he doesn't look too bad. Especially after his bath.'

Sam managed a rueful smile, recalling how wet both she and the bathroom had been afterwards. 'He seemed to like it.'

Emily pulled a face. 'I'm not sure his fleas did, but it takes more than soap and warm water to get rid of them.' She paused, reaching into her bag and pulling out a handheld scanner. 'And now to find out who owns him.'

Sam watched as the vet passed the device across the dog's haunches and frowned. 'Something wrong?' she asked.

Emily tried again. 'That's weird. There's no chip.'

Now it was Sam's turn to frown. She didn't know much about owning a dog, but she did know that microchips were a legal requirement. 'But I thought all dogs were supposed to have them.'

'They are,' Emily said. 'But there's no Microchip Police, unfortunately. Technically, no one is responsible for enforcing the law – vets will insist on their patients having a microchip, but there's not much we can do if a client doesn't bring their animal to see us.'

Sam stared at the dog, who was sniffing Emily's trousers with interest. 'So now what?'

The vet sighed. 'I checked the database of missing pets to see if any dogs matching his description have been reported as lost, but I didn't get anything. The local shelter might have something – we should contact them next.'

'And if they don't?'

'Then they'll take him in and start the process of rehoming him.' Emily gave Sam a speculative look. 'They'll probably ask whether you're interested in having him, subject to satisfactory checks.'

Sam thought back to Laurie's terrified expression and shook her head regretfully. 'I don't think we can.'

Emily nodded. 'Don't worry. There's still a chance we'll find his rightful owner.'

'And everything can end happily ever after,' Sam said, dropping one hand to ruffle the dog's ears. 'Hang in there, boy.'

Chapter Thirty

'Oh no.'

Nessie stared down at the sheet of paper on the desk and felt a chilly sense of foreboding creep over her, in spite of the hot June sunshine that threatened to turn the small office into a sauna by lunchtime. How had she made such a stupid mistake?

Both Sam and Laurie looked up, but it was Sam who spoke first. 'Problem?'

'I think so,' Nessie said, flicking through the pages of her diary. 'Connor gave me his holiday dates a few weeks ago and I signed them off. Except that I must have looked at the diary for July, not June. And now we don't have a cellarman for Midsummer Merriment.'

Laurie shrugged. 'That's hardly a problem. I'll do it.'

An awkward silence filled the air, during which Nessie didn't dare look at Sam. Laurie was keen and desperate to get more involved with the day-to-day running of the Star and Sixpence, but there was still a lot he didn't know. And there was no way he could manage the cellar during what promised to be one of the busiest weekends of the year so far, especially not with the additional demands being made by the guest cidermakers taking part in the festival.

'We'd be happy for you to help out,' Sam said, her tone carefully encouraging. 'But managing the cellar while Connor is away will be a big responsibility, especially with the extra pressure of the cider festival. I'm not sure you're ready for it.'

Nessie's heart sank when she saw the bullish look that crossed Laurie's face. 'I don't suppose we could ask Joss, could we?' she asked Sam quickly. 'He did say he'd like to get more involved.'

Her sister sighed as one hand curled protectively around her bump. 'I think he meant with the baby, but he did mention the pub too, so I suppose he is the logical choice.'

Laurie stood up, pushing his chair back so fast that it screeched against the polished floorboards. '*I'm* the logical choice. I've watched Connor run the cellar for months now – I know everything he does. Why drag in a stranger when I can do the job with my eyes closed?'

He looked furious, Nessie thought, an emotion they seemed to see more and more frequently these days. 'Laurie—' she began, but Sam interrupted.

'Joss isn't a stranger – he knows our cellars better than anyone,' she said, her tone sharp. 'It's thanks to him that the Thirsty Bishop is an award-winner.'

'So it's got nothing to do with you wanting to play happy families?' Laurie countered. 'Nothing to do with you wanting to keep the father of your baby dangling while you flirt with Gabe?'

Sam's expression darkened. 'Can I remind you, *yet again*, that my relationship with Joss or Gabe is none of your business?' She glared at him, green eyes flashing with undisguised irritation. 'This is exactly why we won't give you more responsibility, Laurie – you throw a tantrum when you don't get your own way.'

Nessie wanted to groan out loud. Laurie's behaviour *was* toddler-like, but she could understand his frustration too; it was almost ten months since he'd revealed himself as the brother they hadn't known they had and he'd been working hard to prove himself for most of that time. And here they were basically saying they didn't trust him.

'Sam is right,' she said, summoning up what she hoped was the same sympathetic-but-firm look she used on Luke. 'But perhaps we could ask Joss to mentor you while he's here – get him to share his knowledge and assess whether he thinks you're ready to step into Connor's shoes next time?'

Laurie let out a snort of derision. 'Oh, please. Spare me the patronising bullshit – it's obvious you're both determined to treat me like a staff member instead of your brother.'

It was a grossly unfair accusation, Nessie thought, but she was beginning to recognise a pattern to Laurie's behaviour; he lashed out every time he felt he'd been slighted or overlooked. And it didn't take a psychologist to work out that was almost certainly the result of Laurie being abandoned by their father all those years ago. It might seem like water under the bridge, but Nessie knew Laurie was still nurturing his anger and the undercurrents of resentment ran deep. She had no doubt they also extended to Sam and herself; their father had left them the Star and Sixpence. He hadn't left anything at all to Laurie.

Sam cleared her throat. 'I'm sorry you feel that way, Laurie. But there's no room for negotiation on this – providing Joss is free, he'll be taking over the cellar while Connor is away.'

His glower was so fierce that Nessie half-expected him to throw something. 'One of these days you're going to need me for something,' he ground out. 'And you might find that I'm not so willing to help.'

He spun on his heels, slamming the door as he left and causing the clock on the wall to fall from its nail. It clattered to the floor. Nessie used the silence that followed to draw in a deep calming breath and let it out as slowly as she could.

'That temper is a problem,' Sam said, after a moment or two. 'He must get that from his mother.'

Nessie had to agree; when she looked back now, she saw that their father had often broken things around their childhood home, but it had been through the clumsiness that alcohol brought on, not rage. 'He'll calm down,' she told Sam. 'Give him some time.'

Her sister shook her head. 'But that's just it – I feel as though we're always giving him time, making allowances.

All that stuff about Gabe and Joss and me – it really is none of his business and I'm getting tired of telling him that.'

'It's hard for him too—'

Sam threw up her hands in exasperation. 'Don't defend him! Bloody hell, Ness, I know you've got the patience of a saint, but even you must see his behaviour has got to improve?'

Reluctantly, Nessie nodded. 'I'll speak to him.'

'Okay,' Sam said, although Nessie could tell from her tone that she didn't believe it would make the slightest bit of difference. 'And I'll contact Joss, see if he fancies moonlighting as our cellarman for a couple of weeks.'

'And if he doesn't?'

'Then we'll get someone in from one of the other pubs,' Sam replied. 'Or an agency. In fact, I'd rather roll those barrels myself than let Laurie do it.'

It was such a ridiculous statement that Nessie couldn't help smiling. 'Let's hope it doesn't come to that.'

Sam's lip twitched. 'I'm not sure I've got the biceps for it, to be honest.' She gave Nessie a sidelong look. 'Unlike Owen. Those blacksmith's muscles might come in very handy.'

'He'd help if we needed him to,' Nessie said. 'But the most he knows about Thirsty Bishop is how good it tastes. Joss is a much better man for the job.'

Her sister nodded and sighed. 'He might have his faults, but he's a superstar in the cellar.' She paused, as though thinking about Joss, then fixed Nessie with a direct look. 'There is something I wanted to talk to you about.'

'Oh?' Nessie tried her hardest not to tense. The last

time Sam had said words to that effect it had been to tell her she was pregnant, and the news had tipped both their worlds upside down. But it couldn't be anything that earth-shattering now. Could it?

Sam puffed out a breath. 'How do you feel about a pub dog?'

Nessie's tension deflated; she'd been expecting this, right from the moment she'd seen her sister's eyes soften as she stared at the stray she'd found in the garden just over a week earlier. 'I wouldn't be totally against it,' she said. 'Why?'

'The people at the shelter asked if we'd be willing to rehome the dog we found, if they couldn't locate his owners,' Sam said. 'And I had a message from them today to say they haven't had any luck. So I wondered . . .'

'Whether we'd adopt him instead?' Nessie shook her head in amused disbelief. 'Don't you think we're going to have enough to cope with over the coming months?'

Sam leaned forward. 'The baby isn't due until August – plenty of time to get a new pet settled in. And you know how much you and Owen love walking in the woods – you'd have a really good reason to sneak off with a dog to walk.'

Nessie almost laughed; Sam knew her weak spots all right. 'And how does Gabe feel about a new flatmate?'

'He's fine with it,' Sam said airily. 'I think he was even more smitten than I was, to be honest.'

'Then it's okay with me,' Nessie said. Her good humour faded slightly as she thought of something else. 'I'll tell you who won't be happy. Laurie.'

Sam's smile slipped a little too. 'He'll have to get over it.'

Her determination caused a ripple of uneasiness in Nessie. 'Sam—'

'He will,' Sam cut in. 'Okay, the dog was a little bit unsettled when they first met each other in the bar, but I'm sure that won't happen again.'

It wasn't just the dog who'd been unsettled, Nessie thought, but she knew better than to argue with her sister once she'd set her heart on something. 'When are you picking him up?' she said, surrendering to the inevitable.

'There's some paperwork to complete, and we need to have a visit to check we'll give him a good home,' Sam replied. 'But, all being well, we could be dog owners in around a week.'

'Just in time for the cider festival,' Nessie observed.

'Exactly,' Sam said, her eyes gleaming. 'We'll have to take it easy at first, but just think of all the fuss he'll get from the punters. He's going to be a huge hit.'

The satisfaction in her voice made Nessie eye her with some suspicion. 'A dog is for life, Sam. Not just PR.'

'I know that,' Sam said, sounding wounded. 'But there's no reason we can't make the most of him being here. I wonder if I can pitch an article to one of the broadsheets ...' She reached for her notebook and started scribbling down notes.

Nessie watched for a few seconds, then returned her attention to her own work. But moments later, she found herself staring into space, her mind returning to Laurie. His outbursts were definitely becoming more frequent. And short of giving him the responsibility he wasn't really ready for, she had no idea how to fix things.

'She doesn't look like a tarot reader.'

Martha's gaze was narrow as she studied the slender blonde-haired woman who was tucked away at a table in a shadowy corner of the Star and Sixpence. Nessie could see her point; she'd been expecting someone a little more mysterious-looking too, but there was no doubt Lydia Lake was doing a roaring trade among the pub's customers, especially for Thursday night. The Tarot Evening had been Sam's idea, of course, and Lydia had come highly recommended; Sam had hinted that she had a number of celebrity clients but had predictably refused to name names. And retired actress Ruby Cabernet, one of Little Monkham's very own celebrities, had been first in the queue to have her future told.

'Sam says she's good,' Nessie told Martha, placing a Silver Sixpence cocktail on the bar in front of the village baker. 'Are you going to cross her palm with silver?'

Martha let out a long sigh. 'Of course. I'm hoping she's going to predict a torrid affair with a tall, dark stranger.' She glanced sideways to where Gabe was chatting to Ruby. 'Or maybe a tall, dark chef.'

Nessie laughed. The truth was that Martha was very happily married to Rob, who ran the neighbouring butcher's shop. That didn't stop her flirting shamelessly with any man who caught her eye, however. Gabe took it all in his stride, as had Nick Borrowdale, the target of Martha's previous crush, and Rob just smiled, safe in the knowledge that his wife would be going home with him at the end of the night. 'How about a cute and cuddly butcher?' Nessie said, winking.

'You don't need the second sight to predict that,' Martha replied. 'A girl needs to dream a little, right?'

Ruby Cabernet sashayed up the bar in time to catch the last sentence. 'Absolutely right, darling.' Her eyes twinkled as she looked from Martha to Nessie. 'The lovely Lydia predicted wedding bells in my future. I'm not sure whether to tell Micky or not.'

Ruby had been devoted to Nessie and Sam's father until his death some four years earlier, but lately, she'd rekindled an old love affair with Micky Holiday, ex-lead singer of the world-famous Flames rock band. Both Sam and Nessie had doubted his decision to settle into retirement in Little Monkham, but he certainly showed no signs of missing his rock and roll lifestyle. It didn't seem beyond the realms of possibility that he might propose to Ruby, either; as far as Nessie could tell, they were besotted with each other.

Martha took a long sip of her cocktail and shook her head. 'Better let him think he came up with the idea all by himself,' she advised Ruby. 'I can't wait to see the size of the rock he buys you!'

Over the course of the evening, Nessie watched the steady flow of comings and goings at Lydia's table. Once or twice, she took advantage of a slight lull in the tarot reader's visitors to check she had something to drink, casting a curious look at the deck of cards as she did so. As closing time drew near, she was surprised to see Henry Fitzsimmons take a seat opposite Lydia. Her heart ached as she watched Lydia look up from the spread of cards to smile sadly at him.

'Poor Henry,' Sam said, materialising beside Nessie. 'Do you suppose he asked about Franny?'

It had been just over six weeks since Franny's tragic death and Henry had taken the loss of his wife hard. 'Probably,' Nessie replied, sighing. 'I hope Lydia is gentle with him.'

Sam placed a hand on her arm. 'I know you don't believe in it – I don't either. But I've heard enough about Lydia to know she's very good at what she does. I'm sure she'll be able to offer Henry some comfort.'

They watched as the tarot reader made a comment that elicited a smile from the white-haired man opposite her. Whatever she said made him sit up a little straighter too and by the time he got up to leave, Nessie thought he looked as though a weight had been lifted from his shoulders. 'Never mind predicting the future, Lydia should set up as a bereavement counsellor,' she murmured to Sam.

Her sister gave her a sidelong look. 'Fancy having yours done?' she said with an impish grin. 'I will if you will.'

Nessie felt her eyes widen. 'No!'

'Spoilsport,' Sam teased. 'What's the worst that can happen?'

It was a fair question, Nessie thought. Owen had been fascinated by the idea of getting his cards read, but he was a blacksmith and Welsh; Nessie often had the sense that there was something wild and magical buried beneath his practical exterior. But that didn't mean she was ready to let Lydia peek into her future.

'Nothing will happen,' she said to Sam, 'because it's not real.'

Sam cocked her head. 'Then there's no reason not to give it a whirl, is there?'

'Apart from the queue of paying customers,' Nessie pointed out. 'I'm sure Lydia will be exhausted by the time she's finished with them.'

But it seemed Sam wasn't letting Nessie off the hook. Once the door of the pub was firmly closed, she turned a meaningful look on her sister. 'Lydia says we can choose one card each.'

'Sam!' Nessie protested, with an embarrassed glance at the tarot reader. 'I'm sure she just wants to go home.'

The blonde woman smiled serenely and held out her pack of cards. 'Not at all. Shuffle the deck and think of what you want to ask, then spread the cards and select whichever you are most drawn to.'

There was no way Nessie could refuse, not without seeming rude. Deciding to have strong words with Sam later, she took the pack and did as Lydia instructed. And although she hadn't expected to feel anything as she spread the ornately-decorated cards face-down on the table, there was one her hand hovered over longer than the others. 'This one,' she said, placing it face down in front of Lydia.

'Ah,' Lydia said thoughtfully, once she'd turned the card over. 'The Moon.'

Nessie gazed at the image, which featured a woman's face in a full yellow moon. A wolf and a dog howled beneath it. At their feet, water lapped at a path that led into the mountains, and a scorpion waved its pincers as though trying to nip them. 'What does it mean?' she asked, before she could stop herself.

Lydia tilted her head. 'Illusion. Duality. Something is not as it seems. Or perhaps someone.'

Blinking in surprise, Nessie gazed into her clear blue eyes. 'What?'

The tarot reader pointed at the two towers that flanked the mountains. 'These can sometimes represent good and evil, and the difficulty of deciding which course of action will place us on the right path.' She sighed and peered more closely at the card. 'There is uncertainty and anxiety in your future, but you must trust in the light of the moon to reveal the truth to you. Your intuition will show you the way, if you allow yourself to trust it.'

Nessie nodded, trying to find some meaning in Lydia's words in spite of her determination not to. When it seemed there was no more to be said, she smiled. 'Thank you.'

Sam stepped forward eagerly. 'My turn,' she said, taking the gathered pack from Lydia and closing her eyes to shuffle it.

Lydia's face brightened as she turned Sam's card over. 'The Lovers,' she said, beaming with approval. 'A happy union is in your future.'

Was it Nessie's imagination or did Sam blush? 'Oh. Er ... good,' she mumbled, firing an embarrassed look Nessie's way.

Lydia's finger tapped at the colourful image, coming to rest on the handsome man. 'This card suggests a strong and lasting relationship is about to enter your life – a partnership that will both empower and enrich you. But it can also mean there is a choice to be made – perhaps between two potential suitors – and you must take the time to consider the options before making your decision.'

Sam's blush deepened. Nessie had no doubt what her sister's question had been, and she was clearly hoping that the happy union might be with Gabe, although there was the small matter of being pregnant with Joss's baby to consider. And the strangest thing was that it was unexpectedly accurate, Nessie thought; Lydia's prediction for Sam had been very near the mark, even though Nessie was sure the other woman couldn't have any idea what was going through Sam's head.

'Does that mean anything to you?' Lydia said, gathering up her cards.

Sam nodded. 'Yes. Thanks for doing it for us.'

Lydia smiled as she slipped the pack into a velvet bag and reached for her coat. 'A pleasure. Thank you for having me here tonight.'

'That wasn't at all weird, was it?' Sam asked when Lydia had left. 'Do you forgive me for making you do it?'

'Just about,' Nessie replied, smiling. 'No prizes for guessing what yours means.'

'No,' Sam admitted. 'I'm not sure I like the bit about making a choice, though. My baby brain is so bad that I can't even decide which socks to wear most mornings.'

Nessie pulled a face. 'Consider yourself lucky,' she said ruefully. 'At least you don't have a scorpion snapping at your feet.'

They finished clearing up. Yawning, Nessie made her way towards the door. 'See you tomorrow.'

'Sleep well,' Sam called back. 'Wait. You didn't tell me what your question was.'

'That's because the card I pulled didn't make any sense,' Nessie said. 'I wanted to know what to do about Laurie.'

Sam frowned. 'Oh. Yeah, that doesn't make any sense.'

'Just as I expected,' Nessie said, shrugging. 'Night, Sam.'

Chapter Thirty-one

'Have you got a minute, Nessie?'

She looked up to see Connor hovering in the office doorway, his large frame taking up most of the space. He was frowning in a way that made Nessie's heart sink; as an ex-firefighter, Connor usually took everything in his stride and it was rare for him to trouble Sam or Nessie. Something must be wrong.

'Of course,' Nessie said, twisting in her seat to face him. 'What's up?'

'That delivery that arrived from the brewery just now . . .' He paused and looked even more puzzled. 'Is there any reason you ordered double what we needed?'

Nessie felt her mouth fall open. 'Double? What are you talking about?' She reached for the lever arch folder where she kept copies of all the pub's orders. 'It should have been a standard Monday delivery.'

Connor shrugged. 'And it was – just twice as much as

usual. I'm struggling to find room for everything in the cellar – come and see for yourself. It's like Tetris down there.'

She shook her head in bewilderment as she flicked through the paperwork. 'No, I believe you. But I don't understand how it's happened – I placed the order on Friday morning, right after the Tarot Evening.' She pointed at a sheet of paper in the folder. 'Look – here it is.'

Connor took a few steps forwards and dutifully scanned the order. 'Looks like exactly half of what came. I had to send three barrels of Thirsty Bishop back.'

'Maybe the order was duplicated somehow,' Nessie said. She picked up her phone. 'Let me give them a ring.'

The mystery was solved by the brewery's sales rep a few moments later: the email containing Nessie's order had been delivered once, at nine-twenty on Friday morning, and then it had arrived again just after midday. The automated ordering system hadn't been clever enough to realise the same order had been placed twice, hence the double quantities.

'I'm so sorry,' the sales rep's voice crackled on speakerphone. 'The system is programmed to flag up two identical orders that come through within seconds of each other. But there were a few hours between these two, so it would have treated them as separate requests.'

Nessie ran a weary hand over her face. 'I've got no idea how it happened. A glitch in the matrix, I suppose.'

The sales rep apologised again and Nessie rang off. 'It's not the end of the world, I suppose,' she said to Connor. 'We can probably find somewhere secure to stash the wine and spirits for a week or so. It's a good thing you sent the Bishop back.'

'No choice,' Connor replied. 'There's not enough room to swing a cat, let alone squeeze in three barrels of beer.'

'Squeeze in as much as you can,' Nessie said sympathetically. 'I'll see what I can sort out for the stuff you don't have room for.'

A few calls later, Nessie was satisfied that she'd found a secure location for the excess alcohol and set about going through the Star and Sixpence messages to see if she could work out what had gone wrong. Sure enough, there were two emails showing in the Sent Items folder, their date stamps matching the times given by the brewery's sales rep. Nessie had no idea how they'd come to be duplicated; it had never happened before. But hopefully it was a one-off anomaly – no real harm had been done.

'At least it will come in handy for the cider festival,' Sam said later that morning, when Nessie explained what had happened. 'It's not as though alcohol is perishable.'

'True,' Nessie replied. 'But I'm not sure there's space for Connor in the cellar.'

Sam shrugged cheerfully. 'We'll just have to think of a way to encourage everyone to drink more. It shouldn't be a problem now that the weather is warming up.'

It was true; after a dismal rainy May, the sun seemed to be winning the battle to bring summer to the country and the Met Office was predicting soaring temperatures for the end of June.

'Maybe our new member of staff will help too,' Nessie said with a smile. 'When are you picking him up?'

Sam's eyes gleamed. 'Tomorrow morning. Gabe and I will drive over to the shelter first thing. I think we'll keep him upstairs for a few days, until he gets used to being around us, and then we can bring him downstairs for short bursts.'

'I hope he'll be allowed visitors,' Nessie said. 'I know a nine-year-old boy who is – and I quote – "epically excited" to meet him.'

'Of course,' Sam replied. 'And we'll need to give him a new name – maybe Luke can help with that?'

'I'm sure he can,' Nessie said, imagining how thrilled Luke would be with the news. 'As long as you don't mind him being named after some weird character from an online game that no one over the age of fifteen understands?'

Sam laughed. 'Good point. Maybe we'll take suggestions and put it to a vote.'

'Very wise,' Nessie said. She paused. 'How did Laurie react when you told him?'

'I – erm – thought we'd surprise him,' Sam said, not quite able to meet Nessie's gaze.

Nessie blinked at her sister in dismay. 'That's possibly the worst idea you've ever had. What if he's dog-phobic? Or allergic to them?'

'He told me he had a dog when he was growing up. So he can't have a phobia or an allergy.'

'Unless they developed recently,' Nessie suggested. 'All I'm saying is that you should mention it anyway, to be on the safe side. I'm sure you've told Connor and Tilly.'

'Neither of whom had a problem,' Sam said, raising her chin in a defiant gesture Nessie recognised well. 'And, actually, I don't need Laurie's permission to get a dog.'

Nessie raised her hands placatingly. 'Of course you don't. But this is about common sense and courtesy, not permission.'

'You tell him, then,' Sam said. 'I think he'd accept it coming from you.'

The idea was so ridiculous that Nessie almost laughed. 'Don't be daft. I don't think Laurie sees either of us as being in charge.'

Sam fell silent for a moment. 'Doesn't that strike you as odd?'

And now that she came to think about it, Nessie had to admit that it did. 'A bit.'

'Me too,' Sam said. 'So you'll understand why I'm not prepared to let him stand in the way of something that will be good for everyone else involved.'

It was a fair point, Nessie had to concede; there were lots of plusses to having a pub dog and only one negative. Perhaps Sam was right and Laurie would come round to the idea eventually. The question was, how long would it take him to get there?

'You can't call him Stumpy,' Sam told Luke on Tuesday evening, as he reached down for the hundredth time to ruffle the Border collie's ears. 'I don't care how much he looks like something from your game.'

Luke looked disappointed and Sam thanked her lucky stars that Nessie had given her a heads-up about the kind of names he might put forward; the suggestion had been innocent enough, but Sam could just imagine the outright sniggers among the pub's patrons if they named the poor creature Stumpy.

'Keep thinking,' Nessie said, with an encouraging nod. 'If you had a dog of your own what sort of name would you choose?'

He leaned back against the sofa and screwed up his freckled nose in concentration. 'If he was a girl, I'd say Twinkle. Like the star in the Star and Sixpence.'

Sam gazed down at the dog, remembering the way he'd bounded around the village green earlier that day, apparently determined to sniff every blade of grass and greet every passer-by he saw. He was already looking much healthier than he had when she'd first found him; his brown eyes shone and his coat was glossy. But regardless of sex, Twinkle didn't seem like the right name for him.

'How about Blackheart?' Luke suggested. 'After Elijah.'

He meant the ghost who was rumoured to haunt the pub, dating back to the sixteenth century when it had been a coaching inn and allegedly frequented by one particular highwayman. Sam had spent many nights alone in the building and had never noticed even a hint of a supernatural presence, but she wasn't above encouraging the rumours for the benefit of ghost-hunting guests in the bed-and-breakfast rooms in the attic.

'But he's so friendly,' Nessie said, as the dog thumped his tail on the floor. 'Blackheart makes him sound like a villain.'

Luke glanced impatiently around the living room. 'I don't know. Spidey. Hawkeye. Steve.' His eyes brightened. 'Bucky.'

'Bucky isn't bad,' Sam said, slowly. 'Is that from your game too?'

'No, from the Marvel comics. He's Steve Rogers' best friend,' Luke said, the words tumbling out fast. 'He's loyal and protective and looks after him . . .'

'Those are good, dog-like characteristics,' Sam mused, casting a covert sideways look at Nessie for confirmation.

'And then he gets captured by Hydra and they give him a metal arm,' Luke said, warming to his theme. 'He becomes this deadly assassin who no one can defeat, except for Steve when he becomes Captain America. And he almost kills Nick Fury but he escapes at the last minute.'

'Maybe we won't mention that bit,' Sam said, laughing. She tilted her head at Nessie. 'What do you think – is Bucky a good name?'

Nessie opened her mouth to reply, but the dog cut her off with a single enthusiastic bark. 'I think that's a yes,' she said, grinning. 'Welcome to the Star and Sixpence, Bucky. I think you're going to fit right in.'

Beaming, Luke jumped off the sofa to bury his face in the dog's black-and-white fur. 'This is going to be awesome!'

Sam watched Bucky lick his face and smiled. All they had to do now was convince Laurie . . .

*

Laurie's face was stony when Sam took him to one side later that evening.

'It doesn't look like I've got much choice,' he said, when she explained. 'Although an employment tribunal might take a dim view of your actions.'

She stared at him, genuinely shocked. 'An employment tribunal? What on earth are you talking about?'

He shrugged. 'You failed to ask whether introducing a dog to the workplace might cause me health problems. For all you know, I might be allergic or have mental health issues that might be triggered by having to face a dog every day.'

It was so ridiculous that Sam wanted to laugh. And yet she could tell from her brother's expression that he was serious. 'You told me you had a pet dog when you were younger,' she said. 'I assumed that meant you weren't allergic to them. Are you?'

'No, but that's not the point,' Laurie said, frowning. 'You didn't check – you just went ahead with your own plans. And, as it happens, I do like dogs. Just not that dog.'

Sam shook her head, nonplussed. 'So you're going to take us to an employment tribunal over it?'

'Of course not,' he replied, glaring at her. 'My point is that you didn't ask, Sam. It's like I said the other day – what I want or think doesn't seem to matter around here. And I'm sick of it. I think you owe me an apology.'

Sam took in the self-righteous anger behind Laurie's eyes, battling her own irritation. Was that all he wanted – an apology?

'I'm sorry I didn't check with you first,' she said, after a long calming breath. 'I'm sorry we overlooked your feelings.'

His smile was instant, transforming his face from sulky to sunny in less than a heartbeat. 'There, that wasn't so bad, was it?'

Sam had to dig deep to find an answering smile. It felt thin and insincere. 'Bucky will be upstairs for the next few days, so he won't be under your feet.'

'Good,' Laurie said, turning his back to leave the office with an air of finality. 'The less our paths cross, the better.'

Chapter Thirty-two

'If it's no good, you can always send it back.'

Nessie stopped pushing the steak and kidney pudding around her plate and blinked at Owen. 'Sorry?'

'The food,' he said, nodding at the fork in her hand. 'You've hardly eaten any of it. Isn't it up to standard?'

Nessie felt the start of an embarrassed blush creep up her cheeks. Owen had booked a table at the Prancing Pony on her request, because Gabe had raved about the chef and his menu, and here she was behaving as though the meal she'd been presented with wasn't melt-in-the-mouth delicious. 'No, it's fine,' she said, glancing guiltily around the busy restaurant in case the staff had noticed her less-than-enthusiastic response. 'How's yours?'

Owen waved a hand at the almost empty plate in front of him. 'I've no complaints.'

With another wary look at the Friday night diners around

them, Nessie took another mouthful of the pudding, savouring the steak that fell apart the moment she began to chew and the suet pastry that had no business being as light as it was. Gabe had been right: the food was to die for. And now she felt even more guilty for giving it, and Owen, less than her full attention.

'Sorry,' she said, once she'd finished chewing. 'I'm terrible company tonight.'

Owen's forehead creased as he regarded her with concern. 'You couldn't be bad company if you tried. Quiet, maybe. A little preoccupied.'

Nessie groaned. 'I'm sorry. Our first date in over a month and I'm ruining it.'

'Stop,' Owen said, reaching across the pristine white tablecloth to take her hand. 'You're not ruining anything. I know work has been getting on top of you lately – that's one of the reasons I suggested a night out, to give you some space. And I'm always happy to listen. You know what they say – a problem shared ...'

'Is a problem that has two people worrying about it instead of just one,' Nessie said, but she felt the start of a smile pulling at the corner of her mouth. Maybe talking to Owen about the mountain of mistakes she seemed to be piling up would help to get things in perspective. 'You're going to think I'm a total idiot.'

'Never,' Owen said solemnly, squeezing her fingers.

'Not even when I remind you that I somehow managed to send the same order twice to the brewery,' Nessie said. 'Or that I forgot I'd reset the password for their online portal and locked myself out yesterday.'

Owen sipped his pint. 'Worse things happen.'

'I haven't finished,' Nessie replied, sighing wearily. 'I gave Gabe the wrong breakfast orders for the B and B guests this morning, and then somehow managed to lose my car keys for almost an hour when it was time to go to the wholesalers. Honestly, I think I might be losing the plot.'

'You're not losing anything,' Owen observed thoughtfully, once Nessie had petered out into red-faced silence. 'You've just got too much going on. It's partly my fault – you're so good with Luke that I've let some of my responsibilities become yours.'

A wave of discomfort washed over her. 'No, that isn't what I mean at all – I love looking after Luke.'

He smiled. 'I know you do. But there's no denying you do a lot to keep our lives running smoothly. It used to drive Kathryn crazy when she lived with us – all the things she did that I didn't even notice. The mental load, she called it.'

Kathryn was Owen's irrepressibly blunt younger sister and Nessie could practically hear her explaining the phrase at length.

'What I'm saying is that I don't want you to feel you have to carry that load,' Owen went on, his dark eyes warm. 'Let's share it.'

The trouble was that it wasn't her home life that she needed help with, Nessie thought. But the stresses and strains of running the Star and Sixpence definitely weren't Owen's problem and he was offering what he could to help.

'You're a good man, Owen Rhys,' she said, smiling.

'Not as good as I should be,' he replied with a shrug. 'But I'm always happy to raise my game. For you.'

There was something about the way he looked at her then that sent a tiny shiver of anticipation down Nessie's spine. Suddenly, she couldn't wait to get back to Snowdrop Cottage.

'Your game is already strong,' she told him, placing her knife and fork together on her plate. 'Shall we skip dessert?'

It was still dark when Sam woke up. At first, she wasn't sure what had disturbed her; the inky blackness was so complete that she knew dawn was still a few hours away. She lay for a few seconds, feeling the baby kick as she waited for her quickened heartbeat to slow down, and the sound of a muffled bark solved the mystery. Bucky had settled in perfectly in the week since Sam and Gabe had collected him and seemed more than happy with his bed in the living room. In fact, Sam thought as another woof broke the silence, this was the first time she'd heard him bark. She frowned; it didn't sound as though he was in the living room, though. It sounded as though he was—

'Sam?' Gabe's voice was low outside her bedroom door. 'Are you awake?'

Pushing back the covers, Sam padded across the room. 'I am now,' she said, opening the door.

He stood in a T-shirt and boxer shorts, his cheek still creased from sleep, and Sam felt the usual sharp burst of heat radiate from deep inside her. She'd slept mere centimetres away from that face once, listening to his steady breath punctuate the night and wishing she could put her arms around him. It seemed like a half-remembered dream now, although she often thought of it.

'Bucky is downstairs,' Gabe said, his expression wary and tense. 'I think there's someone in the kitchen.'

A spike of adrenaline caused Sam's heart to thud again. 'Are you sure?'

Gabe nodded. 'I can hear them moving around. And Bucky has been barking like crazy for around ten minutes.'

Sam considered their options. Gabe was tall and strong, but if someone had broken in, she wouldn't be much help. 'We should call the police.'

'They won't get here in time,' Gabe replied grimly. 'You wait here – I'll take Bucky and see if we can scare them off.'

'Not a chance,' Sam said, with a firm shake of her head. 'At the very least, let me call Owen. He's only got to cross the yard to be here.'

'No time,' Gabe whispered, heading for the stairs that led to the bar. 'Stay here.'

Before she could stop him, he was gone, leaving Sam shivering with anxiety. She strained her ears, catching a creak as Gabe reached the bottom of the staircase and a faint whimper from Bucky, then there was silence. A few more seconds ticked by, during which she imagined Gabe grappling with the intruder. Bucky let out a volley of excited barks and suddenly Sam couldn't stand it any longer. Pausing only to grab her phone from the bedside table, she hurried downstairs as fast as she could.

The kitchen was fully lit. Gabe stood at the furthest end, gazing into the storeroom, and Bucky was still barking and growling furiously, although all Sam could see of him was his bristling tail. Had the burglar hidden in the cupboard, she wondered as she ventured forward. 'Gabe? What's going on?'

He turned around and she saw his expression was set. 'We've got a big problem,' he said. 'Our intruder is a rat.'

Sam's mouth fell open in dismay. 'A rat? But how – when?'

'I've got no idea,' Gabe said. 'It scurried across the floor when Bucky and I came in here.'

'We've never had rats before.' Sam shook her head. 'Not even a hint of them.'

'Me either,' he said. 'You know I run a clean kitchen – all the food is put away at the end of the night and this store cupboard is usually locked. But tonight, the door was open – I can only assume that's what attracted our visitor.'

'What are we going to do?' Sam asked, her gaze shifting to Bucky. 'Can we catch it?'

'*We* are not going to do anything,' he said, in a tone that suggested no argument. 'Rats carry diseases, Sam. You are going to wait in the bar while I decide how to trap it until we can get expert advice.'

An involuntary shiver ran down Sam's spine. She wasn't scared of rats, but she had to admit the thought of them scurrying around made her stomach churn. 'What if there's more than one?'

Gabe shook his head. 'I haven't seen any evidence of that, but I suppose we'll have to cross that bridge when we get to it. Right now, Bucky and I need to deal with this one.'

She hesitated for a moment; technically, she was Gabe's boss – shouldn't she stay near at hand to offer moral support? But then there was a flurry of frenzied scrabbling inside the cupboard and Bucky's growls grew fiercer and Sam decided that Gabe was more than capable of managing the problem. She fled to the bar.

A few minutes passed before Gabe joined her, a still-wary Bucky at his heels. 'The cupboard is locked and I've plugged up any gaps with some hessian sacks. I can't really do more than that until the morning.'

Sam eyed the solid kitchen door with some trepidation. 'Do you think it might come in here?'

Gabe frowned as he considered the question. 'I think it's unlikely. But we don't actually know how it got into the building in the first place. Perhaps there's a nest somewhere we don't know about—' He saw her expression. 'Or maybe he's working alone and just found a way into the kitchen tonight. We'll have to call in a pest specialist to know for sure.'

The implications were not lost on Sam. She swallowed a groan. 'Are we going to have to close down until that happens?'

'The kitchens, yes,' Gabe replied without hesitation. 'Everything will need to be cleaned, preventative measures have to be taken and any entry points must be closed so that this doesn't happen again.'

She glanced around the now brightly lit bar, her worst fears confirmed. 'And the pub itself?'

'It depends what the experts say,' Gabe answered, and stifled a yawn. 'We should be able to get an emergency visit in the morning.'

His yawn was catching; Sam covered her mouth in embarrassment as she gave in to the sudden wave of tiredness. 'We should go to bed.'

He gave her a knowing look. 'Will you be able to sleep?'

'Of course,' she replied indignantly. 'I'm not scared. Besides, I'll have Bucky to defend me.'

Gabe studied her for a moment, and for a few wild seconds she wondered whether he was going to offer to share a bed again. But then he nodded. 'He'll probably sleep better in your room. We'll close the door at the foot of the stairs too, in case he decides to go on rat patrol again.'

Sam dropped a hand to stroke the dog's silky ears and he wagged his tail in response. 'Come on, then,' she told him. 'Let's try and get some rest, shall we?'

Back on the landing, Gabe stopped outside her bedroom door. 'There's really nothing to worry about.'

'I know,' Sam said. She pulled a wry face. 'See you in a few hours.'

He smiled. 'Yes. Sleep well.'

It was quite ridiculous, but Sam had to admit she felt happier knowing Bucky was lying on the floor beside her bed. Not as happy as she would have been with Gabe next to her, but at least this way was less complicated. And given the tumult of feelings that coursed through her whenever she spent time with Gabe these days, complication was probably something she needed to work harder to avoid.

Keith from Simply the Pest puffed out a long breath and scratched his head in obvious bewilderment. 'What you've got here,' he said, flicking on a torch to peer underneath the stainless-steel units that lined the kitchen walls, 'is a genuine locked-room mystery.'

Sam and Nessie exchanged uncertain looks, while Gabe looked equally puzzled. 'In what way?' Sam asked, politely hiding her scepticism.

Keith got to his feet and tracked back to the storage cupboard, now conspicuously empty of its nocturnal visitor. 'I've been doing this job for twenty years, so I know what I'm talking about,' he said. 'And I can't for the life of me work out how it got in. There're no gnawed floorboards. No damage to any of the walls that I can see. It's a mystery, right enough.'

'Could ... could it have used the back door?' Sam asked, hoping she didn't sound as stupid as she felt. 'If it was left open, I mean?'

'Unlikely,' Keith said. 'With all due respect, this isn't Disney. Rats don't generally saunter in like they own the place. And there's no droppings, or urine, other than in the cupboard where your intruder spent the night. No sign of an infestation at all.'

Nessie cleared her throat. 'That's good news, at least. So what happens now?'

Keith shrugged. 'I'll check the rest of the premises. Then we can talk about preventative measures and you can make a start on disinfecting the place.'

Sam's nose wrinkled; she didn't want to think about what preventative measures meant. 'Can you recommend a good industrial cleaning company?'

'I can,' Keith said. 'Don't you worry – we'll have this sorted and get you open again within twenty-four hours. Now, who's going to give me the tour?'

'Follow me,' Gabe said, before either Sam or Nessie could reply, and he led the man out of the kitchen.

'What a nightmare,' Nessie said, glancing into the cupboard with a shudder. 'I'm sorry you had to deal with it on your own.'

'I wasn't on my own,' Sam pointed out. 'Gabe pretty much took care of everything. The worst part was imagining it creeping up the stairs, but I was far too tired to worry about that for more than ten seconds.'

Nessie managed a weak smile. 'I suppose we should be glad it wasn't on Friday – we'd have lost all the weekend trade.'

'Or nearer to the weekend coming,' Sam replied. 'We'd have had to cancel the cider festival.'

'It doesn't bear thinking about,' Nessie said grimly. 'I think we got lucky.'

Sam thought back to the sound of tiny claws scuttling across the tiled floor and shuddered. 'I'll tell you what was lucky – having Bucky here. I think he's more than earned his place on the team – even Laurie can't argue.'

Nessie let out a heartfelt sigh. 'If only that was true. I'm starting to think he'd argue the sky was green if he thought there was something in it for him.'

Sam eyed her sister in surprise; Nessie had always been the one who'd suggested they cut Laurie some slack and give him a chance. Could her patience finally be running out?

'Not this time,' Sam said firmly. 'Bucky stays, just in case our visitor has some friends after all.'

'Of course he's staying,' Nessie responded with a smile. 'I just hope he doesn't demand a pay rise!'

Chapter Thirty-three

The closure of the pub while they dealt with the rat issue caused no end of speculation among the villagers. In the past, Nessie would simply have confided the truth to Franny and relied on her to spread the news in a way that would limit any damage to their reputation, but that was sadly no longer an option; the new postmistress was pleasant and well-organised, but she wasn't Chairwoman of the Little Monkham Preservation Society, and her sphere of influence didn't extend much past how much a first-class parcel to London might cost. All of which meant Nessie had to field curious questions from every villager she encountered on Monday afternoon and Tuesday morning.

'Just some emergency maintenance,' she said, ensuring her crossed fingers were hidden from sight. 'Don't worry, we'll be up and running in good time for the cider festival!'

Joss was due to arrive on Wednesday to take over Connor's duties. Nessie and Sam had already agreed that they wouldn't hide the rat encounter from him; apart from anything else, he needed to know that there were now humane traps down in the cellar, along with less-humane poison, safely tucked out of harm's way in the kitchen. Both sisters had argued hard with Gabe about the need for such cruel methods, but he had been insistent that the health of his customers must come first. And when he'd put it like that, Nessie had found it almost impossible to stand her ground.

'Rats?' Joss said when Nessie called him into the office to explain the situation. His fair eyebrows beetled in astonishment. 'I've never known this place to have trouble with any kind of rodent before. Has your fancy new chef been leaving food out?'

His tone was level, but Nessie thought she detected the faintest hint of something altogether less professional underneath. She shouldn't be surprised; Joss had always been unnecessarily jealous where Sam was concerned and he'd clearly worked out that a good-looking chef living on the premises might catch her eye. Nessie paused, wondering whether it was something she needed to address right away, and then decided it could wait. It wasn't as though Sam and Joss were in any danger of rekindling their relationship, after all. She was having his baby, nothing more.

'Rat singular,' Nessie corrected Joss in a low voice. 'And no sign of any more, thankfully.'

Joss frowned. 'Just one? That's weird.'

'That's what the pest control man said,' Nessie said. 'But

maybe we just caught things early. Anyway, we're all clear for now – I just thought you should be aware.'

'Noted,' Joss said, nodding. 'Anything else I need to know?'

Nessie hesitated again, then sighed. 'I should probably tell you that Laurie isn't exactly over the moon that you're here. Just in case you pick up any . . . hostility.'

Joss grinned. 'Let me guess – he thinks he can run the cellar while Connor is away.'

'Got it in one,' Nessie confirmed. 'And I think it's something he could definitely do, in the future. But not right now. And not when we've got ten independent cider makers arriving on Friday, plus a gaggle of apple aficionados, and who knows what else?'

'Don't worry,' Joss said, 'I'll go easy on Laurie.'

'Great,' Nessie said, observing once again that he hadn't extended a similar professional courtesy to Gabe. 'Let me show you to the living room – a brand new sofa bed awaits!'

If Sam had noticed the tension in Joss's body language where Gabe was concerned, she didn't say anything to Nessie. In fact, she was being resolutely positive about his presence, even though Nessie knew it must be weird to be living right next door to him again. Gabe, on the other hand, had definitely noticed something was off with Joss – he'd mentioned it to Nessie once, after Franny's funeral, and had never asked about the former cellarman again, although he was as professional and polite as always. It was something else that kept Nessie awake at night but providing Joss could keep his jealousy under control for as long as it took to get the job done, maybe disaster could be avoided. She hoped, anyway.

Friday was the summer solstice – a day Nessie wasn't sure she'd ever really paid much attention to before she'd fallen for a blacksmith. Both the solstices were important to Owen; he made sure she had a yule log to mark the winter festival and he'd marked the summer one on the family calendar in red. So Nessie wasn't surprised when he leaned over to her side of the bed on Friday morning to kiss her and declare, 'Happy Solstice.'

'And to you,' she replied, smiling. 'May the sun shine all day.'

His dark eyes crinkled with approval. 'I certainly hope so. I've got something special lined up for us.'

Nessie's pleasure was replaced by an instant buzz of anxiety. 'I can't do anything today, Owen. The cider festival starts this afternoon – there are a million and one jobs to be done.'

'Nothing that can't wait,' he said, his voice even but firm. 'I've spoken to Sam and she says she can spare you for a few hours at lunchtime. No arguments – meet me by the back door at midday.'

Nessie swallowed the protests that were jostling on her tongue; what on earth was Sam playing at when they were so busy? But it wasn't the first time her sister had conspired to get her together with Owen and Nessie knew when she'd been outmanoeuvred. 'Okay. Two hours and no more.'

The morning whirled by in a flurry of last-minute panic and worries as the cider festival started to take shape. The village green was taken over by a large marquee that would house the cider makers and form the hub of the festival. In the evenings, the space in the centre of the huge white tent would become a dance floor, playing host to a number of local bands, plus Owen's sister's band, Sonic Folk, as the headline act on Saturday night. Micky Holiday had even promised to perform with Kathryn and Nessie knew she was beyond excited at the prospect.

'You and half the village,' Nessie had told Kathryn when she'd rung to confirm the band would be arriving midway through Saturday. 'Martha has had T-shirts printed for her and Ruby that say "Sonic Flames". I think she's imagining a worldwide tour!'

Joss had slipped into his old role with the minimum of fuss and the consummate skill of someone who was at the top of their game, much to Nessie's relief. She watched him liaise with the cider makers in the marquee, ensuring they had everything they needed and double-checking their pumps were primed and ready to supply the hordes of thirsty visitors set to descend on Little Monkham. What would they have done without him, she wondered, trying not to imagine the chaos that Laurie might have caused. In the kitchen, Gabe had finally taken delivery of ingredients for the special Sausage Fest menu he'd planned to go across the weekend; Nessie spent even more hours awake the night before wondering whether she'd somehow managed to get that order wrong too. It had been a relief when it turned up, all present and correct, just before she left to meet Owen at midday.

She knew what he had planned the moment she saw him, picnic hamper in hand and a tartan rug tucked under his arm. 'Let me take that,' she said, reaching for the hamper, but he swung it out of her reach.

'You're in charge of the drinks,' he said, tilting his head towards another bag on the ground beside the back door of Snowdrop Cottage. 'Try not to shake it up too much.'

Champagne, Nessie thought, when she saw the foiled bottle top poking out of the bag and a little shiver of delight ran through her. 'I'll do my best,' she said gravely. 'Where are we going?'

'You'll see,' Owen said. 'Ready?'

The sun was hot and there wasn't a cloud in the sky; the Met Office had been as good as their word with the pre-dicted heatwave. Nessie fanned her face as Owen led her alongside the village green, past Martha's bakery and St Mary's Church, and across the bridge that spanned the river. She knew where they were going long before he turned off into the blissfully cool woods; how long had it been since they'd last done this – it must be well over a year, surely, and maybe even two?

'I wonder if we'll see Squirrel Nutkin again,' she said, as the green canopy over their heads rustled and shimmered in the slight breeze. 'Do you remember?'

He glanced at her then and the warmth of his gaze caused her cheeks to heat up. 'I remember.'

It had been their first date, Nessie thought, although it hadn't felt like one at the time. Sam and Kathryn had manipulated Owen into taking her for a walk in the woods; the two matchmakers had even packed a surprise picnic, in the hope that it might encourage romance to bloom. And Owen had kissed her for the first time then too, before being overcome with guilt about his dead wife, Eliza. They were taking the same route today, Nessie realised with a jolt. Surely Owen didn't mean to have their picnic by the same waterfall as before?

'I'm sure you recognise the path,' Owen said, glancing at her as though reading her mind. 'But so much has changed since the last time we were here. I hope it doesn't make you uncomfortable.'

She opened her mouth to reassure him, but the right words didn't come. 'A bit,' she said, and instantly wished she could take it back. 'What I mean is, I know this was a special place for you and Eliza. I don't want to intrude on your memories, that's all.'

Owen was quiet for a moment. 'I've thought about the time you and I came here quite a lot lately,' he said eventually, his lilting voice solemn. 'And I don't think I was very fair to you, Nessie. In fact, I often wish I had a time machine so I could go back and do it all differently.'

Nessie held her breath, waiting for him to go on, but he was silent as they turned the corner and the crystal-clear waterfall came into view, exactly as she remembered. There'd been a carpet of bluebells then; she could still see flashes of colour here and there, but it was later in the year than it had been before. The scene was no less beautiful, however, and she took a moment to savour it.

'This way,' Owen said and guided her across the rocks to the exact spot he'd laid the picnic blanket last time.

Nessie tried to squash her anxiety. She didn't dare speak as they unpacked, sensing that Owen had more to say. But it wasn't until he'd popped the cork on the champagne and handed her a brimming glass of golden buttery bubbles that he seemed ready to continue.

'I used to think Eliza was here,' he said, gazing at the babbling water that tumbled across the slick grey stones. 'And maybe she was, for a while. But she wasn't here the day we had our first picnic and . . . well, I'm not proud to admit that I used her memory as an excuse. I knew I'd fallen in love with you, but I was too scared to acknowledge it. So I let myself believe it was too soon to meet someone else. And I treated you badly.'

His forehead was heavy with lines that Nessie longed to smooth away. 'It doesn't matter,' she said, feeling her own anxiety lessen as she understood at last. 'None of that matters now.'

'Except that it does,' Owen insisted. 'I'll never forget Eliza – how could I when I see her every time I look at Luke? But I think it's time I stopped hiding behind her.'

Nessie's eyes misted up as she studied him. 'I would never expect you to forget her, Owen. And I'll always be grateful to her for Luke – he's such a wonderful boy and I am so very honoured to be part of his life.'

Owen managed a wavering smile. 'Thank you. I know he loves you too, in the same way that he loved Eliza.' He paused and took a deep breath. 'But I also think it's time to let the past go, once and for all.'

Placing his glass on a nearby rock, he reached in his pocket. Nessie felt a stab of mingled shock and unreality as she saw the small, emerald-green velvet box nestled in his palm.

'I love you, Nessie Chapman,' he said, lifting the lid to reveal a sparkling emerald and diamond ring. 'Will you marry me?'

She almost dropped her glass of champagne as she stared first at him and then at the ring. The breath caught in her lungs, she couldn't speak. The air around her seemed to freeze. The birds stopped singing. And then a gurgle of wild delight bubbled up from somewhere deep inside and she gasped out her reply. 'Yes! Oh, yes, I will!'

The glass was taken from her hand then and Owen was kissing her, his lips gentle and adoring. Seconds later, he drew back and took her left hand in his, easing the ring onto the third finger where it sat as though it had been made for her. She gazed at it in awe for a moment, then up at him. 'Is this real?'

He smiled and kissed her again. 'I hope it's real. I've been waiting a long time to ask that question. I'm glad you said yes.'

Letting go of her hand, he collected the champagne flutes again and passed one to her. 'Here's to new memories,' he said, touching his glass to hers.

'Here's to us,' she whispered back, as tears of joy tumbled down her cheeks.

Chapter Thirty-four

It took Sam less than five minutes to work out what was different about Nessie when she came back after the picnic. The first clue was her slightly dazed expression; for a few seconds, Sam worried she and Owen had fallen out again, but there was a glow in her sister's eyes that suggested otherwise. Maybe they'd done more than just picnic in the fresh air, she thought in amusement; *good for them*. And then Nessie reached for a pint glass to serve Henry and a flash of green caught Sam's eye. She swallowed a squeak of excitement, checking to make sure it had been Nessie's left hand, and then hovered impatiently at her elbow until she'd finished serving Henry.

'What?' Nessie said, meeting Sam's avid gaze with an air of not-quite-suppressed happiness.

'You need to take a coffee break,' Sam said in a firm tone.

Nessie laughed. 'I've only just come back from lunch!'

Sam glanced along the bar to where Tilly and Laurie were

chatting with Father Goodluck. 'They can manage for a few minutes.' Her gaze dropped to the ring sparkling on Nessie's finger. 'I want to hear every detail. Every single one.'

A hint of rosy pink tinged Nessie's cheeks and she buried her hand behind her back. 'I don't know what you mean.'

'It's far too late for that,' Sam said, grinning. She ran a hand over her swollen belly. 'Come on. If I can't have a love life of my own, at least I can get a vicarious thrill through yours.'

Nessie refused to say a word until they were sitting around the kitchen table upstairs. Even then, she checked Joss and Gabe were nowhere to be seen before she relayed the details of Owen's proposal.

'Oh,' Sam said, her eyes moistening when Nessie told her what he'd said about making new memories. 'Oh, Ness, I'm so thrilled for you. Congratulations!'

'We're keeping it quiet for now,' Nessie said, staring down at the ring as though she was surprised to find it there. 'Obviously, we want Luke to know first, and Kathryn when she gets here tomorrow.'

Sam's mouth quirked. 'Good luck with hiding it from Ruby. She can spot a diamond at a hundred metres.'

Nessie sighed. 'I should take it off, shouldn't I? But I like seeing it there – it reassures me I didn't dream the whole thing.'

'It's either that or wear gloves for the next twenty-four hours,' Sam replied. 'But your secret is safe with me, as long as you promise not to have a whirlwind engagement.' She gestured at her stomach. 'I don't want to look like this in the wedding photos.'

'Deal,' Nessie said. 'You will be my maid of honour, won't you?'

Sam laughed. 'I think it's a bit late for me to be maid of anything, Ness. But I'd be honoured to be part of your day.'

And now it was Nessie's turn to laugh. 'Matron of honour, then.'

'Excellent,' Sam said. 'I can channel my inner Hattie Jacques. Be very afraid for the hen party!'

By six o'clock, the cider festival was well underway. Sam watched from the doorway of the marquee, noting the pleasingly packed benches and crowds around the pumps. The beautiful weather was doing its part; outside, Gabe was already doing a roaring trade at the Sausage Fest stand and the smell alone was enough to make Sam's stomach rumble. Ferrelli's, the Cornish ice-cream stall, was doing a brisk trade too – Sam made a mental note to try their Afternoon Cream Tea gelato before the weekend was over. But right now, she couldn't wait for darkness to fall so she could switch on the twinkling fairy lights that wreathed the trees and hear the music and laughter that would fill the air; it was one of her favourite things about the Star and Sixpence events that spilled out onto the village green.

'It's not looking too bad, is it?'

She turned to see Joss at her shoulder, gazing around with an attitude of obvious satisfaction.

He winked. 'I obviously haven't lost my touch.'

Sam laughed in spite of herself. 'Yes, it's all down to you. How are things in the cellar? Has Connor kept up to your exacting standards?'

'He runs a tight ship,' Joss said approvingly. 'I've got no complaints.'

'Good,' Sam said. 'We were lucky to get him after you left. The fire brigade's loss is our gain.'

Joss gave her a sideways look but said nothing. They stood in companionable silence; it might have taken some adjustment, Sam reflected, but it had been good for both of them to work together again. And it didn't hurt to be reminded how well they'd got on professionally before emotions and jealousy had soured everything; apart from anything else, it gave her hope that they might make a decent job of parenting too.

Joss obviously felt the same way because he touched her arm. 'It's great to be back, Sam. Thanks for letting me help out.'

'There wasn't anyone else for the job,' Sam said, smiling. 'As much as it pains me to admit it, you are the best cellarman I know.'

He accepted the compliment with an uncharacteristically modest shrug. 'I know. But I appreciate the gesture.' His blue eyes met hers and he hesitated. 'Thanks for letting me be part of your life again.'

Sam rested a hand on the top of her bump. 'You might not feel that way when you're up to your eyes in dirty nappies and you haven't slept for a month.'

His gaze was steady. 'I'm pretty sure I will.'

The baby chose that moment to kick. Impulsively, Sam reached out to guide Joss's hand to her stomach. 'Feel that?'

Joss's eyes widened. 'Yes! Wow, that's some kick – is it that strong all the time?'

'Not all the time,' she replied and pulled a face. 'Usually only at three o'clock in the morning.'

'Oh,' Joss said, not moving his hand. 'I had no idea. Sorry about that.'

'Don't be,' Sam said gently. 'I like it. It's as though he or she is reassuring me that everything is okay.'

He opened his mouth to answer but was interrupted by a meaningful cough. Gabe was standing nearby, his expression unreadable. 'Sorry to disturb you, but Tilly says the Thirsty Bishop needs changing.'

'No problem,' Joss said easily, his hand falling from the stretched fabric of Sam's T-shirt. 'I'll get right on it.'

With a swift smile at Sam, he made his way out of the tent. Gabe made to follow, but Sam stopped him. 'Everything okay at Sausage Central?'

He nodded stiffly. 'Fine. Bucky is putting his big brown eyes to good use – you won't need to feed him all weekend.'

'Oh, is he being a pest?' Sam exclaimed. 'I can take him inside if he is.'

Gabe shook his head. 'People love him. And Luke is looking after him – they're practically inseparable.'

Sam laughed. 'I wouldn't be surprised if that boy plans to steal Bucky away someday.'

But Gabe didn't join in with her laughter. Instead, he stared at the ground, lips tight. 'You and Joss seem to be getting along well.'

'We are,' Sam said, feeling the start of a frown tug at her forehead. 'I don't think we have much choice.'

'That's true,' Gabe answered, just a little too fast. 'Especially since we are all flatmates now.'

'Temporarily,' Sam said, staring at him. 'Until Connor comes back.'

He looked at her then. 'And when the baby comes? I don't know about Joss, but if it were me, I'd want to be as close as possible to my newborn child.'

It was a question Sam had given some thought to, not least because Joss had suggested more than once that he and Sam should consider getting back together for the sake of the baby. 'It's true that he plans to move back to Little Monkham,' she told Gabe. 'But that doesn't necessarily mean he'll live at the Star and Sixpence. We don't have room, for a start.'

Gabe was silent for a moment, as though trying to work out how to frame his words. 'You would if I moved out.'

The thought almost caused Sam to rock back on her heels. 'Move out? But that's not . . . I don't . . .' She stopped and took a breath. 'Why would you even think that?'

His brown eyes were candid. 'It makes sense, Sam. You and Joss need the space and I don't really need to be on the premises overnight.'

But I need you to be there, Sam thought desperately, but

pushed the thought away. Maybe Gabe was sick of being at her beck and call 24/7. Maybe he'd grown tired of cooking her breakfast each day, saying goodnight every evening. Maybe he'd lost interest in her.

'Of course you can move out, if that's what you want,' she said, and now it was her turn to sound stiff. She tried to soften her voice, 'I'd miss you, obviously.'

Several seconds passed before he answered. 'That's the thing,' he said, so quietly that she had to lean forward to hear. 'I don't think you would.'

He was gone before she could respond, leaving her to stare after him in hurt and bewilderment. She'd known for some time that her own feelings towards Gabe were jumbled and complicated and much more than platonic, but she hadn't suspected he might feel the same about her. Could it be that he was jealous of Joss, of the role he would undoubtedly play in her life once the baby came? And short of confessing to Gabe the tumultuous mess of feelings she had for him, what on earth could Sam do about it?

Sam didn't see much of Joss or Gabe for the rest of the evening, something she was wearily grateful for. At Nessie's insistence, she'd gone over to a deserted Snowdrop Cottage and spent a blissful few hours dozing on the sofa and failing to follow the latest BBC crime drama. By the time Owen and Luke came home and woke her, it was almost closing time. Stretching, she gathered up the glossy magazine that had slithered to the floor as she slept, thanked Owen for the use of his sofa and made her way over to the Star and Sixpence to help close up.

'Leave that,' Nessie told her, when Sam eased behind the bar and reached for a cloth to wipe down the sticky surface. 'Laurie can do it. Go and sit down.'

'I've been sitting down all evening,' Sam said, looking round for something else to do. There was no sign of Gabe; she assumed he was either finishing up in the kitchen or had taken himself off to bed so he wouldn't have to look at her. Joss was conspicuous by his absence too, although the sound of distant clattering suggested he was busy in the cellar. 'Is Laurie still here, then?'

'Somewhere,' Nessie said as she extracted the till drawer and balanced it on one hip. 'Tilly has taken Bucky for a quick walk around the green.'

'She's a good girl,' Sam said and nodded at the cash drawer. 'So how is it looking?'

Nessie followed her gaze. 'Pretty good. I won't know for sure until I've checked the figures from the marquee system, but there were certainly plenty of happy faces around tonight.' She threw Sam a sympathetic look. 'You missed Sax Appeal's set – they seemed to go down well with the crowd.'

'I've heard them before,' Sam reminded her. 'The band I don't want to miss is Kathryn's tomorrow night – I won't be sprawled out on your sofa then, believe me.'

Nessie nodded. 'All the more reason to get some beauty sleep now. Go on – it's been a long day and tomorrow will be even busier. We can manage down here.'

Sam couldn't deny she was tired; somehow, dozing all evening had only made her more exhausted. 'Okay, thanks. See you in the morning.'

She hesitated when she reached the top of the landing, craning for a sound that would tell her Gabe had opted for an early night too, but everything was still. With a heavy sigh, Sam opened her door and went to bed.

'We need to talk, Sam.'

Joss met her in the kitchen doorway early the following morning, his expression tense. Sam felt a stab of anxiety when she saw Gabe behind him, looking equally grim-faced. Had they argued? Was she about to discover they couldn't bear to be in the same room?

'What's wrong?' she asked, glancing back and forth between them as Bucky snuffled at her hand in greeting.

Joss waited until she was seated and Gabe had placed a mug of decaf coffee in front of her before speaking again. 'Remember how bad the pub's electrics were when you first moved in? How the fuses used to trip at the worst possible times?'

She nodded. 'Of course. The electrician who did the rewiring said he was amazed the place hadn't burned down years ago. Why?'

'I think it might be happening again,' Joss said. 'I woke up in the middle of the night and couldn't get back to sleep, so I figured I'd go downstairs and do a stock-check.'

'Joss!' Sam exclaimed, amused in spite of the seriousness

in his voice. 'Only you would count beer bottles instead of sheep.'

'It was a good thing I did,' he went on, unsmiling. 'The cellar fuses had tripped – every single one of them, including the cooling systems. If I hadn't gone downstairs, our kegs would be far too warm to serve today.'

Sam felt her mouth fall open in dismay. 'Oh no!'

Joss raised his hands. 'It's okay, I switched everything back on and disaster was averted. I've checked this morning and the fuses seem to be behaving themselves.' He paused and rubbed the fair hair of his beard. 'But it's the timing that worries me most – I can't work out what made them trip in the first place. I was in the cellar just after Nessie closed the pub door and everything was fine then – the load on the electrics would have been minimal. So what caused the problem?'

An awful suspicion crossed Sam's mind. 'You're thinking rats.'

Gabe nodded. 'The man from the pest control company did say they often gnawed through electrical cables. It could be that there are still some rats inside the building.'

'And that has big implications,' Joss added. 'Although I can see from the reports that Simply the Pest have done a pretty thorough job in laying traps and poison. You won't necessarily have to close down again.'

Sam thrust her head into her hands and groaned. 'It's just one bloody thing after another, isn't it?'

'Hey, I might be wrong,' Joss said, dropping his hands to rub her shoulders sympathetically. 'It could be a one-off. I'll keep a closer eye on things – make sure there's no danger of the kegs overheating.'

Gabe frowned and looked away. 'But you should probably call an electrician, just to be safe.'

Sam couldn't tell if it was Joss's familiarity or the situation with the fuses that made him look so thunderous. 'I will,' she said, sighing. 'Thank you both.'

On the floor beside her, Bucky licked her palm and gazed up at her with liquid brown eyes.

'Thank you to you too,' Sam said, ruffling his fur. 'And no, I don't have any sausages to give you.'

Chapter Thirty-five

The electrician scratched his head and shrugged at Nessie.

'I don't know what to tell you,' he said, once he'd completed his check of the Star and Sixpence. 'There's nothing wrong that I can see – no obvious equipment issues, no dead spots or overloads. I can't even see any evidence of rodent activity, although that could be inside the walls, I suppose.'

Nessie cast an uneasy glance around and decided she'd ignore the idea of rats running riot behind the plaster. 'So there's no reason for the fuses to trip, that's what you're saying?'

He nodded. 'That's exactly what I'm saying. Maybe you just had a localised power surge that caused the safety mechanisms to engage.'

She sighed. On one hand, it was reassuring that there was no apparent reason for the problem in the night. But, on the other, it was just another mystery to add to a growing list of unexplained things that seemed to have been happening lately. 'Thanks for coming out on a Saturday.'

The electrician smiled. 'No problem. I've been hearing good things about the Somerset Scrumpy you've got on sale here – it'd be rude to leave without having a quick taste, right?'

That raised Nessie's spirits. 'Tell the guys over in the marquee that your first pint is on the house,' she said warmly.

Joss kept a sharp eye on the fuse box for the rest of the day, but it showed no sign of causing them any further problems. Nessie was glad; the sun was even hotter than it had been the day before and they needed the cellar's cooling system to keep doing its job, not to mention the hundreds of other systems that relied on a steady supply of electricity. It was something they took entirely for granted until it stopped, Nessie thought.

By the time the fairy lights came on that evening, the atmosphere on the village green was merry. Everywhere Nessie looked, she saw strangers mingling with Star and Sixpence regulars, laughing and drinking. Ruby seemed particularly taken by a group of scruffy-looking men whom she introduced to Nessie as detectorists, because the hobby that brought them together was exploring with metal detectors.

'And drinking,' a white-bearded man called Jim said, raising his pint of amber cider in salute to Nessie. 'We love that too.'

'But mostly old stuff,' another said. 'If it's old, we like it.'

Ruby winked at the group. 'That must be why you darling gentlemen are so taken with me.'

Predictably, they all disagreed and one suggested she couldn't be a day over forty, which caused Ruby to hoot with laughter.

'That's not what my birth certificate says, believe me.'

'Ah, birth certificates,' Jim snorted derisively. 'Hardly worth the paper they're printed on. When I traced my family tree, I found all kinds of mistakes and discrepancies.'

Was it Nessie's imagination or did Ruby lean forward? 'Oh? Is that so?'

Jim nodded. 'Mostly to do with handwriting – you'd be amazed at how easy it is to mistake a two for a five on an old, handwritten document. Or an e for an o. That kind of thing. Once, I found entirely the wrong parental name had been recorded. That caused some ructions, let me tell you.'

Ruby's eyes narrowed. 'Fascinating,' she breathed. 'Tell me more, Jim.'

Nessie stared at her in confused amusement as Jim warmed to his theme. Ruby was an incorrigible flirt, but she had a low threshold for boring anecdotes. If she was prepared to listen to someone list his entire family tree, there must be a good reason for her patience, but Nessie had no idea what that might be. She hung around for a few more minutes, in case Ruby flashed her a sign that said she needed to be rescued, but the actress seemed totally engrossed so Nessie made her excuses and headed further into the marquee. If there was one thing she'd learned about Ruby Cabernet, it was that she knew how to extricate herself from any situation that had lost its sparkle.

She found Kathryn and her bandmates doing their final preparations before their set at nine o'clock.

'You haven't seen Micky, have you?' Kathryn asked, peering over Nessie's shoulder into the crowds. 'We haven't agreed the final set list yet.'

Nessie frowned. 'He's over by the Somerset Scrumpy stall, I think. Want me to send him your way?'

'Would you?' Kathryn threw her a harried look as she tuned her violin. 'I know he's used to winging it like the true rock and roll legend he is, but we're not!'

'Leave it with me,' Nessie promised.

Once she'd delivered Micky, Nessie set about finding Owen. She'd spent most of the day on her feet, running from one piece of festival business to the next, and she had barely seen him or Luke all day. But there was one promise she'd made to Owen that she intended to keep; once Sonic Folk started to play, she would get two pints of ice-cold cider and dance the rest of the night away with him.

She found him on the edge of the dance floor, two pints in hand.

'Great minds think alike,' he said, lifting the glasses he carried.

She laughed as she joined him and took a long gulp from one of her own pints. 'I'm sure we'll cope.'

Sonic Folk were every bit as brilliant as Nessie remembered – better, in fact; all the months on tour were showing and they played with the ease of familiarity and practice. Kathryn's vocals were excellent too – melodic, throaty or plaintive in turn. Once or twice, Nessie observed Micky throw an unexpected spanner in the works, but the other musicians adapted with lightning-speed and she doubted many people in the audience even noticed. The band ran through a playlist of crowd-pleasing covers and well-known classics that soon had people up and dancing, and Micky's rasping voice caused ripples of appreciation when he sang some of The Flames' greatest hits. Nessie spotted Sam and Joss tapping their feet in the crowd, and wondered briefly whether Gabe was there too, but she soon gave up trying to spot anyone and let her herself enjoy the music.

Owen put his arms around her and pulled her close. 'Come and dance with me, wife-to-be.'

Nessie reached up to plant a soft kiss on his lips and tasted apples. 'Happily, husband-to-be.'

'We'll tell Kathryn and Luke tomorrow, shall we?' he said, as they swayed to the music. 'And then it doesn't have to be a secret any more.'

Nessie snuggled against his shoulder and closed her eyes. 'Yes, I'd like that. Please don't think I'm shallow but I can't wait to start wearing my ring!'

The heatwave showed no sign of abating after the weekend. Monday morning dawned bright and sunny and by lunch-time, Sam was dreaming of frost and snow.

'It's all right for you,' she told Joss as he handed her an ice-cold glass of water. 'You don't have an additional heating system on the go.'

'Never mind, at least it's Midsummer's Day,' he said, cheerfully leaning against the fridges that lined the back of the bar. 'Soon be winter again.'

'Can't come soon enough for me,' Sam grumbled, but she felt guilty even saying it. Part of her bad mood was due to being too hot, but most of her grumpiness had been brought on as the cider festival progressed: everywhere she'd looked, she seemed to see glamorous women in pretty summer dresses, sipping cider and having a wonderful time. And then she had caught sight of herself, frizzy-haired, frumpy and definitely not drinking cool pints of cider, and she'd wanted to cry. It didn't matter that there was a very good explanation for all of those things, or that she only had two more months of pregnancy to go. What mattered, when she was wallowing in her pit of heat-induced misery, was that she was pregnant right now. And she couldn't complain to Nessie, who would always be silently wishing her own pregnancy hadn't ended so tragically, so she'd suffered in sullen silence and escaped to bed as soon as she could on Sunday evening.

'No Gabe today?' Joss asked, glancing at the closed door that led to the restaurant kitchen.

'It's his day off,' Sam said. She puffed a sticky strand of hair off her forehead. 'And no, I don't know where he's gone.'

Joss raised an eyebrow at her irritable tone. 'Why should you know? You're not joined at the hip.'

She didn't like to say that Gabe's absence was another reason she felt out of sorts. They'd barely spoken since their conversation in the marquee on Friday evening and the weekend had flown by so fast that she'd barely had time to think. It wasn't until she'd gone to the kitchen for breakfast this morning and found it conspicuously empty of Gabe that her mood had sunk to its lowest point. It wasn't that she begrudged him his time off, more that she'd grown used to seeing him every morning, even when he wasn't working. She missed him.

'Of course we're not,' she said to Joss, frowning as a wave of fuzziness washed across her vision. 'It's just . . .'

He studied her in sudden concern. 'Are you okay? You've gone very pale.'

Pins and needles prickled at her fingers and her tongue felt too large for her mouth. 'No, I think I'm going to—'

She made a grab for the smooth wood of the bar as her legs buckled, but her fingers slid off the edge and she would have hit the floor hard if Joss hadn't caught her.

'Sorry,' she mumbled, digging her fingers into his T-shirt in an effort to stay upright.

'Easy, now. Let's get you sitting down.'

Concerned customers hurried to help and, together with Joss, they guided Sam to a seat.

'Here,' he said, pressing the glass of cold water to her lips. 'Sip this.'

The coolness made Sam's dizziness recede a bit. Her vision cleared and she blinked at the circle of worried faces, embarrassed and feeling more than a little silly. 'Sorry,' she said again, more distinctly this time. 'I think I must have overheated.'

'A woman in your delicate condition needs to take better

care of herself,' Henry said, his white moustache bristling as he surveyed Sam. 'If Franny was here, she'd order you to bed.'

'And who would argue with Franny?' Joss observed. 'There's a fan in your room, it might help you to cool down.'

Sam didn't want to go, but she suddenly felt overcome with tiredness. And at least if she was upstairs she wouldn't be surrounded by anxious onlookers. 'Okay,' she agreed. 'I'll go for a lie-down.'

'Keep an eye on the bar, will you, Henry?' Joss said, helping Sam to her feet. 'I'll be back in a minute.'

By the time they reached the top of the stairs, Sam could hardly keep her eyes open. She lay on the bed without a murmur, blinking sleepily as Joss switched the fan on and positioned it so that it would cool her down as she rested. She was almost asleep when she felt his lips brush her forehead. 'Sleep well, Sam,' he whispered, drawing a sheet across her. 'Sleep well, baby.'

She wanted to thank him, but the words wouldn't come. And then she tumbled into darkness and it was too late.

'No, Bucky!'

Nessie was in the kitchen of Snowdrop Cottage on Thursday evening, washing up after dinner, when she heard Luke shouting. At first, she assumed he and Bucky were playing, but the undertone of panic caught her attention; if it was a game, something was badly wrong. Dropping the saucepan into the sink, she hurried to the back door and wrenched it open.

'Luke? Where are you? What's going on?'

'It's Bucky,' Luke called back, from what sounded like the beer garden of the pub. 'He's got something he shouldn't have – come quickly!'

She did as he asked. As she rounded the corner of Owen's forge, she wondered briefly whether she should pull back the door to fetch him but there was a real risk he might be handling molten metal. She decided to see what the problem was first; no point in disturbing him if whatever Bucky had found turned out to be harmless.

Amid the fading sunlight of the deserted beer garden, it wasn't immediately obvious what Luke was upset about. He and Bucky were facing each other, but the dog's gaze wasn't fixed on the boy. There was something on the grass just behind Luke. And whatever it was, Bucky wanted it.

Nessie walked slowly forwards, taking care not to startle the dog. 'What is that on the floor behind you, Luke?'

His face was pale and unhappy. 'Some kind of smelly meat. Bucky went into the bushes to fetch the ball and came back with this in his mouth. I made him drop it, but he wasn't very happy and keeps trying to eat it.'

She squinted at the object and saw patches of livid red in amongst its coating of dust. Where on earth had it come from? she wondered. And, more to the point, what was she going to do with it? A lump of raw meat was probably the kind of treat Bucky would enjoy, but until they knew exactly where it had come from, and where it had been, she wasn't going to risk feeding it to the dog.

Leaning against the wall of the pub was the thick-bristled

broom they used to sweep the outdoor smoking area. Nessie reached out an arm to take it and edged round Luke to drag the meat towards her. The dog tensed, as though preparing to pounce.

'Bucky,' Nessie said, hoping her voice was stern and forbidding. 'No. Leave it, Bucky. Sit.'

He whined but did as she commanded.

A second later, the meat was at her feet. Nessie peered downward. 'It looks like steak.'

Gabe materialised in the back door of the Star and Sixpence. 'What's going on?'

'Everything is under control,' Nessie said. 'I just need something to put this lump of meat in before Bucky gobbles it up in one bite.'

Understanding dawned on Gabe's face and he vanished for a few long seconds. When he returned, he was carrying a thick blue plastic bag. 'Here,' he said, passing it to Nessie. 'If you put this on your hand like a mitten, you won't even have to touch it.'

She kept her eyes on Bucky as she slowly bent to scoop his prize into the plastic and let out an audibly relieved sigh when it was no longer in temptation's way.

'Can I see?' Gabe asked.

Nessie passed him the bag. 'Be my guest.'

Opening the bag a fraction, he stared downwards. Then he put his nose nearer to the top and sniffed with care. 'It is steak,' he said, shutting the bag with a sharp rustle. 'With a dressing of something that smells a lot like rat poison.'

Instantly, Nessie's heart was in her mouth. 'Did you touch it, Luke?'

Eyes wide, Luke shook his head. 'No. But Bucky did. He carried it in here.'

Nessie turned a concerned gaze onto the dog; he looked perfectly normal, but she knew rat poison was slow-acting and even a small amount could prove lethal. 'Someone needs to tell Sam she'd better call the emergency vet. And, Luke, you need to wash your hands, right now.'

'But—' Luke started to say, but Nessie was in no mood for arguments.

'Now, Luke. And use soap. Plenty of it.'

'I'll go and give Sam the bad news,' Gabe said, his expression grim.

Nessie threw him a grateful look. 'Thank you. Let's hope Emily hasn't finished for the day and can squeeze in a house call.' She glanced at the bag he held in disgust. 'What I don't understand is where the wretched meat came from.'

'I can answer that,' Gabe said over one shoulder as he went in search of Sam. 'It came from my fridge. I had a plate of sirloin there ready for tonight's menu and I noticed earlier today that one was missing.'

Nessie felt her mouth drop in a horrified circle as she worked out what that meant. Rats couldn't open fridges and they certainly didn't use poison as a dip. A human being had taken the steak and doused it in poison. The question was, who?

Chapter Thirty-six

At first, Emily thought Bucky might need his stomach pumped.

'I'll try to induce vomiting first,' she said, 'but if he won't, then we'll have to take him into the practice for treatment.'

Thankfully, Bucky had obliged in the most disgusting way, by throwing up everything he'd eaten in the previous few hours. Emily had then compounded his misery by giving him activated charcoal to eat to absorb any remaining toxins. And then several anxious days had rolled past, during which Sam and the rest of the Star and Sixpence team watched for any of the terrifying symptoms caused by poisoning. By the time his check-up came round the following Tuesday, Emily happily reported to Sam and Joss that the dog had escaped his experience unscathed.

'He had a lucky escape,' the vet said, ruffling Bucky's silky ears. 'I don't suppose you ever worked out how it happened, did you?'

Sam sighed. The problem was that it had to have been a deliberate action by someone who worked at the Star and Sixpence, and neither she nor Nessie were keen to throw unsubstantiated accusations around when there was little or no chance of uncovering any proof. 'Not really, no,' she told Emily. 'Probably just a mix up.'

'You don't really believe that, do you?' Joss asked Sam as they drove back to Little Monkham. 'Who could possibly have left a chunk of poisoned steak lying around for Bucky to find?'

Sam shrugged; she hadn't shared her suspicions with anyone so far and she wasn't about to start now. 'No idea.'

Joss frowned and cast a sideways look her way. 'It's certainly a strange thing to do. I must admit, I'd feel better about going back to Chester next week if we knew who the culprit was.'

'Whoever it was, I don't think any humans were the target,' she said, choosing her words with care. 'I think we'll all be safe enough.'

'That's not what worries me,' Joss replied as he manoeuvred the car off the main road and down the narrow lane that led to the village. 'It's the collateral damage that scared me – the unintended consequences. What if Luke had touched it and forgotten to tell anyone? What if you had?'

Both were thoughts that had occurred to Sam and Nessie and Gabe as they'd talked things through in the immediate aftermath of the drama. But they'd all agreed that events had probably scared the would-be poisoner and a repeat performance was unlikely. 'No one got hurt,' Sam told Joss firmly. 'Bucky is okay. Honestly, there's no need for you to worry.'

Joss grunted in acknowledgement then was silent for several long seconds. 'I'm going to miss you when I leave.'

Sam hesitated. The truth was she'd got used to having Joss around; she would miss him too. But Connor would soon be back from holiday, meaning Joss would be surplus to requirements, and he had his own job at Castle Court to consider. And, quite apart from anything else, there wasn't anywhere for him to stay at the Star and Sixpence; the sofa was fine as a short-term solution, but it couldn't work for more than a few weeks. Her mind slipped back to the conversation she'd had with Gabe at the cider festival, causing a stab of disquiet – the last thing she wanted was for him to feel pressured into moving out because of Joss.

'I'll miss you too,' she finally said to Joss. 'But the baby will be here in a couple of months and we'll see more than enough of each other then.'

He glanced at her ever-growing bump and shook his head. 'Two months. It doesn't seem possible, does it?'

'No,' Sam replied. 'It only seems like five minutes since I came to Chester to give you the news.'

'But I bet the time will fly by,' Joss went on. 'I'll need to hand my notice in soon and start looking round for somewhere to live nearer to the Star and Sixpence.'

This was it, Sam realised, the moment to tell him what Gabe had suggested. But once she'd put that out there, there would be no going back. 'Great Bardham is nice.'

'Yeah,' Joss said and puffed out his cheeks. 'There are lots of lovely villages. The trouble is, none of them are quite as nice as Little Monkham.'

Sam gnawed on her lip and fixed her gaze on the scenery flashing by. 'You'll find somewhere.'

He sighed. 'Yeah, I'm sure I will. I've got time after all.'

The hot weather finally broke in the first days of July. In some ways, Nessie was sorry when she awoke to the gentle patter of raindrops against the bedroom window, but she knew the parched grass on the green would be grateful. Sam would be relieved too; Nessie had watched her struggle with the soaring temperatures and, perhaps for the first time, didn't envy her sister's pregnancy.

Luke was less impressed by the grey skies.

'He grumbled for the entire journey,' Owen said, when he returned from the school run. 'You'd think he'd never seen rain before.'

'It has been a while,' Nessie said, pouring him a cup of tea and placing it on the kitchen table.

'Not that long,' Owen said, raising a dark eyebrow. 'He acted like we needed to start building an ark.'

She laughed. 'Luke being overly dramatic? Doesn't sound like him.'

Owen tipped his head in agreement. 'Speaking of being dramatic, I saw something curious on the drive home. Is it Gabe's day off today?'

'Yes, it is. Why?'

'I think he and Ruby are taking a trip somewhere. They were in his car, heading for the main road pretty early this morning.'

Nessie frowned. Ruby wasn't famed for being an early riser and she never left the house without a full face of make-up, so if she was going somewhere early enough to pass Owen on the school run, there had to be a good reason. 'No Micky?'

'Just Ruby and Gabe,' Owen replied. 'I half-wondered if it was a hospital appointment, but surely she'd have asked you.'

'She has in the past,' Nessie agreed, her frown deepening. 'She didn't mention a trip, either. Not that she tells me everything.'

Owen shrugged. 'I thought it was odd, that's all. I'm sure there's a perfectly simple explanation.'

But Nessie didn't get the opportunity to ask. Laurie went down with flu, which left them short-staffed now that Joss had gone back to Chester. And since she refused to allow Sam to cover any of his shifts, Nessie was left with no option but to work the extra hours herself. Although she saw both Gabe and Ruby over the days that followed, there never seemed to be time to manoeuvre the conversation around to their unmentioned trip.

Gabe took a very dim view of Laurie's continued absence. 'Flu? In July?'

'You can catch flu at any time,' Sam pointed out. 'And I definitely don't want it, so in some ways I'd rather he stayed away.'

Gabe's dark eyebrows drew together in a severe line. 'If he actually has the flu.'

The thought had crossed Nessie's mind too; there'd been something just a tiny bit insincere about Laurie's croaky apologies down the phone. But it felt disloyal to admit that to Gabe. 'I'm sure he does.'

Gabe threw her an enigmatic look. 'I wouldn't be so quick to trust him, Nessie.'

Nessie stared at him, while Sam didn't even try to hide her confusion. 'What's that supposed to mean?'

'My lips are sealed,' Gabe said, with a resolute shake of his head. 'For now, at least.'

He refused to be drawn further, leaving Nessie to spend yet another sleepless night, this time wondering just what it was Gabe knew that she didn't.

'If Gabe doesn't intend to explain himself, why say anything at all?' Sam grumbled on Saturday morning, when Laurie texted to say he wouldn't be in for his lunchtime shift. 'It's not exactly helpful.'

Nessie sighed as she looked at the rota again. 'We can just about manage over the weekend, if we pull Luiz from Gabe's waiting staff.'

Luiz was a young man from Brazil, who'd followed the girl he'd met while travelling back to the UK and had somehow ended up in Little Monkham. His light brown curls and forget-me-not eyes made him popular with the pub's female patrons, but he was also one of the few waiters who had experience of working a bar.

'Gabe won't be happy about that,' Sam said.

'He'll cope,' Nessie said stoutly. 'And in the meantime, I'm starting to feel guilty about Laurie. What if he's much worse than we think? What if it's more than just flu?'

Sam gave the idea some thought. 'Do you think one of us should go over to see him?'

'Maybe,' Nessie said. 'We could take him some meals, make sure he's eating properly.'

Sam pulled a hesitant face. 'I don't mean to suggest that you're more expendable than me, but it's probably not a good idea for me to go. It isn't very caring to drop a food parcel on someone's doorstep and run away in case they infect you, is it?'

Nessie threw her an affectionate smile. 'No, Sam. It's not exactly sisterly, either.'

'Ah, sisterliness,' Sam repeated with a solemn nod. 'You're much better at that than me. Just don't bring any germs back with you, okay?'

It was midway through Monday morning before Nessie found the time to drive over to the address she had for Laurie. The curtains were drawn at the windows of the little cottage and that morning's milk was still on the doorstep. Nessie felt a pang of sympathy; just how sick was he?

She had her answer a few minutes later when he opened the door, yawning and bare-chested. His sleep-filled eyes widened when he saw her.

'Nessie!' he said, clutching at the door and pulling it almost closed behind him. 'What are you doing here?'

There was a noticeable lack of croak in his voice, and his cheeks were pink and healthy-looking. Nessie felt some of her sympathy ebb away. 'You sounded so poorly that Sam and I thought we should check you were okay.' She lifted up the insulated bag she carried. 'We brought you some meals in case you weren't well enough to cook.'

Laurie had the grace to look guilty. 'Oh. Well, thanks.' He cleared his throat. 'I'm actually feeling a bit better today.'

Nessie did her best to squash her rising sense of outrage. Had Gabe been right – had Laurie been feigning illness? 'So I see,' she said. 'These need to go in the freezer. Shall I come in?'

A momentary flash of panic crossed Laurie's face. 'I can take care of that. I'm sure you're keen to get back to the pub.'

He wasn't alone, Nessie realised with a sinking heart. And, sure enough, a female voice called out, 'Hurry up, Laurie. I'm getting bored in here.'

'I didn't realise you had a girlfriend,' Nessie said, her tone cool to the point of iciness. 'Has she been taking good care of you?'

'Something like that,' he said evasively. 'Look, this isn't a great time.'

'It's not, is it?' Nessie said, wondering how she could have been so gullible. 'Why don't you come to the pub tomorrow – say two o'clock in the afternoon? I'm sure Sam will want to be there and we can discuss your behaviour then.'

His head jerked up. 'Discuss my behaviour?' he repeated,

his eyes hardening. 'I've been ill, Nessie. That's not a disciplinary offence.'

She thrust the freezer bag at him. 'Enjoy your meals. See you tomorrow – don't be late.'

She felt him watching her all the way back to her car, but it wasn't until she'd started the engine and driven away that she called Sam on the hands-free.

'Everything okay?' Sam asked the moment she answered. 'How is he?'

Nessie pictured Laurie's healthy glow and sighed. 'Well, on the plus side, I don't think you need to worry about catching the flu.'

There was a short pause. 'Ah.'

'And on the down side, we might need to look up how to handle things when an employee who is also your brother lies about being ill.'

Nessie heard a low mumbling, as though Sam was relaying what she'd heard to someone else in the room.

'Gabe says he's dealt with something like this before.'

'Really?' Nessie asked as she negotiated a corner.

'Not exactly like this, obviously,' Sam said. 'But he's had employees lie about being ill in order to get time off. It's not the most original work-related crime, after all. Anyway, he says he'll help us work out how to handle things with Laurie.'

'Great,' Nessie said, recalling the hard look Laurie had given her as she'd left. 'I think we're going to need all the support we can get.'

*

They decided to hold the meeting with Laurie in the upstairs kitchen, out of earshot of Tilly and Connor, who were running the bar.

'It'll be cosy with four of us in here,' Nessie said. 'But the office feels too formal.'

Gabe grunted. 'I think formality is exactly what you need.'

Nessie gave a small shake of her head. 'Maybe, but this is Laurie we're talking about. Different rules apply for family.'

'And, actually, it's four and a bit,' Sam said, easing down onto one of the chairs with a sigh.

'Or five and a bit,' a clear smooth voice added.

Nessie whirled around to see Ruby standing in the doorway, a manila folder in her arms. 'Ruby! What are you doing here?'

'I've come to add my two penn'orth,' the older woman said, as though it was the most reasonable thing in the world. 'What else?'

Nessie glanced at Sam, who looked equally confused. 'But—'

'I have evidence to present,' Ruby said, her eyes gleaming. 'Gabe and I have been doing some detective work.'

'Detective work?' Sam said. 'What are you talking about?'

Ruby tapped her nose. 'Don't worry, darling, you'll understand later.'

Laurie's expression was incredulous when he arrived at 2.15 p.m. 'What, no Henry?' he said, his voice thick with sarcasm. 'Maybe we could hold a séance and channel Franny.'

'Would you like a tea or a coffee?' Nessie offered, determined not to be side-tracked. Gabe was right; a little formality might help focus Laurie's mind on the consequences of his actions.

'No, I don't want a cup of tea,' Laurie said, his lip curling as he sat down. 'Let's just get this over with.'

Sam fixed him with a level stare. 'I must say, you don't look like someone who has dragged themselves off their sickbed to be here.'

He shrugged. 'What can I say? The meals Nessie delivered have worked miracles – I'm feeling better.'

'You've been off for over a week,' Sam went on, as though she hadn't heard. 'We're going to need a doctor's certificate to confirm your illness.'

'Seriously?' Laurie said, with an incredulous-sounding laugh. 'You can't just take it on trust? I'm your brother, for god's sake.'

Leaning against the kitchen counter, Gabe muttered under his breath.

Laurie turned to glare at him. 'Got something to say? Or are you just sticking your nose into family business again?'

Gabe glowered at him. 'Okay, Laurie, let's talk about *family*, shall we?'

Nessie blinked, nonplussed, and Sam didn't seem to understand the conversational switch either.

Laurie went still. 'What's that supposed to mean?'

'I'd like to tell you a little story,' Ruby cut in, causing Laurie's gaze to swivel her way. 'It's about a man called Andrew, who had his faults but was still trusting and good at heart. He always tried to do the right thing, even though there were many times when he didn't quite manage it.'

Now it was Laurie's turn to mutter, although Nessie thought she detected a hint of pallor beneath his rosy complexion now.

'Andrew liked to believe the best of people,' Ruby went on. 'So when a woman he'd become romantically involved with assured him the baby she was carrying was his, he took her at her word.'

'I wondered when this would come up again,' Laurie said scornfully. 'I've shown Sam and Nessie my birth certificate. Andrew Chapman is clearly listed under *Father*.'

'I don't doubt that he is,' Ruby said, and Nessie had the sense that the older woman was starting to enjoy herself. 'As I said, Andrew wouldn't have questioned such a colossal statement. But just because he believed it to be true does not make it so.' The last few words came out whip-fast.

Laurie shook his head. 'You're crazy.'

'We took a trip to the place where you grew up,' Gabe said. 'Had a very nice chat with a man called Peter Henderson. He remembered you and your mum very well.'

Ruby leaned forwards. 'As you'd expect, considering they were married. Peter seemed to think the wrong paternal name had been recorded on your birth certificate, Laurie. He seemed to think it should have been him.'

Nessie gasped. 'Is that true?' she asked, turning to stare at Laurie.

There was a hunted look in his eyes and a sheen of sweat glistened on his forehead. 'Nice try. But, legally, Andrew Chapman is my father.'

430

'Legally?' Sam echoed in disbelief. 'What about biologically? Are you actually related to us at all?'

Laurie didn't meet her gaze. 'He treated me like his own son. What does it matter if I wasn't biologically his child?'

Nessie felt as though she'd been punched in the chest. 'Bloody hell, Laurie. How could you lie about something like that? What else have you lied about?'

'Nothing,' he insisted. 'Everything else is true, I swear.'

Gabe folded his arms. 'Except even that is a lie. Tell them about the duplicate brewery order you placed using Nessie's log-in so she'd think she'd made a mistake. Tell them about the rat catcher you know in Purdon who gave you a live rat to plant in my kitchen so the restaurant would have to close down.'

'Tell them about switching off the fuses so that the cellar temperature would fail and Joss would look bad,' Ruby went on, her voice as hard as diamond. 'And how you stole some steak from Gabe's kitchen and covered it in rat poison to kill Bucky.'

'No!' Nessie exclaimed, utterly aghast. 'Oh, Laurie, you didn't!'

He looked a little like a rat now, cornered and snarling. 'Oh, grow up. No one got hurt, did they?'

'Only by sheer luck,' Sam blazed furiously. 'What the hell were you thinking?'

'None of you would give me a chance to prove what I could do,' Laurie snapped, scowling. 'You held every little mistake over my head. So I thought it wouldn't do you any harm to realise that you weren't so perfect yourselves.'

It was almost too much for Nessie to take in. She slumped back in her seat, horrified. 'But Luke might have touched that meat. What if he'd somehow ingested some of the poison? I can't believe you could be so reckless.'

He shook his head. 'You're overreacting. No one got hurt.'

Sam had clearly heard enough. 'Leave, now. Put your keys on the table and walk out of here this minute.' She drew in a long shaking breath. 'And if I ever hear your name or see your face again, I won't be responsible for what happens next.'

Laurie pushed back his chair so fast it screeched across the floor. 'You'll be sorry once I'm gone. You don't have the staff to cope without me.'

'Believe me, we'll manage,' Nessie said. She held out a hand. 'Keys.'

Reaching into his jeans, Laurie pulled the keys that opened the pub front door, the office and the cellar. 'Take them,' he said, tossing them onto the floor in disgust. 'I'm sick of working here anyway.'

The heavy thud of his feet on the stairs receded and there was a hefty bang as he slammed the door at the bottom of the stairs. Then silence fell over the kitchen.

'Well, that happened,' Sam said weakly, after several long seconds had ticked by. She glanced first at Gabe, and then at Ruby. 'How the hell did you know all that?'

Gabe shrugged. 'It was a hunch at first. Some of the things he said didn't quite add up. And once I started to explore the idea, I realised that there was really only one person who linked everything that had gone wrong.'

Ruby held up a hand. 'You'll remember I never accepted his stories about what a terrible father Andrew was – I knew the truth, no matter what Laurie said. So when I met those darling detectorists at the cider festival, things began to fall into place.'

'We went investigating,' Gabe added. 'Like Holmes and Watson.'

Ruby laughed. 'I've always thought I'd make a rather good Jane Marple, actually.' She patted her elegant red chignon. 'If Miss Marple had style, obviously. And a delectable toy boy.'

Sam slumped her head on the table for a moment, then looked up at Gabe and Ruby. 'Thank you. I don't quite know how you put it all together, but I'm really glad you did.'

'No problem,' Gabe said, and it seemed to Nessie that his eyes held a special gleam of pride as he basked in Sam's praise. 'I'm just pleased we finally confronted him.'

Still reeling from the revelation that Laurie was not their brother after all, Nessie glanced across at Sam. 'I guess it's just you and me again.'

'I guess so,' her sister replied. 'Luckily, you're all the family I need.'

'Well if that isn't rude, I don't know what is,' Ruby declared in mock outrage. 'But if it helps, don't think of it as losing a brother. Think of it as getting rid of an arsehole.'

Sam let out a shout of laughter and Nessie couldn't stop herself from smiling a little, in spite of the sadness she felt. Beside her, Ruby sighed. 'You know, for what it's worth, I wish things had turned out differently – I wish we'd been wrong about Laurie, for your sakes.'

'Me too,' Nessie said.

'I'm not,' Sam cut in. 'Good riddance, I say. Let's celebrate the fact that our dynamic duo saved us before Laurie could swindle us out of the Star and Sixpence!'

Ruby beamed at Gabe. 'Dynamic duo – I like it!' She paused and made a restless gesture Nessie recognised. 'You know, it's at times like these that I wish I still drank. A gin and tonic would go down perfectly right now.'

To anyone else, it might have sounded like an innocuous comment but Nessie recognised it as a tiny cry for help in Ruby's constant battle against alcohol. She reached across to press a grateful kiss on the older woman's cheek. 'I'll join you for a celebratory virgin mojito if you like.'

'Me too,' Sam said, with a rueful glance at her swollen belly.

'Sounds perfect,' Gabe said, pushing himself off the kitchen counter and making for the door. 'I'll do the honours, shall I?'

'Thank you, darling,' Ruby said, flashing him a grateful smile. 'And then we can toast our new business venture – Santiago and Cabernet Investigate! I think it's got Netflix series written all over it.'

Nessie shook her head and laughed. 'I'll definitely drink to that!'

Chapter Thirty-seven

'And you're sure you'll be okay?' Nessie asked for the third time in as many minutes. 'You've got the name and the number of the hotel?'

Sam laughed. 'And your mobile number, obviously. And Owen's. I'm not worried I won't be able to contact you, Ness.'

Her sister appeared not to have heard. 'I'll let you know the room number when we get there. It's only Birmingham, not far. I can always come back if you need me.'

'Relax,' Sam said, wincing as a particularly vigorous kick landed against her ribcage. 'I've still got six weeks to go, and this baby is having far too much fun kicking me to make an early appearance. Go and have some fun.'

Nessie nodded slowly. 'Kathryn is next door, taking care of Luke, and, of course, Gabe will be here.' She paused and gave Sam a meaningful look. 'Don't do anything without me.'

'You're my birthing partner,' Sam said with a grin. 'I've got no idea what to do without you.'

Owen poked his head around the door of the Star and Sixpence. 'We should really get going if we want to beat the Friday-night traffic, Nessie.'

'Okay,' Nessie said, taking a deep breath. 'Okay, you're going to be fine. I'm going to be fine. We're all going to be fine.'

'Go!' Sam said, giving her a little push towards the door. 'See you tomorrow.'

Together with Gabe, Sam followed Nessie outside and waved as she and Owen got into their car. Once the Land Rover had vanished around the curve of the village green, Sam let out a long sigh. 'I thought she was never going to leave.'

'She worries about you,' Gabe said. 'We all do.'

It wasn't anything he hadn't told her before, but the words still sent a tiny thrill through Sam. 'I know,' she said. 'You all worry too much. I'm fine.' She gasped as the baby kicked again and Gabe raised his eyebrows. 'Well, mostly fine,' she said, in response to his unspoken disagreement.

'What shall I cook you this evening?' he asked, as they crossed the bar. 'Pickled gherkins with bananas again?'

Sam grinned. She'd prided herself on having the most mundane pregnancy ever, but the weird food cravings had really started to kick in now that she was well into her third trimester. Gabe had taken her peculiar requests in his stride and Sam thought he was even enjoying the challenge. 'Ham and pineapple pizza,' she said, licking her lips at the thought. 'But not made by you – yours is far too healthy. I'll order one from Domino's, thank you.'

Gabe raised his hands in despair. 'She has a world-class chef at her disposal and all she wants is Domino's.'

Seated at the bar, Ruby caught Sam's eye and winked. 'Ah, but sometimes quick and dirty is just what a lady wants. Isn't that right, Sam?'

Gabe flicked an amused glance between the two of them and shook his head. 'Quick and dirty. Got it.'

Unable to stop herself from blushing, Sam made for the stairs. 'Sometimes, Gabe. Sometimes that's exactly what we want.'

When Sam awoke in the night, cold and distinctly damp, she thought for one horrific moment that she'd wet the bed. A sense of incredulity washed over her; she was pretty sure she hadn't done that since she was a toddler. But there was no escaping the fact that both her pyjamas and the sheets were uncomfortably wet; they'd need to be changed if she was going to get any more sleep.

Groaning, Sam swung her legs over the side of the bed and got slowly to her feet. She was halfway across the room when the contraction hit, gripping her sides and squeezing as though she'd been caught in an invisible vice.

'Ow!' she gasped, reaching for the end of the bed to support herself. 'Shit, shit, shit. Ow!'

Once the wave had passed, Sam stood still for a moment and tried to get her head around what was happening. It couldn't be a real contraction, she thought in panic; she wasn't due for at least six more weeks. The baby hadn't been anywhere near in the right place during her last midwife check-up. And that wet patch in the bed couldn't possibly be her waters breaking . . . could it?

Nessie was going to kill her, Sam thought, closing her eyes. And then an altogether more embarrassing realisation occurred to her. She was going to have to tell Gabe what had happened and maybe even ask him to drive her to the hospital.

Shuffling towards the chest of drawers, she wriggled out of her wet pyjama bottoms and thought hopefully of the shower across the landing. Did she have time to sneak in there before she woke Gabe? Perhaps if she was quick . . .

Her body had other ideas. The next contraction was so strong that she had to grasp the chest of drawers for support. When the pain had stopped, Sam abandoned all pretence at dignity and lifted her head to shout. 'Gabe? Gabe! Wake up!'

He burst through the door, just as she tied the belt of her dressing grown, a barking Bucky at his heels. Gabe looked wildly around before hurrying to her side. 'What is it? What's wrong?'

'My waters have broken,' she said, and watched as his face paled in comprehension. 'I think the baby is coming.'

To his credit, he didn't panic. 'But it's too early.'

'Tell me about it,' Sam ground out. She puffed out a short, unsteady breath as Bucky sniffed at her ankles. 'All the same, something is definitely happening here.'

He eyed her sweat-beaded forehead and nodded. 'Any

contractions yet? We should check how far apart they are – the hospital will ask.'

She stared at him. 'Yes! But how do you—?'

He offered a lopsided grin. 'I have a big extended family. My cousins are always having babies – I know roughly what happens. Do you want me to call Nessie?'

Another contraction began, causing Sam to swear and grip his hand tightly. 'I think you'd better call the hospital first. They might not want me to go in yet,' she managed.

Gabe looked askance but did as Sam asked. She panted her way through the pain, listening as he explained the situation to the person on the other end of the phone. And then he covered the handset and looked at Sam. 'They want you to go in.'

It was all she could do to nod.

'What about Nessie?' Gabe asked again, once he'd hung up. 'Shall I call her?'

There wasn't anyone she wanted to see more. But Nessie and Owen were away for a rare romantic mini-break and Sam was reluctant to summon her sister until she knew she wasn't being fooled by Braxton Hicks contractions. 'No, not yet. I don't want to wake her unless we absolutely have to.'

Gabe's eyes were steady on hers. 'As you wish. Let's get you downstairs.'

Slowly, watched by a whining Bucky, they made their way one step at a time down the stairs and into the darkened bar. They reached the door of the pub before Sam remembered her hospital bag, which Nessie had insisted on packing and leaving in the living room. Gabe dashed upstairs to retrieve it, then brought his car to the front of the pub and eased Sam into the passenger seat.

'Just try to hold on until we get to the hospital,' he said, as Sam gasped her way through another contraction. 'I'm not sure I could cope with delivering a baby by the side of the road!'

It seemed to Sam that the journey took forever, even though she was well aware that Gabe was taking the deserted country roads much faster than the speed limit dictated. When the lights of the hospital finally loomed, she didn't try to hide her sob of relief. She had no idea how often the contractions were coming, but it felt as though the next one began as soon as the previous wave ebbed away.

'Almost there,' Gabe said, braking sharply to turn into the car park. 'Keep breathing.'

'I am breathing,' Sam snapped, her fingers gripping the door handle so hard her knuckles turned white. 'Just drive the bloody car.'

There was an ambulance parked outside the entrance to the hospital. Gabe pulled to an untidy stop behind it and leapt out to run around to the passenger door. He yanked it open and crouched at Sam's side. 'Can you walk?'

Blowing her hair from her sweaty forehead, Sam considered the question. 'I . . . I think so . . .'

But at that moment, one of the paramedics materialised next to Gabe with a wheelchair. 'Need any help?' she asked.

Gratitude whooshed over Sam; the truth was, she wasn't at

all sure she could walk, but there hadn't seemed to be much of an alternative, until now.

'Yes,' she said, before Gabe could send the paramedic away. 'Oh god, yes.'

The green-clad woman laughed. 'No problem. Let's get you inside so the midwives can check you over.'

Everything seemed to happen very fast after that. There were lots of questions and tests; Sam was tucked into a white-sheeted bed and hooked up to a monitor so the nurses could keep an eye on the baby's heart rate. And, throughout it all, Gabe didn't leave her side. For the most part, Sam was grateful he was there; despite the cool, matter-of-fact attitude of the hospital staff, her heart was thudding with the terrible fear that there was something wrong, that the baby would be born too early. The warmth of Gabe's hand in hers calmed the panic that threatened to overwhelm her and reminded her she wasn't alone, although she couldn't help cringing as she wondered what he must be thinking; she was still his employer, after all. But that didn't seem to matter.

'I think it's safe to say you're in labour,' a midwife called Nina told her after a thorough check-up. 'You're six centimetres dilated already, which means the baby is well on the way. But the good news is there's no sign of infection and the heartbeat is strong and steady.'

'But I've still got six weeks to go,' Sam said, feeling her eyes fill with hot tears. 'It's too soon.'

Nina smiled. 'It's definitely an early appearance. But babies are usually born between 36 and 38 weeks anyway, so he or she isn't that premature. And those born after 34 weeks don't usually need much special care, providing there are no complications.'

Sam opened her mouth to ask what the complications might be, but another contraction began and she pressed her lips together instead.

Nina kept a practised eye on the monitor as she jotted some notes on Sam's file. When the contraction had passed, she gave Sam a sympathetic look. 'Have you given any thought to the kind of pain relief you might like?'

'Not really,' Sam replied, her mind a blank as she tried to remember the options she and Nessie had discussed. 'I thought I had plenty of time to decide.'

'You're too far along for some things,' Nina said. 'Why don't I go and see what your options are, and then you can decide what's best for you?'

Once she'd disappeared along the corridor, Gabe fixed Sam with a determined look. 'Six centimetres, Sam. I think it's time to call Nessie.'

She couldn't argue; her sister would be very unhappy if they didn't call her. And if Sam was completely honest, she'd feel better for having Nessie beside her.

'And,' Gabe said, his voice even more uncompromising, 'Joss should know too. I don't suppose he'll get here in time, at the rate things are progressing, but he has a right to know what's happening at least.'

Once again, Sam decided not to argue. How could she

when Gabe was right? 'Okay,' she said wearily. 'His number is in my phone.'

He waited until Nina had returned before heading outside to make the calls. Sam watched him leave, overcome once more by a mixture of embarrassment and gratitude. He'd done everything she asked and more, she acknowledged with an uncomfortable shudder, fulfilling a role that was definitely above and beyond his responsibilities as an employee. But he'd been more than an employee almost from the start. And even though things hadn't worked out romantically between them, she was proud and thankful to count him as something altogether more valuable than an employee or a fling; he was her friend.

Gabe arrived back at Sam's side just as Nina was showing her how to use the gas and air mask.

Sam paused, the mask just inches from her face. 'Did you get through?'

He nodded. 'Nessie and Owen are on their way. I've left a message for Joss.'

Too late, Sam thought to wonder what he would make of hearing Gabe's voice telling him the baby was on its way. Would he understand that events had moved too fast for any of them to control? And then a contraction forced the question out of her head; she jammed the mask over her mouth and breathed in the heady mixture.

The next thing she knew, her head was against the pillow and a jumble of concerned faces were staring down at her. 'What happened?' she mumbled, her tongue thick in her mouth.

Holly Hepburn

'You passed out,' Gabe said. His features swam into focus and Sam saw he was grinning. 'Again.'

'A little too much gas and air,' Nina said in a kind tone. 'Try not to breathe so deeply next time.'

The gas definitely helped to dull the contractions, Sam thought as time went by; she could still feel the relentless squeeze of her muscles and the ever-increasing ache deep inside her that somehow managed to push and pull at the same time.

'Don't leave me,' she gasped at Gabe during one wave of agony that seemed to last forever. 'I can't do this on my own.'

He smiled and held her fingers almost as firmly as she grasped his. 'Don't worry, I'll stay as long as you need me.'

In the end, Nessie arrived just before the baby. She hurried into the room, her hair wild and unbrushed, her eyes panicky. 'How are you?' she asked Sam, who grimaced and moaned. Nessie's gaze transferred to Gabe. 'How is she?'

'She's doing brilliantly,' Gabe said, barely taking his eyes from Sam.

'Not long now,' Nina called from the bottom of the bed. 'Keep going, Sam. Push!'

Gritting her teeth, Sam did as she was told. The effort caused her to groan.

Nessie took the hand that was tangled in the rumpled sheets and wrapped her fingers around it. 'I'm here. You can do it.'

The pain was so intense that it was all Sam could focus

444

on. She was only dimly aware of Gabe speaking to her; the words were lost among the waves and it took her a moment to realise he had let go of her hand. But a thin, reedy wail split the air, cutting through the fog in Sam's mind like a siren. Almost instantly, the pain stopped. Blearily, she looked at Nina, who beamed at her.

'It's a girl – congratulations!'

Dazed, Sam stared at the impossibly small body the midwife held. 'Is everything . . . is she okay?'

'Everything is fine,' Nina reassured her. 'Small but perfectly formed. And as you can hear, there's nothing wrong with her lungs – she's breathing all on her own!'

Sam sank into the damp bedsheets, relief washing over her like a flood. 'Oh, thank god for that.'

Beside her, Nessie's cheeks were wet as she smiled down at her. 'Bloody well done, Sam. She's gorgeous.'

Sam allowed her eyes to drift shut for a moment. She'd done it – she'd actually done it.

'Here,' Nina said, after a few more minutes had ticked by. 'You can hold her now.'

The midwife placed the tiny bundle of white sheets and mottled pinky-blue skin into Sam's arms. Sam gazed down at her daughter, utterly transfixed, for what felt like hours, then looked into Nessie's damp-eyed gaze. 'She's got my nose. Joss is going to be furious.'

Nessie shook her head. 'He is not. He's going to be just as delighted as the rest of us. I'm so proud of you, Sam. You did wonderfully well.'

'I couldn't have done it without Gabe,' Sam said, and noticed for the first time that he was no longer in the room. 'Where's he gone?'

'He said something about trying Joss again,' Nessie said gently. 'I'm sure he'll be back soon.'

But Sam was finding it hard to focus on anything but her tiny baby. She stared down at her again, not quite able to take in the fact that she was here already. 'Hello,' she whispered. 'You caught us a bit by surprise. But the good news is that we know your name already.' She hesitated and glanced up at Nessie, who nodded. 'I think we're going to call you Frances, after a very special friend of ours.'

There were more tests and checks, more doctors and nurses, but eventually both Sam and the baby were given a clean bill of health.

'We'll have to keep an eye on her,' Nina said, as the room began to empty. 'But as long as she continues to breathe and feed well, she shouldn't need any special care.'

'Good,' Sam said, glancing across at Frances, who lay in a transparent cot, swamped by a too-large Babygro. 'Thank you.'

'My pleasure,' Nina replied, smiling.

Sam opened her mouth to speak again and was surprised by a sudden yawn.

Nessie laughed, before leaning back into the chair next to the bed and yawning herself. 'You must be shattered. Why don't you get some rest?'

'Oh no, I couldn't,' Sam said, a spike of anxiety stabbing through her. 'What if she wakes up?'

'Then I'll wake *you* up,' Nessie answered. 'I'll be here, Sam. Go to sleep.'

'But what about Joss? What if he arrives while I'm sleeping?'

The look Nessie gave her was half-amused, half-exasperated. 'See my previous answer.'

Sam didn't want to give in, but she could feel her eyelids sinking even as she fought them. 'Promise you'll wake me up if she needs me.'

'Of course I will,' Nessie said. 'Now rest.'

When Sam opened her eyes again, it was Joss and not Nessie she saw.

'Hello,' he said softly, leaning forward in the chair. 'I see you've been busy.'

Sam's gaze flickered sideways to the cot; the baby's outfit had been changed to one that no longer swamped her tiny frame. Someone had been shopping while she slept. 'I have. Sorry.'

He laughed, an incredulous, delighted sound. 'Bloody hell, Sam, don't apologise. It's me who should be saying sorry to you – I wasn't there when you needed me.'

A frown creased Sam's forehead then, because although she wished Joss had been there to see his daughter born, the truth was she hadn't needed him at all. They'd both been well looked after by Gabe. 'How long have you been here?'

'About an hour,' he replied, then hesitated. 'Gabe came and picked me up.'

Sam blinked at him, wondering if she'd misheard. 'Who did?'

'Gabe – I rang him as soon as I got his message,' Joss said. 'Actually, I rang Nessie, but she'd turned her phone off. So I found Gabe's number in my missed calls and he told me what had happened – offered to come and collect me. It would be quicker, he said.'

A sudden lump formed in Sam's throat. It was so kind of Gabe – so typically him – that she found it hard to swallow. 'He must be dead on his feet. Has he gone back to the pub for a rest?'

Joss shook his head. 'He's outside.' Again, he paused, but this time he seemed to be fighting some kind of internal battle. 'He's a good bloke. I like him.'

'He is,' Sam said, an involuntary smile pulling at her lips. 'The best.'

'Yeah, I thought you might say that.' He puffed out his cheeks and then met Sam's eyes in rueful resignation. 'I think I knew the first time I saw you two together, to be honest.'

'Knew what?' Sam said warily.

Joss opened his mouth and closed it again. He was silent for several long seconds, then pushed himself out of the chair and headed for the door. 'I'll let you work it out for yourself.'

'Where are you going?' Sam called in bewilderment.

'I'm not going anywhere,' Joss said, tilting his head.

'But try opening your eyes to see what's really in front of you, Sam.'

For a moment, Sam lay against the pillows, struggling with a burst of intense irritation at Joss's enigmatic comments. What did he mean, try opening her eyes? Obviously, they were already open. But then her gaze was drawn to their daughter, so small and perfect, and her annoyance drained away until she couldn't feel anything but love. She slid out of bed and reached out a hand to touch the pink clenched fingers with their minuscule fingernails. Had this little person really been safely cocooned inside her less than twenty-four hours ago? It didn't seem possible.

'She's beautiful,' Gabe said from the doorway, and Sam didn't need to turn around to know he was smiling.

'I can't argue with that,' Sam said.

'Just like her mother.'

Now Sam did turn to look at him, suddenly aware of her matted hair and crumpled hospital gown. At least they'd given her another to wear like a dressing gown, so she wasn't flashing bare skin to the world. 'I'm pretty sure I've never looked worse.'

Gabe's dark-eyed gaze was level. 'Not to me.'

'Spoken like a true friend,' she said dryly.

He watched her in silence for a moment. 'I will always be your friend, Sam. Even though I wish—' His eyes slid away as he stopped talking.

'You wish what?' Sam asked as her heart started to thud.

'Forget it,' he replied, glancing at the cot with an expression that was both longing and sad. 'I am a fool.'

449

And then Sam thought she understood. 'It was kind of you to go and get Joss.'

Gabe shrugged, staring at the floor. 'It was the decent thing to do. I knew he must be beside himself with worry – I would have been, in his place.'

Sam took a small step towards him. 'He told me he thinks you're a good man.'

'Really?' He looked up briefly and she saw his mouth was twisted into a sardonic smile. 'Then he doesn't know me at all.'

'But I do,' Sam said, closing the distance between them a little more. 'I know you pretty well, Gabriel Santiago, and I think you're a very good man. The kind who makes me breakfast every day, who tells me off for not resting enough and catches spiders from the ceiling in my room.'

He shook his head dismissively and seemed to be marshalling an argument. Sam wasn't going to give him the chance; this time, she would say what was on her mind.

She kept walking until she was standing right in front of him. 'You're the sort of man who feeds stray dogs and investigates liars and comforts a pregnant woman when she's scared in the night, even though her feet are like blocks of ice and she can't stay still.'

A ghost of a smile crossed his face then.

She took his hand and waited until he looked into her eyes. 'The type of man I've thought about kissing every day that I've known him, but didn't because I thought maybe it would make life too complicated for both of us.'

'Sam—'

She touched one finger to his lips to silence him. 'But someone told me today that I should open my eyes and see what was in front of me. And what I see is you.'

Gabe tilted his head to stare at her, almost as though he wasn't sure he'd heard correctly. 'But—'

Sam took a deep breath and ploughed on. 'I love you, Gabe. And I know things are stupidly complicated, but I'm pretty sure we can work things out . . . if you love me too.'

'If I love you too,' he echoed slowly and took a long deep breath. '*Dios mío*, Sam, you must know I have loved you from the first moment we met.'

The room seemed to spin for a moment. Sam pressed her feet hard against the ground and focused on staying present as a gasp escaped her. 'How could I know?'

Gabe took her hands in his. 'I tried to show you each day – I tried to take care of you. But then I realised you were still in love with Joss, and him with you, and I didn't want to stand in your way.'

'But I'm not in love with Joss,' she said, the words tumbling over each other in her hurry to make him understand. 'He doesn't love me either, at least not the way you mean. In fact, it was Joss who made me see what I really wanted – you, Gabe. It's been you all this time.'

He didn't speak for a moment, then let out a sigh that made Sam's heart flutter. 'We are both fools, then.'

'Agreed,' Sam said. 'Can we stop being foolish now, though? Please?'

Gabe smiled. 'It is definitely time.'

Pulling her gently towards him, he lowered his face to hers and brushed her lips with his. Sam lifted her hand to touch his cheek and he responded by kissing her with such tender passion that she felt something soften and melt inside. Closing her eyes, she gave in, hardly caring that anyone walking past could see them. And then an indignant wail split the air. Sam and Gabe sprang apart, turning as one to stare at the cot, where Frances had started to wriggle.

'I suppose I should get used to this,' Sam said, leaving the warmth of Gabe's embrace with some reluctance.

'You should,' he agreed.

A shiver passed over Sam as the magnitude of what she was asking of him hit home for the first time. Joss had made it sound so simple; open her eyes and see what was in front of her. And Gabe had responded in a way she'd never allowed herself to dream he would, but she wasn't asking him to love just her; she and Frances came as a package now and she'd never be truly free to give all of herself to him the way he might want her to. Could she expect him to love another man's child? Would Joss allow him to?

Something of the sudden onslaught of worry must have shown in her face because Gabe tilted her chin up towards him and smiled deep into her eyes. 'But it's okay. I'm going to be right there beside you. We'll get used to it together.'

And Sam burst into tears of relief and happiness at the thought.

Epilogue

It was August Bank Holiday Monday. The sun was sinking below the horizon, sending tendrils of red and gold winding through the cherry blossom clouds. Sam and Nessie sat on a picnic blanket that was spread on the dry yellowing grass of the village green and watched as the last few sunbeams danced across the sky. Beside them, baby Frances, now firmly nicknamed Franny, gurgled in her basket and, at the far end of the green, Nessie could just about make out Luke, playing with his friends, Bucky bounding along at their heels.

'Happy?' Nessie asked Sam.

'Half-dead from exhaustion,' Sam replied instantly. But then a smile tugged at her mouth and creased the corners of her eyes. 'But yeah, I'm happy. Are you?'

Nessie reached across to brush the back of her hand against her niece's plump downy cheek. 'Of course. I've got everything I want.'

The movement caused the diamond and emerald ring on her wedding finger to flash.

'Almost everything,' Sam corrected. 'You and Owen still need to set the date. I know I told you to wait until I no longer looked like a beached whale, but there's such a thing as too long an engagement, you know.'

Nessie hesitated. Should she tell Sam now? Was this the right time? But if the last year had taught her anything, it was that there was never a right time for news like this.

'It might be a slightly longer engagement than anyone expected,' she said slowly. 'Around nine months longer, in fact.'

Sam's head whipped around to stare at her in bewilderment, then a delighted smile wreathed her face. 'You mean—'

Nessie's eyes prickled with tears. 'Yes, Sam. Franny's going to have a little cousin. Owen and I had our twelve-week scan on Friday. Everything is fine.'

Sam threw her arms around her and pulled her into a hug. 'Oh my god, I am so thrilled for you, Ness!' She drew back and Nessie saw she was crying too. 'This is such amazing news!'

'You're the first person I've told,' Nessie whispered. 'And I know it's going to be hard, with two babies instead of one to look after. But we'll find a way to make it work.'

'We will,' Sam told her fiercely. 'It's going to be a dream come true for Joss – he'll finally be the one in charge. It's a good thing he and Gabe are practically best friends now – imagine if they hated each other!'

Nessie laughed. 'It's a shame we can't make it a double wedding,' she teased. 'Joss could be best man for both grooms.'

'One step at a time,' Sam said, rolling her eyes in exaggerated derision. 'Gabe and I aren't even sharing a room yet.'

'Okay, maybe not a double wedding, then,' Nessie conceded. 'But you'll still be my matron of honour, though, when Owen and I finally make it down the aisle?'

'Of course – I'm planning a Carry On hen do, remember?' Sam grinned, as Franny waved her legs in the air. 'And you'll have a ready-made flower girl on the day itself – she might even be walking by then.'

Nessie leaned into her and kissed her on the cheek. 'Thanks, Sam. I'm so lucky to have you for a sister.'

Sam's eyes glistened in the fading sunlight. 'Same. But you're more than just my sister,' she murmured, resting her head against Nessie's. 'You're my best friend.'

A swell of contentment washed over Nessie as she hugged Sam. 'Best friends,' she agreed, smiling as the sun set over the Star and Sixpence. 'Always.'

Acknowledgements

The first drink of any round must always go to Jo Williamson at Antony Harwood Ltd, whose limitless encouragement, support and patience enables me to do what I do. As always, I couldn't write a word without knowing you have my back – thank you so much. Lunch soon, yes?

My editorial thanks are split between the ever-wonderful Emma Capron (still not over you leaving me, although I am sure you are sleeping better) and equally fabulous Bec Farrell, who between them have nursed this book into being. Thank you to Jade Craddock and Elizabeth Dobson for correcting my mistakes. And, of course, eternal thanks to the whole team at Simon and Schuster UK for allowing me to return to my very favourite pub.

Some might say that a writer is only as good as her (drinking) friends and I am uncommonly blessed in mine: Cally Taylor, Julie Cohen, Kate Harrison, Miranda Dickinson and Rowan Coleman, I can only aspire to your genius. Please stay with me forever.

Special thanks to literal life-saver Charlotte Dennis, who is always ready to help when I need medical advice; please continue to take my calls and save everyone, Charlotte.

As always, love, thanks and big squishy hugs to T and E for giving me a reason to work hard.

And last of all, thank you to everyone who reads my books. I know you love the Star and Sixpence as much as I do – see you at the bar!

FIRST CLASS
HOLIDAYS

Booking your dream holiday is not a decision to be taken lightly, whether that be a touring holiday, a luxury honeymoon or a holiday to celebrate a special occasion.

That's where award-winning First Class Holidays come in. Specialising in tailor-made holidays to Canada & Alaska, America, Australia, New Zealand, South Africa and the Pacific Islands, they take away the hard work when it comes to planning the trip you've always imagined and provide an outstanding level of service while doing so, and with over 750 years' experience between the team, over 100,000 satisfied customers and 23 years delivering exceptional service, they'll plan your journey to absolute perfection, offering first-hand advice with the knowledge they've garnered throughout their own travels.